THE
CLOCKMAKER'S
DAUGHTER

THE
CLOCKMAKER'S
DAUGHTER

A Novel

KATE MORTON

ATRIA PAPERBACK

New York   London   Toronto   Sydney   New Delhi

ATRIA
PAPERBACK

An Imprint of Simon & Schuster, Inc.
1230 Avenue of the Americas
New York, NY 10020

Map endpapers by Antiqua Print Gallery / Alamy Stock Photo

This Atria Paperback Canadian export edition October 2018

ATRIA PAPERBACK and colophon are trademarks of Simon & Schuster, Inc.

For information about special discounts for bulk purchases, please contact Simon & Schuster Special Sales at 1-866-506-1949 or business@simonandschuster.com.

The Simon & Schuster Speakers Bureau can bring authors to your live event. For more information, or to book an event, contact the Simon & Schuster Speakers Bureau at 1-866-248-3049 or visit our website at www.simonspeakers.com.

Manufactured in the United States of America

10   9   8   7   6   5

ISBN 978-1-9821-1052-9
ISBN 978-1-4516-4943-7 (ebook)

To Didee, for being the sort of mother who took us to live on a mountaintop and for giving me the best piece of writing advice I've ever received

Part One

THE SATCHEL

I

We came to Birchwood Manor because Edward said that it was haunted. It wasn't, not then, but it's a dull man who lets truth stand in the way of a good story, and Edward was never that. His passion, his blinding faith in whatever he professed, was one of the things I fell in love with. He had the preacher's zeal, a way of expressing opinions that minted them into gleaming currency. A habit of drawing people to him, of firing in them enthusiasms they hadn't known were theirs, making all but himself and his convictions fade.

But Edward was no preacher.

I remember him. I remember everything.

The glass-roofed studio in his mother's London garden, the smell of freshly mixed paint, the scratch of bristle on canvas as his gaze swept my skin. My nerves that day were prickles. I was eager to impress, to make him think me something I was not, as his eyes traced my length and Mrs. Mack's entreaty circled in my head: "Your mother was a proper lady, your people were grand folk, and don't you go forgetting it. Play your cards right and all our birds might just come home to roost."

And so I sat up straighter on the rosewood chair that first day in the whitewashed room behind the tangle of blushing sweet peas.

—

His littlest sister brought me tea, and cake when I was hungry. His mother, too, came down the narrow path to watch him work. She adored her son. In him she glimpsed the family's hopes fulfilled. Dis-

3

tinguished member of the Royal Academy, engaged to a lady of some means, father soon to a clutch of brown-eyed heirs.

Not for him the likes of me.

———

His mother blamed herself for what came next, but she'd have more easily halted day from meeting night than keep us apart. He called me his muse, his destiny. He said that he had known at once, when he saw me through the hazy gaslight of the theater foyer on Drury Lane.

I was his muse, his destiny. And he was mine.

It was long ago; it was yesterday.

Oh, I remember love.

———

This corner, halfway up the main flight of stairs, is my favorite.

It is a strange house, built to be purposely confusing. Staircases that turn at unusual angles, all knees and elbows and uneven treads; windows that do not line up no matter how one squints at them; floorboards and wall panels with clever concealments.

In this corner, there's a warmth, almost unnatural. We all noticed it when first we came, and over the early summer weeks we took our turns in guessing at its cause.

The reason took me some time to discover, but at last I learned the truth. I know this place as I know my own name.

———

It was not the house itself but the light that Edward used to tempt the others. On a clear day, from the attic windows, one can see over the river Thames and all the way to the distant mountains. Ribbons of mauve and green, crags of chalk that stagger towards the clouds, and warm air that lends the whole an iridescence.

This was the proposal that he made: an entire summer month of paint and poetry and picnics, of stories and science and invention. Of light, heaven-sent. Away from London, away from prying eyes. Little wonder that the others accepted with alacrity. Edward could make the very devil pray, if such were his desire.

Only to me did he confess his other reason for coming here. For although the lure of the light was real enough, Edward had a secret.

———

We came on foot from the railway station.

July, and the day was perfect. A breeze picked at my skirt hem. Someone had brought sandwiches and we ate them as we walked. What a sight we must have made—men with loosened neckties, women with their long hair free. Laughter, teasing, sport.

Such a grand beginning! I remember the sound of a stream close by and a wood pigeon calling overhead. A man leading a horse, a wagon with a young boy sitting atop straw bales, the smell of fresh-cut grass— Oh, how I miss that smell! A clutch of fat country geese regarded us beadily when we reached the river before honking bravely once we had passed.

All was light, but it did not last for long.

You knew that already, though, for there would be no story to tell if the warmth had lasted. No one is interested in quiet, happy summers that end as they begin. Edward taught me that.

———

The isolation played its part, this house, stranded on the riverbank like a great inland ship. The weather, too; the blazing hot days, one after the other, and then the summer storm that night, which forced us all indoors.

The winds blew and the trees moaned, and thunder rolled down the river to take the house within its clutches; while inside, talk turned to spirits and enchantments. There was a fire, crackling in the grate, and the candle flames quivered, and in the darkness, in that atmosphere of delicious fear and confession, something ill was conjured.

Not a ghost, oh, no, not that—the deed when done was entirely human.

Two unexpected guests.

Two long-kept secrets.

A gunshot in the dark.

———

The light went out and everything was black.

Summer was curdled. The first keen leaves began their fall, turning to rot in the puddles beneath the thinning hedgerows, and Edward, who loved this house, began to stalk its corridors, entrapped.

At last, he could stand it no longer. He packed his things to leave and I could not make him stop.

The others followed, as they always did.

And I? I had no choice; I stayed behind.

Chapter One

SUMMER 2017

I⊤ was Elodie Winslow's favorite time of day. Summer in London, and at a certain point in the very late afternoon the sun seemed to hesitate in its passage across the sky and light spilled through the small glass tiles in the pavement directly onto her desk. Best of all, with Margot and Mr. Pendleton gone home for the day, the moment was Elodie's alone.

The basement of Stratton, Cadwell & Co., in its building on the Strand, was not an especially romantic place, not like the muniment room at New College where Elodie had taken holiday work the year she completed her master's. It was not warm, ever, and even during a heat wave like this one Elodie needed to wear a cardigan at her desk. But every so often, when the stars aligned, the office, with its smell of dust and age and the seeping Thames, was almost charming.

In the narrow kitchenette behind the wall of filing cabinets, Elodie poured steaming water into the mug and flipped the timer. Margot thought this precision extreme, but Elodie preferred her tea when it had steeped for three and a half minutes exactly.

As she waited, grains of sand slipping through the glass, Elodie's thoughts returned to Pippa's message. She had picked it up on her phone, when she'd ducked across the road to buy a sandwich for lunch: an invitation to a fashion launch party that sounded as tempting to Elodie as a stint in the doctor's waiting room. Thankfully, she already had plans—a visit to her father in Hampstead to collect the recordings he'd put aside for her—and was spared the task of inventing a reason to say no.

Denying Pippa was not easy. She was Elodie's best friend and had been since the first day of grade three at Pineoaks Primary School. Elodie often gave silent thanks to Miss Perry for seating the two of them together: Elodie, the New Girl, in her unfamiliar uniform and the lopsided plaits her dad had wrestled into place; and Pippa, with her broad smile, dimpled cheeks, and hands that were in constant motion when she spoke.

They'd been inseparable ever since. Primary school, high school, and even afterwards when Elodie went up to Oxford and Pippa to Central Saint Martins. They saw less of one another now, but that was to be expected: the art world was a busy, sociable place, and Pippa was responsible for a never-ending stream of invitations left on Elodie's phone as she made her way from this gallery opening or installation to the next.

The world of archives, by contrast, was decidedly *unbusy*. That is, it was not busy in Pippa's sparkling sense. Elodie put in long hours and engaged frequently with other human beings; they just weren't the living, breathing sort. The original Messrs. Stratton and Cadwell had traversed the globe at a time when it was just beginning to shrink and the invention of the telephone hadn't yet reduced reliance on written correspondence. So it was, Elodie spent her days communing with the foxed and dusty artifacts of the long-dead, stepping into this account of a soirée on the Orient Express or that encounter between Victorian adventurers in search of the Northwest Passage.

Such social engagement across time made Elodie very happy. It was true that she didn't have many friends, not of the flesh-and-blood variety, but the fact did not upset her. It was tiring, all that smiling and sharing and speculating about the weather, and she always left a gathering, no matter how intimate, feeling depleted, as if she'd accidentally left behind some vital layers of herself she'd never get back.

Elodie removed the tea bag, squeezed the last drips into the sink, and added a half-second pour of milk.

She carried the mug back to her desk, where the prisms of afternoon sunlight were just beginning their daily creep; and as steam curled voluptuously and her palms warmed, Elodie surveyed the day's remaining tasks. She had been midway through compiling an index on the younger James Stratton's account of his 1893 journey to the west coast of Africa; there was an article to write for the next edition of *Stratton, Cadwell & Co. Monthly*; and Mr. Pendleton had left her with the catalogue for the upcoming exhibition to proofread before it went to the printer.

But Elodie had been making decisions about words and their order all day, and her brain was stretched. Her gaze fell to the waxed-cardboard box on the floor beneath her desk. It had been there since Monday afternoon when a plumbing disaster in the offices above had required immediate evacuation of the old cloakroom, a low-ceilinged architectural afterthought that Elodie couldn't remember entering in the ten years since she'd started work in the building. The box had turned up beneath a stack of dusty brocade curtains in the bottom of an antique chiffonier, a handwritten label on its lid reading, "Contents of attic desk drawer, 1966—unlisted."

Finding archival materials in the disused cloakroom, let alone so many decades after they'd apparently been delivered, was disquieting, and Mr. Pendleton's reaction had been predictably explosive. He was a stickler for protocol, and it was lucky, Elodie and Margot later agreed, that whoever had been responsible for receiving the delivery in 1966 had long ago left his employ.

The timing couldn't have been worse: ever since the management consultant had been sent in to "trim the fat," Mr. Pendleton had been in a spin. The invasion of his physical sphere was bad enough, but the insult of having his efficiency questioned was beyond the pale. "It's like someone borrowing your watch to tell you the time," he'd said through frosted lips after the consultant had met with them the other morning.

The unceremonious appearance of the box had threatened to tip him into apoplexy, so Elodie—who liked disharmony as little as she did disorder—had stepped in with a firm promise to set things right, promptly sweeping it up and stashing it out of sight.

In the days since, she'd been careful to keep it concealed so as not to trigger another eruption, but now, alone in the quiet office, she knelt on the carpet and slid the box from its hiding place . . .

The pinpricks of sudden light were a shock, and the satchel, pressed deep inside the box, exhaled. The journey had been long and it was understandably weary. Its edges were wearing thin, its buckles had tarnished, and an unfortunate musty odor had staled in its depths. As for the dust, a permanent patina had formed opaquely on the once-fine surface, and it was now the sort of bag that people held at a distance, turning their heads to one side as they weighed the possibilities. Too old to be of use, but bearing an indefinable air of historic quality precluding its disposal.

The satchel had been loved once, admired for its elegance—more importantly, its function. It had been indispensable to a particular person at a particular time when such attributes were highly prized. Since then, it had been hidden and ignored, recovered and disparaged, lost, found, and forgotten.

Now, though, one by one, the items that for decades had sat atop the satchel were finally being lifted, and the satchel, too, was resurfacing at last in this room of faint electrical humming and ticking pipes. Of diffuse yellow light and papery smells and soft white gloves.

At the other end of the gloves was a woman: young, with fawnlike arms leading to a delicate neck supporting a face framed by short black hair. She held the satchel at a distance, but not with distaste.

Her touch was gentle. Her mouth had gathered in a small, neat purse of interest, and her dark eyes narrowed slightly before widening as she took in the hand-sewn joins, the fine Indian cotton, and the precise stitching.

She ran a soft thumb over the initials on the front flap, faded and sad, and the satchel felt a frisson of pleasure. Somehow this young woman's attention hinted that what had turned out to be an unexpectedly long journey might just be nearing its end.

Open me, the satchel urged. *Look inside.*

Once upon a time the satchel had been shiny and new. Made to order by Mr. Simms himself at the royal warrant manufactory of W. Simms & Son on Bond Street. The gilt initials had been hand-tooled and heat-sealed with enormous pomp; each silver rivet and buckle had been selected, inspected, and polished; the fine-quality leather had been cut and stitched with care, oiled, and buffed with pride. Spices from the Far East—clove and sandalwood and saffron—had drifted through the building's veins from the perfumery next door, infusing the satchel with a hint of faraway places. *Open me . . .*

The woman in the white gloves unlatched the dull silver buckle and the satchel held its breath.

Open me, open me, open me . . .

She pushed back its leather strap and for the first time in over a century light swept into the satchel's dark corners.

An onslaught of memories—fragmented, confused—arrived with it: a bell tinkling above the door at W. Simms & Son; the swish of a young woman's skirts; the thud of horses' hooves; the smell of fresh paint and turpentine; heat, lust, whispering. Gaslight in railway stations; a long, winding river; the wheat fragrance of summer—

The gloved hands withdrew and with them went the satchel's load.

The old sensations, voices, imprints, fell away, and everything, at last, was blank and quiet.

It was over.

Elodie rested the contents on her lap and set the satchel to one side. It was a beautiful piece which did not fit with the other items she'd taken from the box. They had comprised a collection of rather humdrum office supplies—a hole punch, an inkwell, a wooden desk insert for sorting pens and paper clips—and a crocodile leather spectacle case, which the manufacturer's label announced: "The property of L.S-W." This fact suggested to Elodie that the desk, and everything inside, had once belonged to Lesley Stratton-Wood, a great-niece down one of the family scions of the original James Stratton. The vintage was right— Lesley Stratton-Wood had died in the 1960s—and it would explain the box's delivery to Stratton, Cadwell & Co.

The satchel, though—unless it was a replica of the highest order—was far too old to have belonged to Ms. Stratton-Wood; the items inside looked pre–twentieth century. A preliminary riffle revealed a monogrammed black journal (E.J.R.) with a marbled fore-edge; a brass pen box, mid-Victorian; and a faded green leather document holder. There was no way of knowing at first glance to whom the satchel had belonged, but beneath the front flap of the document case, the gilt-stamped label read, "James W. Stratton, Esq. London, 1861."

The leather document holder was flattish, and Elodie thought at first that it might be empty; but when she opened the clasp, a single object waited inside. It was a delicate silver frame, small enough to fit within her hand, containing a photograph of a woman. She was young, with long hair, light but not blond, half of which was wound into a loose knot on the top of her head; her gaze was direct, her chin slightly lifted, her cheekbones high. Her lips were set in an attitude of intelligent engagement, perhaps even defiance.

Elodie felt a familiar stirring of anticipation as she took in the sepia tones, the promise of a life awaiting rediscovery. The woman's dress was looser than might be expected for the period. White fabric draped over her shoulders, and the neckline fell in a V. The sleeves were sheer and billowed, and had been pushed to the elbow on one arm. Her wrist was slender, the hand on her hip accentuating the indentation of her waist.

The treatment was as unusual as the subject, for the woman wasn't posed inside on a settee or against a scenic curtain, as one might expect in a Victorian portrait. She was outside, surrounded by dense greenery, a setting that spoke of movement and life. The light was diffuse, the effect intoxicating.

Elodie set the photograph aside and took up the monogrammed journal. It fell open to reveal thick cream pages of expensive cotton paper; there were lines of beautiful handwriting, but they were complements only to the many pen and ink renderings of figures, landscapes, and other objects of interest. Not a journal, then: this was a sketchbook.

A fragment of paper, torn from elsewhere, slipped from between two pages. A single line raced across it: *I love her, I love her, I love her, and if I cannot have her I shall surely go mad, for when I am not with her I fear—*

The words leapt off the paper as if they'd been spoken aloud, but when Elodie turned over the page, whatever the writer had feared was not revealed.

She ran her gloved fingertips over the impressions of the text. When held up to the last glimmer of sunlight, the paper revealed its individual threads, along with tiny lucent pinpricks where the sharp nib of the fountain pen had torn across the sheet.

Elodie laid the jagged piece of paper gently back inside the sketchbook.

Although antique now, the urgency of its message was unsettling: it spoke forcefully and currently of unfinished business.

Elodie continued to leaf carefully through the pages, each one filled with cross-hatched artist's studies with occasional rough-sketched facial profiles in the margins.

And then she stopped.

This sketch was more elaborate than the others, more complete. A river scene, with a tree in the foreground and a distant wood visible across a broad field. Behind a copse on the right-hand side, the twin-gabled roofline of a house could be seen, with eight chimneys and an ornate weather vane featuring the sun and moon and other celestial emblems.

It was an accomplished drawing, but that's not why Elodie stared. She felt a pang of déjà vu so strong it exerted a physical pressure around her chest.

She knew this place. The memory was as vivid as if she'd been there, and yet somehow Elodie knew that it was a location she'd visited only in her mind.

The words came to her then as clear as birdsong at dawn: *"Down the winding lane and across the meadow broad, to the river they went with their secrets and their sword."*

And she remembered. It was a story that her mother used to tell her. A child's bedtime story, romantic and tangled, replete with heroes, villains, and a Fairy Queen, set in a house within dark woods encircled by a long, snaking river.

But there had been no book with illustrations. The tale had been spoken aloud, the two of them side by side in her little girl bed in the room with the sloping ceiling—

The wall clock chimed, low and premonitory, from Mr. Pendleton's office, and Elodie glanced at her watch. She was late. Time had lost its shape again, its arrow dissolving into dust around her. With a final glance at the strangely familiar scene, she returned the sketchbook with the other contents to its box, closed the lid, and pushed it back beneath the desk.

Elodie had gathered her things and was halfway through the usual motions of checking and locking the department door to leave, when the overwhelming urge came upon her. Unable to resist, she hurried back to the box, dug out the sketchbook, and slipped it inside her bag.

CHAPTER TWO

ELODIE caught the 24 bus north from Charing Cross to Hampstead. The Underground would have been faster, but she didn't use the Tube. There was too much crowding, too little air, and Elodie didn't do well in tight spaces. The aversion had been a fact of life since she was a child and she was used to it, but in this instance it was a regret; she loved the *idea* of the Underground, its example of nineteenth-century enterprise, its vintage signs and tiles and fonts, its history and dust.

The traffic was grindingly slow, especially near Tottenham Court Road where the Crossrail excavation had left the backs of a row of brick Victorian terraces exposed. It was one of Elodie's favorite views, providing a glimpse of the past so real it could be touched. She imagined, as she always did, the lives of those who'd dwelt within these houses long ago, back when the southern part of St. Giles was home to the Rookery, a teeming, squalid slum of crooked alleys and cesspits, gin shops and gamblers, prostitutes and urchins; when Charles Dickens was making his daily walks, and alchemists plied their trade in the sewer-lined streets of the Seven Dials.

The younger James Stratton, sharing with so many of his fellow Victorians a keen interest in the esoteric, had left a number of journal entries recording visits to a particular spiritualist and seer in Covent Garden with whom he'd enjoyed a long-running dalliance. For a banker, James Stratton had been a gifted writer, his diaries providing vibrant, compassionate and at times very funny glimpses of life in Victorian London. He had been a kind man, a *good* man, committed to improving the lives of the poor and dispossessed. He believed, as he wrote to friends when he tried to enlist them to his philanthropic causes, that "a human being's life and prospects must surely be improved by having a decent place to lay his or her head of a night."

Professionally he had been respected, even liked, by his peers: a bright, sought-after dinner party guest, well traveled and wealthy, successful by every measure a Victorian man might care to name; yet, in his personal life, he'd cut a lonelier figure. He had married late, after a number of short-lived, improbable romances. There was an actress who'd run off with an Italian inventor, an artist's model who was pregnant with another man's child, and in his midforties he developed a deep and abiding affection for one of his servants, a quiet girl called Molly, upon whom he bestowed frequent small kindnesses without ever declaring his true feelings. It seemed to Elodie almost as if he'd set out purposely to choose women who wouldn't—or couldn't—make him happy.

"Why would he do that?" Pippa had asked with a frown when Elodie mentioned this thought to her over tapas and sangria one night.

Elodie wasn't sure, only that although there was nothing overt in his correspondence, no declaration of unrequited love or confession of deep-seated unhappiness, she couldn't help but sense something melancholy lurking beneath the pleasant surface of his personal letters; that he was a seeker for whom true fulfillment remained forever out of reach.

Elodie was used to the skeptical look that settled on Pippa's face whenever she said that sort of thing out loud. She would never be able to describe the intimacy of working day after day amongst the artifacts of another person's life. Elodie couldn't understand the modern urge to share one's innermost feelings publicly and permanently; she guarded her own privacy carefully and subscribed to the French notion of *le droit à l'oubli*—the right to be forgotten. And yet it was her job—more than that, her passion—to preserve, and even to reanimate, the lives of people who had no choice in the matter. She had read James Stratton's most private thoughts, journal entries written without a view to posterity, yet he had never even heard her name.

"You're in love with him, of course" was Pippa's comment whenever Elodie tried to explain.

But it wasn't love; Elodie simply admired James Stratton and felt protective of his legacy. He had been granted a life beyond his lifetime, and it was Elodie's job to ensure it was respected.

Even as the word "respect" took form in her mind, Elodie thought of the sketchbook, deep inside her bag, and her cheeks flushed.

What on earth had come over her?

Panic mixed with a terrible, wonderful, guilty sense of anticipation. Never in the decade that she'd worked in the archive room at Stratton, Cadwell & Co. had she transgressed so emphatically across the edicts laid down by Mr. Pendleton. His rules were absolute: to take an archive from the vault—worse, simply to shove it in one's bag and force upon it the sacrilege of being transported on a twenty-first-century London bus—was beyond disrespectful. It was inexcusable.

But as the number 24 skirted Mornington Crescent station and started up Camden High Street, with a quick glance to reassure herself that no one was watching, Elodie took the sketchbook from her bag and opened the pages quickly to the drawing of the house in its river setting.

Once again she was struck by a sense of profound familiarity. She *knew* this place. In the story that her mother used to tell, the house had been a literal gateway to another world; for Elodie, though, curled up in her mother's arms, breathing in the exotic fragrance of narcissus that she wore, the story itself had been a gateway, an incantation that carried her away from the here and now and into the land of imagination. After her mother's death, the world of the story had become her secret place. Whether at lunchtime in her new school, or at home in the long, quiet afternoons, or at night when the darkness threatened suffocation, all she had to do was hide herself away and close her eyes and she could cross the river, brave the woods, and enter the enchanted house . . .

The bus arrived at South End Green and Elodie stopped briefly to make a purchase at the stall by the Overground station before hurrying up Willow Road towards Gainsborough Gardens. The day was still warm and very stuffy, and by the time she arrived at the door of her father's tiny house—originally the gardener's cottage—Elodie felt as if she'd run a marathon.

"Hello, Dad," she said, as he gave her a kiss. "I've brought you something."

"Oh, dear," he said, eyeing the potted plant dubiously. "Even after how things ended last time?"

"I believe in you. Besides, the lady selling them told me this one only needs watering twice a year."

"Good God, really? Twice a year?"

"That's what she said."

"Miraculous."

Despite the heat, he'd prepared duck à l'orange, his speciality, and they ate together at the table in the kitchen as they always did. They'd never really been a dining room family, only on special occasions, like Christmas or birthdays, or the time Elodie's mother had decided they should invite the visiting American violinist and his wife for Thanksgiving.

As they ate they spoke of work: Elodie's curation of the upcoming exhibition and her father's choir, the music lessons he'd been giving recently at one of the local primary schools. His face lit up when he described the little girl whose violin was almost as long as her arm, and the bright-eyed boy who'd come to the practice room of his own accord and begged for cello lessons. "His parents aren't musical, you see."

"Let me guess: The two of you came to your own arrangement?"

"I hadn't the heart to say no."

Elodie smiled. Her father was a soft touch when it came to music and wouldn't have dreamt of denying a child the opportunity to share his great love. He believed that music had the power to alter people's lives—"their very minds, Elodie"—and nothing made him quite as excited as discussing brain plasticity and MRI scans showing a connection between music and empathy. It made Elodie's heart clench to watch him watching a concert: the utter transfixion of his face beside

18

her in the theater. He had been a professional musician once himself. "Only second violinist," he always qualified when the subject arose, a trace of reverence entering his voice as he continued predictably: "Nothing like she was."

She. Elodie's gaze drifted to the dining room on the other side of the hall. From where she was sitting, only the edges of a few frames were visible, but Elodie didn't need to look upon the wall to know exactly which picture was hanging where. Their positions never altered. It was her mother's wall. That is, it was Lauren Adler's wall. Striking black-and-white photographs of a vibrant young woman with long, straight hair and a cello in her embrace.

Elodie had made a study of the photographs when she was a child and they were thus printed indelibly on her mind's eye. Her mother, in various attitudes of performance, concentration fine-tuning her features; those high cheekbones; the focused gaze; her clever articulated fingers on strings that gleamed beneath the lights.

"Fancy a bit of pudding?"

Her father had taken a quivering strawberry concoction from the refrigerator, and Elodie noticed suddenly how old he was compared with the images of her mother, whose youth and beauty were locked in the amber of her memory.

Because the weather was glorious, they took their wineglasses and dessert upstairs to the rooftop terrace that overlooked the green. A trio of brothers were tossing a Frisbee, the smallest one running back and forth across the grass between the others, while a pair of adults sat together nearby, their heads bent close in conversation.

The summer twilight cast a soporific glow, and Elodie was reluctant to spoil things. Nonetheless, after a few minutes of the easy, companionable silence in which she and her father had always specialized, she ventured, "Do you know what I was thinking of today?"

"What's that?" He had a spot of cream on his chin.

"That bedtime story from when I was little—the one about the river, and the house with the moon and stars weather vane. Do you remember it?"

He laughed with soft surprise. "Goodness! That's taken me back. Yes, of course, you used to love that one. It's been a long time since I've thought of it. I always wondered that it might not be a bit too scary for a child, but your mother believed that children were much braver than they were given credit for. She said that childhood was a frightening time and that hearing scary stories was a way of feeling less alone. It seemed that you agreed: whenever she was away on tour, you were never happy with the books I read. I used to feel quite rejected. You'd hide them under your bed so I couldn't find them and demand that I tell you instead about the clearing in the deep, dark woods and the magic house on the river."

Elodie smiled.

"You were not pleased with my attempts. Feet were stomped, words like 'No!' and 'Not like that!' bandied about."

"Oh, dear."

"It wasn't your fault. Your mother was a wonderful storyteller."

Her father fell into a melancholy silence, but Elodie, who was usually mindful not to trespass on her father's old grief, pressed on gingerly. "I wonder, Dad—is it possible that the story actually came from a book?"

"Would that it had. I'd have been saved a lot of time trying to console my inconsolable child. No, it was an invention, a family story. I remember your mother saying it had been passed down to her when she was young."

"I thought so, too, but perhaps she got it wrong? Maybe whoever told her the story had read it in a book? One of those illustrated Victorian books for children."

"It's possible, I suppose." He frowned. "But what's all this about?"

With a prickle of sudden nerves, Elodie withdrew the sketchbook from her bag and handed it to her father, open to the drawing of the house. "I found this at work today, in a box."

"It's lovely . . . and obviously drawn by a fine artist . . . wonderful penmanship . . ." He looked at it a little longer before glancing at Elodie uncertainly.

"Dad, can't you see? It's the house from the story. An illustration of the very same house."

He returned his attention to the sketch. "Well, it's *a* house. And I see there's a river."

"And woods, and a weather vane with a sun and moon."

"Yes, but . . . lovey, I daresay there are dozens of houses fitting that description."

"So precisely? Come on, Dad. This is the same house. The details are identical. More than that, the artist has captured the same *feel* as the house in the story. You must be able to see it." The possessive instinct came upon her suddenly, and Elodie took the book back from her father. She couldn't explain more emphatically than she already had: she didn't know how, or what it meant, or why the sketch had turned up in the archives at work, but she *knew* it was the house from her mother's story.

"I'm sorry, love."

"Nothing to be sorry for." Even as she said it, Elodie felt the sting of impending tears. Ridiculous! To cry like a child over the provenance of a bedtime story. She grasped for a different subject, something—anything—to move the conversation on. "Have you heard from Tip?"

"Not yet. But you know what he's like. He doesn't believe in the telephone."

"I'll go and see him at the weekend."

Silence fell once more between them, but this time it was neither easy nor companionable. Elodie watched the warm light at play on the leaves of the trees. She didn't know why she felt so agitated. Even if it *were* the same house, what did it matter? Either the artist had made sketches for a book that her mother had read, or it was a real-life house that someone had seen and enfolded into the story. She knew she ought to let it go, to think of something pleasant and benign to say—

"They're predicting fine weather," her father said, at the very same moment Elodie exclaimed, "The house has eight chimneys, Dad. Eight!"

"Oh, lovey."

"It's the house from her story. Look at the gables—"

"My dear girl."

"Dad!"

"This all makes sense."

"What does?"

"It's the wedding."

"What wedding?"

"Yours, of course." His smile was kind. "Big life events have a way of bringing the past back to bear. And you miss your mother. I should have anticipated that you'd be missing her now more than ever."

"No, Dad, I—"

"In fact, there's something I've been wanting to give you. Wait here a minute."

As her father disappeared down the flight of iron stairs that led back to the house, Elodie sighed. With his apron tied around his middle and his too-sweet duck à l'orange, he just wasn't the sort of person with whom one could maintain a state of prolonged irritation.

She noticed a blackbird watching her from one of the twin chimney pots. It stared intently before responding to a command she couldn't hear to fly away. The littlest of the children on the green began to wail, and Elodie thought of her father's account of her own petulance in the face of his best bedtime story efforts: the years that had stretched out afterwards, just the two of them.

It couldn't have been easy.

"I've been saving this for you," he said, reappearing at the top of the stairs. She had presumed that he was going to fetch the tapes she'd asked him to put aside, but the box he was holding was too small for that, not much bigger than a shoe box. "I knew that one day—that the time would be right—" His eyes were beginning to glisten and he shook his head, handing her the box. "Here, you'll see."

Elodie lifted the top.

Inside was a swath of silk organza, light ivory in color, its scalloped edge trimmed with a fine ribbon of velvet. She knew at once what it was. She had studied the photograph in its gilt frame downstairs many times before.

"She was so beautiful that day," her father said. "I'll never forget the moment she appeared in the doorway of the church. I'd half convinced myself she wouldn't show. My brother teased me mercilessly in the days beforehand. He thought it was great sport and I'm afraid I made it easy for him. I couldn't quite believe that she'd said yes. I was sure there'd been some sort of mix-up—that it was too good to be true."

Elodie reached to take his hand. It had been twenty-five years since her mother's death, but for her father it might as well have happened yesterday. Elodie had only been six, but she could still remember the way he used to look at her mother, the way they'd intertwined their fingers when they walked together. She remembered, too, the knock at the door, the low voices of the policemen, her father's awful cry.

"It's getting late," he said with a quick pat to the top of her wrist. "You should be heading home, love. Come on downstairs—I've found the tapes you were after, too."

Elodie replaced the lid of the box. She was leaving him to the burdensome company of his memories, but he was right: the journey home was a long one. Besides, Elodie had learned many years before that she was not equal to the task of healing his sorrow. "Thanks for keeping the veil for me," she said, brushing a kiss on his cheek as she stood.

"She'd be proud of you."

Elodie smiled, but as she followed her father downstairs, she wondered if that was true.

Home was a small, neat flat that sat at the very top of a Victorian building in Barnes. The communal stairwell smelled like chip grease courtesy of the fish shop below, but only the merest hint remained on Elodie's landing. The flat itself was little more than an open-plan sitting room and kitchenette and an oddly shaped bedroom with a tacked-on bathroom; the view, though, made Elodie's heart sing.

One of her bedroom windows overlooked the back of a row of other Victorians: old bricks, white-sash windows, and truncated roofs with terra-cotta chimney pots. In the gaps between drainpipes she could glimpse the Thames. Better yet, if she sat right up on the sill, she could look all the way upriver to the bend where the railway bridge made its crossing.

The window on the far wall faced the street, lining up with a mirror house on the other side. The couple who lived there were still eating when Elodie arrived home. They were Swedish, she had learned, which seemed to explain not only their height and beauty, but also their exotic Nordic habit of dining after ten. There was a lamp above their kitchen bench, which looked to be made of crepe and sent light shimmering pinkly onto the surface below. Beneath it, their skin glowed.

Elodie drew her bedroom curtains, switched on the light, and took the veil from its box. She didn't know much about fashion, not like Pippa, but she knew this was a special piece. Vintage by dint of its age, covetable owing to Lauren Adler's fame, but precious to Elodie because it had been her mother's and there was surprisingly little of her left. Surprisingly little of a private nature.

After a moment's hesitation, she lifted the veil and held it tentatively at the crown of her head. She slipped the comb into place and the organza unfurled over her shoulders. She let her hands fall to her sides.

Elodie had been flattered when Alastair asked her to marry him. He had proposed on the first anniversary of the day they'd been introduced (by a boy Elodie had gone to school with who now worked in Alastair's firm). Alastair had taken her to the theater and then to dinner in a fancy Soho restaurant, whispering into her ear as the cloakroom attendant stowed their coats that it took most people *weeks* to get a reservation. Whilst the waiter was fetching them dessert, he had presented the ring in its robin's egg blue box. It had been like something from a movie, and Elodie had seen the two of them as if from outside, he with his handsome, expectant face, his perfect white teeth, and she in the new dress Pippa had made for her when she'd given the Stratton Group 150-Year Presentation speech the month before.

An elderly woman sitting at the table beside them had said to her companion, "Isn't that lovely. Look! She's blushing because she's so in love." And Elodie had thought, *I'm blushing because I'm so in love,* and when Alastair lifted his eyebrows she'd watched herself smile and tell him yes.

Out on the dark river a boat sounded its foghorn, and Elodie slipped the veil from her head.

That was how it happened, she supposed. That is how people become engaged. There would be a wedding—in six weeks, according to the invitation, when Alastair's mother said the Gloucestershire gardens would be at "their late summer best"—and Elodie would be one of those married people who met up at weekends to talk about houses and bank loans and schools. For there would be children, presumably, and she would be their mother. And she wouldn't be like her own mother, talented and sparkling, alluring and elusive; but her children would look to her for advice and comfort and she would know what to do and say because people just seemed to, didn't they?

Elodie set the box on the brown velvet chair in the corner of her room.

After a moment's uncertainty, she slid it under the chair instead.

The suitcase she'd brought back from her father's house was still standing by the door where she'd left it.

Elodie had imagined getting started on the tapes tonight, but she was suddenly tired—intensely tired.

She showered and then, guiltily, switched off the lamp and slunk into bed. She would start on the tapes tomorrow; she had to. Alastair's mother, Penelope, had already called three times since breakfast. Elodie had let the calls go through to voice mail, but any day now Alastair would announce that "Mummy" was cooking Sunday lunch and Elodie would find herself in the passenger seat of the Rover being transported up the tree-lined driveway to that enormous house in Surrey where the inquisition would be waiting.

Choosing the recording was one of only three tasks she'd been set. The second was visiting the reception venue owned by Penelope's best friend, "just to introduce yourself, of course; leave the rest to me." The third was liaising with Pippa, who'd offered to design her dress. So far, Elodie had completed none.

Tomorrow, she promised, pushing all thought of the wedding aside. Tomorrow.

She closed her eyes, the faint sounds of late-night customers buying battered cod and chips drifting up from downstairs, and without warning, her thoughts returned to the other box, the one beneath her desk at work. The framed photograph of the young woman with the direct gaze. The sketch of the house.

Again that strange sensation, like the glimpse of a memory she couldn't grasp, disquieted her. She saw the sketch in her mind's eye and heard a voice that was her mother's, but somehow also wasn't: "*Down the winding lane and across the meadow broad, to the river they went with their secrets and their sword . . .*"

And when she finally fell asleep, at the very moment that consciousness slid away, the pen-drawn picture in her mind dissolved into sunlit trees and the silver-tipped Thames, and a warm wind brushed her cheeks in an unknown place she somehow knew like home.

II

It has been a quiet existence, here at Birchwood. Many summers have passed since ours, and I've become a creature of habit, following the same gentle rhythms from one day into the next. I haven't a lot of choice. I rarely have visitors and those that do come these days don't stay long. I am not a good host. This is not an easy place to live.

People, by and large, are fearful of old buildings, just as they fear the elderly themselves. The Thames Path has become a favorite rambling route, and sometimes in the evenings and early mornings people stop in the laneway and peer over the garden wall. I see them but I do not let them see me.

I rarely leave the house. I used to run across the meadow, my heart thumping in my chest, my cheeks warm, the movement of my limbs strong and bold, but such feats are beyond me now.

Those people in the laneway have heard rumors about me, and they point and dip their heads together in the way of gossips everywhere. "That's where it happened," they say, "That's where he lived," and "Do you think she did it?"

But they do not trespass when the gate is shut. They have heard this is a haunted place.

I confess to paying little attention when Clare and Adele spoke of spirits. I was busy, my thoughts elsewhere. Many a time since I have regretted my distraction. Such knowledge would have come in useful over the years, especially when my "visitors" have come to call.

27

I have a new one, just arrived. I *felt* it first, as I always do. An awareness, a slight but certain change in the stale currents that lick and settle in the treads of the stairs at night. I kept my distance and hoped that it would not bother me as I waited for the stillness to return.

Only the stillness did not return. Nor the silence. It—*he*, for I have glimpsed him now—is not noisy, not like some of them, but I have learned how to listen, what to listen for, and when the movements took on a regular rhythm, I knew that he intended to stay.

It has been a long time since I've had a visitor. They used to bother me with their whispering and thumping, the chilling sense that my things, my spaces, were no longer my own. I kept about my business, but I studied them, one after the other, just as Edward might have done, and with time I learned how best to move them on. They are simple creatures, after all, and I have become practiced at helping them on their way.

Not all of them, mind you, for there are some to whom I have warmed. The Special Ones. The poor, sad soldier shouting in the night. The widow whose angry weeping fell between the floorboards. And, of course, the children—the lonely schoolgirl who wanted to go home, the solemn little lad who sought to mend his mother's heart. I like the children. They are always more perceptive. They have not yet learned how not to see.

I am still deciding about this new one, whether or not the two of us can live peaceably together, and for how long. He, for his part, has not yet noticed me. He is much intent on his own activity. The same each day, traipsing a path across the brewhouse kitchen, always with that brown canvas bag slung over one shoulder.

They are all like that at first. Unobservant, caught in their own loop, absorbed by whatever it is that they believe they must get done. I am patient, though. I have little else to do besides watch and wait.

I can see him now through the window, making his way towards the little churchyard on the edge of the village. He stops and seems to read the headstones as if he is searching for someone.

I wonder for whom. There are so many buried there.

I have always been curious. My father used to say that I was born wondering. Mrs. Mack said that it was only a matter of time before I ended up as flat as the curious cat.

There. He is gone now, over the top of the rise so that I can no longer tell which way he walks, or what it is that he carries inside his bag, or what he intends to do here.

I think I might be excited. As I said, it has been a while, and wondering about a new visitor is always buoying. It takes my thoughts away from the bones of habit upon which they usually pick.

Bones like these . . .

When they all packed up and fled, as the carriages tore like demons from hell along the coach way, did Edward glance behind him and glimpse in the dusk-lit window a sight to replace his nightmare?

Repaired to London and back behind his easel, did he blink sometimes to clear my image from his sight? Did he dream of me during the long nights, as my thoughts have dwelt on him?

Did he remember then, as I do now, candlelight flickering on the mulberry wall?

There are others, too. Bones that I have forbidden myself to polish further. There is little use wondering when there is no one left to ask.

They have all gone. They are all long gone. And the questions remain mine. Knots that can never be untied. Turned over and over again, forgotten by all but me. For I forget nothing, no matter how I try.

CHAPTER THREE

THE odd, unsettled feeling was still with Elodie the following day and she spent the train ride into work jotting down everything she could remember of her mother's bedtime tale. As London blurred on the other side of the window, and a group of schoolboys further down the carriage sniggered at a phone screen, she rested a notepad on her knee and let the real world disappear. Her pen raced across the page, but as the train drew nearer to Waterloo, her enthusiasm began to wane, her pace to slow. She glanced over what she'd written, the tale of the house with its celestial weather vane, and the mercurial wending river and the wonderful, terrible things that happened in the woods at night, and Elodie felt slightly embarrassed. It was a children's tale, after all, and she a grown woman.

The train stopped at the platform and Elodie gathered her bag from the floor beside her feet. She eyed the sketchbook—wrapped now in a clean cotton tea towel—and a wave of uncertainty washed over her as she recalled her recklessness the afternoon before, the sudden compulsion she'd felt to take it, her growing conviction that the sketch presaged some sort of mystery. She'd even harbored a suspicion—thank God, she'd had enough sense not to share it with her father!—that the sketch had been waiting for her all of these years.

Elodie's phone rang as she was passing St. Mary le Strand and Penelope's name appeared on-screen. As a butterfly swooped in Elodie's stomach, it occurred to her that her father might have had a point. That perhaps it was the wedding after all, and *not* the sketch of the house, that was stirring up these strange feelings. She ignored Penelope's call, tucking the phone away in her pocket. She would log in with her formidable mother-in-law-to-be that afternoon, after she'd met with Pippa and had something concrete to report.

For the many thousandth time, Elodie wished that her own mother were still alive to create some balance in the force. She had it on good authority—and not just from her father—that Lauren Adler had been extraordinary. Elodie had gone on a research binge when she was seventeen, the internet first and then beyond that by applying for a Reader Pass at the British Library, collecting every article and interview that she could find relating to Lauren Adler's glittering career. In her bedroom at night, she'd read all of the articles, forming a picture of an exuberant young woman with a stunning talent, a virtuoso whose mastery of her instrument was complete. But it was the interviews that Elodie had savored, for there, between the inverted commas, she'd discovered her mother's own words. Her thoughts, her voice, her very turns of phrase.

Elodie had read a book once, found beneath the bed in a hotel room in Greece, about a dying woman who wrote her children a series of letters about life and how to live it in order that she might continue to guide them from beyond the grave. But Elodie's mother had had no warning as to her impending death and had thus left no such sage advice for her only daughter. The interviews, though, were the next best thing and seventeen-year-old Elodie had studied each one, learning them by heart and whispering certain choice phrases to the oval mirror above her dressing table. They had become like revered lines of poetry, her very own list of life commandments. Because, unlike Elodie, who'd been struggling with bad skin and a hopeless case of teenage insecurity, seventeen-year-old Lauren Adler had been radiant: as modest as she was talented, she'd already played solo at the Proms, cementing herself forever as the nation's musical sweetheart.

Even Penelope, whose self-confidence was as old and established as the string of perfect pearls around her neck, spoke of Elodie's mother in tones of nervous awe. She never referred to "your mother"; it was always "Lauren Adler": "Did Lauren Adler have a favorite concert piece?" "Was there a venue that Lauren Adler preferred above all others?" Such questions Elodie answered to the best of her ability. She did not mention that much of her own knowledge had been acquired from interviews that were freely available if one knew where to look. Penelope's interest was flattering and Elodie clung to it. In the face of Alastair's grand estate, his tweed-and-twill parents, the weight of tradition in a family whose walls were covered with ancestral portraits, Elodie needed every advantage she could claim.

Alastair had mentioned in the early days of their relationship that his mother was a classical music buff. She used to play herself when she was a girl, but had given it all up when she became a debutante. He'd told stories that endeared him to Elodie, of the concerts his mother had taken him to when he was a boy, the excitement of the London Symphony Orchestra opening night at the Barbican or the conductor's arrival on stage at the Royal Albert Hall. It had always been just the two of them, their special time. ("My father finds it all a bit over-the-top, I'm afraid. His favorite cultural activity is rugby.") They still had a long-standing "date night" each month, a concert followed by dinner.

Pippa had arched her brows when she heard that, particularly when Elodie admitted that she hadn't ever been invited to join them, but Elodie had brushed it off. She was sure she'd read somewhere that men who treated their mothers well made the best partners. Besides, it was nice for a change for people not to assume that she must be a classical music aficionado. Throughout her life she'd had the same conversation over and over: strangers asking what instrument she played, the look of confusion when she told them that she didn't. "Not even a little?"

Alastair had understood, though. "I don't blame you," he'd said, "No point competing with perfection." And although Pippa had bridled when she heard this ("You're perfect at being you"), Elodie had known that wasn't what he'd meant—that he wasn't being critical.

It had been Penelope's idea to include a film recording of Lauren

Adler in the wedding ceremony. When Elodie said that her father kept a full video set of Lauren Adler's performances and that she could ask him to pull them out of storage if Penelope wished, the older woman had looked at her with what could only be described as genuine fondness. She'd reached out to touch Elodie's hand, the first time she'd ever done so, and said, "I saw her play once. She was stunning, so focused. A technician of the highest order, but with that added quality that made her music soar above all others. It was terrible when it happened, just terrible. I was bereft."

Elodie had been taken by surprise. Alastair's family did not "reach out" and they did not broach subjects like loss and bereavement in casual conversation. Sure enough, the moment was over as quickly as it had come, Penelope moving on to general musing about the early arrival of spring and its implications for the Chelsea Flower Show. Elodie, less adept in quicksilver changes of subject, had been left with a lingering sensation on her hand where the other woman's touch had been, and the memory of her mother's death had shadowed her for the rest of the weekend.

Lauren Adler had been the passenger in a car driven by the visiting American violinist, the two of them making their way back to London after a performance in Bath. The rest of the orchestra had returned the day before, straight after the show, but Elodie's mother had stayed behind to take part in a workshop with local musicians. "She was very generous," Elodie's father had said many times, practiced lines that formed part of the adoring litany of the bereaved. "People didn't expect it from her, someone so impressive, but she loved music and she went out of her way to spend time with other people who loved it, too. It didn't matter to her if they were expert or amateur."

The coroner's report, accessed by Elodie from the local archives during her summer of research, said that the accident had been caused by a combination of loose gravel on the country lane and poor judgment. Elodie had wondered why they hadn't been on the motorway, but coroners didn't offer speculation as to travel arrangements. Thus: the driver had taken a hairpin bend too quickly and the car

33

had lost traction, skidding across the verge; the impact had thrown Lauren Adler through the windscreen, breaking her body in countless places. She would never have played the cello again had she survived, a fact that Elodie had learned from a couple of her mother's musician friends whose conversation she'd overheard from her hiding place behind the sofa at the wake. The implication seemed to be that death was the lesser of two ills.

Elodie had not seen it that way, and neither had her father, who'd made it through the immediate aftermath, the funeral, in the grip of a shock-induced composure that was more alarming for Elodie in some ways than his plunge into the grey depths of despair afterwards. He had thought he was concealing his grief by remaining behind the closed door of his bedroom, but the old brick walls were not as thick as all that. Mrs. Smith from next door had smiled with grim knowing as she stepped into the breach, serving up soft-boiled eggs and toast for dinner each night and telling Elodie vivid stories about London in the war: her girlhood nights spent amidst the bombs and the Blitz, and the day the black-rimmed telegram came with news of her missing father.

Thus, the death of her mother was something Elodie could never quite untangle in her memory from the sound of explosives and the smell of brimstone and, on some deep sensory level, the fierce longing of a child in need of a story.

"Morning." Margot was boiling the kettle when Elodie arrived at work. She pulled down Elodie's favorite mug, sat it beside her own, and dropped a tea bag over the side. "A word to the wise: he's on the rampage this morn. The time management fellow has issued a list of 'recommendations.'"

"Oh, dear."

"Quite."

Elodie took the tea to her desk, careful not to catch Mr. Pendleton's eye as she passed his office. She felt a collegial affection for her crotchety old boss, but when the mood took him he could be punitive, and Elodie had enough to get done without the assignment of a gratuitous index revision.

She needn't have worried: Mr. Pendleton was well and truly distracted, glaring blackly at something on his monitor.

Elodie settled herself at her desk and without wasting a moment transferred the sketchbook from its toweling shroud within her handbag back to the box from the disused cloakroom. It had been a temporary madness and it was over. Best thing now was to catalogue the items and assign them a place in the archives once and for all.

She donned her gloves and then took out the hole punch, the inkwell, the wooden desk insert, and the spectacle case. Even the most cursory of glances revealed them as mid-twentieth-century office paraphernalia; the initials on the spectacle case meant that they were safely enough recorded as having belonged to Lesley Stratton-Wood; and Elodie was glad to relax into the ease of preparing a clear contents list. She fetched a new archive box and packed the items, carefully affixing the list of contents to one side.

The satchel was more interesting. Elodie began a meticulous inspection, noting the worn edges of the leather and a number of scuffs on the back, closer towards the right-hand side; the needlework in the joins was of a very high quality, and one of the buckles bore a set of five hallmarks suggesting that it was sterling and British-made. Elodie fitted the monocle magnifying glass to her left eye and took a closer look: yes, there was the lion for sterling; the leopard for London—uncrowned, which placed the item after 1822; a lowercase g in old English font connoting the year (a quick consultation of her London Date Letters chart revealed it as 1862); the duty mark showing Queen Victoria's head; and, finally, the maker's mark, a set of initials that read "W.S."

Elodie consulted the directory, running her finger down the list until she reached "William Simms." She smiled in recognition. The satchel had been made by W. Simms & Son, a high-end manufacturer of silver and leather goods with a Royal Warrant and, if Elodie remembered correctly, a shop situated in Bond Street.

Satisfying, but not a complete story, for the other marks on the satchel, the scuffs and patterns of wear, were of equal importance in determining its past. They showed that the satchel, no matter how exclusive its provenance, had not been purely decorative. It had been used and used well, slung over its owner's shoulder—the right shoulder, Elodie noted, as she ran her gloved fingers gently along the unevenly worn strap—and knocked habitually against the owner's left thigh. Elodie mimed hanging a satchel over one of her shoulders and realized that her instinct would have been to drape it in the other direction. There was a strong chance then that the satchel's owner had been left-handed.

That ruled out James Stratton, even though his document holder had been inside the satchel; but then, the gilt initials sealed to the leather flap of the satchel had done that already. "E.J.R." Elodie traced a gloved fingertip lightly over the cursive *E*. The same initials were on the sketchbook. It seemed safe to assume, then, that the person who had made the sketches was the same person to whom the initials belonged and that this was his (or her) satchel. An artist, then? James Stratton had liaised with a number of well-known artists of the day, but the initials were not immediately familiar. There was always Google, but Elodie had an even faster line to information about art. She pulled out her phone, quelled a heart flutter as she noticed that Penelope had left a second message, and then sent a text to Pippa:

> *Morning! Can you think of an artist, probably mid-Vic., with the initials EJR??*

The response was immediate:

> *Edward Radcliffe. Still on for today? Can we make it 11 instead of 12? Will text address.*

Edward Radcliffe. The name was vaguely familiar, though he was not one of the artists with whom James Stratton had kept up a regular correspondence. Now Elodie typed him into Google and clicked on the Wikipedia page. The entry was brief and she skimmed the first half, noting that Edward Radcliffe's birth year of 1840 made him a close peer to James Stratton, and that he had been born in London but spent some of his childhood in Wiltshire. He'd been the eldest of three children, the only son of a man who sounded like something of a dilettante and a woman with artistic pretensions, and had been raised for a number of years by his grandparents, Lord and Lady Radcliffe, while his parents were away in the Far East collecting Japanese ceramics.

The next paragraph described a wild youth, a fierce temper, and a precocious talent, discovered by chance when an elderly artist (unfamiliar to Elodie but evidently of some renown) stumbled upon his work and took the young man beneath his wing. There had been some promising early exhibitions, a patchy relationship with the Royal Academy, a brief but fiery public spat with Dickens after a poor review; and then, finally, vindication when the great John Ruskin commissioned a painting. By all accounts, Edward Radcliffe had been on track for a distinguished career, and Elodie was just starting to wonder why she wasn't familiar with his work, when she reached the final paragraph:

> *Edward Radcliffe was engaged to be married to Miss Frances Brown, the daughter of a Sheffield factory owner; however, when she was killed tragically during a robbery, at the tender age of twenty, he withdrew from public life. Rumors abound that Radcliffe was working on a masterpiece at the time; but, if so, neither the painting, nor any bona fide preliminary work, has ever seen the light of day. Radcliffe drowned off the coast of southern Portugal in 1881, but his body was returned to England for burial. Although his artistic output was not as prodigious as it might have been, Radcliffe remains an important figure in mid-nineteenth-century art for his role as a founding member of the Magenta Brotherhood.*

37

The Magenta Brotherhood. The name rang a distant work-related bell and Elodie made a note to cross-reference it with her Stratton correspondence database. She reread the paragraph, lingering this time over the violent, untimely death of Frances Brown; Radcliffe's withdrawal from public life; his lonely death in Portugal. Her mind stitched links of cause and effect between these points, arriving at a picture of a man whose promising career had been cut short by a broken heart and whose constitution had been weakened ultimately to the point of physical exhaustion.

Elodie took up the sketchbook and turned over its pages until she found the loose sheet containing the scrawled love note: *I love her, I love her, I love her, and if I cannot have her I shall surely go mad, for when I am not with her I fear—*

Was it true that there was a love so powerful that its loss could drive a person mad? Did people really feel like that? Her mind went to Alastair and she blushed, because of course to lose him would be devastating. But to be driven mad? Could she honestly imagine herself sliding into irredeemable despair?

And what if she were the one to go? Elodie pictured her fiancé in one of the immaculate bespoke suits made by the same tailor his father used; the smooth, handsome face that drew admiring glances wherever they went; the voice warmed by inherited authority. He was so assured, so clean-cut and contained, that Elodie couldn't imagine him being driven mad by anything. Indeed, it was sobering to reflect on how quickly and quietly the gap made by her absence might close over. Like the surface of a pond after a pebble is dropped.

Not like the turbulent aftermath of her mother's death, the high emotion and public grieving, the newspaper columns that ran alluring black-and-white photographs of Lauren Adler and used words like "tragedy" and "sparkling" and "fallen star."

Perhaps Frances Brown had also been a sparkling person?

A thought occurred to Elodie. The document holder that had once belonged to James Stratton was still inside the satchel, and now she took the framed photograph from inside.

Was this Frances Brown? The age was about right, for this face could not belong to a person much older than twenty.

Elodie stared closely, captured by the young woman's gaze, her direct expression. Self-possession, that's what it was. This was someone who knew her own mind, her own worth. The sort of woman about whom a passionate young artist might write: . . . *if I cannot have her I shall surely go mad . . .*

She typed "Frances Brown" into Google and an image search brought up multiple copies of the same portrait, a young woman in a green dress, also beautiful but predictably so—not the person whose likeness had been captured by the photograph.

Elodie felt a dull wash of disappointment. The feeling was not unfamiliar. It was the archivist's lot, for they were treasure hunters, in a way, sifting through the everyday detritus of their subject's life, sorting it methodically, constructing records, always hoping for that rare precious find.

It had been a long shot: the sketchbook and note had been found in the same satchel as the document holder containing the photograph, but there was no apparent connection beyond that. The satchel and sketchbook had belonged to Edward Radcliffe; the document case had belonged to James Stratton. At this point, there was no evidence that the two men had even been acquainted.

Elodie took up the framed photograph once more. The frame itself was of a high quality: sterling silver, intricately patterned. James Stratton's document holder was dated 1861 and it seemed reasonable to assume that the photograph inside it had belonged to him and that it had been acquired after that time. Also, that the woman in it had meant enough for him to keep it. But who was she? A secret romance? Elodie couldn't think that she had ever come across any of the telltale references in his journals or letters.

She looked again at the beautiful face, searching it for clues. The longer she stared at the image, the stronger the pull it exerted. The photograph was over a hundred years old, more likely a hundred and fifty, and yet the woman in it was unmarked by time; her face was strangely contemporary, as if she might have been one of those girls outside now on the summery streets of London, laughing with her friends and enjoying the sun's warmth on her bare skin. She was confident and amused, staring at the photographer with a familiarity that was almost uncomfortable to perceive. As if Elodie were trespassing on a private moment.

"Who are you?" she said beneath her breath. "And who were you to him?"

There was something more, something difficult to articulate. The woman in the photograph was *illuminated*: it was that face, of course, with its beautiful features and the enlivened expression, but it was the styling of the image, too. The long, unfussy hair, the romantic dress, loose and earthy, but also alluring where it caught her waist, where a sleeve had been pushed up her arm to reveal sunlit skin. Elodie could almost feel the warm breeze coming off the river to brush against the woman's face, to lift her hair and heat the white cotton of her dress. And yet, that was her mind playing tricks, for there was no river in the picture. It was the freedom of the photograph she was responding to, its atmosphere. Now, that was the sort of dress Elodie would like to wear at her wedding—

Her wedding!

Elodie glanced at the clock and saw that it was already a quarter past ten. She hadn't even responded to Pippa's message, but she was going to have to get moving if she expected to be at King's Cross by eleven. Gathering her phone and notebook, her diary and sunglasses, Elodie loaded her bag. She surveyed the desktop for anything she might have forgotten and, on a whim, picked up the framed photograph, the woman in that wonderful dress. With a glance at where Margot was hunched over by the filing cabinet, she wrapped it in the tea towel and tucked it in her bag.

Making her way through the office door and up the stairs into the warm summer's day, Elodie started texting her reply.

11 is fine, she typed; *Leaving now—send me the address and I'll see you soon.*

CHAPTER FOUR

PIPPA was working that day at a publishing house on New Wharf Road, putting together an installation in the foyer. When Elodie arrived at quarter past eleven, her friend was perched at the top of a very tall ladder in the center of the contemporary white room. She'd been stringing long dresses and other antique items of clothing—skirts and bloomers and corsets—from the high ceiling and the effect was enchanting, as if a dance floor of ivory ghosts had swept in on the breeze. Words came to Elodie's mind from one of her favorite Wilde poems:

> *We caught the tread of dancing feet,*
> *We loitered down the moonlit street,*
> *And stopped beneath the harlot's house*
> *. . .*
> *We watched the ghostly dancers spin,*
> *To sound of horn and violin,*
> *Like black leaves wheeling in the wind . . .*

Pippa spotted Elodie and exclaimed around the wooden ruler clenched horizontal in her teeth.

Elodie waved back and held her breath while her friend leaned to fasten a petticoat strap to a thread of fishing line.

After an excruciating moment, Pippa made it back to the ground in one piece. "Won't be long," she said to the man behind the desk as she shrugged on her backpack. "Just out for a coffee."

As they pushed through the large glass door, Elodie fell into step beside her friend. Pippa was wearing dark wartime dungarees and the sort of puffed-up sneakers favored by the teenage boys who gathered at the fish-and-chip shop on Friday evenings. The items were not individually notable, but somehow on Pippa their effect was magnified so that Elodie felt like a dreary little minnow in her jeans and ballet flats.

Pippa drew on her cigarette as they cut through a tall locked gate (to which she somehow had the code) and skirted the canal. "Thanks for coming early," she said on an exhalation. "I'm going to have to work through lunch to get it finished. The author's coming in tonight to launch the book. Have I shown you? It's *gorgeous*—an American who found out that the English aunt she'd known only as an ancient woman in a home had once been mistress to the king and had collected the most extraordinary wardrobe of dresses, all in mothballs in a storage unit in New Jersey. Can you imagine? The only thing my aunt left me was a nose I could steer a boat with." They crossed the street and made their way over the bridge towards a glass-faced restaurant adjacent to the tube station.

Inside, a friendly waitress seated them at a round table in the back corner. "Macchiato?" she said, to which Pippa replied, "Perfect. And a . . . ?"

"Flat white, please," said Elodie.

Pippa wasted no time in pulling a bulging scrapbook from her bag, letting it fall open to reveal all manner of loose papers and samples. "Here's what I'm thinking," she began, before launching into an enthusiastic description of sleeves and skirts, the pros and cons of peplums, the benefits of natural fabrics, switching from one illustration to another, barely pausing for breath, until the table was covered in magazine pages, fabric swatches, and fashion sketches. Finally she said, "So, what do *you* think?"

"I love it. All of it."

Pippa laughed. "I know it's a bit of a muddle; I just have so many thoughts flying around. How about you—do you have any ideas?"

"I have a veil."

"Ooh la la."

"Dad dug it out for me." Elodie handed over her phone with the photo she'd taken that morning.

"Your mum's? Lucky thing, it's gorgeous. Designer, I'm sure."

"I think so. Not sure which one."

"Hardly matters: it's beautiful. Now we just have to make sure the dress deserves it."

"I found a photograph of something I like."

"Come on, then, give us a look."

Elodie took the tea towel out of her bag and slid the silver frame from inside.

Pippa lifted a single amused brow. "Have to admit, I was expecting a torn page from *Vogue*."

Elodie handed the frame across the table and waited, a flutter of unplaceable nerves at the pit of her stomach.

"Wow, she's beautiful."

"I found her at work. She'd spent the past fifty years in a leather bag at the bottom of a box under some curtains in a cabinet beneath the stairs."

"No wonder she looks so pleased to be out." Pippa brought the photograph closer. "The dress is divine. The whole thing is divine. It's more of an art shot than a portrait, like something Julia Margaret Cameron might have taken." She looked up. "Does this have anything to do with the text you sent me this morning? Edward Radcliffe?"

"I'm still trying to figure that out."

"I wouldn't be surprised. This photo is classic aestheticism. The engaging expression, the loose dress and fluid posture. Early to mid-1860s, if I had to guess."

"It reminded me of the Pre-Raphaelites."

"Related, definitely; and of course the artists of the time were all inspired by one another. They obsessed over things like nature and truth; color, composition, and the meaning of beauty. But where the Pre-Raphaelites strove for realism and detail, the painters and photographers of the Magenta Brotherhood were devoted to sensuality and motion."

"There's something moving about the quality of light, don't you think?"

"The photographer would be thrilled to hear you say so. Light was of principal concern to them: they took their name from Goethe's color wheel theories, the interplay of light and dark, the idea that there was a hidden color in the spectrum, between red and violet, that closed the circle. You have to remember, it was right in the middle of a period when science and art were exploding in all directions. Photographers were able to use technology in ways they hadn't before, to manipulate light and experiment with exposure times to create completely new effects." She paused while the waitress delivered their coffees. "Edward Radcliffe was very well regarded, but not as famous as some of the other members of the Magenta Brotherhood went on to become."

"Remind me?"

"Thurston Holmes, Felix and Adele Bernard—they met at the Royal Academy and bonded over their anti-Establishment ideas; tight-knit, but with all the lies, lust, and split loyalties you'd expect in the cutthroat nineteenth-century art world. Radcliffe was prodigiously talented, but he died young." Pippa returned her attention to the photograph. "What makes you think he might have something to do with her?"

Elodie explained about the archive box and the satchel with Edward Radcliffe's initials on it. "There was a document holder inside that belonged to James Stratton; the only thing in it was this framed photo."

"And Radcliffe was a friend of your main man?"

"I've never come across the connection before," Elodie admitted; "That's one of the strange things about it all." She took a sip of her flat white as she decided whether to continue. She was torn between two opposing urges: a desire to tell Pippa everything and draw on her best friend's knowledge of art history; and an odd sensation that had come over her when she'd handed the photograph to Pippa, an almost jealous drive to keep the photo, the sketch, all for herself. It was an inexplicable and not particularly worthy impulse, and so she made herself continue: "The photo wasn't the only item inside the satchel. There was a sketchbook. I think it belonged to Edward Radcliffe."

"What sort of sketchbook?"

"Leather cover, about so big"—she demonstrated with her hands—"page after page of pen and ink sketches, handwritten notes. I think it belonged to Edward Radcliffe."

Pippa, who was never surprised by anything, drew breath. She caught herself quickly. "Was there anything in it you could use to date the work?"

"I haven't been all the way through—not carefully—but Stratton's document holder was made in 1861. I've no way of knowing if they're related, of course," she reminded Pippa, "beyond somehow, having wound up in the same satchel over the course of a hundred and fifty years."

"What were the drawings like? What were they of?"

"Figures, profiles, landscapes, a house. Why?"

"There were rumors of an abandoned work. After Radcliffe's fiancée's death, he continued to paint, but not with the same spirit as before, and very different subjects, and then he drowned. It was all very tragic. The idea of this 'abandoned work,' something he was working on before her death, has taken on a sort of mythology in art history circles: people keep hoping and guessing and positing theories. Every so often an academic takes it seriously enough to write a paper, even though to this point there hasn't been a lot of evidence to support the idea. It's one of those whispers that's so tantalizing it refuses to die."

"You think the sketchbook might have something to do with it?"

"Hard to say for sure without seeing it. I don't suppose you've any more tea towel surprises in that bag of yours?"

Elodie's cheeks warmed. "I could never take the sketchbook out of the archive."

"Well, why don't I drop in next week and have a look?"

Something tightened unpleasantly in Elodie's stomach. "You'd better call first: Mr. Pendleton's on the warpath."

Pippa flapped her hand, unperturbed. "Course." She leaned back in her chair. "In the meantime I'll get started on your dress. I can already picture it: romantic, gorgeous. Very *now*—in an 1860s sort of way."

"I've never been particularly fashionable."

"Hey, nostalgia's very much in vogue, you know."

Pippa was being affectionate, but today it rankled. Elodie *was* a nostalgic person, but she hated the charge. The word was terribly maligned. People used it as a stand-in for sentimentality, when it wasn't that at all. Sentimentality was mawkish and cloying, where nostalgia was acute and aching. It described yearning of the most profound kind: an awareness that time's passage could not be stopped and there was no going back to reclaim a moment or a person or to do things differently.

Of course, Pippa had only meant to make a light, humorous comment and had no idea as she gathered up her scrapbook that Elodie was upset. Why was she thinking along such lines? Why *was* she so sensitive today? Ever since she'd looked inside the satchel, she'd been unsettled. She felt constantly distracted, as if there were something she was supposed to be doing that had slipped her mind. Last night she'd even had the dream again: she'd been at the house in the sketch, when suddenly it turned into a church and she realized that she was late for a wedding—her own—and she started to run, but her legs wouldn't work properly—they kept collapsing as if they were made of string—and when she finally arrived, she found that it was no longer a wedding at all, she was too late, it was now a concert and her mother—still only thirty years old—was onstage playing her cello.

"How are the rest of the wedding plans coming along?"

"Fine. They're fine." It had come out crisply, and Pippa noticed. The last thing Elodie wanted was to get mired in a deep-and-meaningful that might expose her malaise, so she added, airily, "Of course, if it's details you're after, you'd best to speak with Penelope. I'm told it's going to be beautiful."

"Just make sure she remembers to tell you where and when to show up."

They smiled at one another, allies again, and then Pippa continued with blistering politeness. "And how is the fiancé?"

Pippa and Alastair had got off on the wrong foot, which wasn't entirely surprising, as Pippa had strong opinions and a sharp tongue and didn't suffer fools gladly. Not that Alastair was a fool—Elodie winced at her own mental slip of the tongue—only that he and Pippa weren't at all alike. Regretting her earlier sharpness, Elodie decided to wear some disloyalty to let her friend score a point. "He seems reassured that Mother is calling the shots."

Pippa grinned. "And your dad?"

"Oh, you know Dad. He's happy if I'm happy."

"And are you?"

Elodie gave a firm look.

"Okay, okay. You're happy."

"He's given me the recordings."

"He was okay with it, then?"

"Seemed to be. He didn't say much. I think he agrees with Penelope that it will be like having her there."

"Is that how you feel?"

Elodie didn't want to be having this discussion. "We have to have some sort of music," she replied defensively. "It makes sense to keep it in the family."

Pippa looked as if she were about to say something further, but Elodie got in first. "Did I ever tell you that my parents had a shotgun wedding? They were married in July and I was born in November."

"A little stowaway."

"You know how I feel about parties. Always looking for somewhere to hide."

Pippa smiled. "You do realize you're going to have to attend this one? That your guests will be expecting to see you?"

"Speaking of my guests, do you think you could be a dear and send back your RSVP?"

"What? In the post? With a stamp?"

"Apparently it's important. It's a thing."

"Well, if it's a *thing* . . ."

"It is, and I've been reliably informed that my friends and family are bucking the system. Tip's next on my list."

"Tip! How is he?"

"I'm off to see him tomorrow. Don't suppose you want to come?"

Pippa wrinkled her nose in disappointment. "I have a gallery event. Speaking of which . . ." She signaled the waitress to bring the bill and pulled a ten-pound note from her wallet. While she was waiting, she indicated the framed photograph, lying beside Elodie's empty coffee cup. "I'm going to need a copy so I can start thinking about your dress."

Elodie was seized again by the odd, possessive urge. "I can't lend it to you."

"'Course not. I'll take a pic now with my phone." She lifted the frame, angling the picture to make sure her shadow didn't fall across it.

Elodie sat on her hands, willing her friend to finish quickly, and then she rewrapped the photo in its cotton shroud.

"You know what?" said Pippa, inspecting the shot on her phone screen. "I'm going to run this by Caroline. She wrote her master's on Julia Margaret Cameron and Adele Bernard. I bet she'll be able to tell us something about the model, perhaps even who it was that took the photo."

Caroline was Pippa's mentor from art school, a filmmaker and photographer, renowned for her ability to find moments of beauty where they were least expected. Her images were wild and alluring, with lots of lean trees and houses and wistful landscapes. She was sixty or so, with the lithe movements and energy of a much younger woman; she had no children of her own and seemed to look upon Pippa as a daughter of sorts. Elodie had met her a couple of times socially. She had striking silver hair, cut straight and thick across her shoulder blades, and was the sort of woman whose self-possession and authenticity made Elodie feel like a bad fit for her own skin.

"No," she said quickly. "Don't do that."

"Why not?"

"I just . . ." There was no way of explaining that the photo had been hers alone and now it wasn't without sounding petty and, frankly, a bit unhinged. "I just meant . . . there's no need to bother Caroline. She's so busy—"

"Are you kidding? She'd love to see it."

Elodie managed a weak smile and told herself that it would be helpful to have Caroline's input. Unpleasant personal feelings aside, it was her job to learn as much as she could about the photograph and the sketchbook. And if a genuine tie to Radcliffe heralded any new information on James Stratton, it would be a very good thing for the archive team at Stratton, Cadwell & Co. New information on well-known Victorians did not surface often.

CHAPTER FIVE

Elodie walked the long way back, detouring down Lamb's Conduit Street because it was pretty and the dove-grey chocolate box of the Persephone storefront always managed to lift her spirits. She ducked inside—force of habit—and it was there, while she was leafing through the war diaries of Vere Hodgson, soaking up a 1930s swing-dance track, that her phone began to shrill.

It was Penelope again, and Elodie suffered an immediate clutch of panic.

She left the bookstore, cutting quickly across Theobalds Road, and then High Holborn, through to Lincoln's Inn Fields. Elodie picked up her pace as she passed the Royal Courts of Justice, darted behind a red bus to cross the street, and was almost jogging as she made her way along the Strand.

Rather than go straight back to work where Mr. Pendleton was in exactly the sort of mood to relish catching one of them making personal calls, she slipped down a cobbled laneway that dog-legged towards the river and found a bench on the Victoria Embankment, right near the pier.

She fished out her notebook and flipped to where she'd written the phone number of the wedding reception venue in Gloucestershire; Elodie dialed and made an appointment to visit the following weekend. Leaving no time for her commitment to cool, she telephoned Penelope, apologized for having missed her calls, and launched into a report of the progress she'd made with respect to the venue, the veil, the dress, and the videos.

After she hung up, Elodie sat for a few minutes. Penelope had been very pleased, particularly when Elodie reported the suitcase of her mother's recordings she now had in her possession. She had suggested that, rather than featuring only one clip of Elodie's mother playing the cello, they might feasibly include another at the end of the ceremony. Elodie had promised to make a short list of three tracks so that they could look at them together and decide. "Best make it five," Penelope had said. "Just in case."

So, that was the weekend sorted.

The ferry carrying tourists to Greenwich pulled out from the pier and a man in a Stars and Stripes cap pointed a long-lens camera at Cleopatra's Needle. A skein of ducks swooped in to take the boat's place, landing expertly on the choppy surface.

The ferry left ripples that washed against the low-tide bank, filling the air with the scent of mud and brine, and Elodie thought of a description in James Stratton's journal of the Great Stink of 1858. People didn't realize how badly London had smelled back then. The streets had been covered with animal dung, human waste, rotting vegetables, and the carcasses of slaughtered animals. All of it, and a lot more besides. had found its way into the river.

In the summer of 1858, the smell coming in off the Thames was reportedly so fetid that the Palace of Westminster had to be closed and those who could afford it were evacuated from London. The young James Stratton had been inspired to form the Committee to Clean Up London; he'd even published an article in 1862 in a journal called the *Builder*, agitating for progress. Amongst the archives were letters exchanged between Stratton and Sir Joseph Bazalgette, whose London sewer system was one of the great triumphs of Victorian England, funneling excrement away from the built-up center so that not only was the smell improved, but the incidence of waterborne disease was significantly reduced.

The thought of Stratton reminded Elodie that she had a workplace she was supposed to be at and a job she was meant to be doing. She went quickly, mindful of how long it had been since she'd left to meet Pippa, and was glad when she arrived to find that Mr. Pendleton had been called away and would be out of the office for the rest of the day.

Eager to capitalize on her return to efficiency, Elodie spent the afternoon cataloguing the remaining items from the lost archive box. The sooner it was filed and finished, the better.

She started by running a database search for "Radcliffe" and was surprised when the results delivered two items. One of the first jobs that Elodie had been assigned when she started at the firm was transferring the index card system onto the computer; she prided herself on having a near-photographic memory for the people and places that James Stratton had known and couldn't remember ever having come across the name Radcliffe before.

Curious, she fetched the corresponding documents from the file room and brought them back to her desk. The first was an 1861 letter from James Stratton to the art dealer John Haverstock, with whom he'd had plans to dine the following week. In the final paragraph of the letter, Stratton expressed a desire to "find out what you know about a painter whose name I came across recently—Edward Radcliffe. I am told he is a man of rare talent, although having had an opportunity to glimpse samples of his work I observe that his 'talent,' at least in part, is an ability to charm his young female subjects into revealing more than they otherwise might—all in the name of art, naturally."

As far as Elodie could remember, James Stratton did not own any of Radcliffe's paintings (though she made a note to confirm that fact); so, despite his interest in the painter, he must ultimately have been disinclined to acquire Radcliffe's work.

The second mention occurred some years later in Stratton's 1867 journal. At the end of a day's entry he had written:

> *The painter, Radcliffe, called to see me this evening. His arrival was unexpected and the hour was very late. I confess to having fallen asleep with my book in hand when*

the knocker startled me awake; poor Mabel was abed and I had to ring to summon her so that refreshments might be brought. I may as well not have bothered and let the weary girl sleep, for Radcliffe did not deign to touch one crumb of the supper provided. He fell, upon arrival, to treading this way and that across the carpet in a most harried state and could not be calmed. His manner was that of a crazed beast, his eyes wild and his long hair disheveled by the constant raking to which it was subjected by his fine, pale fingers. He emanated a captured energy, like a man possessed. He muttered as he paced, something incomprehensible about curses and fate, a sorry state of affairs indeed and one that gave me cause for grave concern. I know the loss that he has suffered, better than most, but his grief is wretched to watch; he is a reminder of what heartbreak can do to the most sensitive of souls. I confess that I had heard tell of his ruinous state, but I would not have believed the description had I not seen it with my own eyes. I have determined to do what I can, for it will surely right the scales in some way if I can help him to regain his former self. I encouraged him to stay, assuring him that it was no hardship at all to have a room made up, but he refused. He asked instead that I keep a couple of his personal effects for him, and of course I agreed. He was nervous to make the request and I sensed that he had not come to see me with the intention of leaving the items; rather, that the idea had come to him on the spur of the moment. It is only a leather satchel, empty but for a single book of sketches. I would never have broken a confidence to look inside, but he insisted on showing me before he left. He made me swear to keep the bag and sketchbook safe, poor soul. I did not press him on the question of from whom it is to be kept, and he gave me no answer when I asked as to when he might return. He only looked at me sadly, before thanking me for the supper he did not eat, and

leaving. His wretched presence stayed with me afterwards,
and is with me even now, as I sit by the dying fire writing
this record.

The journal extract painted a melancholy picture, and the "wretched presence" described within its pages lingered with Elodie, too. The account answered her question as to how James Stratton came to possess Edward Radcliffe's satchel, but there was still the intriguing question of how Radcliffe had come to know James Stratton well enough in the space of six years to turn up at his door in the middle of the night when beset by his private demons. Also, why he had chosen Stratton, of all people, to safeguard his bag and book. Elodie made a note to cross-reference some of the archives of Stratton's friends and associates to see whether Radcliffe's name appeared there.

Another wrinkle was Stratton's reference to wanting to "right the scales." It was an odd turn of phrase, almost suggesting that he had played some part in the man's decline, which made no sense at all. Stratton couldn't have known Edward Radcliffe well: he'd made no mention of the other man in any of the private or public documents within the archive at any time between 1861 and 1867. And it was established fact, according to Pippa and Wikipedia, that Radcliffe had slid into despair after the death of his fiancée, Frances Brown. The name was not familiar to her within the context of Stratton's archives, but Elodie made another note to cross-reference his associates' papers.

She opened a new archive form on her computer and typed in a description of the satchel and sketchbook, adding a brief summary of the letter and journal entry and the corresponding file reference details.

Elodie leaned back in her chair and stretched.

Two down, one to go.

The identity of the woman in the photo, however, was going to be more difficult. There was just so little to work with. The frame was of a fine quality, but then, James Stratton had owned very few items that weren't. Elodie attached her magnifying eyepiece and searched the frame for silver markings. She jotted them down on a piece of scrap paper, even as she knew they were unlikely to yield any clues as to the subject of the photo and her relationship to James Stratton.

She wondered how the photograph had found its way into Radcliffe's satchel. Was the placement accidental or was there some meaning to it? It all depended, she supposed, on the identity of the woman. It was possible, of course, that she had not been special to Stratton and that the frame had, in fact, been placed within the satchel by the great-niece to whom the desk had belonged—a random act of storage at some point during the decades after Stratton's death. But it was an outside chance. The way the woman was dressed, the styling and look of the photo itself, suggested that it—and she—had been contemporaneous with Stratton. Far more likely that he had stored, even concealed, the photograph inside his document holder and slipped it inside the satchel himself.

Elodie finished her inspection of the frame, making notes so that she could provide a description of its condition on the archive sheet—a dent at the top, as if it had been dropped; some fine, feathery scratches on the back—and then she returned her attention to the woman. Again the word that came to mind was "illuminated." It was something in the quality of the woman's expression, the flow of her hair, the light in her eyes . . .

Elodie realized that she was staring as if she expected the woman to explain herself. But no matter how hard she tried, she could find no identifying feature in the face, the clothing, even in the background of the image that suggested where to turn next. Although the photograph was well composed, there was no studio signature in any of the corners, and Elodie wasn't familiar enough with Victorian photography to know whether anything else inherent to the image might give a clue as to its origin. Perhaps Pippa's mentor, Caroline, would be able to help after all.

She set the frame down on her desk and rubbed her temples. The photo was going to be a challenge, but she refused to be cowed. The detective thrill of the chase was one of the best parts of her job, a counterbalance to the satisfying but repetitive work of creating neat records. "I'll find you," she said softly. "Make no mistake about that."

"Talking to yourself again?" Margot was beside Elodie's desk, hunting through the handbag she had slung across her shoulder. "First sign of trouble, you know." She found a tin of peppermints and shook them, dropping a couple into Elodie's waiting palm. "Staying late?"

Elodie glanced at the clock, surprised to find that it was already half past five. "Not tonight."

"Alastair picking you up?"

"He's in New York."

"Again? You must be missing him. Don't know what I'd do without Gary to go home to."

Elodie agreed that she was missing her fiancé, and Margot gave her a sympathetic smile which turned swiftly into a cheery farewell. Fishing her neon earbuds out of her bag, she swiped her iPhone and sashayed off into the weekend.

The office resettled into papery silence. The strip of sunlight had arrived on the far wall and was beginning its daily approach towards her desk. Elodie cracked one of the mints open with her back teeth and hit PRINT on the archive label she'd made for the new box. She started to tidy her desk, a task she performed religiously on Friday afternoons so that she could begin the upcoming week with a clean slate.

Not that she'd admit it, and certainly not to Margot, but there was a small part of Elodie that looked forward to Alastair's weeks in New York. She missed him, of course, but it was restful in some way knowing that for six whole nights she could stay at her own place, in her own bed, with her own books and her favorite teacup, without having to negotiate and explain herself.

It was true what he said: her flat was tiny and there was that old chip grease smell in the stairwell, whereas his was large, with two bathrooms, and always enough hot water, and never any need to listen to the neighbor's television through the whisper-thin floors. But Elodie was fond of her little flat. Yes, there was a trick to getting the kitchen sink to drain properly and the shower only ever managed a half flow when the washing machine was running a cycle, but it felt like the sort of place where real human lives could be and had been led. There was history in its natty old cupboards and creaking floorboards, the loo that was reached only by climbing three carpeted stairs.

Alastair seemed to consider it endearing that she found comfort in such diminished surrounds. "You should be staying at my place when I'm away," he always said, his place being a sleek apartment at Canary Wharf. "You don't need to go back to your lair."

"I'm happy here."

"Here? Really?" They'd had a variation on the same conversation at least fifteen times, and he always reserved his most skeptical glance for deployment at this point, its target invariably the corner in which Elodie had arranged her dad's old velvet armchair beneath a fairy-lighted shelf of treasures: the painting Mrs. Berry had presented to her when she turned thirty, the charm box Tip gave her after her mother died, a framed strip of funfair photos taken with Pippa when they were both thirteen.

Alastair favored mid-century Danish design and believed that if an item couldn't be purchased from the Conran Shop, it had no business being on display at all. Elodie's flat was "homely," he was willing to concede, but only before adding, "Of course, you'll have to give it up when we're married—we can't very well put the crib in the bathroom."

Obviously, it was churlish to feel anything other than excited at the prospect of living in such a grand, glossy place, but Elodie just wasn't a very grand, glossy person, and she was terrible with change. "Little wonder"—this was the psychologist she'd seen for a time when she first went up to Oxford. "You lost your mother. It's one of the most significant and frightening changes that a child can experience." Such loss, Elodie was reliably informed by Dr. Judith Davies ("Call me Jude") after three months of weekly sessions in the warm front room of her Edwardian house, couldn't help but embed itself within a person's psyche.

"You mean it's going to affect my every life decision?" Elodie had asked.

"I do."

"Forever?"

"Most likely."

She had stopped seeing Dr. Davies ("It's Jude") soon after that. There hadn't seemed much point, though she *had* missed the pot of citrus mint tea that appeared on the scuffed wooden table at the start of each session.

The doctor had been right: Elodie had got no better with change. Picturing other people in *her* flat, hanging their pictures on the hooks she'd hammered into the wall, arranging their teacups on the sill where she grew her herbs, enjoying the view from her window, gave Elodie the same dread feeling she'd experienced sometimes on holiday when she woke in an unfamiliar room utterly lost because none of her touchstones were there.

She hadn't had the heart to break the news about the move to her landlady yet. Mrs. Berry was eighty-four years old and had grown up in the house in Barnes, when it was still a family home and not three and a half flats above a fish-and-chip shop. She lived now in the garden flat behind the shop. "This used to be my mother's morning room," she liked to reminisce after a glass or two of her favorite sherry. "Such a lady she was, such a fine lady. Oh, not in the aristocratic sense, I don't mean that, it was just her nature." Mrs. Berry's eyes took on a particular shine when she started to slip into the past and she became less careful with her cards. "What are trumps?" she'd ask at the start of each round. "Spades? Or was it Curlies?"

Elodie was going to have to cancel the game they'd penciled in for that evening. She'd promised Penelope a list of recordings and a selection of clips by Monday. Now she was on a roll, she couldn't let anything get in the way of ticking items off her list.

She shut down the computer and capped her pen, lining it up against the top of the jotting pad. The desk was clear except for the satchel, the sketchbook, and the framed photograph. The first two could be reboxed and stored; the latter faced another weekend amidst the jumble of office supplies within the lost box.

Before tucking the photograph away, Elodie took a picture with her phone, just as Pippa had done. She would need it if she were to give more thought to her dress. It wouldn't hurt to look at it beside the veil, either.

After a moment's hesitation, she took a photo of the house in the sketchbook, too. Not because she was allowing herself any longer to entertain the notion that it was somehow, magically, the house from her mother's fairy tale. She took the photo simply because she liked the sketch. It was beautiful, and it made her feel things: a connection to her mother and a tethering to the unbroken part of her childhood.

And then Elodie slipped the satchel and sketchbook into a new archive box, affixed the label she'd printed out, and filed them in the storeroom on her way out the door and into the busy London street.

III

Mrs. Mack used to say that a needy man's budget was full of schemes. She'd say that sort of thing whenever she wanted one of us to try a new scam, we kids that lived like rats in the runners within the set of small rooms above the bird shop on Little White Lion Street.

I've been thinking about Mrs. Mack lately. And Martin and Lily and the Captain. And even Pale Joe, who was the first person I ever truly loved. (The second if you include my father, which I don't always.)

Mrs. Mack was kind enough in her way. It was a way that included plenty of beatings for those that got on her wrong side and a tongue so sharp it lashed, but she was fairer than most. In her way. She was good to me; she took me in when I was desperate; I believe she even loved me. I betrayed her in the end, but only when I had to.

It is different on this side. Human beings are curators. Each polishes his or her own favored memories, arranging them in order to create a narrative that pleases. Some events are repaired and buffed for display; others are deemed unworthy and cast aside, shelved belowground in the overflowing storeroom of the mind. There, with any luck, they are promptly forgotten. The process is not dishonest: it is the only way that people can live with themselves and the weight of their experiences.

But it is different over here.

I remember everything, memories forming different pictures depending on the order in which they fall.

Time passes differently when I'm alone in the house; I have no way of marking the years. I am aware that the sun continues to rise and set and the moon to take its place, but I no longer feel its passage. Past, present, and future are meaningless; I am outside time. Here and there, and there and here, at once.

My visitor has been with me for five of his days now. I was surprised when he first arrived, with his scuffed suitcase and that brown bag over his shoulder, which makes me think of Edward's satchel; even more so when the doors were locked on the house that night and he remained. It has been a long while since anyone stayed here overnight. Ever since the Art Historians' Association opened the house to the public, I have seen only weekend day-trippers with sensible shoes and tour books.

The people from the Association have put the young man in the rooms of the old malthouse, part of the closed area that was once used briefly to accommodate a caretaker and into which the visiting public are NOT PERMITTED. It wouldn't do to have him take up residence inside the house, for it is set up like a museum now. Antique furniture, much of it from Edward's own collection, purchased with the house when he bought it, has been "arranged," taking care to leave room for the tourists to mill about on weekends. Bunches of lavender with velvet bows have been placed on the seats so that no one tries to use them as intended.

Just before my clock strikes ten each Saturday morning, a group of volunteers arrives, positioning themselves about the house so that there is one per room. They wear tags that read, "Guide" around their necks, and it is their job to remind people DO NOT TOUCH! They are primed with partially correct historical anecdotes so that when they catch the eye of a half-willing tourist they can ensnare them with their spiel.

There is one in particular, Mildred Manning, who likes to sit on a Quaker-style chair at the top of the attic staircase, baring her teeth in the grim approximation of a smile. Nothing makes her happier than to catch an unwitting guest in the process of setting down their pamphlet on the table beside her. This infraction grants her the prized opportunity to intone that "*nothing* should be placed upon Edward Radcliffe's furniture."

Edward would have hated her. He couldn't bear the zealous over-protection of "things." He believed that beautiful objects should be cherished but not revered. And so, with Edward in mind, some days when the year is creeping towards autumn, I spend my afternoons draped around Mildred's shoulders. No amount of clothing can keep a person warm when I get too close.

———

I have taken a preliminary inventory: my visitor's hair is dirty blond in color and his skin is sun-browned. His hands are weathered and capable. They are not the fine hands of a painter. They are the hands of a man who knows how to use the tools that he carries with him when he heads out on his daily rounds.

He has been very busy since he arrived. He wakes early, before sunrise, and although he does not seem pleased about the fact, groaning and then squinting at the phone he keeps beside his bed to tell the time, he nonetheless elects to rise rather than to remain in bed. He makes a cup of tea, quickly and sloppily, and then showers and dresses, always in the same clothing: a T-shirt and faded blue denim jeans, tossed the night before across the bentwood chair in the corner.

Whatever it is that he is doing requires him to frown at a map of the manor grounds and a series of handwritten notes. I have taken to standing at a distance behind him as I try to discover what it is that he is up to. But it is no use. The handwriting is too small and faint to read and I dare not go nearer. We have not yet been acquainted long enough for me to know how close I can get. I can be an oppressive companion and I do not wish to scare him off.

Yet.

And so I wait.

I do at least know what it is he keeps in that brown bag of his; he unpacked it last night. It is a camera, a proper camera of the sort that Felix might recognize were he to rematerialize suddenly in the here and now.

Something that Felix would not recognize, however, is the way my visitor is able to connect the camera to a computer and have the images appear, like magic, upon the screen. No need anymore for a darkroom or developing solutions with their acrid smell.

I watched last night as he scrolled through picture after picture. Photographs of the churchyard; headstones, mainly. No one that I knew, but I was transfixed all the same. It was the first time in many years that I have been able to "leave" this place.

What do his photographs tell me about his purpose here? I wonder.

Not nearly enough.

He is out there somewhere now; he has been gone since breakfast time. But I am patient, far more patient now than before.

I have been watching from the window in the stairwell, looking beyond the chestnut tree towards my old friend the Thames. I do not expect my young man to return that way: unlike others who came to Birchwood before him, he does not favor the river. He considers it at times, as one might a painting, but only from a distance and not, I think, with pleasure. No boat rides for him thus far.

No, I watch the river for myself. The Thames flowed through my life just as surely as blood flows through a body. I can only go as far now as the wall of the field barn in the north, the Hafodsted Brook to the west, the orchard to the east, and the Japanese maple in the south. I have tried to travel further over the years, but, alas, to no avail. The sensation, if I dare, is like an anchor being pulled. I do not understand the physics; I only know that it is so.

My visitor is not as young as I first thought. He is muscular and able, with the pulsing physicality of an animal made to come inside against his will, but there is something that weighs on him. Hardships tell upon a man: my father aged by a decade during the months after my mother's death, when the landlord began to knock on our door and the two of them engaged in tense discussions that became more and more heated over time, until at last, on a bleak wintry day, the landlord shouted that he'd been as patient as a saint, that he wasn't a charity and it was high time my father found himself a new situation.

My visitor's hardship is of a different nature. He keeps a printed photograph inside a scuffed leather wallet. I have seen him take it out late at night and pore over it. The image is of two small children, little more than babies. One of them grins with juicy happiness at the camera; the other is more circumspect.

The way he frowns at that photograph—the way he rubs his thumb across its surface, as if by doing so he might enlarge it and permit himself a closer view—makes me certain that they are his.

And then, last night, he made a call on his mobile telephone to someone he called Sarah. He has a warm voice and was polite, but I could see by the way he clenched his pen and clawed his hand in his hair that he was struggling.

He said, "But that was a long time ago," and "You'll see, I've changed," and "Surely I deserve a second chance?"

As all the while he stared at that photograph, worrying at its top left corner with his fingertips.

It was that conversation which put me in mind of my own father. Because before Mrs. Mack and the Captain there was my father, always looking for his second chance. He was a clockmaker by trade, a master craftsman, his skills unsurpassed and his expertise sought by those with the most elaborate timepieces to repair. "Each clock is unique," he used to tell me. "And just like a person, its face, whether plain or pretty, is but a mask for the intricate mechanism it conceals."

I went with him sometimes on repair jobs. He called me his helper, but I did not really help. When he was ushered into the library or study, I was invariably taken downstairs by a dutiful serving maid into one of the vast steaming kitchens that fueled the stately houses of England. Each had a rotund cook laboring away in her engine room, pink of cheek, sweaty of brow, keeping the larders stocked with sweet lumpy jam and fresh loaves of bread.

My father used to tell me that my mother had grown up in such a house. She had been sitting in the grand upstairs window, he said, when he arrived to mend her father's clock. Their eyes had met, they'd fallen in love, and nothing after that could keep them apart. Her parents had tried, her little sister had pleaded with her to stay, but my mother was headstrong and young and used to being indulged, and so she ran away. Children as a rule are literal creatures, and whenever I heard this story I pictured my mother running, her skirts flying behind her in a satin wake, as she fled from the looming castle, leaving behind her beloved sister and the raging horror of her overbearing parents.

This is what I believed.

My father had to tell me stories, as I did not have the chance myself to know my mother. She was two days shy of twenty-one when she died, and I a child of four. It was consumption that killed her, but my father had the coroner put "bronchitis" on her death certificate, as he thought it sounded more refined. He needn't have bothered: having married my father and left the bosom of her titled family, she was removed to the great mass of ordinary people of whom history takes no account.

There was a single likeness, a small sketch, that he kept inside a gold locket, and which I treasured. Until, that is, we were forced to move into the pair of drafty rooms in the pinched alleyway in a pocket of East London, where the smell of the Thames was always in our noses and the calls of gulls and sailors mingled to form a constant song, and the locket disappeared to the rag-and-bone man. I do not know where the likeness went. It slipped through the cracks of time and went to where the lost things are.

——

My father called me Birdie; he said I was his little bird. My real name was beautiful, he said, but it was the name of a grown-up lady, the sort of name that wore long skirts and fine silks, but had not the wings to fly.

"Do I want a name with wings?"

"Oh, yes, I should think so."

"Then why did you give me one without?"

He became earnest then, as he always did when talk grazed the subject of *her*: "You were named for your mother's father. It was important to her that you should carry something of her family."

"Even if they did not wish to know me?"

"Even if," he said with a smile, and then he ruffled my hair, which never failed to make me feel assured: as if no deprivation could matter in the face of his love.

My father's workshop was a place of wonder. The great tall bench beneath the window was a sea of springs and rivets, scales and wires, bells, pendulums, and fine arrow hands. I used to sneak in through the open door to kneel on a wooden stool and explore the bench while he was working, turning over the curious and clever contraptions, gently pressing the tiny, fragile parts beneath my fingertips, holding the different metals in the streaming sun to make them shine. I asked question after question, and he peered over his glasses to answer; but he made me promise not to breathe a word to anyone about the things that I observed, for my father was not merely repairing clocks; he was working on an invention of his own.

His Great Project was the creation of a Mystery Clock, the construction of which involved long sessions at his workbench and frequent surreptitious visits to the Court of Chancery, where patents of invention were enrolled and issued. My father said that the Mystery Clock, when he mastered it, would make our fortune—for which man of means would not desire a clock whose pendulum appeared to move without the benefit of a mechanism?

I nodded solemnly when he said such things—the gravity with which he spoke required it—but in truth I was equally impressed by the regular clocks that lined his walls from floor to ceiling, their hearts beating, their pendulums swinging, in constant gentle dissonance. He showed me how to wind them, and I would stand back in the center of the room afterwards, gazing at their mismatched faces as they tut-tut-tutted me in chorus.

"But which one shows the *right* time?" I would ask.

"Ah, little bird. The better question is: Which one doesn't?"

There was no such thing as the right time, he explained. Time was an idea: it had no end and no beginning; it could not be seen or heard or smelled. It could be measured, sure enough, but no words had been found to explain precisely what it was. As to the "right" time, it was simply a matter of agreeing to agree. "Do you remember the woman on the railway platform?" he asked.

I told him that I did. I had been playing one morning while my father repaired the large clock at a station west of London, when I'd noticed a smaller version hanging on the wall by the ticket office. I'd stopped what I was doing and was looking between the two disparate faces when a woman came up beside me. "That there's the real time," she'd explained, pointing at the little dial. "And that one"— she frowned at the clock my father had just finished winding—"that there's London time."

Which is how I learned that while I could not be in two places at once, I could most certainly be in one place at two times.

Soon after, my father suggested that we take a trip to Greenwich, "the home of the meridian."

Greenwich meridian. The new words were like an incantation.

"A line from which time begins," he continued. "From the north to the south pole, it splits the earth in two."

So impressive did this sound, so vivid was my child's imagination, that I suppose it was inevitable the reality would disappoint.

Our journey took us to the well-tended lawn of a grand stone palace, from which I searched in vain for the great, jagged tear I had envisaged in the earth's surface.

"There it is"—he indicated with a straightened arm—"right in front of you, a direct line. Zero degrees longitude."

"But I cannot see anything. All I see is . . . grass."

He laughed when I said that, and ruffled my hair, and asked whether I would like to take a look through the Royal Observatory telescope instead.

We took the journey along the river to Greenwich a number of times in the months before my mother died, and on the boat back and forth my father taught me how to read—the words in books, the tides in the river, the expressions on the faces of our fellow travelers.

He showed me how to tell the time by the sun. Human beings had ever been captivated by the great burning sphere in the heavens, he said, "for not only does it give us warmth, but also light. The foremost craving of our souls."

Light. I took to watching it on the spring trees, noticing how it turned the delicate new leaves translucent. I observed the way it threw shadows against walls; tossed stardust across the surface of the water; made filigree on the ground where it fell through wrought-iron railings. I wanted to touch it, this marvelous tool. To hold it in my fingertips the way I did the tiny objects on my father's workbench.

It became my mission to capture light. I found a small hinged tin, emptied of its contents, and drove a nail through the top several times with one of my father's hammers to make tiny perforations. I took the contraption outside with me, sat it in the sunniest place that I could find, and waited until the top was burning hot. Alas, when I slid the box of wonder open, there was no glittering captive waiting for me. It was just the empty inside of a rusty old tin.

—————

Mrs. Mack used to say that when it rained, it poured—which wasn't a comment on the weather, although it took me a while to work that out, but an observation of the way misfortune seemed to invite further misfortune.

After my mother died, it began to pour for my father and me.

For one thing, it was the end of our trips to Greenwich.

For another, we saw a lot more of Jeremiah. He was my father's friend, of sorts, the two of them having grown up in the same village. He had visited occasionally when my mother was alive, for my father had taken him along sometimes as an apprentice on large railway clock repair jobs; but I was aware, in the vague, instinctive manner of small children, that Jeremiah was a source of tension between them. I can remember my father offering placatory assurances like "He does the best with what God gave him," or "He means well," and reminding her that although Jeremiah had been blessed with few of life's gifts, he was "a good fellow, really, and certainly very enterprising."

The latter was undeniably true: Jeremiah turned his hand to whatever opportunity came his way. He was by turns a rag-and-bone man, a tanner, and at one time became convinced his fortune lay in the door-to-door distribution of Steel's Aromatic Lozenges, the professed benefits of which included "magnificent male stamina."

After my mother's death, when my father began his tumble into the dark crevasse of grief, Jeremiah started taking him out for long stretches in the afternoon, the pair of them stumbling back after dark, my father half-asleep and slumped across his friend's shoulder. Jeremiah would then bed down for the night on the sofa in our drawing room, all the better to "help" us out the following day.

And my father had longer days to fill by then. His hands had started to shake and he had lost the ability to concentrate. He received fewer offers of work, which in turn made him bitter. Jeremiah, though, was always there to prop him up. He convinced my father that he'd been wasting his time on repairs anyway; that his future lay in perfecting his Mystery Clock; that with Jeremiah as his agent they couldn't help but make a fortune.

When the landlord finally reached the end of his patience, it was Jeremiah, through his contacts, who helped my father to find rooms in a building that huddled in the shadows of the steeple of St. Anne's. He seemed to know a lot of people and always had an opinion to venture and a "bit of business" to transact. It was Jeremiah who oversaw the sale of my father's patents and Jeremiah who told me not to worry when the bailiff started knocking on the door at all hours, complaining that my father owed him money; he knew a man who ran a gambling outfit in the Limehouse, he said. All my father needed was a little bit of luck to see him right.

And when my father took to spending every night down at the public house on Narrow Street, dragging himself back at first light smelling of tobacco and whisky to collapse at the empty table with his pipe—when he sold off the last of his brass and rivets in order to pay his gambling debts—it was Jeremiah who shook his head sadly and said, "Your old man's just unlucky. I never did meet a man with an unluckier star."

———

The bailiff continued to knock, but my father ignored him. He began, instead, to talk obsessively about America. In his battered state, the idea made perfect sense. We would leave behind the sorrow and unhappy memories and start afresh in a new place. "There's land, little bird," he said, "and sunshine for the taking. And rivers that run clean and soil that can be turned over without fear of unearthing bones from the past." He sold the last of my mother's dresses, pieces that he had been saving for me, and booked cheap passage for us both on the next ship to America. We packed our possessions, such as they were, in one small suitcase apiece.

The week that we were due to leave was cold, the first snow of the season, and my father was eager that we should have as much extra coin as possible for the journey. We spent each day down by the river, where a supply ship had recently overturned and there were prizes hidden in the mud for those that wanted most to find them. We labored each hour, from dawn until dusk, through rain and sleet and snow.

Mudlarking was ever tiring work, but one evening I was more exhausted than usual. I fell upon my mattress, soaking wet, and was unable to rise. The dizziness came on suddenly, along with aches that made my bones feel cold and heavy. My teeth chattered even as my forehead burned, and the world began to darken as surely as if someone had pulled down its curtains.

I was adrift, my perception as unsteady as a small wooden boat in rough seas. I heard my father's voice sometimes, and Jeremiah's, but they were brief snatches followed by long stretches of surrender to the vivid stories in my mind's eye, dreams most fruity and peculiar.

My fever raced, creating shadows and jagged monsters in the room; they lurched across the walls, widening their crazy eyes, reaching their taloned fingers to grab at my bedclothes. I turned and twisted away from them, my sheets wet from the exertion, my lips moving around incantations that seemed of vital importance.

Words pierced my delusions like hot needles, familiar words like "doctor" . . . "fever" . . . "America" . . . that had once held meaning and importance.

And then I heard Jeremiah say, "You must go. The bailiff will be back, and he's promised to put you in jail this time, or worse."

"But the child, my little bird—she is not well enough to travel."

"Leave her here. Send for her when you're settled. There are people who'll mind a child for a small fee."

My lungs, my throat, my mind, all burned with the effort to shout, "No!"; but whether the word passed my lips I could not tell.

"She depends on me," said my father.

"Worse, then, if the judge decides that you must pay for your debts with your life."

I wanted to shout, to reach out and grab my father, to cleave him to me so that we could never be parted. But it was no use. The monsters pulled me under again and I heard no more. Day dissolved into night; my boat pushed out once more into stormy seas—

And that is the last I remember of that.

The next thing I knew, it was morning, bright, and the first sound to my ears was of birds calling outside the window. But these were not the birds that sing of morning's arrival here at Birchwood Manor, or those that used to nest beneath the sill in our little house in Fulham. This was a great cacophony of birds, hundreds of them squawking and jeering in languages foreign to my ears.

A church bell pealed and I recognized it at once as the bell of St. Anne's, but it was *different* somehow from the sound that I knew so well.

I was a shipwrecked sailor, washed up on a foreign shore.

And then a voice, a woman's voice I did not know; "She's waking."

"Papa," I tried to say, but my throat was dry and a mere airy sound arrived.

"Shhh . . . there, now," said the woman. "There, now. Mrs. Mack is here. Everything's going to be all right."

I cracked open my eyes to find a large figure looming above me.

Beyond, I saw that my little suitcase was on a table by the window. Someone had opened the lid and my clothing was sitting now in a neat pile beside the case.

"Who are you?" I managed to say.

"Why, I'm Mrs. Mack, of course, and this lad here is Martin, and that over there's the Captain." There was a note of cheery impatience in her voice.

I looked about, absorbing quickly the unfamiliar surrounds and the strange people to whom she was pointing. "Papa?" I started to cry.

"Shhh. Lordy, child, there's no need to blubber. You know very well that your father's gone on to America and will send for you when he's ready. In the meantime, he's asked that Mrs. Mack look after you."

"Where am I?"

She laughed. "Why, child! You're at home, of course. Now, stop that bawling or else the wind might change and spoil that pretty face of yours."

———

And so I was born twice.

Once, to my mother and father, in a small room in our family home in Fulham, on a fresh summer's night when the moon was full and the stars were bright and the river was a shimmery-skinned snake beneath the window.

And once again, to Mrs. Mack, when I was seven years old, in her house tucked above the shop selling birds and cages, in the area of Covent Garden referred to as the Seven Dials.

CHAPTER SIX

Mrs. Berry was out amongst the hollyhocks and larkspur when Elodie arrived home from work. The garden door at the back of the hall was wide-open and Elodie could see her old landlady inspecting the blooms. It never failed to amaze her how someone who relied on Coke-bottle glasses to tell the difference between diamonds and hearts could remain such a sharpshooter when it came to the grubs on her flowers.

Rather than duck straight upstairs, Elodie went down the hall, past Mrs. Berry's grandfather clock—still softly, patiently, sweeping time aside—to stop at the doorway. "Are you winning?"

"Scoundrels," Mrs. Berry called back, plucking a fat green caterpillar from a leaf and holding it up for Elodie's distant inspection. "Sneaky little devils, and greedy, too—frightfully greedy." She dropped the offender into an old jam jar with a smattering of others. "Fancy a drink?"

"Love one." Elodie dropped her bag on the concrete step and headed out into the summery garden. A quick Friday catch-up and then she'd start on the recordings as she'd promised Penelope.

Mrs. Berry set the jar of wrigglers on the elegant iron table beneath the apple tree and disappeared into her kitchen. At eighty-four she was exceptionally spry, a fact she credited to her refusal to earn a driver's license. "Terrible polluting machines. And the way people charge about in them! Dreadful. Much better to walk."

73

She reappeared carrying a tray loaded with a jug fizzing orange. Mrs. Berry had been on a trip to Tuscany with her watercolor group the previous year and had developed a penchant for Aperol Spritz. She filled a generous glass for each of them and passed one across the table. "*Salute!*"

"Cheers."

"I sent that RSVP of yours off today."

"Brilliant news. That's one, at least, for my side of the church."

"And I've been giving more thought to my reading. There's a lovely Rossetti—reads like a piece of Morris fabric, all peacocks and fruit and halcyon seas . . ."

"Sounds divine."

"But trivial. Too trivial for you. I prefer the Tennyson: *If I were loved, as I desire to be, / What is there in the great sphere of the earth, / And range of evil between death and birth, / That I should fear,—if I were loved by thee?*" She was smiling beatifically, a small hand planted on her heart. "Oh, Elodie, what truth! What liberty! What joy, to be released from life's fear by the simple knowledge of love."

Elodie found herself nodding with equal enthusiasm. "It's beautiful."

"Isn't it?"

"There's the small matter of what Alastair's mother will think of a wedding reading that describes life as a range of evil between death and birth . . ."

"Pah! What business is it of hers?"

"Well, none, I suppose."

"It's not the point of the poem anyway. The point is that no matter what evil might come one's way, to be loved is to be protected."

"Do you think that's true?"

Mrs. Berry smiled. "Did I ever tell you how I met my husband?"

Elodie shook her head. Mr. Berry had died before she moved into the attic flat. She'd seen photos of him, though, lots of photos of a beaming man with glasses and a rim of white hair around an otherwise smooth pate; they were all over the walls and atop the sideboards in Mrs. Berry's flat.

"We were children. His name was Bernstein back then. He came to England on one of the trains from Germany at the start of the Second War. The Kindertransport, you know? My mother and father had put their names down as foster parents and in June 1939 we were sent Tomas. I still remember the night he arrived: we opened the door and there he was, all alone, skinny legs and a battered suitcase in hand. Funny little thing, with his very dark hair and eyes, and not a word of English. Ever so polite. He sat at the dinner table and endured my mother's attempt at sauerkraut and was then taken upstairs to the room they'd made up specially. I was fascinated, of course—I'd asked many times for a brother—and there was a fissure in the wall back then between my room and his, a mousehole that my father had never got around to fixing. I used to spy through it, and that's how I knew he lay down each night in the bed my mother had prepared, but when the house got dark and quiet he carried his blanket and pillow to the cupboard and climbed inside to sleep. I think it was this that made me love him.

"He had a single photograph with him when he arrived, wrapped up with a letter from his parents. He told me later that his mother had sewn the little parcel inside the lining of his jacket so it couldn't get lost along the way. He kept it all his life, that photograph. His two smartly dressed parents, and he a happy little lad between them with no idea of what was coming. They died at Auschwitz, both of them. We found that out later. We got married as soon as I turned sixteen and the two of us went off to Germany together. There was so much confusion after the war, still so much horror to be sorted through, even then. He was very brave. I kept waiting for it to hit him, all that he'd lost.

"When we learned that we couldn't have children, when his best friend and business partner swindled him and it looked like we might be bankrupted, when I discovered a lump in my breast . . . he was always so brave. So *resilient*, I suppose—that seems to be the word du jour. It wasn't that he didn't feel things—many's the time I saw him weep—but he dealt with his disappointment, with his hardship and grief; he picked himself up and went on, every time. And not like a mad person who refuses to recognize adversity, but like someone who accepts that life is inherently unfair. That the only truly fair thing about it is the randomness of its unfairness." She topped up their glasses. "I'm telling you all this not because I feel like a stroll down memory lane or because I like to tell my young friends sad stories on sunny Friday evenings; I just— I wanted you to understand. I wanted you to see what a balm love is. What it is to share one's life, to really share it, so that very little matters outside the certainty of its walls. Because the world is very noisy, Elodie, and although life is filled with joy and wonder, there's evil and sorrow and injustice, too."

There was little Elodie could think to say. To utter agreement in the face of such hard-won wisdom sounded glib, and really, what of life's experience did she have to add to the thoughts of her eighty-four-year-old friend anyway? Mrs. Berry didn't appear to expect a response. She was sipping from her drink, her attention focused on something beyond Elodie's shoulder, and so Elodie fell to her own musing. She realized that she hadn't heard from Alastair all day. Penelope had mentioned on the phone that he'd had the meeting with the New York board and that it had all gone very well. Perhaps he was out with his colleagues celebrating the merger?

Elodie was still not entirely sure what it was that Alastair's company did. Something to do with acquisitions. He had explained it more than once—it was all about consolidation, he said, the joining of two entities so that their combined value might be increased—but Elodie was always left with the sort of questions a child might think to ask. In her line of work, an acquisition referred to the delivery and possession of an object. Something solid and real that could be held in one's hands and which told a story through its every mark.

"When Tomas was dying," said Mrs. Berry, picking up the thread of her story, "right towards the very end, I started to fret. I was so worried that he'd be frightened; I didn't want him to have to go alone. At night, my dreams were filled with the image of that little boy, alone on our doorstep. I didn't say anything, but we'd always been able to read each other's thoughts, and one day he turned his head towards me, unprompted, and told me that he'd never been frightened of anything in life since the day we met." Her eyes glistened and her voice filled with wonder. "Do you hear that? Nothing in life had had the power to frighten him, because he knew how much I loved him."

Elodie had a lump in her throat. "I wish I'd known him."

"I wish you had, too. He'd have liked you." Mrs. Berry took a large sip of her drink. A starling swooped down to land on the table between them, eyeing the jar of grubs keenly before giving a loud call and removing himself to a bough of the apple tree for a further inspection. Elodie smiled and Mrs. Berry laughed. "How about you stay for dinner," she said. "I'll tell you a happier story, about the time Tomas and I accidentally bought a farm. Then I'm planning to beat your socks off. I have my deck shuffled and ready to go."

"Oh, Mrs. Berry, I'd really love to, but I can't tonight."

"Not even cards?"

"I'm afraid not. I'm on a deadline."

"More work? You work too hard, you know."

"Not this time; it's wedding business."

"Wedding business! Honestly, people do complicate things these days. What more do you need than two people who love one another and someone to hear them say it? If you ask me, even the latter's surplus to requirements. If I had my time again, I'd run away to Tuscany and speak my vows to my Tomas on the edge of one of those medieval hilltop villages, with the sun on my face and a wreath of honeysuckle in my hair. And then I'd enjoy a jolly good bottle of Chianti."

"Is there any other sort?"

"That's my girl!"

Upstairs, Elodie kicked off her shoes and opened the windows. The honeysuckle from Mrs. Berry's garden had grown voraciously over the summer, clinging to the brick back of the house, so that its fragrance drifted up on the warm afternoon breeze to infuse the flat.

She knelt on the floor and opened the suitcase of tapes her father had packed for her. Elodie recognized the suitcase as one he'd bought about twelve years earlier when she convinced him to go on a classical music tour in Vienna. It had seen better days and was an unprepossessing choice to hold such precious cargo. No one would ever have guessed that it held his heart, which Elodie supposed was part of his thought process: all the better to keep it safe.

There were at least thirty videocassettes inside, all labeled meticulously in her father's careful hand by date, concert, location, and piece of music. Thanks to Mrs. Berry, Elodie was in possession of what was surely one of the last video players in London, and she connected it now to the back of her TV. She chose a tape at random and inserted it into the player. Sudden nerves swirled in her stomach.

The tape had not been rewound fully and the room filled immediately with music. Lauren Adler, celebrated cello soloist and Elodie's mother, was in close-up on the screen. She hadn't started yet, but was embracing the cello, its neck entwined with her own as the orchestra played behind her. She was very young in this video. Her chin was lifted, her eyes fixed on the conductor; long hair cascaded over her shoulders and down her back. She was waiting. The stage lights illuminated one side of her face, throwing the other into dramatic shadow. She was wearing a black satin dress with spaghetti straps, and her fine arms—deceptively strong—were bare. She wore no jewelry except for her simple gold wedding band; her fingers, resting on the strings, were poised, ready.

The conductor was on-screen now, a man in a white bowtie and black jacket. He brought the orchestra to a pause and, after a few seconds of silence, nodded at Lauren Adler. She drew breath and then she and her cello began their dance.

Amongst the many articles Elodie had devoured about her mother, one adjective had appeared over and over: Adler's talent was sublime. The critics all agreed. She had been put on earth to play the cello and each piece of music, no matter how well-known, was reborn in her hands.

Elodie's father had kept all of the obituaries, but the one from the *Times* had pleased him especially and so it had been framed to hang on the wall amongst the stage photos. Elodie had read it many times and there was a passage that always stuck in her memory: "Lauren Adler's talent opened a fissure in ordinary experience through which purity and clarity and truth could be glimpsed. That was her gift to her audience; through Lauren Adler's music they experienced what religious people might call God."

The label on the videotape said that this performance had taken place at the Royal Albert Hall in 1987 and that the piece of music was the Dvořák Concerto in B Minor, Op. 104. Elodie jotted a note.

Her mother was playing unaccompanied now, and the orchestra—a blurred sea of women with straight faces and men with dark-rimmed glasses—sat very still behind her. The heart-stripping cello notes sent a shiver up Elodie's spine.

Lauren Adler had believed that a recording was a dead thing. She'd given an interview to the *Times* in which she'd said so, going on to describe live performance as the precipice on which fear, anticipation, and joy met, a unique experience shared between audience and performer, which lost all potency when pressed into permanence. But the recording was all Elodie had. She had no memories of her mother the musician. She'd been taken to see her play once or twice when she was a very small child, and of course she'd heard her practicing at home, but Elodie couldn't actually *remember* hearing her mother play professionally—not that she could separate her from her experience of other concerts, performed by other musicians.

She would never have confessed as much to her father, who was wholly invested in the idea that Elodie carried those memories inside her; moreover, that they were an intrinsic part of who she was. "Your mother used to play for you when she was pregnant," he'd told her more times than she could count. "She used to say that the human heartbeat was the first music that a person heard, and that every child was born knowing the rhythm of her mother's song."

He often spoke to Elodie as if she shared his memories. "Remember when she played for the Queen and the audience stood in ovation at the end for over three minutes? Remember the night she played all six Bach cello suites at the Proms?"

Elodie didn't remember. She didn't know her mother at all.

She closed her eyes. Her father was part of the problem. His grief was just so pervasive. Rather than allowing the chasm left when Lauren Adler died to close—even to *help* it close—his own sorrow, his refusal to let her go, had kept it wide-open.

One day, in the weeks following the accident, Elodie had been in the garden when she overheard a couple of well-meaning women who'd come to offer consolation and were now returning to their car. "A good thing the child's so young," one of them had said to the other as they reached the front gate. "She'll grow up and forget and she'll never know what she's missing."

They were right, in part: Elodie *had* forgotten. She simply had too few memories of her own with which to fill the hole made by her mother's death. But they were wrong, too, for Elodie knew exactly what she was missing. She hadn't been allowed to forget.

Now she opened her eyes.

It was dark outside; night had swept the dusk aside. Inside, the television screen was fizzing with static. Elodie hadn't noticed when the music stopped.

She climbed off the window seat and ejected the tape, selecting another to replace it.

This one was labeled *Mozart String Quintet No. 3 in C Major, K. 515, Carnegie Hall, 1985*, and Elodie stood watching the preamble for a few minutes. The video had been shot documentary-style, starting with a biographical introduction to the five young string players—three women and two men—coming together in New York to perform a concert. As the narrator spoke about each one in turn, the footage showed her mother in a rehearsal room, laughing with the others while a violinist with dark curly hair joked around with his bow.

Elodie recognized him as her mother's friend, the American violinist who had been driving the car from Bath to London on the day they were both killed. She remembered him vaguely: his family had come to dinner once or twice when they were visiting London from the States. And, of course, she'd seen his photograph in some of the newspaper articles published after the accident. There'd been a couple, too, amongst the boxes of loose photos at home that her father had never got around to sorting.

She watched him for a moment as the camera followed his movements, trying to decide how she felt about this man who had unwittingly taken her mother from her; who would remain linked to Lauren Adler forever by the circumstances of their deaths. But all she could think was how impossibly young he looked, and how much talent he possessed, and how right Mrs. Berry was that life's only nod to fairness was the blindness with which it dealt unfair blows. After all, he had left a young family behind, too.

Lauren Adler was on-screen now. It was true what all the newspaper columns said: she had been breathtaking. Elodie watched as the group performed in concert, jotting down notes as she considered whether the piece would be a good choice for the wedding ceremony and, if so, which portions they might decide to use.

When the tape ended, she started another.

She was halfway through her mother's 1982 performance of the Elgar Cello Concerto Op. 85, with the London Symphony Orchestra, when her phone rang. Elodie glanced at the time. It was late, and her first instinct was to worry that something had happened to her dad, but it was only Pippa.

Elodie remembered the book launch at the publishing house in King's Cross; her friend was probably on her way home now, wanting conversation on the walk.

Her thumb hesitated above the answer button, but the call rang out.

Elodie considered ringing back and then silenced the phone and tossed it onto the sofa.

A peal of laughter carried up from the street below, and Elodie sighed.

Some of the disquiet from her meeting with Pippa earlier that day lingered. Elodie had felt possessive about the photo of the Victorian woman in the white dress, but it had been more than that. Now, sitting in a room filled with the melancholy strains of her mother's cello lines, she knew that it was the way Pippa had asked about the recordings.

They'd already talked about the subject, back when Penelope had first suggested using clips of Lauren Adler in the wedding ceremony. Pippa had wondered then whether Elodie's dad might not have reservations, given that he could barely talk about Elodie's mother without welling up. Frankly, Elodie had held the same concerns, but it turned out he'd been quietly pleased, echoing Penelope's sentiment that it was the next best thing to having her there.

Today, though, when Elodie had said as much, rather than dropping the subject and moving on, Pippa had pushed further, asking whether Elodie agreed.

Now, watching Lauren Adler as she brought the Elgar to its aching conclusion, Elodie wondered whether perhaps Pippa had her own reasons. Within their friendship Pippa had always occupied the more dynamic space, inviting attention where Elodie, naturally shy, preferred to play the support act; maybe in this one instance, when Elodie could lay claim to an extraordinary parent, Pippa resented the intrusion?

Even as the thought occurred to her, Elodie was ashamed of it. Pippa was a good friend who was even now busy designing and making Elodie's wedding dress. She had never done anything to suggest that she begrudged Elodie her parentage. In fact, she was one of the few people who'd never seemed particularly interested in Lauren Adler. Elodie was used to people, when they learned of the connection, tripping over themselves to ask questions, almost as if from Elodie they could absorb some of the talent and tragedy that had surrounded Lauren Adler. But not Pippa. Although over the years she'd asked plenty about Elodie's mother—whether Elodie missed her, whether she remembered much from before her mother died—her interest had been limited to Lauren Adler's maternal role. It was as if the music and fame, though interesting enough, was inconsequential in all the ways that mattered.

The Elgar recording ended and Elodie switched off the TV.

Without Alastair there to insist on "a proper weekend lie-in," she planned to get up early and take a long walk east along the river. She wanted to get to her great-uncle Tip before his shop opened.

She showered and climbed into bed, closing her eyes and willing herself to sleep.

The night was still warm and she was restless. Free-floating anxiety circled in the air above her like a mosquito looking to land a sting.

Elodie turned and tossed and then turned again.

She thought of Mrs. Berry and her husband, Tomas, and wondered if it was true that the love of one person—and such a tiny person as Mrs. Berry, five feet tall on a good day and as wiry as they come—was comfort enough to alleviate another person's fears.

Elodie was frightened of so many things. Did it take time, she wondered, for the certainty of another person's love to accumulate such power? Would she discover, somewhere down the track, that the knowledge of Alastair's love had made her fearless?

Did he love her that way? How was she to know?

Her father had certainly loved her mother that way, but rather than make him brave, the loss of her had made him timid. Edward Radcliffe, too, had loved with a depth that made him vulnerable. *I love her, I love her, I love her, and if I cannot have her I will surely go mad, for when I am not with her I fear—*

Her. The woman in the photograph came to Elodie's mind. But, no, that was her own obsession. There was nothing to link the woman in the white dress to Radcliffe; it had turned up in his satchel, certainly, but the photo was in a frame that had belonged to James Stratton. No, Radcliffe had been writing about Frances Brown, the fiancée whose death, it was well known, had driven him to his own demise.

If I cannot have her . . . Elodie rolled over onto her back. It was an odd thing to write about a woman to whom he was engaged. Surely the very act of engagement meant the opposite? She was already his.

Unless he wrote the message after Frances's death, when he was facing the same abyss of absence that had confronted her own father. Is that when Radcliffe had drawn the house, too? Was it a real house? Had he stayed there after his fiancée's death—to recuperate, perhaps?

Elodie's thoughts swarmed, dark feathered birds circling closer and closer.

Her father, her mother, the wedding, the woman in the photo, the house in the sketch, Edward Radcliffe and his fiancée, Mrs. Berry and her husband, the little German boy alone on the doorstep; life, fear, the inevitability of death . . .

Elodie caught herself entering the dreaded nighttime thought loop and stopped.

She pushed back her sheet and slid out of bed. She'd been down this road enough times to know that she was as far away from sleep as one could be. She might as well do something useful.

The windows were still open and the sounds of the nocturnal city were a familiar comfort. Across the road, all was in darkness.

Elodie turned on a lamp and made a cup of tea.

She loaded another tape into the video player, this one labeled *Bach Suite No. 1 in G Major, Queen Elizabeth Hall, 1984*, and then she sat cross-legged on the old velvet armchair.

As the clock ticked over past midnight and the new day slid into position, Elodie pressed PLAY and watched as a beautiful young woman with the world at her feet walked out onto the stage, lifted her hand to acknowledge the applauding audience, and then, taking up her cello, began her magic.

CHAPTER SEVEN

ELODIE'S great-uncle lived in a garden flat at the end of Columbia Road. He was eccentric and something of a recluse, but had used to come to lunch at the weekends when her mother was alive. As a child, Elodie had found him somewhat startling; even then he'd seemed old, and she'd been vitally aware of his great tufting eyebrows and runner-bean fingers, and the way he would start to fidget when the lunch conversation turned to topics that didn't interest him. But where Elodie might have been told off for sticking her fingertips in the warm wax of the lunch table candle and peeling the prints off once they'd cooled, nobody said a word to great-uncle Tip, who would quietly amass a considerable pile, arranging them in elaborate patterns on the linen cloth, before losing interest and brushing them aside.

Elodie's mother had been very fond of her uncle. She was an only child and had become close to him when he moved into her family home for a year when she was young. "She used to say that he was different from other adults," Elodie could remember her father telling her. "She said your great-uncle Tip was like Peter Pan, the boy who never grew up."

Elodie had glimpsed this for herself in the aftermath of her mother's death. Amidst all the adult well-wishers, there'd been Tip and his pottery charm box, its surface covered with a wondrous array of shells and pebbles, broken tiles and shiny pieces of glass—all the things that children noticed but grown-ups walked right by.

"What's a charm box?" Elodie had asked him.

"A little bit of magic," he'd replied, with no hint of the indulgent

85

smile adults usually adopted when speaking on such themes. "And this one's just for you. Do you have any treasures?"

Elodie had nodded, thinking of the little gold signet ring her mother had given her for Christmas.

"Well, now you have a place to keep them safe."

It had been kind of Tip to make an effort, to seek her out when everyone else was focused on their own grief. They hadn't had a lot to do with one another since, but Elodie had never forgotten the kindness and hoped that he would come to the wedding.

It was a bright morning and, as she walked along the river path, Elodie was glad to be out in it. She had fallen asleep eventually on the brown velvet chair, and the night had passed in a series of fractured dreams and stirrings until she woke with the dawn birds. Now, as she neared Hammersmith Bridge, she realized that she still hadn't shaken it off: she had a stiff neck and a haunting cello line stuck in her mind.

A clutch of gulls wheeled above a nearby patch of water, and by the distant boathouses rowers were making the most of the fine weather to get out early. Elodie stopped at one of the bridge's grey-green pillars and leaned against the railing to watch the swirling Thames below. This was the spot from which Lieutenant Charles Wood had leapt in 1919 to rescue a woman who was drowning. Elodie thought of him every time she crossed the bridge. The woman had survived, but Wood had died from tetanus due to injuries sustained in the rescue. It seemed a particularly cruel fate to survive service with the RAF in the First World War, only to die after an act of bravery in peacetime.

By the time she reached the Chelsea Embankment, London was waking up. Elodie walked as far as the Charing Cross railway bridge and then caught the number 26 bus from outside the Royal Courts of Justice. She managed to get a front seat on the top level: it was a childhood pleasure that gladdened her still. The bus route followed Fleet Street all the way into the City of London, past the Old Bailey and St. Paul's, along Threadneedle Street, before turning towards the north at Bishopsgate. Elodie pictured, as she always did, the streets as they must have looked in the nineteenth century, back when London had belonged to James Stratton.

Elodie hopped off at Shoreditch High Street. Beneath the railway bridge a group of kids were having a hip-hop dance lesson while their parents stood around cradling cups of takeaway coffee. She crossed the road and then cut through the backstreets, turning the corner onto Columbia Road, where the shops were just starting to open.

Columbia Road was one of those vibrant, hidden streets in which London specialized: a run of short brick terraces with colorful storefronts of turquoise, yellow, red, green, and black, in which vintage clothing, artisan jewelry, handcrafted treasures, and tastefully distressed miscellanea could be bought. On Sundays, when the flower market took over and fragrance filled the air, it was difficult to move for the abundance of bright blooms and bustle; but today, at this time, the street was almost empty.

There was an iron gate on the side of Tip's building, behind which a path overgrown with violets led to the back garden. Black letters and a pointed finger had been stenciled on the white brick pillar out front, indicating that the "Garden Flat" was accessed that way. The gate was unlatched and Elodie let herself through. At the end of the path, in the back corner of the garden, was a shed with a carved sign above the door which read, "The Studio."

The studio door was ajar. Elodie pushed it open and was met, as ever, by an incredible collection of intriguing objects. A blue racing bicycle was propped against a Victorian printing press, and a series of wooden work desks braced the walls. Their surfaces were covered with old-fashioned contraptions: lamps and clocks, radios and typewriters, jostling for space with metal trays of vintage typeset letters. The cabinets beneath overflowed with oddly shaped spare parts and mysterious tools, and the walls were hung with an array of oil paints and ink pens that would have put any art shop to shame. "Hello?" she called as she stepped inside. She spotted her great-uncle at his tall desk at the back of the studio. "Tip, hello."

He glanced over the tops of his glasses but otherwise registered no sign of surprise at the arrival of his great-niece on his doorstep. "Good timing. Could you pass me the smallest Pfeil tool?"

Elodie fetched it from the wall where he was pointing and handed it across the workbench.

"That's better," he said, making a fine cut. "So . . . what's new in your world?" As if Elodie had just stepped out an hour ago to fetch groceries.

"I'm getting married."

"Married? Aren't you ten years old?"

"A little older than that now. I was hoping you could come. I sent you an invitation."

"Did you? Did I receive it?" He gestured towards a pile of papers on the end of the bench nearest the door. Amongst a stack of energy bills and estate agents' flyers Elodie spotted the cream cotton-thread envelope selected and addressed by Penelope. It had not been opened. "Shall I?" she said, holding it aloft.

"You're here now. You might as well give me the highlights in person."

Elodie sat at the bench, opposite Tip. "It's next month, Saturday the twenty-sixth. Nothing to do but turn up. Dad said he'd be happy to drive you there and back."

"Drive?"

"It's in a place called Southrop, a village in the Cotswolds."

"Southrop." Tip focused on a line he was about to cut. "How did you settle on Southrop?"

"My fiancé's mother knows someone who owns a venue. I've never actually been there, but I'm heading out to have a look next weekend. Do you know it?"

"Pretty place. Haven't been there for years. Hopefully they haven't ruined it with progress." He sharpened his blade on a Japanese stone, holding it up to the hanging light to inspect his work. "Still that same fellow, is it? David, Daniel—"

"Danny. No."

"Shame, I liked him. Interesting ideas about health care, I seem to remember. Is he still working on that thesis of his?"

"As far as I know."

"Something to do with adopting the same system as Peru?"

"Brazil."

"That's it. And this one? What's his name?"

"Alastair."

"Alastair. Is he a doctor, too?"

"No, he works in the City."

"Banking?"

"Acquisitions."

"Ah." He ran a soft cloth across his blade. "I take it he's a good fellow, though?"

"Yes."

"Kind?"

"Yes."

"Funny?"

"He likes a joke."

"Good. It's important to pick someone who can make you laugh. My mother told me that, and she knew a thing or two about everything." Tip ran his blade along a sweeping curve of his design. He was working on a river scene; Elodie could see this line forming part of the water's flow. "You know, your mother came and saw me before her wedding, too. She sat right there where you are now."

"Was she also chasing an RSVP?"

Elodie was joking, but Tip didn't laugh. "She came to talk about you, in a manner of speaking. She'd only recently discovered that she was pregnant." He smoothed his piece of linoleum, thumbing a fine loose shard along the top edge. "It was a hard time; she wasn't well. I was worried about her."

Elodie had a vague memory of having been told that her mother suffered with bad morning sickness in the first few months. According to her father, Lauren Adler's pregnancy was responsible for one of the only occasions on which she'd needed to cancel a performance. "I don't think I was planned exactly."

"I should say not," he agreed. "But you were loved, which is arguably more important."

It was strange to picture her mother, a young woman over thirty years before, sitting on the same stool as she was now, talking about the baby who would become Elodie. It sparked in Elodie a sense of kinship. She wasn't used to thinking of her mother as a peer. "Was she worried that having a baby would put an end to her career?"

"Understandably. Times were different then. And it was complicated. She was lucky Winston, your dad, stepped up."

The way he spoke of her father, as if he'd been conscripted into service by her arrival, made Elodie defensive. "I don't think he saw it as a sacrifice. He was proud of her. He was forward-thinking in his way. He never presumed that because she was a woman she should be the one to stop working."

Tip considered her over his glasses. He seemed about to speak but didn't, and the silence sat awkwardly between them.

Elodie felt protective of her father. Protective of herself, too, and of her mother. Their situation had been unique: *Lauren Adler* had been unique. But her father was no martyr, and he didn't deserve pity. He loved being a teacher; he'd told Elodie many times that teaching was his calling. "Dad was always clear-sighted," she said. "He was a very good musician, too, but he knew her talent was of a different caliber; that her place was on the stage. He was her biggest fan."

It sounded corny when she said it out loud, but Tip laughed and Elodie felt the odd tension slip away. "That he was," said Tip. "You won't get any argument from me there."

"Not everyone can be a genius."

He gave her a kindly smile. "Don't I know it."

"I've been watching the recordings of her concerts."

"Have you, now."

"We're going to play some during the ceremony, instead of an organist. I'm supposed to choose, but it isn't easy."

Tip set down his blade. "The first time I heard her play, she was four years old. It was Bach. I was lucky if I could get my shoes on the right feet at that age."

Elodie smiled. "To be fair, shoes are tricky." She fiddled with the corner of the wedding invitation on the bench beside her. "It's strange watching the videos. I thought I'd feel a connection—some sort of recognition . . ."

"You were very young when she died."

"Older than she was when you first heard her playing Bach." Elodie shook her head. "No, she was my mother. I should remember more."

"Some memories aren't the obvious sort. My dad died when I was five and I don't remember a lot. But even now, seventy-seven years later, I can't walk past someone smoking a pipe without being hit with the strongest memory of hearing typewriter keys being struck."

"He used to smoke while he typed?"

"He used to smoke while my mother typed."

"Of course." Elodie's great-grandmother had been a journalist.

"Before the war, on nights when my father wasn't working, the two of them used to sit together at a round wooden table in our kitchen. He'd have a glass of beer and she a whisky, and they'd talk and laugh and she'd work on whatever article it was that she was writing." He shrugged. "I don't remember any of that with pictures, like a film. So much has happened since to take its place. But I can't smell pipe smoke without being overwhelmed by a visceral sense of being small and content and knowing that my mother and father were together in our house while I was drifting off to sleep." He eyed his blade. "You'll have memories in there somewhere. It's just a matter of working out how to trigger them."

Elodie considered this. "I can remember her telling me stories before I went to bed at night."

"There you are, then."

"There was one in particular—I remember it so vividly. I thought it must've come from a book, but my dad said it was one she'd been told when she was young. Actually"—Elodie straightened—"he said it was a family story, passed down to her, about a wood and a house on the bend of a river?"

Tip brushed his hands clean on his trousers. "Time for a cuppa."

He pottered over to the nearby Kelvinator and reached for the paint-splattered kettle on top.

"Have you heard it? Do you know the one I mean?"

He held up an empty mug and Elodie nodded.

"I know the story," said Tip, unwinding first one tea bag and then another. "I told it to your mum."

It was warm in the studio, but Elodie felt a chill brush lightly on the skin of her forearms.

"I lived with them for a while when your mother was small, with my sister Beatrice's family. I liked your mum. She was a bright kid even without the music. I was an unholy mess at the time—I'd lost my job, my relationship, my flat; but kids don't care about that sort of thing. I'd have preferred to be left alone to surrender myself fully to the slough of despond, but she wouldn't have it. She followed me around the place like the chirpiest bad smell you can imagine. I begged my sister to call her off, but Bea always did know best. I told your mum the story about the river and the woods so I could have a moment's reprieve from that chipper little voice with its constant comments and questions." He smiled fondly. "I'm glad to think that she told it to you. Stories have to be told or else they die."

"It was my favorite," said Elodie. "It was real to me. I used to think about it when she was away and dream about it at night."

The kettle started to sing. "It was the same for me when I was a lad."

"Did your mum tell the story to you?"

"No." Tip fetched a glass bottle of milk from the fridge and poured some into each mug. "I was evacuated from London when I was a boy; we all were: my mum, my brother and sister, and me. Not officially. My mum organized it. Our house was bombed and she managed to find us a place in the country. Wonderful old house it was, filled with the most incredible furniture—almost like the people who'd lived there before had left for a stroll and never come back."

Elodie's mind went to the sketch she'd found in the archives—her idea that the tale might have come originally from an illustrated book for which the sketch was an early draft. An old, furnished house in the country seemed like just the sort of place where a Victorian book might have been tossed onto a shelf, forgotten until a little boy unearthed it midway through the next century. She could almost picture the boy, Tip, finding it. "You read the story there?"

"I didn't read it. It wasn't from a book."

"Someone told it to you? Who?"

Elodie noticed just the merest hesitation before he answered. "A friend."

"Someone you met in the country?"

"Sugar?"

"No, thanks." Elodie remembered the photo that she'd taken on her phone. While Tip was finishing preparing the tea, she pulled it out, swiping past another missed call from Pippa and scrolling to the photo of the sketch. She handed it to him as he set down her mug.

His woolly brows lifted and he took the phone. "Where did you get this?"

Elodie explained about the archives, the box discovered beneath the curtains in the antique chiffonier, the satchel. "As soon as I saw the sketch I felt a jolt of familiarity, as if it were somewhere that I'd been. And then I realized it was the house, the one from the story." She was watching his face. "It is, isn't it?"

"That's it all right. It's also the house my family and I lived in during the war."

Deep inside her, Elodie felt something lighten. So, she'd been right. It *was* the house from the story. And it *was* a real house. Her great-uncle Tip had lived there as a boy during the war, where a local person had invented a story that had captured his imagination and which, in turn, he'd told many years later to his little niece.

"You know," said Tip, still inspecting the sketch, "your mother came to ask me about the house, too."

"When?"

"A week or so before she died. We had lunch together and then went for a walk, and when we got back here she asked me about the house in the country where I'd stayed during the Blitz."

"What did she want to know?"

"At first she just wanted to hear me speak about it. She said that she remembered me telling her about it, that it had taken on magical proportions in her mind. And then she asked me if I could tell her where it was exactly. The address, the closest village."

"She wanted to go there? Why?"

"I only know for certain what I've told you. She came to see me, she wanted to know about the house from the story, I never saw her again."

Emotion had made him gruff and he moved to clear the photo of the sketch from the phone's screen. Instead, the picture swiped backwards. As Elodie watched, every bit of color drained from his face.

"What is it?" she said.

"Where did you get this?" He was holding out the phone to show the picture she'd taken, the Victorian woman in the white dress.

"I found the original at work," she said. "It was with the sketchbook. Why? Do you know who she is?"

Tip didn't answer. He was staring at the image and didn't appear to have heard.

"Uncle Tip? Do you know the woman's name?"

He looked up. His eyes met hers but all the openness had gone. They were the defensive eyes of a child caught lying. "Don't be ridiculous," he said. "How could I? I've never seen her before in my life."

IV

It is just before first light and I am sitting on the foot of my visitor's bed. It is an intimate thing to do, to watch another person sleep; once upon a time I might have said that there was no other moment in which a human being was more vulnerable, but I know now from experience that's not true.

I can remember the first time that I stayed overnight in Edward's studio. He had painted until well after midnight, the candles that stood in green glass bottles burning one by one to rippled pools of molten wax, until, at last, it was too dark to continue. We fell asleep together on the cushions that littered the floor of the corner nearest the furnace. I woke before he did, as dawn was creeping softly across the pitched glass ceiling, and I lay on my side with my face in my hand, watching his dreams skate beneath his eyelids.

I wonder what this young man dreams of. He returned just prior to dusk last night and I felt the energy inside the house shift instantly. He went straight to the malthouse room where he has set up camp and I was with him in a flash. He peeled off his shirt in one liquid movement and I found myself unable to look away.

He is handsome in the way of men who do not think about being handsome. He has a broad chest and the arms a man gets from working hard and lifting heavy things. The men on the wharves along the Thames had bodies like that.

Once upon a time I would have left the room or turned away when a man I did not know undressed; the learned privacies go surprisingly deep. But my observation can take nothing away from him, and so I watched.

He has a stiff neck, I think, for he rubbed the palm of his hand against it and then tilted it this way and that as he walked to the small adjoining bathroom. The night had continued warm and humid and my attention lingered on the back of his neck, the place where his hand had been, where the ends of his hair curl.

I miss touch.

I miss being touched.

Edward's body was not that of a man who toiled on the wharves, but it was stronger than one might have expected for a man who spent his days lifting brush to canvas and eyes to subject. I remember him in candlelight; at his studio in London, and here, in this house, on the night of the storm.

My visitor sings in the shower. Not very well, but then, he does not know he has an audience. When I was a child in Covent Garden I used to stand sometimes and listen to the opera singers practicing in the theaters. Until the managers came, waving their arms and their threats, and I ran back into the shadows.

Although my visitor left the door to the bedroom open, the cubicle is so small that steam filled it, and when he was finished he stood in front of the mirror, wiping the center clear with his hand. I remained at a distance behind him and if I'd had breath it would have been held. Once or twice, when the condition of the light has been just right, I have caught a glimpse of myself in the looking glass. The circular mirror in the dining room is best—something to do with its curved sides. Rarely, I have been able to make others see me, too. No, not *make* them, for I have not been aware of doing anything differently.

But my visitor did not see me. He rubbed his hand across his bristled jaw and then went to find his clothing.

I miss having a face. And a voice. A real voice that everyone can hear.

It can be lonely in the liminal space.

—•—

Mrs. Mack lived with a man known only as "the Captain," whom I took at first for her husband but who turned out to be a brother. He was as thin as she was round and walked with a lopsided gait due to the wooden leg he'd gained after an altercation with a carriage on Fleet Street.

"Got stuck in a wheel, 'e did," I was told by one of the children who lived in the streets outside. "Dragged 'im for a mile before 'is leg broke plain off."

The wooden leg was a handmade contraption that attached below the knee with a series of leather straps and silver buckles. It had been fashioned by one of his friends down at the docks, and in it the Captain took great pride, lavishing the limb with careful attention, polishing the buckles and waxing the straps, sanding every splinter away. Indeed, so smooth was the wood, so waxed were the straps, that on more than one occasion, the leg slipped out of place, causing great alarm to those around who weren't familiar with his plight. He had been known to take the leg from his knee and shake it at those whose actions had displeased him.

I was not the only child whose care had fallen to Mrs. Mack. Alongside her various other businesses, which were only ever discussed in low voices and veiled language, she had a small side interest taking in children. She ran an advertisement in the newspaper each week that read:

> *Wanted, by a respectable widow with no young children of her own, care of or to adopt a child of either sex. The Advertiser offers a comfortable home and a parent's care. Small premium; age under ten years. Terms: 5s a week, or would adopt entirely infants under three months for the sum of £13.*

I did not understand at first the special mention of infants under three months, but there was a girl, older than I was, who knew a little bit of everything, from whom I learned that there had been infants in the past, adopted by Mrs. Mack. Lily Millington was that girl's name, and she told me of a baby boy called David, a girl called Bessie, and a set of twins whose names no one remembered anymore. Sadly, though, they had all been sickly and died. This had seemed to me then like terribly bad luck, but when I said as much, Lily Millington merely raised her brows and said there wasn't much luck about it, good or bad.

Mrs. Mack explained that she had taken me in as a favor to my father, and to Jeremiah, whom it turned out she knew well; she had special plans for me and was certain that I wasn't going to disappoint. In fact, she said, eyeing me sternly, my father had assured her that I was a good girl who would do as I'd been told and make him proud. "Are you a good girl?" she'd asked. "Is your father right in that?"

I told her that I was.

The way it worked, she continued, was that everyone did their bit to afford their upkeep. Anything left over she would send to my father to help him with his new start.

"And then he'll be able to send for me?"

"Yes," she agreed, with a wave of her hand. "Yes, yes. Then he'll be able to send for you."

———

Lily Millington laughed when I told her that Mrs. Mack had special plans for me. "Oh, she'll find you something to do, all right, make no mistake about *that*. She's nothing if not creative, and she demands her pound of flesh."

"And then I'm going to America with my father."

Lily tousled my hair whenever I said that, just as my father had always done, which made me even more disposed to like her. "Are you, poppet?" she said, "What a lark that'll be," and, when she was in an especially good mood: "Do you think you'll have room for me in that suitcase of yours?"

Her own father had been "no good," she said, and she was better off without him. Her mother, though, had been an actress ("That's a fancy way of putting it," Mrs. Mack snorted if ever she heard this claim), and when she was littler, Lily herself had been in the pageants at Christmastime. "Gaslight fairies, they called us. Because we glowed yellow on the front of the stage."

I could imagine Lily as a fairy, and as an actress, which is what she planned to be. "An actor-manager like Eliza Vestris or Sarah Lane," she would say as she strutted across the kitchen, chin up, arms wide. Mrs. Mack, should she hear such utterances, could always be counted on to toss a damp cloth across the room and huff, "Best be managing those dirty dishes back into the kitchen racks, if you know what's good for you."

Lily Millington had a sharp tongue and a hot temper, and a knack for provoking Mrs. Mack's ire, but she was funny and clever and, in the first weeks after I woke to find myself in the rooms above the shop selling birds and cages in the Seven Dials, she was my salvation. Lily Millington made everything brighter. She made me braver. Without her I do not think I would have survived my father's absence, for I was so used to being the clockmaker's daughter that I did not know myself without him.

It is a strange thing, though, the human instinct for survival. I have had many opportunities whilst resident in this house, to observe firsthand the ability of people to bear the unbearable. And so it was for me. Lily Millington took me under her wing and the days passed.

It was true what Mrs. Mack had said, that everyone in the house worked to earn their keep, but due to the nature of her "special plans," I was granted an initial brief reprieve. "A little bit of time to get yourself settled," she said, with a pointed nod at the Captain. "While I get things in order."

In the meantime I did my best to stay out of her way. For someone who took in children, Mrs. Mack did not appear to like them very much, bellowing that should she find one "underfoot" she would not spare the strap. The days were long and there were only so many corners within the house to keep oneself hidden, and so I fell to trailing Lily Millington when she left for work each morning. She was unimpressed at first, worried that I'd get her "caught," but then she sighed and said that I was as green as grass and it was just as well for someone to show me the ropes before I got myself into trouble.

The streets back then were chaotic with horse-drawn omnibuses and colorful carriages; ducks and pigs being driven to Leadenhall Market; sellers of every type of food one could imagine—sheep's trotters, pickled periwinkles, eel pie—trumpeting their wares. Further south, were we to steal down the shadowy cobbled lanes of Covent Garden, was the market square, where costermongers lined up by the dozen to buy the best strawberries from the delivery cart, market porters carried stacked baskets loaded with fruit and vegetables on their heads, and traveling vendors wove through the thronging crowds selling birds and snakes, brooms and brushes, Bibles and ballads, penny slices of pineapple, china ornaments, ropes of onions, walking sticks, and live geese.

I came to recognize the regulars, and Lily Millington made sure that they knew me. My favorite was the French magician who set up every second day on the southern corner of the market, closest to the Strand. There was a farmer's stall behind him where the best eggs could be bought, so a constant stream of traffic bustled by and he always gathered a crowd. He caught my attention first for his elegant appearance: he was tall and thin, an effect accentuated by his black top hat and stovepipe trousers; he wore a tailcoat and vest, and his moustache was tapered and curled above his dark goatee. He said little, communicating instead with his large kohl-rimmed eyes as he made coins disappear from the table in front of him only to reappear within the bonnets and scarves of people in his audience. He was able, too, to conjure wallets and items of jewelry from members of the crowd who were amazed and indignant in equal measure to discover their valuables in the hands of this exotic stranger.

"Did you see, Lily?" I exclaimed, the first time I observed him pull a coin from behind a child's ear. "Magic!"

Lily Millington only bit into a carrot she'd procured from somewhere and told me to watch more closely next time. "Illusion," she said, flicking a long plait over one shoulder. "Magic's for those that can afford it, and that's not the likes of us."

I was still coming to understand exactly who "us" was and just what Lily Millington and the others did for work. They were good at it, I suppose, and that's the point. I knew only that it involved hours of loitering, occasional instances when I was instructed to wait while Lily mingled briefly with the crowd, and then, sometimes, a hot-cheeked flight—from whom, I was not sure—through a tangle of cluttered lanes.

Some days, though, were different. From the moment that we set out from Mrs. Mack's place, Lily Millington would be jumpier than usual, like a skinny cat that does not take kindly to petting. On such occasions, she would find me a spot to stand at the markets and make me promise to wait for her. "Don't you go nowhere, you hear? And don't talk to nobody. Lily'll be back for you soon." Where she went then, I did not know, only that she was always gone longer than usual, and often returned with a grim, secretive expression on her face.

It was on just such a day that I was approached by the man in the black coat. I'd been waiting for what felt to me then like an eternity and, growing weary, had wandered from the spot where Lily had left me, to crouch instead against a brick wall. I was half watching a shop girl sell roses and didn't notice the man in the black coat until he was right above me. His voice made me startle: "Well, now, what have we here?" He reached down to take my chin roughly in his hand and turned my face towards him, eyes narrowing as he carried out his inspection, "What's your name, then, girl? Who's your father?"

I was about to answer, when Lily appeared, like a flash of light, to stand between us.

"There you are," she said, grabbing my arm in her strong, skinny fingers; "I've been looking all over for you. Ma's waiting on those eggs. It's time we got them home."

Before there was time for me to utter so much as a sneeze, Lily yanked me after her and we were zigzagging through the alleyways.

Not until just before the Seven Dials did she finally stop. She spun me around to face her, her cheeks blotchy red. "Did you tell him anything?" she said. "That man?"

I shook my head.

"You sure about that?"

"He wanted to know my name."

"Did you tell him?"

Again I shook my head.

Lily Millington put both of her hands on my shoulders, which were heaving still from the effort of running so far, so fast. "Never tell nobody your real name, you hear me, Birdie? *Never*. And certainly not him."

"Why not?"

"Because it isn't safe. Not here. The only way to be safe is to be someone else when you're out here."

"Like an illusion?"

"Just like that."

And then she explained to me about the workhouse, for that's where the man in the black coat was from. "If they find out the truth, they'll lock you up, Birdie, and they'll never let you out. They'll make you work until your fingers bleed and flog you for the merest fault. Mrs. Mack has her moments, but there's far worse can happen to the likes of us. A girl I heard of was given sweeping duties. She left a spot of dirt on the floor and they stripped off her clothes and beat her black and blue with a broom. Another lad was strung up in a sack and hung from the rafters for wetting his bed."

My eyes had begun to sting with tears and Lily's face became kinder. "There, now. No need for the waterworks or I'll have to thrash you myself. But you must promise me solemn that you'll never tell no one your real and proper name."

I swore that I wouldn't and at last she seemed satisfied. "Good." She nodded. "Then let's get home."

We turned the corner into Little White Lion Street, and when the shop selling birds and cages came into view, Lily said, "One more thing, while we're giving undertakings. You're not to go tattling to Mrs. Mack that I left you on your own, all right?"

I promised that I wouldn't.

"She has her 'special plans' for you, and she'd have my head if she knew what I'd been doing."

"What were you doing, Lily?"

She glanced at me and stared hard for a few seconds, and then she leaned close to my ear, so that I could smell the tang of perspiration. "I'm saving up," she whispered. "It's all very well to work for Mrs. Mack, but you'll never get free if you don't earn a little for yourself."

"Have you been selling things, Lily?" I was doubtful because she did not carry fruit or fish or flowers like the other traders.

"In a manner of speaking."

She never told me more than that, and I never thought to ask. Mrs. Mack used to say that Lily Millington had "a mouth on her," but Lily could be tight-lipped when it suited.

I never had the chance to ask her much anyway. I only knew Lily Millington for six weeks before she was killed by a sailor with too much whisky under his belt who didn't agree the price that she was asking for her services. The irony is not lost on me that I know so little about a girl to whom I tied myself for eternity. Yet she is precious to me, Lily Millington, for she gave me her name: the most valuable thing she had to give.

———

Although she hadn't a spare two pennies to rub together, Mrs. Mack had a way about her that could almost be described as airs and graces. There was an abiding narrative in her household that the family had once been destined for Better Things, dislodged from their rightful place by an Incident of Cruel Misfortune a couple of generations before.

And so, as befitting a woman of such illustrious lineage, she kept a room at the front of the house that she referred to as her "parlor," and into which she poured every bit of spare money that she possessed. Colorful cushions and mahogany furnishings, skewered butterflies on velvet backings, bell jars flaunting taxidermy squirrels, autographed images of the royal family, and a collection of crystal oddments with only the merest cracks.

It was a sacred place and children were most certainly not permitted unless a specific invitation had been issued, which it wasn't, ever. Indeed, aside from Mrs. Mack, the only two people granted entrée into the sanctum were the Captain and Martin. And Mrs. Mack's dog, of course, a *boarhund* who had come off one of the boats and whom she'd named Grendel, because she had heard the word in a poem sometime and liked it. Mrs. Mack doted on the dog with the kind of cooing affection I do not recall ever hearing her bestow upon a human being.

After Grendel, the light of Mrs. Mack's affection fell upon Martin, her son, who was ten years to my seven when I came to live with them at their place on Little White Lion Street. Martin was large for his age—not merely tall but imposing, his presence being of the sort whereby he seemed to occupy more space than was his due. He was a boy of little intelligence and even less kindness who had, however, been gifted with a great deal of natural slyness, an attribute which proved a blessing in that particular time and place as, I daresay, it would now.

I have had much opportunity to wonder over the years whether Martin might have turned out differently had he found himself within another situation. If he had been born into the family of Pale Joe, for instance, would he have become a gentleman of refined tastes and proper decorum? The answer, I am all but certain, is yes, for he would have learned the manners and mask required to survive, and indeed to thrive, in whichever station society determined that he must. This was Martin's prevailing skill: an innate ability to see which way the wind was blowing and to hoist his sail accordingly.

His conception had apparently been immaculate, for a father was never mentioned. He was only ever referred to, proudly, by Mrs. Mack as "my boy, Martin." That she was his mother was as clear as the noses on their matching faces, but where Mrs. Mack was a woman of great optimism, Martin tended always towards the negative view of life. He saw losses everywhere and could not receive a gift without wondering at the alternatives he would now be forced to do without. Another trait, it must be said, that served him well in our particular knot of London.

I had been with them in their house above the bird shop for two months and Lily Millington had been dead two weeks when I was invited one night to visit the parlor after dinner.

I was very worried as I made my approach, for I had seen, by now, what happened to children who displeased Mrs. Mack. The door was ajar and I pressed my eye up close against the gap the way I had witnessed Martin do when Mrs. Mack was entertaining one of her "business associates."

The Captain was standing by the window overlooking the street, intoning on one of his favorite subjects, the epic winter fogs of 1840: "Totally white, it was; ships, like ghosts, colliding in the middle of the Thames." Grendel was stretched out along the sofa; Martin was hunched over, biting his nails on a three-legged footstool; and Mrs. Mack, I saw at last, was ensconced in her winged armchair by the fire. For some time she had been engaged of an evening with a secret stitching project, telling anyone who asked about it to mind their own business "or else I'll mind it for you." The project, I could see, was across her lap now.

I must have pressed too hard upon the door, for it swung open with a rude creak.

"There you are, then," said Mrs. Mack, shooting a knowing glance at Martin and the Captain. "Little pitchers and their big ears." She dragged her needle through the fabric with a final triumphant flourish and then snapped the thread with her teeth and secured the end. "Come on, then, let's have a look at you."

I hurried to her side and Mrs. Mack unraveled the item on her lap, shaking it out to present a dress, more beautiful than any I had worn since outgrowing those that my mother had kept so carefully mended when she was alive.

"Turn around, then, girl, arms in the air. Let's see how it fits."

Mrs. Mack undid the button at the top of my smock and then pulled it over my arms and head. It was not cold, but a shiver went through me as the fine dress slipped into place.

I couldn't understand what was happening—why I was being granted such an extravagant and beautiful gift—but I knew better than to ask. Tiny pearl buttons snaked up the back to the nape of my neck and a wide satin sash of the palest blue ribbon was tied around my waist.

I was aware of Mrs. Mack behind me, her warm labored breaths, in and out, as she undertook to put the whole ensemble to rights. When she was finished, she spun me back to face her and said to the room, "Well?"

"Aye, she's a pretty one," the Captain coughed around his pipe. "And with that sweet little toffee voice—we never had one of them before. She's a right proper little lady."

"Not yet she's not," came Mrs. Mack's pleased reply. "But with a good bit of polish, some etiquette lessons, and a curl or two in the hair, she might just pass for one well enough. Doesn't she look a picture, Martin?"

I met Martin's gaze, but I did not like the way he stared.

"What about the pockets?" said Mrs. Mack. "Have you found the pockets?"

I slipped my hands down the sides of the skirt, my fingertips finding the openings. They were deep—in fact, I could not find the bottoms unless I sacrificed my arms. It was like having carry bags stitched within the petticoat of my dress.

I was perplexed, but evidently all was as intended, for Mrs. Mack laughed crowingly and exchanged a glance with the others. "There, now," she said, with a lick of feline satisfaction. "Do you see that? Do you see?"

"There, now, indeed," said the Captain. "Well done, Mrs. Mack. Well done. She looks a right treat and there's none would suspect a thing. I predict a mighty windfall. Doesn't everybody want to help the little girl who's lost her way?"

———

My visitor stirs at last.

I do not think I have ever had a visitor so reluctant to rise and start the day as this one. Not even Juliet, who used to cling to the last few minutes when her children were already up and racing, before they finally came in to drag her to her feet.

I will move closer to the head of the bed and see whether that helps. It is as well for me to know. Some of them are insensitive and I can brush right by them and fail to raise a shiver. Others notice me without the slightest of prompts, like my little friend during the time of the bombs and planes, who reminded me so much of Pale Joe.

And so, a test. I will just shift up the bed now, nice and slowly, and see what happens.

What happens is this:

He shivers and scowls and lumbers out of bed, shooting daggers at the open window as if to punish the breeze.

Sensitive. And it is just as well to know; I will simply have to work around it.

It makes my task harder, but in some way I am pleased. My lingering vanity. It is always nice to be noticed.

He removes the earplugs that he wears when he sleeps and heads towards the bathroom.

The photograph of the two little girls has found a new home on the shelf above the small sink, and after he finishes shaving, he pauses and lifts the image from its place. He could be forgiven anything for the look that crosses his face when he studies that photo.

I heard him speaking to Sarah again last night. He was not as patient as he had been previously, saying, "That was a long time ago; there's been a lot of water under the bridge," and lowering his voice to a slow, calm tone that was worse somehow than if he'd shouted: "But, Sar, the girls don't even know who I am."

Evidently he convinced her of something, for it was agreed that they would meet for lunch on Thursday.

After that phone call, he seemed unsettled, as if the victory were one he hadn't planned on winning. He took a bottle of ale outside to one of the wooden picnic tables that the Art Historians' Association has arranged on the grassy clearing near the crab apple tree, overlooking the Hafodsted Brook. On Saturdays the area is filled with visitors trying not to spill the trays of tea and scones and sandwiches that they've purchased from the café which now fills the old barn where the schoolgirls used to stage their concerts. During the week, though, all is quiet, and he cut a lonely figure, shoulders tight and balled as he drank his beer and watched the gunmetal-grey river in the distance.

He reminded me of Leonard another summer long ago, back when Lucy was on the verge of handing over the house and its administration to the Association. Leonard used to sit in the same place, a hat low down across one eye and a cigarette permanently on his lip. He carried a kit bag rather than a suitcase, neatly packed, everything in it that he thought he would need. He had been a soldier, which explained a lot.

My young man is off to the kitchen now to start the water boiling for his cup of breakfast tea. He will move too quickly and slop some over the bench and curse at himself, but not with any real malice, and then he will take a few deep slurping gulps, leaving the rest to sit and cool in its mug, forgotten on the windowsill while he has his shower.

I want to know why he is here; what he does with the shovel and whether the photographs relate to his task. When he heads outside again, with his shovel and his brown camera bag, I will wait. But I am becoming less patient, less content to observe.

Something, somewhere, has changed. I can feel it, the way I used to be able to tell when the weather was turning. I feel it like a shift in atmospheric pressure.

I feel *connected*.

As if something or someone out there has flicked a switch, and although I do not know what to expect, it is coming.

Chapter Eight

ELODIE sat in the window of her flat, wearing her mother's veil and watching the river heave silently towards the sea. It was one of those rare, perfect afternoons when the air is infused with the scent of clean cotton and clipped grass, and a thousand childhood memories glint in the lingering light. But Elodie wasn't thinking about childhood.

There was still no sign of Pippa on the High Street. It had been an hour since her call and Elodie had been unable to settle to anything since. Her friend had refused to go into detail on the phone, saying only that it was important, that there was something she had to give to Elodie. She'd sounded urgent, almost breathless, which was nearly as unusual as her suggestion that she come down to Barnes on a Saturday evening.

But then, it seemed that nothing was normal this weekend. Nothing had been normal since Elodie found the archive box at work and unearthed the sketchbook and photograph.

The woman in the white dress. Tip had continued to deny all knowledge that morning, clamming up when Elodie pressed him further. He'd bundled her out of the studio as quickly as he could, muttering that he was late opening his shop and that, yes, yes, of course he'd see her at the wedding. But his reaction had been unmistakable. He had recognized the woman in the photo. And, crucially, although Elodie still wasn't sure how, his recognition tied the two items together, for Tip had known the house in the sketch, too. He had stayed there with his family as a boy.

After her ejection, Elodie had headed straight back to the Strand and into work. She'd typed in the weekend door code and let herself inside. It had been dark and even colder than usual in the basement, but Elodie hadn't stayed long. She'd retrieved the framed photograph from the box beneath her desk and the sketchbook from the archives and then left again. This time she hadn't felt one bit guilty. In some way that she couldn't yet explain, the photograph and sketchbook belonged with her. She had been meant to find them.

Now she picked up the photograph, cupping it in her palm, and the woman met her gaze, that look of defiance, which was almost a challenge. *Find me*, it seemed to say. *Find out who I am.* Elodie turned the frame over in her hands, running her fingertip along the spider-web-fine scratches in the silver. They were on both sides, close to matching, as if a pin or something similarly sharp had been used to etch the marks on purpose.

Elodie propped the frame on the sill in front of her, the way she imagined James Stratton must once have displayed it.

Stratton, Radcliffe, the woman in white . . . all were connected, but how?

Elodie's mother, Tip's childhood evacuation, the friend who told him the tale of the house on the Thames . . .

Elodie's gaze drifted out the window again to her bend of the river. She was aware, faintly, of the layers of previous occasions on which she'd done the same thing. It was a great, silent carrier of wishes and hopes, of old boots and pieces of silver, of memories. One came to her now suddenly: a warm day when she was still a little girl, the breeze brushing against her skin, her mother and father and a picnic on the riverbank . . .

She traced the ivory scallops of the veil, smooth beneath her fingertips. She supposed her mother might have done the very same thing thirty years before, perhaps as she stood outside the front of the church and prepared to walk towards Elodie's father. What song had played as Lauren Adler made her way down the aisle? Elodie didn't know; she'd never thought to ask.

She had been watching the videos all afternoon, stopping only when Pippa called, and her thoughts swam now with cello melodies. "It will be as if she's there," Penelope had said. "The next best thing to having your mother by your side." But it wasn't like that at all. Elodie saw that now.

Had her mother lived, she would have been a woman approaching sixty. She would not have been young and dewy, with a girlish smile and laugh. Her hair would have been silvering, her skin relaxing. Life would have left its marks on her, body and soul, and the ebullience and emotion that leapt out from the videos would have calmed. People would still have whispered words like "genius" and "extraordinary" when they saw her, but they would not have then lowered their voices to add that great magnifier, "tragedy."

That's what Pippa had been thinking when she'd asked whether Elodie agreed that they should play videos of Lauren Adler at the wedding. She hadn't been jealous and she wasn't being unkind. She'd been thinking of her friend, aware before Elodie was that it would be less like having her mother beside her down the aisle and more like having Lauren Adler walk onstage first, cello in hand, casting a great long shadow for Elodie to follow in.

The intercom buzzed and Elodie jumped up to answer it. "Hello?" she said.

"Hey, it's me."

She pressed the button to release the security door below and opened the door to her flat. Familiar Saturday afternoon street sounds and the faint aroma of fish and chips wafted in on the breeze as she waited for Pippa, who was running up the stairs towards her.

Pippa was out of breath when she reached the top. "Lord, this stairwell makes me hungry. Gorgeous veil."

"Thanks. I'm still deciding. Cup of something?"

"Glass, please." Pippa thrust a bottle of wine into Elodie's hands.

Elodie slipped the veil from her head and draped it over the end of the sofa. She poured two tumblers of pinot noir and brought them to where Pippa was perched now in the window. She'd picked up the framed photograph and was studying it. Elodie handed her a drink. "So?" Anticipation had burned up any small talk.

"So"—Pippa set down the photo and focused on Elodie—"I saw Caroline last night at the party. I showed her the photo on my phone and she thought the woman looked familiar. She couldn't immediately place her, but she confirmed that the styling in the photo was definitely suggestive of the 1860s; more specifically, as we thought, the photographers associated with the Pre-Raphaelites and the Magenta Brotherhood. She said she'd need to see the original to date it with any degree of accuracy, but that the photographic paper might give some clue as to the photographer's identity. Then I mentioned Radcliffe—at that stage I was thinking of the sketchbook you said you'd found with the photo, the possibility that it might give us a hint as to a lost painting—and Caroline said she had a number of books about the Magenta Brotherhood; that I was welcome to come over and pick them up."

"And?"

Pippa dug into her backpack and pulled out an old book in a tattered dust jacket. Elodie tried not to wince as her friend cracked open the spine and flicked rapidly through the powdery, yellowed pages. "Elodie, look," she said, arriving at an illustrated plate in the center and stabbing it with her fingertip. "It's her. The woman from the photo."

The plate was foxed around the edges, but the painting at its center was still intact. The annotation beneath gave the title as *Sleeping Beauty* and the artist's name, Edward Radcliffe. The woman in the painting was lying in a fantastical treetop bower of leaves and flower buds, all of which were waiting in stasis for the chance to bloom. Birds and insects were interspersed amongst the woven branches; long red hair flowed in waves around her sleeping face, which was glorious in repose. Her eyes were closed, but the features of her face—the elegant cheekbones and bow lips—were unmistakable.

"She was his model," Elodie whispered.

"His model, his muse, and, according to this book"—Pippa turned the pages eagerly to reach a later chapter—"his lover."

"Radcliffe's lover? What was her name?"

"From what I could glean this morning, there seems to have been some mystery about it. She used a false name to model. It says here that she was known as Lily Millington."

"Why would she have used a false name?"

Pippa shrugged. "She might've come from a respectable family who didn't approve; or maybe she was an actress with a stage name. A lot of actresses modeled as well."

"What happened to her? Does he say?"

"I haven't had time to read it, but I've done a good bit of dipping. The author starts by saying that it's hard to know for certain when even her true name remains a mystery, but then he relates a new theory that she broke Radcliffe's heart by stealing some jewelry—a family heirloom—and running off to America with another man."

Elodie thought back to the Wikipedia entry she'd read, the robbery in which Edward Radcliffe's fiancée was killed. She shared the outline quickly with Pippa and said, "Do you think it was the same robbery? That this woman, his model, was involved in some way?"

"No idea. It's possible, though I'd be careful about taking the theories too literally. I did a quick JSTOR search this morning and found some criticism pointing out that the author relied on a single unidentified source for a lot of the new information. What *is* useful is the painting of our woman in white; now we've established for certain that she and Radcliffe knew one another."

Elodie nodded, but she was thinking about the loose page in the sketchbook, the scrawled lines about love and fear and madness. Had those desperate lines been written by Radcliffe after the woman in white, his model "Lily Millington," disappeared from his life? Was it she who'd broken his heart by absconding to America with his family's heirloom treasure, and not his pleasant-faced fiancée? And what of Stratton? What had his relationship to the woman been? For it was he who'd kept her framed photograph, tucking it for safekeeping in the satchel belonging to Edward Radcliffe.

Pippa had gone to the kitchen bench for the bottle of pinot and was now topping up their glasses.

"Elodie, there's something else I wanted to show you."

"Another book?"

"Not a book, no." She sat down, a new and unnatural hesitance creeping into her manner, putting Elodie on guard. "I'd mentioned to Caroline that I was asking all of this for you, because of what you'd found in the archives. She's always liked you."

Pippa was being kind. Caroline barely knew Elodie.

"I told her I was making your dress and we got to talking about the wedding, about the recordings, the music, and what it must be like for you to watch all of your mum's concerts, and then Caroline came over quiet. I was worried at first that I'd said something to offend her, but then she apologized to me, excused herself, and went to get something from her studio."

"What was it?"

Pippa dug again inside her backpack and pulled out a thin plastic folder with a piece of card inside it. "One of her photographs. Elodie—it's a photo of your mum."

"Caroline knew my mother?"

Pippa shook her head. "She took it by chance. She said she had no idea who they were until later."

"'They'?"

Pippa opened her mouth, as if to explain, but evidently thought better of it, simply handing the folder to Elodie instead.

The photograph inside was larger than usual, with the rough edges and crop marks indicating that it had been printed from a negative. The image was black-and-white, of two people, a man and a woman, deep in conversation. They were sitting together in a beautiful place, outdoors, with masses of ivy and the very edge of a stone building in the background. There was a picnic blanket and a basket, and detritus suggesting lunch. The woman was wearing a long skirt and strappy sandals and was sitting with her legs crossed, leaning forward so that her elbow rested on one knee and her face was partly turned towards the man beside her. Her chin was lifted and the beginnings of a smile seemed to be playing at the corners of her mouth. A shard of sunlight had broken through a gap in the foliage to bathe the scene. The image was beautiful.

"She took it in July 1992," said Pippa.

Elodie didn't say anything. They both knew the importance of that date. Elodie's mother had died that month. She had been killed in a car with the American violinist, returning from a performance in Bath, and yet here she was, sitting with him in a leafy grove somewhere only weeks—days?—beforehand.

"She said it's one of her favorite photographs. The light, the expressions on their faces, the setting."

"How did she— Where was she?"

"In the country, somewhere near Oxford; she went out for a walk one day, turned a corner, and saw them. She said she didn't think twice; she just lifted her camera and captured the moment."

Most of the questions she wanted to ask wouldn't occur to Elodie until later. For now, she was too distracted by this new image of her mother, who didn't look like a celebrity but like a young woman in the middle of a deep, personal conversation. Elodie wanted to drink in every detail. To study the hem of her mother's skirt where the breeze was brushing it against her bare ankle, the way the fine chain of her watch fell low on her wrist, the elegant fluidity of her hand as it gestured towards the violinist.

It put her in mind of another photograph, a family snapshot she'd discovered at home when she was eighteen years old. She'd been about to graduate from sixth form and the editor of her school newspaper planned to run childhood pictures of the whole class beside their school portraits. Her father was not a neat man, and decades' worth of photos in their Kodak envelopes had been stored inside a couple of boxes at the bottom of the linen cupboard. One of these rainy winter days, he always said, he was going to pull them out and sort them into albums.

From the bottom of one box, Elodie had plucked a series of square, yellow-tinged photographs showing a group of young people laughing around a dining table covered by half-mast candles and wine bottles with elegant necks. A New Year's Eve banner was suspended above them. She'd thumbed through the pictures, noting fondly her father's turtleneck and flares, her mother's slim waist and enigmatic smile. And then she'd come to a shot from which her father was missing—behind the camera, perhaps? It was the same scene, but her mother was sitting now beside a man with dark eyes and an intense bearing, the violinist, the two of them deep in conversation. In that photo, too, her mother's left hand had been blurred in motion. She had always spoken with her hands. As a child, Elodie had thought of them as small, delicate birds, weaving and fluttering in harmony with her mother's thoughts.

Elodie had known at once when she saw that photo. A deep, human, intuitive knowing. The electricity between her mother and the man could not have been clearer had a cable been strung from one to the other. Elodie hadn't said anything to her father, who had already lost so much, but the knowledge cast a shadow; and several months later, when they were watching a film together, a French film in which infidelity was a central theme, Elodie had made a barbed comment about the cheating woman. It had come out sharper and hotter than it sounded in her head; it had been a challenge—she was hurt for him, and angry with him; angry with her mother, too. But her father had not risen to the bait. "Life is long" was all he'd said, his voice calm; he hadn't looked up from the film. "Being human isn't easy."

It struck Elodie now that it was unlikely, given her mother's fame—and Caroline's, too—that a photograph as striking as this one had never been published, particularly if, as Pippa said, Caroline considered it one of her favorites. She said as much to Pippa.

"I asked Caroline about that. She told me she developed the roll a few days after taking it and that she loved the image of your mum immediately. Even while it was still in the solution tray she could see that it was one of those rare magical captures where the subjects, the composition, the light—everything was in harmony. Later that same night, though, she turned on the TV and saw coverage of your mum's funeral. She hadn't made the connection until then, but they put a photo of your mum on the screen and Caroline said she felt a chill of recognition, especially when she realized that he'd been in the car, too. That she'd seen the two of them right before—" She gave Elodie a faint, sorry smile.

"She didn't publish it because of the accident?"

"She said it didn't feel right in the circumstances. Also, because of you."

"Me?"

"The news coverage included footage of you. Caroline said that she saw you holding your dad's hand, walking into the church, and she just knew she couldn't publish the photo."

Elodie looked again at the two young people in the ivy-covered grove. The way her mother's knee was brushing against his. The intimacy of the scene, the comfort of their postures. Elodie wondered if Caroline, too, had perceived the true nature of their relationship. Whether that explained, in part, her decision to keep the image to herself.

"She thought of you on and off over the years, she said, and wondered what had become of you. She felt connected to you because of what had happened—as if by taking the photograph on that day, preserving that particular moment between them, she had become part of their story. When she realized that you and I were friends, when you came to see my final year art show, she told me that the urge to meet you was irresistible."

"That's why she came for supper with us that night?"

"I didn't realize at the time."

It had been a surprise when Pippa mentioned that Caroline was going to join them; at first, Elodie had been intimidated by her presence, this accomplished artist of whom Pippa had spoken so highly, so often. But Caroline's manner had set her at ease; more than that, her warmth had been alluring. She'd asked questions about James Stratton and archive keeping, the sort of questions that made it seem that she was really listening. And she'd laughed—a spirited, musical laugh that had made Elodie feel cleverer than she was and more amusing. "She wanted to know me because of my mother?"

"Well, yes, but not like that. Caroline likes young people; she's interested in them and inspired by them—that's why she teaches. But with you it was more. She felt bonded to you, because of what she saw that day and everything that happened afterwards. She'd been wanting to tell you about the photo since the first moment you met."

"Why didn't she?"

"She was worried it might be overwhelming. That it might upset you. But when I mentioned you this morning—your wedding, the concert recordings, your mum—she asked me what I thought."

Elodie studied the image again. Pippa said that Caroline had developed the photo only days after taking it, and that by then her mother's funeral had made the news. Yet here she was, sharing lunch with the American violinist. They had performed in Bath on the fifteenth of July and died the following day. It seemed likely that this photograph had been taken on their way back to London; that they had stopped for a lunch break somewhere en route. It explained why they had been driving on the country roads instead of the motorway.

"I told Caroline that I thought you'd be glad to have it."

Elodie *was* glad. Her mother had been much photographed, but this, she realized, was the last picture ever taken. She liked that it wasn't a posed image from a photo shoot. Her mother looked very young—younger than Elodie was now. Caroline's camera had caught her in a private moment, when she wasn't being Lauren Adler; there wasn't a cello in sight. "I am," she said now to Pippa. "Thank Caroline for me."

"'Course."

"And thank *you*."

Pippa smiled.

"For the book, too—not to mention, bringing them all the way here. I know it's a trek."

"Yeah, well, turns out I'm going to miss this place. Even if it is halfway to Cornwall. How did your landlady take the news?"

Elodie lifted the pinot bottle. "Top up?"

"Oh, dear. You haven't told her."

"I couldn't. I didn't want to upset her before the wedding. She's put so much thought into selecting the reading."

"You realize she's going to figure it out when the honeymoon's over and you don't come back."

"I know. I feel wretched."

"How much longer do you have on the lease?"

"Two months."

"So, you're thinking . . . ?"

"Ride it out in complete denial and hope something comes to me in the meantime?"

"A solid plan."

"Alternatively, I simply take out another lease and turn up twice weekly to collect my mail. I could come upstairs sometimes and sit right here. I could even leave my furniture in situ, my tatty old chair, my odd assortment of teacups."

Pippa smiled sympathetically. "Maybe Alastair will change his mind?"

"Maybe." Elodie topped up her friend's glass. She didn't feel like another conversation about Alastair; they invariably turned into in-quisitions that led to Elodie feeling like a pushover. Pippa didn't understand compromise. "You know what? I'm hungry. Want to stay for a bite to eat?"

"Sure," said Pippa, a tacit agreement to let the subject drop. "Now you mention it, I've got a hankering for fish-and-chips."

CHAPTER NINE

ELODIE had planned to spend Sunday listening to more recordings so that she could deliver the promised short list to Penelope, but sometime the night before, somewhere between the first and second bottles of red wine, she'd made a decision. She wasn't going to walk down the aisle to a video of Lauren Adler playing the cello. No matter how much Penelope (and Alastair, too?) loved the idea, it made Elodie feel uncomfortable to picture herself in a wedding dress, heading towards a large screen of her mother in performance. It was a bit weird, wasn't it?

"Yes!" Pippa had said as they lounged by the river, finishing their fish-and-chips and watching the last of the day slip behind the horizon. "I didn't think you liked classical music anyway." Which was true. Elodie preferred jazz.

And so, as the first pealing church bells of Sunday morning drifted through the open windows, Elodie packed the videotapes back into her father's suitcase and sat on the velvet chair. The new photograph of her mother was propped on the shelf of treasures between Mrs. Berry's watercolor of Montepulciano and Tip's charm box, and Elodie's thoughts had started to clarify into a list of things she wanted to ask her great-uncle—about her mother, and the house in the sketch, and the violinist, too. In the meantime she was going to dive into Caroline's book and learn as much as she could about the woman in the photograph. As she opened it on her lap, she felt an immensely satisfying sensation of coming home, as if this, right now, was the very thing that she was supposed to be doing.

Edward Radcliffe: His Life and Loves. The title was a bit sappy, but then it had been originally published in 1931, and it didn't do to judge by contemporary standards. There was a photograph of the author, Dr. Leonard Gilbert, on the inside of the dust jacket, a black-and-white image of a serious young man in a light-colored suit. It was hard to guess his age.

The book was divided into eight chapters: the first two gave an account of Radcliffe's childhood, his family background, his interest in folktales, and his early artistic abilities, highlighting his particular affection for houses, and positing that the thematic focus on "home" and enclosed spaces in his art might have been the result of his fractured upbringing. The next two described the formation of the Magenta Brotherhood, profiling its other members and outlining Radcliffe's early achievements at the Royal Academy. The fifth chapter took a turn for the personal, detailing his relationship with Frances Brown and their eventual engagement; the sixth arrived finally at the model known as Lily Millington and the period in Radcliffe's life during which he created his most extraordinary works.

It went against her grain, but Elodie couldn't resist starting at chapter six, sinking into Leonard Gilbert's account of a chance meeting in London between Edward Radcliffe and the woman whose face and bearing would inspire him to create some of the aesthetic movement's most striking pieces of art—a woman with whom Gilbert claimed the artist would fall deeply in love. He likened Lily Millington to the Dark Lady of Shakespeare's sonnets, making much of the mystery of her true identity.

As Pippa had forewarned, a lot of the information, particularly that of a biographical nature, had come from a single "anonymous source," a local woman who had "enjoyed a close association with the Radcliffe family." The source, according to Gilbert, had been especially close to Radcliffe's youngest sister, Lucy, and offered important insights into Radcliffe's childhood and the events of the summer of 1862, during which his fiancée was shot and killed and

Lily Millington disappeared. Gilbert had met the woman when he visited the village of Birchwood to complete his doctoral thesis; he had then conducted a series of interviews with her between 1928 and 1930.

Although Gilbert's intimate portrayal of Radcliffe and his model must necessarily have been largely imagined—extrapolated from fact, if Elodie were to be generous—it was rich and nuanced. Gilbert wrote with insight and care, weaving a story that brought the pair to life, culminating in their final summer together at Birchwood Manor. The tone was unusually affecting, and Elodie was pondering why that might be, when she realized the answer was simple: Leonard Gilbert, the author, had fallen in love with Lily Millington. So appealing was his depiction that Elodie found that she, too, couldn't help but be drawn to this woman of brilliance and beauty. In Gilbert's hands, she was enchanting. Every word caressed her character, from the initial description of a young woman whose "flame brightly burned" to the poignant turn as the chapter reached its end.

For in chapter seven, the story arrived at Radcliffe's downfall, and Gilbert went against conventional wisdom to propose his new theory: that the artist's decline was not the result of his fiancée's death but was in fact due to the loss of his great love and muse, Lily Millington. Based on information gleaned from "never before seen" police reports, Gilbert posited a theory that the model had been an accomplice to the robbery in which Frances Brown was shot dead, fleeing afterwards with the intruder to America, taking with them the Radcliffe family's heirloom pendant.

The official story, Gilbert claimed, had been massaged over the years by the Radcliffe family themselves, whose influence in the village extended to sway with the local constabulary, and the family of Miss Brown, in whose mutual interest it was to erase all mention and memory of "the woman who had stolen Edward Radcliffe's heart." Far more palatable to both families, each of whom took a view to posterity, preferring tragedy to scandal, was the official narrative that an unknown thief had broken into the manor house to steal the necklace, killing Frances Brown and devastating her devoted fiancé. A search was mounted for the pendant, but aside from occasional false reports no trace was found.

Compared with the rest of Gilbert's book, the theory relating to Lily Millington's perfidy was proposed in an almost mechanical tone, the text based heavily on direct quotes from the case notes Gilbert had found in the police files. As a researcher, Elodie could understand Gilbert's reluctance to believe such treachery of the woman he'd conjured into life in the previous chapter. This chapter read as if two aspects of the same man were doing battle: the ambitious academic in possession of an intoxicating new theory, and the writer who had come to feel great affection for a character he'd spent so long depicting. And then there was that face. Elodie considered the way the woman in the silver-framed photograph had got beneath her skin. Even as she reminded herself sternly of the dangers and powers inherent to beauty, Elodie knew that she, too, was resistant to the notion that the woman in white could be capable of such stunning duplicity.

Despite his unwillingness to accept wholeheartedly the idea that Lily Millington was central to its disappearance, Gilbert went into some detail about the pendant, for it turned out that the diamond it contained was no ordinary gem. The twenty-three-carat stone was a blue diamond so rare and valuable that it had its own name: the Radcliffe Blue. The lineage of the Blue could be traced back in time to Marie Antoinette, for whom the remarkable stone had first been set in a pendant; back further to the mercenary John Hawkwood, who obtained the gem during a raid on Florence in the fourteenth century and couldn't bear to be parted from it, going to his deathbed, according to one report, "loaden with honour and riches"; back further still to tenth-century India, where it was said—apocryphally, in Gilbert's opinion—that the stone had been plucked by a traveling merchant from the wall of a Hindu temple. Whatever the case, when the stone fell into the hands of the Radcliffe family in 1816, it was reset in a filigree gold casing and threaded onto a fine chain to sit at the hollow of the neck. Spectacular, but of prohibitive value: for the half century or so that the diamond remained in the possession of the Radcliffe family, it was kept almost exclusively in the family's safe-deposit box at Lloyd's of London.

Elodie wasn't particularly interested in the history of the Radcliffe Blue, but the next line made her sit upright. According to Gilbert, Edward Radcliffe had "borrowed" the pendant from the safe-deposit box in June 1862 in order that his model could wear it in a great work he planned to complete over the summer. This, then, must be the unfinished painting that had come to be regarded by art lovers and academics with mythological longing.

The second half of chapter seven was dedicated to the possibility that such a painting, finished or in process, was extant somewhere. Gilbert posited several possible theories, based on his research into Edward Radcliffe's artistic oeuvre, but in conclusion acknowledged that without proof it was all speculation. For although there were vague references to an abandoned artwork in correspondence between the other members of the Magenta Brotherhood, nothing belonging to Radcliffe himself had yet been unearthed.

Elodie glanced at the sketchbook she'd found in the archives. Was this the proof that Leonard Gilbert had craved? Had the verification for which the art world had longed been sitting all the while in a leather satchel in the house of the great Victorian reformer James Stratton? The thought brought Elodie back to Stratton, for she knew now that Lily Millington was the missing link between the two men. Stratton knew the woman well enough to keep her photograph; Radcliffe had been in love with her. The two men themselves did not appear to have been closely acquainted, and yet it was to Stratton that Radcliffe had turned in the middle of the night when his desperate heartache threatened to overwhelm him. It appeared that it was Stratton, too, to whom Radcliffe had entrusted the plans for his great work. But why? Learning the true identity of Lily Millington was key. The name was not familiar, but Elodie made a note to check the Stratton correspondence database for any mention.

In the final chapter of his book, Gilbert returned his attention to

Edward Radcliffe's interest in houses, especially his love for the country dwelling he referred to in correspondence as his "charming house . . . within its own bend of the river," this time allowing his own story to intersect with that of his subject. For it turned out that Gilbert, too, had spent a summer living within Radcliffe's "charming house," walking in Radcliffe's footsteps as he worked to complete his doctoral thesis.

Leonard Gilbert, the returned soldier, who had suffered his own losses on the French battlefields of the Great War, wrote elegiacally about the effects of displacement, but ended his book on a note of hope, with a meditation on the longing for "home" and what it meant to find oneself at last in a place of comfort after so long in the wilderness. He relied on one of Radcliffe's contemporaries, the greatest Victorian of them all, Charles Dickens, to convey the simple, enormous power of "home": "Home is a name, a word, it is a strong one; stronger than magician ever spoke, or spirit ever answered to . . ." For Edward Radcliffe, Gilbert wrote, this place was Birchwood Manor.

Elodie read the line again. The house had a name. She typed it into the search engine on her phone, held her breath, and then there it was. A photograph, a description, an address. The house was on the border of Oxfordshire and Berkshire, in the vale of White Horse. She chose a link and learned that it had been given to the Art Historians' Association in 1928 by Lucy Radcliffe for use as a Residential Scholarship for students. When the costs of upkeep became too high, there'd been talk of setting it up as a museum to celebrate the art of Edward Radcliffe and the tremendous flowering of creativity that occurred under the umbrella of the Magenta Brotherhood, but the money required was not immediately available. It had taken years of fundraising, and finally, in 1980, a generous bequest from an unnamed donor, to allow the AHA to make good on its plans. The museum was still there; open to the public on Saturdays.

Elodie's hand was shaking as she scrolled to the bottom of the web page and noted the directions to Birchwood Manor. There was another photo of the house, this one taken from a different angle, and

Elodie enlarged it to fill the screen. Her gaze roamed across the garden, the brick face, the dormer windows in the steep roof, and then she drew breath—

At that moment the image left her screen, replaced by an incoming call. It was international—Alastair—but before she knew what she was doing, Elodie had stabbed the screen to cancel, swiping the call aside to return to the photo of the house. She zoomed closer and there it was, just as she'd known it would be: the astrological weather vane.

Radcliffe's sketch was of his own house, on its own bend of the river, which was in turn the house from the story her mother had told her, the house to which Tip had been evacuated during the Second World War. Elodie's own family was somehow connected to Radcliffe and a mystery that had fallen into her lap at work. It made no sense at all, and yet there was more to the connection than that, for Tip, although he hadn't been willing to admit it, had recognized the photograph of Lily Millington, the woman in white.

Elodie picked up the framed photograph. Who was she? What was her real name and what had become of her? For reasons that she couldn't explain, Elodie was overcome with a passionate, almost *desperate* need to find out.

She ran her finger lightly around the edge of the frame, over the fine scratches. As she did so, Elodie noticed that the back of the frame, from which the stand protruded, was not completely flat. She held it up at eye level so that the horizontal plane was directly in front of her; yes, there was a very slim convex bend. Elodie pressed it lightly with her fingertips. Was she imagining that the backing felt ever-so-slightly padded?

Heart beginning to beat faster, with the finely tuned instinct of a treasure hunter, and even as she knew it was absolutely against regulation to tamper with the archives, Elodie looked for a way to jimmy it loose without causing damage. She pulled at the old tape that had been used to seal the backing and it lifted, held not by adhesive anymore but from habit. There, pressed flat and tucked beneath the frame, was a piece of paper that had been folded into quarters. Elodie opened it out and could tell at once that it was old—very old.

It was a letter, written in a lively cursive hand, and it began, *My dearest, one and only, J, what I have to tell you now is my deepest secret . . .* Elodie's breath caught, for here, at last, was the voice of her woman in white. Her attention skittered to the bottom of the page where the letter was signed with a pair of looped initials: *Your most grateful and ever-loving, BB.*

Part Two

THE SPECIAL ONES

V

There was a long stretch, before this new visitor came, and before the Art Historians' Association opened their museum, when there was no one living in this house. I had to content myself with occasional children on weekday afternoons, clambering through the ground floor windows in order to impress their friends. Sometimes, when the mood was upon me, I obliged by slamming a door or shaking a window, making them squeal and trip over themselves trying to get free.

But I have missed the companionship of a proper visitor. There have been some over the century, a precious few, whom I have loved. In their stead, I am forced now to endure the ignominy of a weekly deluge of busybodies and officials merrily dissecting my past. The tourists, for their part, talk a lot about Edward, although they call him "Radcliffe" or "Edward Julius Radcliffe," which makes him sound old and stuffy. People forget how young he was when he lived in this house. He had only just marked his twenty-second birthday when we decided to leave London. They talk in serious, respectful tones about Art, and they look through the windows and gesture towards the river and say things like, "This is the view that inspired the Upper Thames paintings."

There is a lot of interest, too, in Fanny. She has become a tragic heroine, impossible though that is for one who knew her in life to believe. People speculate as to where "it" happened. The newspaper reports were never clear, each one contradicting the other; and although there was more than one person at the house that day, their accounts were uncertain and history has managed to bury the details.

I didn't see it happen myself—I wasn't in the room—but through a quirk of history I have been able to read the police reports. One of my previous visitors, Leonard, obtained lovely clear copies and we spent many a quiet evening together poring over them. Works of utter fiction, of course, but that's how things were done back then. Perhaps they still are.

Edward's portrait of Fanny, the one in which she wears the green velvet dress and a heart-shaped emerald on her pale décolletage, was brought in by the Association when they started opening for tourists. It hangs on the wall of the first-floor bedroom, facing the window that overlooks the orchard and the laneway that runs towards the church-yard in the village. I wonder sometimes what Fanny would think of that. She was easily excited and did not like the idea of a bedroom that looked onto gravestones. "It is just a different type of sleep," I can hear Edward saying, in an attempt to placate her. "Nothing more than that. Just the long sleep of the dead."

People pause in front of Fanny's portrait sometimes, comparing it with the smaller image printed in the tourist brochure; they comment on her pretty face, her privileged life, her tragic end; they speculate on the theories as to what happened that day. Mostly, they shake their heads and sigh in contented lamentation; reflection on someone else's tragedy being one of the most delicious of pastimes, after all. They wonder about Fanny's father and his money, her fiancé and his heart-ache, the letter she received from Thurston Holmes the week before she died. This I know: to be murdered is to become eternally interest-ing. (Unless, of course, you are a ten-year-old orphan living on Little White Lion Street, in which case to be murdered is simply to be dead.)

The tourists also talk, of course, about the Radcliffe Blue. They wonder, with their wide eyes and their excited voices, where the pen-dant could have gone. "Things don't just disappear," they say.

Sometimes they even talk about me. Again, I have Leonard, my young soldier, to thank for that, for it was he who wrote the book which first presented me as Edward's lover. Until that time I was sim-ply one of his models. There are copies of the book for sale in the gift shop and every so often I glimpse Leonard's face on the back cover and remember his time in the house, the cries of "Tommy" in the dead of night.

The tourists who walk about the house on Saturdays with their arms behind their backs and studied expressions of self-conscious learning on their faces refer to me as Lily Millington, which is understandable given how things worked out. Some of them even wonder where I came from, where I went to, who I really was. I am inclined to like those ones, in spite of their wrongheaded speculation. It is nice to be considered.

No matter how many times I hear the name Lily Millington spoken out loud by strangers, it is always a surprise. I have tried whispering my real name into the air around their ears, but only a couple have ever heard me, like my little friend with the curtain of fine hair above his eyes. Not surprising: children are more perceptive than adults, in all the ways that count.

Mrs. Mack used to say that those who seek to know gossip will hear ill about themselves. Mrs. Mack said a lot of things, but in this she was correct. I am remembered as a thief. An imposter. A girl who rose above her station, who was not chaste.

And I was all of those things at different times, and more. But there is one thing they accuse me of which is not just. I was not a murderer. I did not fire the gun that day that killed poor Fanny Brown.

———

My current visitor has been here for a week and a half. A Saturday passed, which saw him scamper away from the house as early as he could—would that I were able to do the same—and another few days after that in which he continued with the same routines as last week. I had begun to despair of ever learning what it is he's up to, for he is not communicative like some of the others have been: he never leaves papers lying around from which I might glean answers, nor does he reward me by carrying out long, informative conversations.

But then, tonight, at last, a phone call. The upshot of which is that I now know why he is here. I also know his name. It is Jack—Jack Rolands.

He had spent the whole day out of the house, as is his habit, having set off in the morning with his shovel and camera bag. When he returned, though, I could see at once that he was changed. For a start, he took that shovel of his down to the tap on the side of the old outhouse and washed it clean. Evidently, there was to be no more digging.

There was something different in his attitude, too. A looseness to his joints; an air of resolution. He came inside and cooked a piece of fish for dinner, which was quite unlike him, having thus far proven himself more of a tinned-soup sort of man.

The hint of ceremony put me further *en garde. He has finished whatever it is that he came here to do*, I thought. And then, as if to prove me right, there came the call.

Jack had apparently been expecting it. He had glanced at his phone a couple of times while he ate his dinner, as if to check the time, and when he finally picked it up he knew already who it was at the other end.

I was worried at first it would be Sarah, telephoning to cancel their lunch appointment tomorrow, but it wasn't; it was, instead, a woman called Rosalind Wheeler, telephoning from Sydney, and the conversation had nothing at all to do with those two little girls in Jack's photograph.

I listened from where I was sitting on the kitchen bench, and that is how I came to hear him speak a name that I know well.

The conversation to that point had been a brief and somewhat stilted exchange of pleasantries, and then Jack, who doesn't strike me as one to mince words, said, "Look, I'm sorry to disappoint you. I've spent ten days checking the places on your list. The stone isn't there."

There is only one stone that people mention with respect to Edward and his family, and thus I knew at once what he'd been seeking. I confess to being slightly disappointed. It is all so predictable. But then, human beings are, for the most part. They cannot help it. And I am hardly one to judge a treasure hunter.

I was interested, though, that Jack should think to seek the Radcliffe Blue here at Birchwood. I knew already, from listening to the museum's day-trippers, that the diamond has not faded from thought—indeed, that a legend has grown around its whereabouts— but Jack is the only person ever to come looking for it *here*. Since the very first newspaper reports were printed, the general wisdom has been that the pendant made its way to America in 1862, where it promptly disappeared underground. Leonard nudged the idea even further, proposing that it was *I* who took the diamond from this house. He was wrong in that, of course, and deep down I am sure he knew it. It was the police reports that swayed him—the curious, wrongheaded interviews conducted in the days after Fanny's death. Still. I had thought we had an understanding, he and I.

That Jack had come to Birchwood—sent by this woman, this Mrs. Wheeler—to seek the Radcliffe Blue intrigued me, and I was pondering the fact when he said, "It sounds as if you're asking me to break into the house," and my other thoughts fell away.

"I know how much this means to you," he went on, "but I'm not going to break in. The people who run this place made it very clear that my accommodation is conditional."

In my eagerness, I had moved too close without realizing it. Jack shivered abruptly and left the phone on the table as he went to shut the window; he must have pressed a button on the device, because suddenly I could hear the other half of the conversation, too. A woman's voice, not young, with an American accent: "Mr. Rolands, I paid you to do a job."

"And I've checked all of the places on your list: the woods, the river bend, the hill in the clearing—all the sites mentioned in Ada Lovegrove's letters to her parents."

Ada Lovegrove.

Such a long time since I'd heard her name; I confess to a wave of deep emotion. Who was this woman on the other end of the phone? This American woman telephoning from Sydney. And what was she doing with Ada Lovegrove's long-ago letters?

Jack continued, "The stone wasn't there. I'm sorry."

"I told you when we met, Mr. Rolands, that if the list of sites didn't yield results, then I'd advise you of plan B."

"You didn't say anything about breaking into a museum."

"This is a matter of great urgency to me. As you know, I'd have gone myself if my condition didn't prevent my flying."

"Look, I'm sorry, but—"

"I'm sure I don't need to remind you that I only pay the second half of your fee if you deliver."

"All the same . . ."

"I will be emailing you with further instructions."

"And I'll go in on Saturday, when the place is open, and have a look around. Not before."

She did not end the call happily, but Jack was unmoved. He is an unflappable sort of person. Which is a fine quality, yet one that makes me inexplicably eager to cause him to flap. Just a little. I have developed a rather perverse streak, I fear; no doubt a consequence of boredom and its miserable twin, frustration. A consequence of knowing Edward, too, for whom ebullience was beauty, and whose ethos was so passionately defended that it was impossible not to be moved.

I was overcome with great agitation after the phone call. As Jack took out his camera and began transferring images onto his computer, I retreated, alone, to the warm corner where the staircase makes its turn, to consider what it all means.

In some ways the cause of my perturbation was clear. The mention of Ada Lovegrove after so long was startling. It brought with it a host of memories; also questions. There was a logic to Ada's association with the Blue; the timing, however, was a mystery. Why now, more than one hundred years since she spent her brief time in this house?

But there was another layer to my distress, too. Less apparent. More personal. Unrelated to Ada. It stemmed, I realized, from Jack's refusal to do as Rosalind Wheeler had asked of him. Not for Mrs. Wheeler's sake; my turbulence was caused by the recognition that as far as Jack is concerned, he has finished the task that he was sent here to perform. It is unrelated to the two little girls in the photograph, with whom he has an ongoing interest, and so he intends to leave.

I do not want him to leave.

On the contrary, I want very much for him to stay; to come inside my house. Not on Saturday with all of the others, but by himself, alone.

It is *my* house, after all, not theirs. More than that, it is my home. I let them use it, grudgingly, because their purpose is a tribute to Edward, who deserved so much better than what he got. But it is mine and I will have my visitors if I wish.

It has been a long time since I've had one of my own.

And so I have come back downstairs and into the old caretaker's accommodation where Jack and I are sitting together now—he in quiet contemplation of his photographs, I in unquiet contemplation of him.

He looks from one image to the next and I watch the minute changes in his features. All is quiet; all is still. I can hear my clock ticking from inside the house, the clock that Edward gave me just before we came here that summer. "I will love you for all time," he promised, on the evening we decided where to hang it.

There is a door on the wall behind Jack that leads into the kitchen of the house. Within the kitchen is the narrow entrance to the smaller set of stairs that winds up to the first floor. There is a window ledge midway up, just wide enough for a woman to rest. I remember a day in July, the scented air that brushed through the panes to caress my bare neck; Edward's sleeves pushed halfway up his forearms; the back of his hand grazing my cheek—

Jack has stopped typing. He is sitting very still, as if trying to hear a distant melody. After a moment he returns his attention to his screen.

I remember the way Edward's eyes searched mine; the way my heart beat fast beneath my breast; the words he whispered in my ear, his warm breath on my skin—

Jack stops again and glances at the door on the wall behind him.

Suddenly, I understand. I move closer.

Come inside, I whisper.

He is frowning slightly now; his elbow is on the table, his chin on his fist. He is staring at the door.

Come inside my house.

He goes to stand right by the door now, resting the palm of one hand flat upon its surface. His expression is perplexed, in the manner of one trying to understand an arithmetical problem that has delivered an unexpected solution.

I am immediately beside him.

Open the door . . .

But he doesn't. He is going. He is leaving the room.

I follow, willing him to return, but instead he goes to the old suitcase that holds his clothing, digging about until he produces a small black tool kit. He stands, looking down at the object, jostling it slightly as if to guess its weight. He is weighing up more than the kit, I realize, for finally, with a set of resolution to his jaw, he turns around.

He is coming!

There is an alarm on one side of the door, installed by the Association after it proved difficult to keep a caretaker, which is set like clockwork every Saturday afternoon when the museum closes for the week. I watch avidly as somehow, with a tool extracted from that kit of his, he manages to circumvent it. He then proceeds to pick the lock of the door with so little fuss that I think at once of the Captain, who would have been most impressed. The door pushes open, and before I know it, Jack has crossed the threshold.

It is dark inside my house and he has not brought a torch; the only light is of the moon, spilling silver through the windows. He walks across the kitchen and into the hallway, where he stops. He makes a slow, considering turn. And then he starts up the stairs, climbing all the way to the top, the attic, where once again he stands still.

And then he retraces his path and returns to the malthouse.

I would have liked for him to stay, to see more. But my mood is tempered by the thoughtful expression on his face as he leaves. I have a feeling, born of long experience, that he will return. People tend to, once I take an interest.

And so, I let him go, and I remain alone in the dark of my house as he bolts the door again from the other side.

I have always found much to admire in a man who knows how to pick a lock. And a woman, for that matter. Blame it on my upbringing: Mrs. Mack, who knew a lot about life and even more about business, used to say that wherever one came across a lock, it was wise to assume that there was something on the other side one ought to see. I was never a picker of locks myself, though, not officially. Mrs. Mack ran a far more complex enterprise than that and believed that diversification was key; or, as she preferred to put it, in words that might have been etched upon her headstone, that there was more than one way to skin a cat.

I was a good thief. As Mrs. Mack had foreseen, it was the perfect sleight of hand: people expected dirty street urchins to steal and were on guard should such a child enter the frame. But clean little girls in pretty dresses, with copper ringlets sitting on their shoulders, were above suspicion. My arrival in her house allowed Mrs. Mack's enterprise to push beyond the bounds of Leicester Square, into Mayfair in the west and Lincoln's Inn Fields and Bloomsbury in the north.

Such expansion had the Captain rubbing his hands together with glee: "That's where all the men of worth are," he would say, "their pockets overflowing with spoils ripe for the picking."

Little Girl Lost was a simple enough scheme, involving nothing more than for me to stand about conspicuously with a look of forlorn concern upon my face. Worried tears were helpful but not essential, and because they required significant additional energy, and could not easily be reversed if I decided that the wrong fish had been hooked, I deployed them sparingly. It did not take me long to develop a sixth sense for knowing for whom I should make the effort.

When the right sort of gentleman arrived at my side, as he always eventually did, inquiring as to where I lived and why I was alone, I would give him my sad story and a suitably respectable address—though not so grand as to risk recognition—and then allow the fellow to put me in a cab with a fare. It was not difficult to slip my hand inside his pocket while he was Being Helpful. There is a very useful sense of righteous importance that overtakes the renderer of assistance; it tends to overwhelm his better judgment and leave him dull to everything else.

But Little Girl Lost required a lot of standing around in the one place, which I found boring and, in the winter months, cold, wet, and unpleasant. I soon realized that there was another way in which I could make the same profit from a position of relative comfort. It also solved the problem of what to do should the Helpful Gentleman insist on seeing me all the way "home." Mrs. Mack appreciated ingenuity: she was a natural-born scammer and lit up with possibility when presented with a fresh scheme; she had also proven herself clever with a needle and thread. And so, when I told her my idea, she was soon able to procure a pair of fine white kid gloves and alter them to fit my purpose.

Thus was Little Girl Passenger born, and a quiet young thing she was, too, for her job was the opposite of Little Girl Lost. Where the latter had sought attention, Little Girl Passenger's wish was to avoid it. She was a frequent traveler on the omnibuses, sitting quietly against the window, her delicate kid gloves folded demurely on her lap. Being small, clean, and innocent, she was the natural choice of seating partner for a lady traveling alone. But once the lady had relaxed into the journey, distracted by conversation or sightseeing, a book or her posy, the Little Girl's hands—heretofore tucked well out of sight—would reach between the voluminous folds of merged skirts until they found her pocket or her bag. I can still remember how it felt: the slip of my hand into the pretty lady's skirt, the coolness of the silk, the smooth, swift sweep of my fingertips, as all the while my false kid gloves sat well beyond reproach upon my lap.

From some of the omnibus drivers, an all-day seat could be procured for a small price. And on days when the conductor couldn't be bought, Little Girl Lost reprised her role, bereft and frightened on a well-heeled street.

I learned a lot about people during those days. Things like:

1. Privilege makes a person, especially a woman, trusting. Nothing in her experience prepares her for the possibility that anyone might mean her harm.
2. There is nothing so sure as that a gentleman likes to be seen to help.
3. The art of illusion is knowing precisely what people expect to see and then ensuring that they see it.

The French magician in Covent Garden helped me with that final one, for I had done what Lily Millington bade me and watched him closely until I knew exactly how he made those coins appear.

I also learned that, should the worst thing happen and a call of "Stop! Thief!" be raised behind me, London was my greatest ally. For a slight child who knew her way, the thrum and throng of the streets provided the perfect cover; it was easy to disappear amongst the moving forest of legs, particularly when one had friends. Once again, I had Lily Millington to thank for that. There was the man with the sandwich board who could always be counted on to turn it back and forth into the shins of an inconvenient policeman; the organ-grinder whose contraption had an uncanny habit of rolling on its wheels to block my pursuer's path; and, of course, the French magician, who, along with his coins, had a knack for producing the right wallet at the right time, leaving my chaser indignant and reduced as I slipped away to freedom.

And so, I was a thief. A good thief. Earning my keep.

As long as I returned each day with a few pilfered spoils, Mrs. Mack and the Captain were kept happy. She told me many times that my mother had been a real and proper lady, that the ladies I picked from were no better than I was, that it was right that I should feel the weight of quality beneath my fingertips. I suppose she meant to counter the rise in me of any pesky conscience.

She needn't have bothered. We all do things in life that we regret; stealing trifles from the rich is not high on my list.

———

I was restless after Jack left my house last night, and he slept fitfully, too, surrendering finally to wakefulness in the light mauve of dawn. It is the day of his meeting with Sarah and he has been dressed for hours. He has made a special effort with his clothing, and the items sit uncomfortably on him.

There was a carefulness to the way he readied himself. I noticed him stop to rub at an imagined spot on his sleeve, and he spent longer than usual in front of the mirror; he shaved and even ran a brush through his wet hair. I have not seen him do that before.

When he was finished, he stood for a moment as if sizing up his own reflection. I saw his eyes shift in the mirror and for a split second I thought that he was looking at me. My heart skipped a beat before I realized that he was looking at the photograph of the two babies. He reached out to touch each one's face in turn with his thumb.

I assumed at first that his unsettlement was due to today's meeting, and no doubt, for the most part, it is. But I wonder now whether there might be more to it than that.

He made his cup of tea, spilling half, as is his wont, and then, with a piece of toast in hand, went to his computer on the small round table in the middle of the room. A couple of new emails had appeared in the night, one from Rosalind Wheeler, as promised (threatened), which seemed to comprise a rather lengthy list and a sketch of some kind. Jack's reaction was to stick a small black contraption in the side of the laptop and press a few buttons before removing the tiny object to his pocket.

I cannot know for certain whether what he found in Rosalind Wheeler's email is responsible for sending him back inside my house this morning. I went closer after he left the table and saw that the subject line read, "Further Instructions: Ada Lovegrove Notes," but I could not learn anything more because the email above was open, an advertisement for a subscription to the *New Yorker*.

Whatever the case, soon after checking his computer, he fetched his miniature tool kit and unlocked the door to my house again.

He is in here with me now.

He has not done much since his arrival; there is little of determined industry in his movements. He is in the Mulberry Room, leaning against the large mahogany desk that abuts the window. It faces towards the chestnut tree in the middle of the back garden, and beyond that the field barn. But Jack's focus is on something further still, the distant river, and he wears that troubled expression on his face again. He blinks as I come nearer and his gaze shifts to the meadow, the barn.

I remember lying in the upper level of the barn with Edward that summer, watching the sun stream through the pinprick holes between the roof slates as he whispered to me of all the places in the world he'd like to go.

It was in this very room, on the chaise longue by the fireplace, that Edward told me the details of his plan to paint the *Fairy Queen*; it was here that he smiled and reached inside his coat pocket, producing the black velvet box and revealing the treasure within. I can still feel the light touch of his fingertips as he fastened that cold blue stone at my throat.

Perhaps Jack is merely seeking distraction—a way to pass the minutes before it is time to leave; certainly, his meeting with Sarah is on his mind, for he glances up at my clock at regular intervals to check the time. When, at last, it delivers the correct answer, he beats a hasty retreat, leaving my house, locking the kitchen door behind him and resetting the alarm, almost before I can catch up.

I follow him as far as the gate, where I watch him get into his car and leave.

I hope he isn't gone too long.

For now, I am going to return to the malthouse. Perhaps there

143

will be something more from Rosalind Wheeler in the email. I crave to know how she came by Ada Lovegrove's letters.

Poor little Ada. Childhood is the cruelest time. A place of extremes, in which one might this day sail carefree amongst the silvery stars, only to be plunged tomorrow into the black woods of despair.

—

After Fanny died and the police finished their investigation, the others left Birchwood Manor and all was still and silent for a long stretch. The house rested. Twenty years passed before Lucy returned. That is how and when I learned that Edward was dead and that he'd left this house, his most beloved possession, to his youngest sister.

It was a quintessentially Edward thing to do, for he adored his sisters, and they him. I know why he chose Lucy, though. He would have reasoned that Clare could take care of herself, by marrying well or convincing someone to look after her, but that Lucy was different. I will never forget my first glimpse of her, that pale watchful face in the upstairs window of the dark brick house in Hampstead, when Edward brought me home to the studio in his mother's garden.

She will always be that child to me: the girl I knew who resented the strictures of London but blossomed as soon as she was set loose in the countryside, free to explore and dig and collect to her heart's content. I have such a clear memory of her when we arrived at the house that summer, the walk from the railway, Lucy lagging behind because her trunk was loaded with precious books and she refused to send it on the carriage with the others.

What a surprise it was to see her when she turned up to inspect the house. Little Lucy turned into an austere and serious woman. Thirty-three years old and no longer young by the standards of the day. But still Lucy, wearing a long, practical skirt, the most unflattering shade of olive green, and a dreadful hat that caused me to suffer a wave of overwhelming fondness. Her hair beneath it was already coming loose—she never could keep a pin in place—and her boots were thick with mud.

She did not view all of the rooms, but then she didn't need to; she knew the house and its secrets as well as I do. She only went as far as the kitchen before shaking the lawyer's hand and telling him that he could leave.

"But, Miss Radcliffe"—a hint of bewilderment flecked his words—"would you not like me to show you the property?"

"It won't be necessary, Mr. Matthews."

She waited, watching him disappear along the coach way, and then she turned back towards the kitchen and stood very still. I went right up close to her, reading the fine lines now written upon her face. Behind them I could see the little Lucy that I knew, for people do not change. They remain, as they age, the people that they were when they were young, only frailer and sadder. I wished nothing more than to put my arms around her. Lucy, who had always been my ally.

All of a sudden she looked up, and it was as if she were staring right at me. Or through me. Something had disturbed her from her contemplation and she brushed me aside, crossing the hallway and starting up the staircase.

I wondered if she intended to live here at Birchwood Manor. I hoped against hope that she would stay. And then the deliveries began to arrive: first the wooden box, followed by the desks and chairs and small iron beds. Blackboards and trays of chalk, and eventually a severe-looking woman named Thornfield, whose desk plaque read, DEPUTY HEADMISTRESS.

A school. And I was pleased to see it. Little Lucy had always quested for knowledge. Edward would have been glad, for he was forever stopping in the street, dragging me with him into this bookshop or that, in order to choose a new tome for Lucy. Her curiosity was unquenchable.

Sometimes I can still hear those schoolgirls. Faint, faraway voices, singing, arguing, laughing, crying into their pillows, pleading for a mother or father to have a change of heart, to come back and reclaim her. Their voices became trapped in the weave of the house.

During the years that I lived with Mrs. Mack and Martin and the

Captain, I longed for my father to return for me, but I did not cry. The letter left with Mrs. Mack had been very clear: I was to be brave, my father instructed, and to do my best to be good; I was to pull my weight and to make myself helpful; I was to do as Mrs. Mack told me, for she had his complete confidence and could be relied upon to protect my best interests.

"When is he coming back?" I asked.

"He will send for you when he's established in his new situation."

There is a wound that never heals in the heart of an abandoned child. It is something that I recognized in Edward and I wonder sometimes if it is that which first drew us together. For of course he was abandoned, too, as a boy. He and his sisters left with their disapproving grandparents while their mother and father traveled the world.

It is something that I recognized, too, in Ada Lovegrove.

I have thought often of her over the years. The unkindness of children. The way she pined. That day in the river.

So long ago, and yet it was yesterday. With only the merest effort I can see her now, sitting cross-legged on the bed in the attic, hot tears of anger on her cheeks, scribbling faster than her pen will permit, entreating her parents to please, please, please come back for her.

Chapter Ten

ADA Lovegrove had a tall, wealthy father and an elegant. clever mother and she hated them both equally. The hatred was only new—she had adored them both as recently as April the twenty-fifth—but it was no less deeply felt for being novel. A holiday, they'd said, a little trip back to England. Oh, Ada-Bear, how you'll adore London—the theaters and the Houses of Parliament! And just you wait until you see how soft and green the countryside is in summer! How gentle and floral, filled with honeysuckles and primroses, narrow laneways and hedgerows . . .

These foreign words, spoken with a romantic longing that Ada could not understand and did not trust, she had turned over with the dispassionate interest of an archaeologist building a picture of a distant civilization. She had been born in Bombay, and India was as much a part of her as the nose on her face and the freckles that covered it. She didn't recognize words like "soft" and "gentle" and "narrow": her world was vast and sudden and blazing. It was a place of unspeakable beauty—of brilliant flowers on the terrace and sweet swooning fragrance in the dead of night—but also of mercurial cruelty. It was her home.

Her mother had broken the news about the upcoming holiday one afternoon in March when Ada was having her evening meal. She had been eating in the library because Mamma and Papa were hosting a dinner that evening and the grand mahogany dining table (shipped from London) was being set. The library was lined with books (also

147

shipped from London) on whose spines were printed names like Dickens and Brontë and Keats, and at the end of the desk was the playbook from which Mamma had been teaching her *The Tempest*. The heat had made her hair stick to her forehead, and a lazy fly was turning loops around the room, its song droning like a barbless threat.

Ada had been thinking about Caliban and Prospero, wondering why Mamma's forehead had creased disapprovingly when Ada said that she felt sorry for Caliban, when the words "little trip back to England" broke her concentration.

As the lace curtains shrugged off a hot, moist breeze, Ada said, "How long will it take to get there?"

"A lot less time than it took before the canal was opened. We used to have to go by rail, you know."

Rail sounded preferable to Ada, who could not swim.

"What shall we do there?"

"All sorts of things. Visit family and friends, take in the sights. I'm looking forward to showing you the places I knew as a girl, the galleries and parks, the palace and gardens."

"We have gardens here."

"We do."

"And a palace."

"Not with a king and queen inside it."

"How long will we be away?"

"Long enough to do what needs to be done and not a moment more or less."

This answer, which was not really an answer at all, was not typical of Mamma, who was usually very good at meeting Ada's many questions, but Ada had no time then to unpick her mother's reticence. "On your way, now," she had said, making a fluttery sweeping motion with her elegant fingers. "Father will be home from his club any minute, and I still have the flowers to set. Lord Curzon is coming, as you know, and everything must be perfect."

Afterwards, Ada turned slow cartwheels on the terrace, watching the world change kaleidoscopically from purple to orange as the queen's crepe myrtles took turns with the hibiscus. The gardener was sweeping the lawn and his helper was cleaning down the curved cane chairs on the wide verandah.

Ordinarily, cartwheeling was one of Ada's favorite things to do, but this afternoon her heart wasn't in it. Rather than enjoying the way the world spun around her, she felt dizzy, even queasy. After a time, she sat instead on the edge of the verandah near the spider lilies.

Ada's father was an important man and their mansion was on the very top of a hill in the center of Bombay; from her vantage point, Ada could see all the way over the Hanging Gardens to where the Arabian Sea rolled its shoulders. She was busy peeling long white tentacles from an enormous spider lily flower, breathing in its sweet perfume, when her *aaya*, Shashi, found her.

"There you are, *pilla*," said Shashi, in careful English. "Come now—your mother wishes us to collect some extra fruits for the dessert."

Ada stood up and took Shashi's outstretched hand.

Usually she loved market chores—there was a man with a snack stall who always gave her an extra *chakkali* to nibble on while she followed Shashi and her enormous basket around to all of the various fruit and vegetable sellers—but today, in the shadow of her mother's worrying announcement, she dragged her heels as they walked together down the hill.

Storm clouds were gathering in the east, and Ada hoped that it would rain. Great, drenching rain, just as the carriages were arriving with her parents' guests. She sighed heavily as she turned over each line of her mother's unexpected proposal in her mind, searching the words for hidden meaning. England. The faraway land of her parents' childhood, the realm of the mysterious and legendary "Grandmother," the homeland of a people Shashi's father called the monkey bottoms . . .

Shashi switched to Punjabi. "You are very quiet, *pilla*. Make no mistake, my ears are enjoying the peace, but I have to wonder, has something happened to hurt your snout?"

Ada hadn't yet finished her considering, but she heard herself blurting out a report of the conversation regardless. She drew breath as she finished. "And I don't want to go!"

"Stubborn little mule! Such a fuss about a trip back home?"

"It is *their* home, not mine. I don't ever want to go to England, and I intend to tell Mamma so as soon as we get back from the markets."

"But, *pilla*"—the setting sun had balanced itself on the horizon and was leaching gold into the sea, which carried it back towards the shore in ripples—"you are going to visit an *island*."

Shashi was wise, for while Ada had no interest in "England," she was exceedingly excited by islands and she had forgotten, in her vexation, that England happened to be part of one in the middle of the North Sea: an hourglass-shaped island, shaded pink, all the way at the top of the map. There was a globe in her father's study, a large cream-colored sphere in a dark mahogany grip, that Ada spun sometimes when she was permitted entrée into the cigar-scented domain, because it made a wonderful clicking noise that sounded like a giant swarm of cicadas. She had spotted the island called Great Britain and commented to her father that it did not look particularly "great" to her. He had laughed when she said that and told her that looks could be deceiving. "Within that small island," he'd said, with a hint of personal pride that made Ada unaccountably flustered, "is the engine that drives the world."

"Yes, well," she conceded now, "an island is good, I suppose. But Britain is an island of monkey bottoms!"

"*Pilla!*" Shashi stifled a laugh. "You must not say such things—certainly not close to your mother and father's ears."

"Mother and Father are monkey bottoms!" Ada blustered hotly.

The delicious risk and irreverence of referring to her dignified parents in such a way was a spark that lit a flame, and Ada felt her commitment to being cross begin to melt. A surprise of laughter threatened. She took her *aaya*'s free hand and squeezed it hard. "But you must come with me, Shashi."

"I will be here when you return."

"No, I will miss you too much. You must come with us. Mamma and Papa will say yes."

Shashi shook her head gently. "I cannot come to England with you, *pilla*. I would wilt like a plucked flower. I belong here."

"Well, I belong here, too." They had reached the bottom of the hill and the line of palms that grew along the coast. The dhows bobbed mildly on the flat sea, their sails down, as white-robed Parsees gathered along the shores to begin their sunset prayers. Ada stopped walking and faced the golden ocean, the dying sun still warm on her face. She was infused with a feeling for which she did not have a name, but which was exquisitely wonderful and painful at the same time. She repeated, more softly now, "I belong here, too, Shashi."

Shashi smiled at her kindly but said nothing further. This, of itself, was unusual, and Ada was troubled by her *aaya's* silence. In the space of an afternoon, it seemed that the world had tilted and everything had slid off-center. All of the adults in her life had broken like once-reliable clocks that had started showing the wrong time.

She'd had that feeling a lot lately. She wondered whether it was something to do with having recently turned eight. Perhaps this was the way of adulthood?

The breeze brought with it the scent of salt and overripe fruit, and a blind beggar held up his cup as they passed him. Shashi dropped him a coin and Ada took a new tack, saying airily, "They can't make me go."

"They can."

"It wouldn't be fair."

"Wouldn't it?"

"Not a bit."

"Do you remember the story of 'The Rat's Wedding'?"

"Of course."

"Was it fair that the rat who had done no wrong ended with nothing but a singed bottom?"

"It was not!"

"And what about 'The Bear's Bad Bargain'? Was it fair that the poor bear did everything asked of him but ended up with no *khichri* and no pears, either?"

"Certainly not!"

"Well, then."

Ada frowned. It had never occurred to her how many of the stories Shashi told contained the moral that life was not fair. "That bear was *bevkuph*! Stupid. I would have punished the woodman's wife if I were him."

"Very stupid," Shashi agreed, "and I know you would have."

"She was a liar."

"She was."

"And a glutton."

"Mmm, speaking of gluttons . . ." They had reached the edge of the busy marketplace, and Shashi led Ada by the hand towards her favorite snack stall. "It seems to me that we need to feed that little snout of yours. I cannot have complaints while I select the fruit."

It was hard to stay cross with a warm, fresh, salty *chakkali* in hand, with the songs of the Parsees drifting up from the water, with candles and hibiscus flowers floating on the sea and dotted around the market stalls, in a world that had turned orange and mauve with the dusk. In fact, Ada felt so happy that she couldn't quite remember now what she'd been so annoyed about. Her parents wanted to take her on a little trip to visit an island. That was all.

Mamma required the fruit back quickly, so they didn't have as long as usual for Shashi to spend picking over each stall to find the *best* papaya and muskmelons, and Ada was still licking the last of her *chakkali* as they started the walk home. She said, "Will you tell me about Princess Aubergine?"

"Again?"

"It is my favorite." Truthfully, Ada liked all of Shashi's stories. Indeed, she would have relished story time even if Shashi chose only to read from one of Ada's father's diplomatic papers; what she really loved was lying with Shashi, whose name meant "moon," as the last of the day's light dissolved into the stars of the nighttime sky, listening to the enchanting sound of her *aaya's* voice, the soft breathy clicking of the Punjabi words with which she wove her tales. "Please, Shashi."

"Perhaps."

"Please!"

"Very well. If you help me carry the fruit to the top of the hill, I will tell you tonight of Princess Aubergine and her clever trick upon the wicked queen."

"Now, while we walk instead?"

"*Bāndara!*" said Shashi, pretending to swat Ada's ear. "Little monkey! What do you take me for to ask such a thing?"

Ada grinned. It had been worth a try, even though she'd known that Shashi would say no. Ada knew the rules. The best storytellers only ever spoke by dark. Many times, as they lay together at night when it was too hot to sleep, side by side on the platform at the top of the house, with the window wide-open, Shashi had told Ada about her girlhood in the Punjab. "When I was your age," she would say, "there were no stories between sunrise and sunset, for there was work to be done. Not for me a life of pleasure like yours! I was busy making fuel cakes all day so that there was something to burn at night, while my mother sat at her spinning wheel and my father and brothers drove the bullocks in the fields. In the village, there was always work to be done."

Ada had received this little lecture many times before, and although she knew it was only intended to highlight the idleness and indulgence of her own life, she did not mind: there was a magic to the way Shashi spoke about her home that made such tales every bit as wondrous as her "Long ago . . ." stories. "All right, then," she said, taking the smaller basket and hooking it over her arm. "Tonight. But if I beat you home, you will tell me the tale of Princess Aubergine twice!"

"Monkey!"

Ada started running, and Shashi gave a whoop behind her. They ran together, each laughing as much as the other; and when Ada glanced sideways at her *aaya's* face, taking in her kind eyes and wide smile, she knew that she had never loved anyone quite so much. If Ada were asked, "In what does your life lie?"—as the wicked queen asked of Princess Aubergine in order to discern her weakness—she would have had to confess that it lay in Shashi.

And so, on that hot afternoon in Bombay, Ada Lovegrove's ill temper disappeared with the day's sun. And when she and Shashi reached the house, its terrace now swept clean, candles flickering in glass jars along the verandah, the scent of freshly cut grass on the warm evening breeze, and the sound of piano music drifting out through the open windows, Ada experienced a swelling sense of ecstatic completeness so overwhelming that she dropped her basket of fruit and ran inside to tell Mamma that yes, she consented, she would accompany them on the trip to England.

But Ada's parents had not been truthful.

After a tortuous journey through the Suez Canal, during which Ada had spent the entire time heaving overboard or lying abed with a damp cloth on her forehead, they'd had a week in London, and a second week touring Gloucestershire—Mamma remarking to the point of delirium on the glory of spring and how little of the "seasons" they saw in India—before arriving one day at a twin-gabled house on the bend of an upper reach of the Thames.

The clouds had begun to darken as their carriage wound south through the village of Burford, and when it took a turn in the road before Lechlade, the first rain began to fall. Ada had been resting her face on the edge of the carriage window, watching the wet fields sweep by and wondering what it was that made the colors of this country appear as if they had been washed in milk. Her parents, meanwhile, had been unusually quiet since they'd bidden farewell to Lady Turner, their host, but this was something Ada noticed only on reflection.

They passed a triangle-shaped green in the middle of a very small village, and a public house called the Swan, and when they reached a stone church and cemetery, the carriage turned into a winding lane with edges that fell away into the verge, making the journey exceedingly bumpy.

Finally, when they had gone as far along the lane as they could go, their carriage cut between a pair of iron gates which were open within a tall stone wall. A barn-like structure stood to one side, overlooking a stretch of very green grass that ran as far as a line of willows beyond.

The horses came to a full stop and the driver leapt down from on high to open Mamma's door. He held aloft a large black umbrella and helped her from the carriage.

"Birchwood Manor, ma'am," he said in a dour voice.

Ada's parents had spent a great deal of time telling her about the people and places that they were going to see when they were in England, but she could not think that they'd mentioned friends who lived in a house called Birchwood Manor.

They followed a flagstone path with roses planted on either side and when they reached the front door were met by a woman with shoulders that hunched forward as if she had spent her whole life hurrying to get where she was going. Her name, she announced, was Miss Thornfield.

Ada noted with mild curiosity how different she was from the other ladies that they had visited during the week, with her scrubbed face and severe hairstyle, before realizing that this woman, although not wearing a uniform, must be the housekeeper.

Ada's parents were being scrupulously polite—Mamma was always reminding Ada that a true lady treated servants with respect—and Ada followed suit. She smiled daintily and stifled a yawn behind her closed lips. With any luck, they would be taken to meet the lady of the house, be offered tea and a slice of cake (something, she had to admit, the English did very well indeed), and be on their way within the hour.

Miss Thornfield led them into a dim passage, through two halls and past a stairwell, to arrive at a room that she called "the library." A sofa and pair of worn armchairs stood at the center of the room, and shelves laden with books and other *objets d'art* lined the walls. Through the window at the back of the room was a garden with a chestnut tree at its center; beyond it, a meadow with a stone barn. The rain had stopped already and weak light was breaking through soft clouds: even rain wasn't really rain in England.

It was at this point that proceedings took a further turn for the unexpected: Ada was instructed to wait while her parents were served tea elsewhere.

She frowned at her mother as they were leaving—it was always wise to register disapproval—but in truth she did not mind the exclusion. Adults, Ada had found during this family trip to England, could be rather dull companions, and at a glance the library was full of curiosities that would be far more pleasant to explore without a chaperone reminding her not to touch.

As soon as the adults were gone she began her inspection, pulling books from shelves, lifting the lids from odd-looking pots and delicate *bonbonnières*, investigating framed wall hangings that included collections of pressed feathers, flowers, and ferns and careful cursive annotations in fine black ink. Finally, she came to a glass display case that housed a number of variously sized rocks. There was a lock, but Ada was pleasantly surprised to find that the top lifted easily and she was able to reach inside, turning the rocks over one by one, noting the curious markings, before realizing that they were not rocks at all but fossils. Ada had read about fossils in the copy of Wood's *New Illustrated Natural History* that her father had ordered from London for her seventh birthday. They were the leftover markings of ancient life forms, some of them no longer existent. Mamma had read to Ada from a book by Mr. Charles Darwin during lessons back home in Bombay, so Ada knew all about the transmutation of species.

On the glass shelf below the fossils was another rock, this one smaller and roughly triangular in shape. It was deep grey and smooth, carrying none of the telltale spiral markings of the fossils. There was a neat hole through one corner and faint linear etchings, mostly parallel, on its side. Ada took it out and turned it over carefully in her hands. It was cold in her palm, and holding it gave her a strange feeling.

"Do you know what that is?"

Ada gasped, fumbling not to drop the stone in her shock.

She spun around, seeking the owner of the voice.

There was no one on the sofa or chairs, and the door was still closed. Movement in her peripheral vision made Ada turn her head sharply. A woman appeared from a nook to the left of the fireplace that Ada had not noticed when she first entered the room.

"I didn't mean to touch," she said, closing her fingers tighter around the smooth stone.

"Whyever not? I should have thought such treasures would prove irresistible. And you haven't answered me: Do you know what that is?"

Ada shook her head, even though Mamma was forever telling her that it was rude to do so.

The woman came near enough to take the stone. Up close, Ada could see that she was younger than she'd first appeared—Mamma's age, perhaps—though not like Mamma in any other way. The woman's skirt, for one thing, was as dirty at the hem as Ada's got when she had been playing in the chicken run behind the kitchen garden in Bombay. The pins in her hair had been put in quickly, too, and not by a proper lady's maid, as they'd wriggled out in many places, and she wore not a jot of paint or powder on her remarkably freckled nose.

"It is an amulet," the woman said, cupping the stone in the palm of her hand. "Thousands of years ago, it would have been worn around someone's neck for protection. That's what this hole is for"—she twisted her smallest finger as far in as it would go—"twine of some sort; it rotted away long ago."

"Protection from what?" said Ada.

"Harm. In all its many forms."

Ada could tell when adults were being truthful; it was one of her special powers. This woman, whoever she was, believed what she was saying. "Where does one find such a thing?"

"I found it years ago, in the woods beyond the house." The woman slipped the stone back onto its shelf within the glass cabinet, withdrew a key from her pocket, and turned it in the cabinet's lock. "Though there are those who say it is the amulet that finds its owner.

157

That the earth knows best when, and with whom, to share her secrets." She met Ada's gaze. "You are the girl from India, I suppose?"

Ada answered yes, that she had come to visit England from her home in Bombay.

"Bombay," said the woman, seeming to taste the word as she said it. "Tell me. What does the sea smell like in Bombay? Is the sand of the Arabian Sea granular or stony? And what of the light: Is it truly much brighter than ours?"

She indicated that they should sit, and Ada obliged, answering these questions and more with the wary compliance of a child who is not accustomed to adults showing genuine interest. The woman, beside her now on the sofa, listened carefully and made occasional small noises signaling surprise or satisfaction, sometimes a mix of both. Finally, she said, "Yes, good. Thank you. I will remember everything you have told me, Miss . . . ?"

"Lovegrove. Ada Lovegrove."

The woman reached out her hand and Ada shook it as if they were a pair of grown women meeting in the street. "It is good to meet you, Miss Lovegrove. My name is Lucy Radcliffe, and this is my—"

The door opened just then and Ada's mother swept into the room on the wave of effervescence that she carried with her everywhere. Ada's father and Miss Thornfield were close behind, and Ada jumped to her feet, ready to leave. But "No, dearest," said her mother with a smile, "you are to stay here for the afternoon."

Ada frowned. "Alone?"

Mamma laughed. "Oh, darling, you are hardly alone. There's Miss Thornfield, and Miss Radcliffe, and look behind you at all those lovely girls."

Ada glanced over her shoulder through the window, and as if on cue a slew of girls—English girls with long blond curls tied back with ribbons—appeared in the garden. They were walking towards the house in a series of small groups, laughing and talking, some of them carrying easels and paint sets.

The whole experience was so unexpected and inexplicable that even then Ada failed to grasp precisely what sort of place this was.

Later, after she had finished castigating herself for her stupidity, a small voice of self-defense would pipe up to remind her that she was only eight years old and had heretofore had no experience with schools; indeed, *nothing* in her life could have hoped to prepare her for what her parents had in store.

At the time, she had simply allowed her mother to hug her good-bye—yet another unexpected turn in a thoroughly strange day—taken a firm shoulder pat from her father teamed with an admonishment to do her best, and then watched as the pair of them linked arms, turned on their heels, and swept, together, out through the door and back along the halls to where their carriage was waiting.

It was Miss Thornfield who told her in the end. Ada had started after her parents, thinking to ask a little more about what it was precisely that they expected her to do that afternoon, when Miss Thornfield grabbed her wrist to stop her. "Welcome, Miss Lovegrove," she said, with a pained smile, "to Miss Radcliffe's School for Young Ladies."

School. Young ladies. Welcome. Ada liked words—she collected them—but those four hit her like bricks.

Panic ensued, and she quite forgot the manners that Mamma was always reminding her to use. She called Miss Thornfield a liar and a baboon; she said that she was a wicked old woman; she might even have shouted "*Bevkuph!*"at the top of her lungs.

Then she pulled her arm free and ran like a cheetah from the house, past the other girls, still milling in the corridors, straight into a tall golden-haired girl who exclaimed loudly. Ada hissed through her teeth and pushed the bigger girl aside, running down the passage, through the front door, and all the way to the drive where the carriage had deposited her with her parents not an hour before.

The carriage was gone now, and Ada let out a cry of angry frustration.

What did it all mean? Her mother had said that she was to stay for the afternoon, but Miss Thornfield had made it sound as if she were to stay here, at this school, for . . . for how long?

159

Longer than the afternoon.

Ada spent the next few hours stalking along the river, pulling reeds from their sheaths and then slaying the tall grasses that lined the bank. She observed the horrible house from a distance, hating it with all of her might. She shed hot, angry tears when she thought of Shashi.

Only when the sun began to set and Ada realized that she was alone in the middle of a darkening copse of trees did she start to head back across the meadow, skirting the stone wall that surrounded the house, to arrive at the front gate. She sat cross-legged on the ground where she could keep an eye on the lane that led from the village. That way she would be able to see the carriage as soon as it turned towards Birchwood Manor. She watched the light turn from yellow to less yellow and her heart ached when she pictured the jagged scars of palm trees on the purple and orange horizon at home, the sharp smells and the bustle, the hymns of the praying Parsees.

It was almost dark when she sensed someone behind her. "Come now, Miss Lovegrove." Miss Thornfield stepped from the shadows. "Dinner is being served. It would not do to go hungry on your first night."

"I will dine with my mother and father when they return," said Ada. "They will be back for me."

"No. They will not. Not tonight. As I tried to explain, they have left you here to go to school."

"I don't want to stay here."

"Be that as it may."

"I won't."

"Miss Lovegrove—"

"I want to go home!"

"You *are* home, and the sooner you start to accept that fact, the better." Miss Thornfield stiffened then, and seemed to grow in length, drawing herself up like a ladder, all the way to her hunched shoulders, so that Ada was put in mind of an alligator stretching its scales. "Now, then, shall we try again? Dinner," she enunciated, "is being served, and no matter what you might have become accustomed to on the subcontinent, Miss Lovegrove, I assure you that *here* we do not serve dinner twice."

CHAPTER ELEVEN

AND SO, here she was, sixty-three days later, crouched in the dark in a secret damp-smelling space in the lining between walls in the first-floor hallway of Miss Radcliffe's School for Young Ladies. Her parents, as she understood it, were now back in Bombay, although she had not heard the news directly because, as Miss Thornfield had explained, they wished to give Ada time to "settle in" before sending any post. "Very considerate of them" was Miss Thornfield's determination. "They wished to give you no cause for upset."

Ada pressed her ear to the wooden panel and closed her eyes. It was already dark, but the act of shutting them helped to focus her other senses. Sometimes she thought that she could actually hear the whorls within the wood. "Whorls" sounded very similar to "worlds," and it was a pleasant distraction to imagine them as such. She could almost believe that the worlds within the wood were speaking to her in a lovely voice. It made her feel better, that voice.

Now, from the hallway outside, came two real voices, muffled, and Ada's eyes snapped open.

"But I saw her come this way."

"You couldn't have."

"I did."

"Well? Where is she, then? Disappeared into thin air?"

There was a pause and then a petulant reply. "I *saw* her come this way. I *know* I did. She *must* be here somewhere; we just have to wait."

Tucked inside her hiding place, Ada exhaled silently. Her foot had gone to sleep; she'd been cramped up in the same position for at least twenty-five minutes now, but if there was one thing she was good at—as opposed to sewing, piano and painting, and almost everything else they tried to teach at this *bevkuph* school—it was being stubborn. Shashi was always calling her "little *khacara*"—little mule. Those girls could wait all they liked in the corridor; Ada would simply wait longer.

Charlotte Rogers and May Hawkins were the names of her tormentors. They were older than she was, twelve years old, and one of them, Charlotte, particularly tall for her age. She was the daughter of a parliamentarian, May of a prominent industrialist. Ada had not had much opportunity to mix with other children, but she was a fast learner and an excellent observer, and it hadn't taken long for her to ascertain that at Miss Radcliffe's School for Young Ladies, there was a small group of big girls who ran things and that they expected willing obedience from the littler ones.

But Ada was not used to being told what to do by other children, and her steel sense of justice rendered her incapable of iniquitous compliance. So when Charlotte Rogers demanded the new ribbons that Mamma had bought for her in London, Ada told her no. She liked the ribbons, thank you very much, and would prefer to keep them for herself. When the two of them cornered her in the stairwell and told her not to make a single noise while May Hawkins saw how far backwards her finger would bend, Ada brought her boot down hard on May's toes and shouted, "Let go of my finger at once!" When they reported (falsely) to Matron that it was Ada who had sneaked into the larder and opened the new jars of jam, Ada spoke up quickly to report that, no, she was not the culprit, adding that in fact it had been Charlotte Rogers who stole down the hallway after dark; she had seen it with her own two eyes.

None of this had endeared her to Charlotte Rogers and May Hawkins, it was true, but their enmity went back further than that, to the beginning. For when Ada had fled from the library, hoping to catch her parents, it had been Charlotte Rogers with whom she had collided in the corridor. Charlotte had been caught by surprise, issuing a banshee-like scream that drew laughter and pointed fingers from the other girls, even the younger ones. The fact that Ada had then hissed into her face had not helped matters.

"There she is, the little Indian wildcat," Charlotte had said the very next time that she'd seen Ada.

They had crossed paths in the front garden, Ada sitting alone beneath the young Japanese maple by the wall, Charlotte in the midst of a giggling flock of ringlet-ribboned girls.

A radiant, hungry smile had spread across Charlotte's pretty face as she drew the attention of the group to Ada. "This is the one I was telling you about, ladies. Her parents brought her all the way from India in the hopes that she could somehow be civilized." One of them sniggered at that and Charlotte, emboldened, widened her cool blue eyes: "I want you to know that we are all here to help you, Ada, so if there's anything you need, anything at all, you must simply ask. While I think of it, there's a water closet inside, but you should feel free to dig yourself a hole out here if that makes you more comfortable."

The girls had all laughed, and Ada's eyes had stung with hurt and anger. An image had come to mind, unbidden, of Shashi's sunshine face as they lay side by side on the platform on the roof in Bombay, her broad, bright smile as she told stories of her childhood in the Punjab and teased Ada gently for her life of privilege in the mansion. In some inexplicable way, when Charlotte spoke derisively of India, it was as if she had poked fun directly at Shashi; as if she had made Ada complicit.

In defiance, Ada had been determined not to give the others the pleasure of a reaction; she swept aside all thought of Shashi and her own painful longing for home, and instead gazed straight ahead, pretending that she could not see them. After a time, in the face of their continued taunts, she started telling herself a story in soft Punjabi, as though she hadn't a care in the world. Charlotte had not liked that; her gleeful smile had slipped and even as she ordered the others to leave with her, she'd fixed Ada with a puzzled frown, as if Ada were a problem that needed to be solved. A nut in need of cracking.

Charlotte had been right in one thing: Ada's parents had left her at Miss Radcliffe's School for Young Ladies in the misguided expectation that she would be magically transformed into a proper English schoolgirl. But while Ada was quite familiar with a water closet, she was not a "young lady" and had no intention of being turned into one. She had never mastered stitching, she asked far too many questions that did not have ready answers, and her piano skills were nonexistent. In India, while her mother had played beautifully, melodies floating from the library on the warm breeze, Ada had only ever managed to torment the keys such that even her father—traditionally disposed to appreciate her every misstep—had hunched down into his collar so his ears might be protected.

Most lessons at Miss Radcliffe's School for Young Ladies were thus a misery. The only subjects from which Ada took some small pleasure were the two actually taught by Miss Radcliffe: science and geography. Ada had also joined Miss Radcliffe's Natural History Society, of which she was the sole member aside from a girl called Meg, who did not appear to have two wits to rub together and was content to wander about humming romantic dance tunes and collecting clover flowers to thread into elaborate crowns.

For Ada, though, the Natural History Society was the single redeeming feature of having been abandoned at Birchwood Manor. Every Saturday morning and Thursday afternoon, Miss Radcliffe would lead them on a brisk walk across country, sometimes for hours at a time, through muddy fields and flowing streams, over hills and into woods. Sometimes they bicycled farther afield, to Uffington to see the White Horse or Barbury to climb the Iron Age hill fort or even on occasion as far as the Avebury stone circle. They became quite expert at spotting the round hollows Miss Radcliffe referred to as "dew ponds": they were made by prehistoric people, she said, in order to ensure that they always had sufficient water to drink. According to Miss Radcliffe, there were signs of ancient communities everywhere, if one only knew where to look.

Even the woods behind the school were filled with secrets from the past: Miss Radcliffe had shown them beyond the clearing to a small hill she called the "dragon mound." "There is every possibility that this was an Anglo-Saxon burial site," she'd said, going on to explain that it was so named because the Anglo-Saxons believed that dragons watched over their treasure. "Of course, the Celts would have disagreed. They would have called this a fairy mound and said that beneath it lay the entrance to fairyland."

Ada had thought then of the amulet in the library and wondered whether this was where Miss Radcliffe had found her protection charm. "Not far from here," Miss Radcliffe had replied. "Not far from here at all."

To Ada, being a member of the Natural History Society was like being a detective, looking for clues and solving mysteries. Every relic they unearthed came with a story, a secret life led long before the object reached their hands. It became a game of sorts to come up with the most exciting (yet plausible, for they were scientists and not creative writers) history for each find.

Miss Radcliffe always let them keep their treasures. She was adamant about it: the earth gives up its secrets in good time, she liked to say, and always to the person it intends. "What about the river?" Ada had asked one Saturday morning, when their adventures had taken them close to the water's edge. She'd been thinking about a story Shashi had told her, about a flood that came to her village and washed away her precious childhood possessions. She realized too late her terrible faux pas, for Ada had heard whispers, by then, that Miss Radcliffe's brother had died by drowning.

"Rivers are different," the headmistress said at last, her voice steady but her face paler than usual beneath her freckles. "Rivers are always on the move. They take their secrets and mysteries with them to the sea."

Miss Radcliffe herself was something of a mystery. For a woman who put her name to a school proposing to turn young girls into civilized ladies, she was not particularly ladylike. Oh, she had all of the "manners" that Mamma liked to talk about—she didn't chew with her mouth open or burp at the table—but in other ways she reminded Ada far more of Papa: her purposeful stride when they were out in the open air, her willingness to talk about subjects like politics and religion, her insistence that it was incumbent on one to strive always for the attainment of knowledge, to demand better information to do so. She spent most of her time outside and had no care for fashion, always dressing in precisely the same way: dark leather button-up boots and a green walking suit, the long skirt of which was always caked with mud about the hem. She had a large woven basket that reminded Ada of Shashi's, and she carried it wherever she went; but where Shashi filled her basket with fruit and vegetables, Miss Radcliffe's was used for carrying sticks and stones and birds' eggs and feathers and all manner of other natural objects that had piqued her interest.

Ada was not the only person to have noticed Miss Radcliffe's eccentricities. The school was hers, and yet—aside from delivering occasional fierce and imploring speeches about the duty of "you girls" to learn as much as possible, and offering the general admonishment that "time is your most precious commodity, girls, and there's none so foolish as those that waste their minutes"—she left matters of administration and discipline to the deputy headmistress, Miss Thornfield. Amongst the other girls, it was rumored that she was a witch. To start with, there were all those plant samples and oddities, not to mention the room in which she kept them. It was a small chamber adjoining her bedroom that students were forbidden from entering on pain of death. "That's where she does her spells," Angelica Barry insisted. "I've heard her from the other side, chanting and intoning." And Meredith Sykes swore that she had glimpsed inside the door one day and, amongst the stones and fossils, seen a human skull upon the bureau top.

One thing was certain: Miss Radcliffe loved her house. The only time she ever raised her voice was in castigation of a girl caught sliding on the banisters or kicking along the skirting boards. On one of their walks across Wiltshire, talk had turned to loneliness and special places and Miss Radcliffe had explained to Ada that Birchwood Manor had once belonged to her brother; that he had died many years before; and that although she still missed him more than anything else she'd ever lost, she felt close to him when she was inside his house.

"He was an artist," Ada's fellow rambler Meg had said once, apropos of nothing, looking up from the clover necklace she was threading; "Miss Radcliffe's brother. A famous artist, but his fiancée was killed with a rifle and afterwards he went mad with grief."

Now, her reverie interrupted by the proximity of her tormentors, Ada shifted carefully in her hiding place within the wall, mindful not to make even the tiniest of noises. She did not know much about lovers or fiancées, but she knew how much it hurt to be separated from a loved one and she felt immensely sorry for Miss Radcliffe. Ada had decided that it was the loss of her brother that explained the expression of deep unhappiness that came upon her headmistress's face sometimes when she thought no one was watching.

As if she had somehow read Ada's thoughts, there came now a familiar voice on the other side of the wall panel: "Girls, what are you doing in the hallway? You know how Miss Thornfield feels about skulking."

"Yes, Miss Radcliffe," they chorused.

"I cannot think what could be keeping you so interested in here."

"Nothing, Miss Radcliffe."

"I hope you are not dragging those hockey sticks along my wall."

"No, Miss Radcliffe."

"Well, then, off you go, and I will consider not mentioning this infraction to Miss Thornfield for her detention list."

Ada heard their footsteps scuttle away and allowed herself a small sigh of satisfied relief.

"Out you climb, then, child," said Miss Radcliffe, rapping gently on the wall. "You must have a class you're missing, too."

Ada slipped her fingers into the hidden latch and unhooked the panel, cracking the door open. Miss Radcliffe had already disappeared, nowhere to be seen, and Ada climbed quickly from the hiding place, marveling once again at how seamlessly the wall panel

Kate Morton

slid back into place. Unless one knew that it was there, it would be impossible to guess.

Miss Radcliffe had been the one to show her the secret chamber. She had caught Ada hiding behind the thick brocade curtains in the library one afternoon when she should have been in a sewing lesson and bade her come to the office, where they would have "a little talk." Ada had prepared herself for a dressing down, but instead Miss Radcliffe had told her to sit wherever she pleased and said, "I was not much older than you are now when I first came to this house. My brother and his friends were adults, and far too busy with other things to be interested in me. I was given a free run, as they say, and being of a somewhat"—she hesitated—"*inquisitive* disposition, I engaged in rather more exploration than might have been expected."

The house was very old, she'd continued, hundreds of years old, and had been built at a time in history when certain people had very good reason to seek concealment. She had invited Ada then to follow her, and while all of the other girls were singing Beethoven's "Ode to Joy" downstairs, Miss Radcliffe had revealed to Ada the secret hideaway. "I am not sure about you, Miss Lovegrove," she'd said, "but there have been times in my life when I have felt a very keen need to disappear."

Now Ada hurried along the passage to the central stairwell. Rather than heading downstairs to the music appreciation class, though, she went all the way up to the attic and into the bedroom labeled "East Loft" that she shared with another boarder, Margaret Worthington.

She didn't have much time; music appreciation class would soon be over and the other girls would be released. Ada knelt on the floor, tossing back the linen valance that was draped around her bed. Her suitcase was still there, exactly where she'd left it, and she slid it out carefully.

Ada lifted the lid and the tiny bundle of fur blinked at her, opening his mouth in a silent, emphatic *Meow!*

She cupped the kitten in one hand and drew him into a close cuddle. "There, now, little one," she whispered against the soft spot between his ears. "Don't worry, I'm here."

The kitten pawed at her dress with his velvet pads and launched into an indignant tale of hunger and need; Ada smiled and dug inside the deep pocket of the pinafore that Mamma had chosen for her at Harrods, retrieving the jar of sardines she'd pilfered earlier from the kitchen.

While her kitten stretched his legs, stalking the room's rim as if it were a wide savannah plain, Ada prized the lid off the jar and withdrew a single slippery fish. Holding it out, she called, softly, "Here, Bilī; here, little cat."

Bilī padded towards her, demolishing the dangled sardine, and each one thereafter, until the jar was empty; he then meowed plaintively until Ada set the jar down on its side and let him lick the juice delicately from within. "Greedy little fellow," she said, with deepest admiration. "You've gone and got your snout thoroughly wet."

A week ago, Ada had saved Bilī's life. She had been avoiding Charlotte and May and had found herself on the far side of the meadow, beyond the house where the river bend turned around the copse and disappeared from sight.

Ada had heard noises coming from the other side of the trees that reminded her of festival time in Bombay and had followed the river westward until she turned a corner and saw a Gypsy camp in the clearing beyond. There were caravans and fires, horses and dogs, and children throwing a floating kite with a long tail of colorful ribbons into the air.

She had noticed one scruffy boy heading towards the river on his own. He had a sack over his shoulder and was whistling a song that she almost recognized. Curious, Ada had followed him. She crouched behind a tree and watched as he started taking things from the sack, one by one, and dunking them in the river. She had thought at first that he was cleaning small items of clothing, just as she had seen people doing in Dhobi Ghat back home. It was only when she heard the first tiny cry that she realized it wasn't clothing he was drawing from the sack, and that he wasn't cleaning anything.

"Hey! You! What do you think you're doing?" she had called, pounding over to his side.

The boy looked up at her, his shock as clear as the dirt on his face.

Ada's voice was quivering. "I said, what do you think you're doing?"

"Putting them out of their misery. Like I been told to."

"You awful, cruel boy! You beastly coward! You great big thug!"

The boy raised his eyebrows, and Ada was galled to realize that he looked amused by the force of her rage. Without a word, he reached into the sack and scooped out the last remaining kitten, holding it aloft by the scruff of its neck with the most indelicate grip.

"*Murderer!*" she hissed.

"My dad'll murder *me* if I don't do what he says."

"Give me that little cat at once."

The boy had shrugged and then thrust the limp kitten into Ada's waiting hands before tossing the empty sack over his shoulder and slinking back towards camp.

Ada had thought a lot about Bilī's brothers and sisters since that day. She woke sometimes in the middle of the night, unable to rid her mind of pictures of their submerged faces and lifeless bodies, tossed and tumbled by the river's current as it carried them out to sea.

Now, Bilī let out a squawk of displeasure as Ada hugged him just a bit too hard.

There was a noise outside on the staircase, footfalls, and Ada fumbled the kitten quickly back into the suitcase, dropping the lid but making sure to leave a crack around the rim for air. It was not an ideal solution but it would do for now. Miss Thornfield, predictably enough, did not tolerate pets.

The door opened just as Ada had climbed to her feet. The valance, she noticed, was still hooked up near her mattress, but there was no time to fix it.

Charlotte Rogers was standing in the doorway.

She smiled at Ada, but Ada knew better than to smile back. She remained *en garde*.

"There you are," said Charlotte sweetly. "Haven't you been a slippery little fish today!" For a split second, aware of the empty sardine jar in her pocket, Ada thought that Charlotte Rogers had somehow guessed her secret. But the older girl continued: "I'm just here to deliver a message—the bearer of bad tidings, I'm afraid. Miss Thornfield knows that you skipped music class and she has asked me to send you to her to receive your punishment." She smiled with mock sympathy. "You would get on so much better here if you just learned to follow the rules, Ada. Rule number one is that I always win." She turned to leave, hesitated, and then looked back. "Better straighten your bed. I wouldn't like to have to tell Miss Thornfield that you've been slovenly."

Ada's fists were clenched so tightly as she took the stairs down towards Miss Thornfield's office that it was hours before the fingernail marks left her palms. It had become clear that she was not going to win a war of attrition with Charlotte Rogers and May Hawkins simply by ignoring or avoiding them. She would never concede, which meant that she was going to have to strike back, and in such a way that it would get them to leave her alone, once and for all.

She hardly even heard Miss Thornfield's lecture about tardiness, and when the punishment was handed down—a fortnight of extra sewing duties, assisting the costumiers for the end-of-term concert, instead of attending Natural History Society—Ada was too distracted even to mount a protest.

She turned over the pieces of the puzzle all afternoon, moving them around, trying to force them to make sense, but it was not until much later that night, while Margaret, her roommate, was snoring softly on the other side of the room and Bilī was purring in her arms, that the idea finally came to her.

When it arrived, it was as clear as if someone had entered the room, tiptoed across the floor beside her bed, knelt down low, and whispered the idea into her ear.

Ada grinned to herself in the dark: the plan was perfect and so very simple. Better yet, thanks to Charlotte Rogers, she had been given the perfect means with which to execute it.

CHAPTER TWELVE

THE end-of-summer-term concert was an institution at Miss Radcliffe's School for Young Ladies, and, as such, rehearsals had begun in the very first week of term. Miss Byatt, the thin, nervous speech and drama teacher, had held a series of auditions, whittling the show to a select group of fifteen performances comprising musical acts, poetry recitals, and dramatic soliloquies.

Ada was to appear in the static, unspeaking role of Mouse Two as part of a scene from the pantomime of Cinderella; Charlotte Rogers, as the second cousin twice removed of Ms. Ellen Terry, was regarded (not least by herself) as a formidable Shakespearean actress and was thus performing thrice within the show: a recital of one of the sonnets, a rendition of Lady Macbeth's "Out, damned spot!" monologue, and a parlor song sung to piano accompaniment provided by her friend, May Hawkins.

Due to the small size of the two halls within the house, it was customary to stage the concert within the long barn that stood at the top of the coach way. In the days leading up to the show, each girl was responsible for carrying chairs across from the house and arranging them in rows; those who had not been fortunate enough to be selected for the cast were automatically assigned to stage management tasks, including the assembly of a raised stage and the suspension of proscenium curtains from the rafters above.

In light of the punishment handed down by Miss Thornfield, Ada was especially busy, corralled into joining the sewing circle whose members were making final touches to the girls' costumes. The occupation was not a natural fit; Ada was terrible at sewing, certainly not capable of making the rows of strong, neat backstitches necessary to anchor two pieces of fabric together. She had, however, been able to demonstrate that she was adept at trimming loose threads and was thus handed a small pair of silver scissors and tasked with "neatening the edges."

"She is the first one to arrive at each meeting, whereupon she barely makes a peep, such is her commitment to her work," the sewing mistress reported to Miss Thornfield, when asked, to which the deputy headmistress gave a thin smile and said, "Very good to hear."

When dawn broke on the day of the concert, the entire school was abuzz. Afternoon lessons were canceled in order to accommodate a full-cast rehearsal, and the show was scheduled to begin promptly at four.

At two minutes before the hour, Valerie Miller, who had auditioned (unsuccessfully) with a rendition of "My Wild Irish Rose" played on the cowbells, was given a nod by Miss Thornfield and started sounding one of her bells to alert the audience that the show was about to begin. Most of the girls and a smattering of parents and siblings, along with certain Very Important community members, were already assembled; but the ringing brought their chatter to an end, at which point the lamps within the hall were dimmed and the black curtains dropped, casting the audience into darkness and allowing the limelights lining the stage to take over.

One by one, the performers took their places within the glow of center stage, singing and reciting with all of their might, to the warm appreciation of the audience. The program was not a short one, however, and as the first hour ticked over, the crowd began to flag. By the time Charlotte Rogers appeared on stage for the third time, the younger children were starting to squirm in their seats and yawn, their stomachs to grumble.

Charlotte, ever the professional, was undaunted. She planted her feet squarely and blinked prettily at her audience. Her golden hair tumbled in curls, one thick ringlet over each shoulder, and from behind the piano, May Hawkins watched for a signal to start playing, deepest admiration writ large upon her face.

Ada's attention, though, was on Charlotte's costume: a rather grown-up blouse and skirt ensemble—modeled, of course, on one of the stage outfits worn recently by Ellen Terry—that made her look older than she was.

From her seat in the dark hall, Ada watched the other girl carefully, as if by the power of her gaze alone she might move matter. She was nervous—far more nervous than she had been when she was performing as Mouse Two. Her hands were balled in damp fists upon her lap.

It happened as Charlotte hit the highest note, one that she had been practicing to reach for the better part of the month. Perhaps it was the significant intake of breath required to make it to high C, or else the way she thrust her arms out wide to entreat the crowd. Whatever the case, as Charlotte attained her note, she dropped her skirt.

The skirt did not drop sluggishly. It dropped suddenly and completely, in one fell swoop, to land in a puddle of white lace and linen on the floor around her dainty ankles.

It was one thousand times better than anything that Ada had dared to imagine.

As she'd trimmed a few of the stitches on Charlotte's waistband, she had hoped that the garment might slip enough to cause agitation and distraction, but never in a million years had she envisaged this. The way the skirt fell! The exceptional timing with which it collapsed completely, almost as if an invisible force, controlled by Ada's very mind, had swept into the hall and, on receiving a silent command, yanked down the skirt . . .

It was by far and away the funniest thing that Ada had seen in many months. And, judging by the thunderous surge of unrestrained laughter that filled the barn, lifting to roll and echo amongst the rafters, the other girls felt the same way.

As Charlotte, pink-cheeked, sang the last few lines, and the crowd continued their rapturous, hooting applause, Ada realized that, for the first time since she had come to Birchwood Manor, she felt almost happy.

According to tradition, the supper after the concert was always a more relaxed affair than regular school dinners, and even Miss Thornfield, who generally considered it deeply improper to approach any school event in the spirit of fun, was induced to conduct the annual presentation of the "Good Sport" awards. These were a series of amusing accolades, nominated and voted for by the students, with the aim of reinforcing the air of celebration and merriment that infused the school body as the academic year drew to a close.

For many of the girls, this would be their last school dinner of term. Only a handful of students—those who did not have homes that could be reached by rail or carriage, or whose parents had traveled to the Continent for the summer and been unable to make other arrangements for their daughters—would be staying on through the holidays. Ada was one of them.

This fact had brought her spirits lower than they might otherwise have been following the spectacular success of the concert, and she was sitting quietly, finishing her second serving of blancmange, turning over the "Little Miss Threadgood" award she had been given for "Services to Stitching" (printed prior to the costuming disaster, one assumed), while the other girls chatted happily about the upcoming summer break, when the daily postal delivery arrived.

Ada was so used to being overlooked at mail time that she had to be nudged twice by the girl beside her when her name was called. Up beside the teacher's table, the senior girl on roster was holding a large box.

Ada jumped to her feet, eager to claim it, almost tripping over in her hurry.

She began untying the twine as soon as she reached her table, slipping out her small silver thread scissors to snip loose the final knots.

Inside was a beautiful decoupage box, which Ada identified at once as the perfect new home for Bilī; within the box was a thick envelope promising a letter from Mamma, a new sun hat, two dresses, and a smaller package that made Ada's heart leap. She recognized Shashi's handwriting on the gift card at once. "*Pilla*," she had written, continuing in Punjabi: "A little something to remind you of home while you're living amongst the monkey bottoms."

Ada tore open the package to find a small black leather book inside. Between its covers were no words, but instead page after page of pressed flowers: orange hibiscus, mauve Queen's crepe myrtle, purple passionflower, white spider lilies, red powder puffs. All of them, Ada knew, had come from her very own garden, and in an instant she was back in Bombay. She could feel the sultry air on her face, smell the heady fragrance of summer, hear the songs of prayer as the sun set over the ocean.

So transported was Ada that she was not aware that Charlotte Rogers had made an approach until the older girl was casting a shadow across Ada's table setting.

Ada looked up, taking in Charlotte's serious expression. As usual, May Hawkins was serving as aide-de-camp, and the arrival of the two girls at Ada's table had caused a hush to descend. From instinct, Ada closed Shashi's flower book and slipped it beneath the wrapping paper.

"I suppose you saw what happened during the performance," said Charlotte.

"Terrible," said Ada. "A spot of very bad luck."

Charlotte smiled grimly. "I've always believed that a person makes her own luck."

There was little for Ada to say in reply. Agreement seemed impolitic.

"I am hoping to have better luck in future." She held out a hand. "Truce?"

Ada eyed the outstretched hand before meeting it finally with her own. "Truce."

They shook solemnly, and when Charlotte gave a small smile, after a moment's consideration Ada allowed herself to match it.

And so, although Ada had not expected to be anticipating the end-of-summer-term picnic with enthusiasm, in light of her recent reconciliation with Charlotte Rogers she found herself rather looking forward to the day. There were to be games like battledore and shuttlecock, quoits and skipping, and some of the older girls had even managed to convince Miss Radcliffe to allow them to carry down the small wooden rowboat that was usually kept stored within the field barn behind the house. The groundsman had looked it over the previous week and, after making a few small repairs, declared the vessel riverworthy.

The day, when it dawned, was warm and clear. An early summer's haze burned off so that by midday the sky was deep blue and the garden glittered. Down by the river, a series of tablecloths were arranged along a stretch of grassy bank that fell beneath two willows, and the teachers were already lounging on them, enjoying the day. Some had brought large white parasols, while others wore sun hats, and a number of woven hampers containing the lunchtime spread were arranged in the shade around the edges of the group. On Miss Radcliffe's instructions, the groundsman had carried a single wooden table over from the house, and it now wore a lace cloth, topped with a vase of delicate pink and yellow roses, jugs of cold lemonade, and a porcelain teapot with assorted glasses, cups, and saucers.

Shashi had always teased Ada for being a greedy little snout, and it was true; she loved and looked forward to mealtimes. Happily, the picnic did not disappoint. She sat on a square of fabric near Miss Radcliffe, who ate a number of hearty cheese sandwiches whilst pointing out the copse of trees and telling Ada about the first time she had seen Birchwood Manor—when her brother, Edward, had made them walk from the railway station in Swindon—and they had traipsed all the way through the woods before emerging, finally, to discover the house, like a vision, before them.

Ada listened intently. She hungered for stories and Miss Radcliffe was not usually so expansive. Only once before had she spoken in such a way. They had been returning from one of their Natural History Society walks when Birchwood appeared suddenly like a great ship against the dusk-darkening sky. One of the top windows had caught the last of the day's sun, glowing orange, and from nowhere a story had unraveled, of magical children and a Fairy Queen. Delighted, Ada had begged her to tell another, but Miss Radcliffe had refused. She'd said that it was the only story she knew.

A game of blindman's buff was just starting up on the sun-warmed grass beyond the picnic. Indigo Harding was "It" and had a white scarf tied over her eyes; a group of six or seven girls were spinning her around, counting each full turn. As they reached the number ten, they all scattered backwards to form a loose circle, and Indigo, dizzy, teetering, and laughing, started to reach for them, arms outstretched. Ada had not exactly meant to join in, but she had walked that way, and before she knew it was amongst the group, dodging Indigo's arms and shouting out her own fun taunts.

Everyone had a turn at being "It," and eventually the scarf was held out to Ada. Her pleasure evaporated, to be replaced at once with apprehension. The game relied on trust and she hardly knew these girls; there was a river not far away and she was frightened of water. These fractured thoughts, and others, flitted through her mind in the space of an instant, and then she caught May Hawkins's eyes and the other girl nodded in a way that made it seem that she understood. "Truce," they had agreed the night before; now, Ada realized, it was time to put that promise to the test.

She stood still while the scarf was tied around her eyes and then allowed the others to spin her, chanting slowly from one to ten. Ada's head spun and she could not help laughing to herself as she tried to keep her balance whilst walking towards the others. She waved her hands, listening to their voices; the air felt warm and dense between her fingers; she could hear crickets burring defiantly in the dry grasses, and somewhere behind her a fish leapt from the water, landing with a satisfying *plonk*. Finally, her fingertips brushed someone's face and laughter ensued. Ada pulled the blindfold from her eyes.

There was a line of perspiration on her upper lip. Her neck was stiff with tension. Blinking into the sudden brightness, she felt a strange surge of relief-tinged triumph.

"Come on," said May, suddenly beside her. "I've thought of something fun to do."

❧

Charlotte was already sitting in the boat when May and Ada reached the river. Her face lit up with a smile when she saw them and she gestured that they should join her. "I've been waiting for ages."

"Sorry," called back May, "we were playing blindman's buff."

"Never mind that, let's go!"

Ada stopped where she was and shook her head. "I can't swim."

"Neither can I," said May, squinting into the sun, "who said anything about swimming?"

"It's shallow here, anyway," said Charlotte; "We're just going to take her upstream a little way and then drift back down. It's such a lovely day."

Ada could see that what Charlotte said was true: reeds were swaying not too far beneath the surface; the water didn't run deep.

Charlotte held up a small paper bag. "I have boiled sweets."

May grinned and skipped over to where the boat was moored against a simple wooden jetty, stepping down to sit on the bench in the middle of the boat.

Ada looked longingly at the bag of sweets, the two smiling girls, the glittery flecks of sunlight on the river's surface; she heard Shashi telling her not to be frightened, that many people lived half lives due to fear . . .

"Come on!" called May. "We'll lose our turn."

So Ada decided to go with them. She hurried to the end of the jetty and let May help her down onto the bench at the very back. "What do I do?"

"You don't need to do anything but sit," said Charlotte, untying the rope. "Let us do the rest."

179

Ada was glad. Frankly, she was too busy holding on for dear life to do much of anything else. She was keenly aware of the boat's subtle rocking motion as the older girl took the oar and pushed them away from the jetty's end. She gripped the sides tightly, her knuckles white.

And then they were floating. And it was *almost* lovely. She didn't feel seasick at all.

"Of course not," said Charlotte, laughing, when Ada said so. "This is hardly the sea."

The older girl rowed and they traveled slowly upstream; a mother duck trailed by nine ducklings floated towards them from the other direction. Birds sang in the willows that lined the water; a horse in a field whinnied. The other girls became smaller and smaller specks in the distance. At last the boat rounded a bend and they were alone.

The Gypsy camp was only a little further on. Ada wondered whether they were going to go that far upstream. Perhaps they would even go as far as St. John's Lock.

But as they were nearing the edge of the copse of trees, Charlotte stopped rowing. "That's enough of that. My arms are tired." She held out the paper bag. "Sweet?"

May took a barley sugar and then passed the bag to Ada, who chose a black-and-white mint humbug.

The river's current was not strong and, rather than begin its drift back downstream, the boat sat happily where it was. Although they were no longer in view of the picnic site, across the fields Ada could see the twin gables at the back of the schoolhouse. She thought of Miss Radcliffe's description of Birchwood Manor as "a vision" and realized warmly that some of her teacher's affection for the house was starting to rub off on her.

"It's a shame we got off to such a bad start," said Charlotte, breaking the silence. "All I ever wanted was to help you, Ada. I know how difficult it is to be the new girl."

Ada, sucking on her humbug, nodded.

"But you never listen, and you never seem to learn."

Although Charlotte was still smiling, Ada experienced a sudden, unpleasant jolt of foreboding. At the other end of the boat, the older girl reached to slide something out from beneath her bench seat.

It was the decoupage box sent from India.

As Ada stiffened, Charlotte removed the lid and reached inside, pulling out the little bundle of fur. "He is rather sweet, I'll admit. But pets are not allowed at Miss Radcliffe's school, Ada."

Ada stood up at her end of the boat, starting it rocking from side to side. "Give him to me."

"You're going to get yourself in a lot of trouble if you don't let me help you."

"Give him to me."

"What do you think Miss Thornfield will say when I tell her?"

"Give him to me!"

"I don't think she understands," May Hawkins piped up.

"No," agreed Charlotte. "Such a shame. I'm going to have to teach her." She slid to the side of her seat and flung her arm out wide so that Bilī was almost touching the water. He was the merest scrap in her hand, cycling his hind legs fearfully as he sought to gain purchase, desperately trying to climb to safety. "I told you, Ada. Rule number one: I always win."

Ada took another step and the boat rocked harder. She needed to save him.

She almost lost her balance but she didn't sit down. She had to be brave.

May was holding on to her legs now, trying to stop her from getting past.

"Time to say good-bye," said Charlotte.

"No!" Ada kicked free of May's hold and lunged towards the other girl.

The boat was rocking violently now, and Ada fell heavily to the planked wooden floor.

Charlotte was still holding Bilī out over the water and Ada scrambled to her feet. She lunged again, and again she fell. This time, though, she didn't hit the planks.

The water was so much colder than she had imagined, so much harder. She was gasping for breath, her hands flapping and her mouth opening, her vision blurring wetly.

She couldn't stay at the surface. She couldn't cry for help. She began to panic.

Down, down, down she went, limbs flailing, mouth filling with water, lungs beginning to burn.

Everything was different under here. The world sounded different. And it was getting darker. The sun was a tiny silvery disc beyond the surface, but Ada was falling further away, like a girl in space, surrounded by stars that slipped between her fingers when she reached for them.

Through the silty water, amongst the furry reeds, she saw Shashi on the terrace, smiling her wide, white smile, and Mamma at the desk in the library, and Papa in his study with the spinning globe. *Tick, tick, tick,* it went when it was spun, *tick, tick, tick* . . .

She was going to have a *chakkali* when they reached the market.

But where was Shashi? She was gone. Candles flickering . . .

Ada was lost.

But she was not alone. There was someone in the water with her, she was sure of it. She couldn't see who it was, but she knew that someone was there. A shadow . . . a sense . . .

The last thing Ada felt was her body hitting the bottom of the river, her arms and legs impacting against the gentle rocks and slippery weeds as her lungs grew larger than her torso, pushing their way into her throat and filling her head.

And then the strangest thing: as her brain was burning, she saw something ahead of her, a bright blue shining light, a jewel, a moon, and she knew, somehow, that if she just reached out and grabbed it, the bright blue light would show her the way.

VI

Something very interesting has happened. This afternoon we had another visitor.

Jack spent the morning in the malthouse poring over a stack of papers that he brought in with him when he got home last night. I glanced over them when he went to put a pie in the oven for lunch and gleaned that they replicate the contents of the email sent yesterday by Rosalind Wheeler. For the most part they are text, but one appears to be a map. A floor plan, more properly, hand-drawn and corresponding largely to the layout of the house, presumably produced by the mysterious Mrs. Wheeler. I suspect that, in combination with the written notes, it is designed to lead Jack to the Radcliffe Blue.

He came back into the house just before midday and we passed a contented hour as he tried to make sense of the plan, staring at it and then measuring out footsteps along the lengths of each room, stopping every so often to make a small adjustment with his pen.

It was around one when the knock came at the door. He was surprised, but I was not, for I had noticed the slight, elegant woman earlier, standing on the edge of the lane that runs alongside the front wall. She had been staring up at the house, arms folded across her middle, and there was something in her bearing that made me wonder whether I had met her before. I hadn't; I knew that when she came closer: I never forget a face. (I never forget anything. Not anymore.)

People often stand in the laneway and look up at the house—people with dogs and muddy boots, guide books and pointed fingers—so there was nothing unusual in that. To venture into the front garden and knock on the door, though, is not usual.

Jack, despite his initial surprise, took the interruption in his stride, glancing through the kitchen window and then thudding down the hallway towards the door in that heavy, purposeful manner of his, opening it with characteristic might. He has been in a black mood ever since he returned from his meeting with Sarah yesterday. Not angry—rather sad and frustrated. Naturally I am filled with curiosity as to what went on between them, but thus far he has not obliged me. He made only one phone call last night and that was to his father; they were marking an anniversary of some sort, because Jack said, "Twenty-five years today. Hard to believe, isn't it?"

"Oh," said the woman, taken aback by the opening door. "Hello— I didn't actually . . . I thought the museum was shut during the week."

"And yet you knocked."

"Yes."

"Force of habit?"

"I suppose so." She collected herself and then reached into her bag to retrieve an ivory-colored piece of card, holding out a small, fine hand to present it to Jack. "My name is Elodie Winslow. I'm an archivist with Stratton, Cadwell & Co. in London. I look after the archives of James William Stratton."

It was my turn then for surprise, and let me assure you, that does not happen often. While Jack's utterance of Ada Lovegrove's name the other night had given me some defense against the return of my past, I was nonetheless momentarily struck. I had not encountered his name in years and had no reason to think that I would ever hear it again.

"Never heard of him," said Jack, turning the card over. "Should I have?"

"Not really. He was a reformer back in Victorian times, improving the plight of the poor, that sort of thing. Are you the person I should speak to about the museum?" She sounded doubtful, as well she might. There is little of Jack that gives any impression of the guides who usually man the door, foisting their rehearsed patter upon visitors no matter how many times they have spouted it before.

"In a manner of speaking. I'm the only person here."

184

She looked unconvinced but said, "I know you're not usually open on Fridays, but I've come from London. I didn't expect to find anyone here. I was just going to peek over the wall, but . . ."

"You want to look around the house?"

"If you wouldn't mind."

Invite her in.

After a moment's consideration, Jack stepped aside and gestured in that generous, physical way of his, indicating that she should come inside. He closed the door quickly behind her.

She stepped into the dim hall and glanced about her, as most people do, leaning close to view one of the framed photographs that the Art Historians' Association has hung along the walls.

Some days, when I am in need of amusement, I haunt the entrance hallway, enjoying the reverent comments made by visitors of a Certain Type while they postulate as to the events behind the photo. "It was at this time, of course," the sensibly outfitted man of advanced years will intone, "that the Magenta Brotherhood were engaged in fierce debate with respect to the artistic worth of photography, wondering whether it might in fact be more properly considered a science than an art." To which the long-suffering companion beside him will invariably reply, "Oh, I *see*."

"Make yourself at home," said Jack. "In a careful sort of way."

She smiled. "Don't worry. I'm an archivist. I spend my life taking care of precious things."

"You'll have to excuse me a minute—I have a pie in the oven, and I can smell it burning." He was already backing away towards the malthouse kitchen, and I left him uttering his expletives to follow our visitor.

She walked from room to room downstairs, an enigmatic expression on her face. Only once did she stop and stifle a small shiver, glancing over her shoulder as if she sensed that she might not be alone.

On the first floor, she hesitated at the window overlooking the woods to glimpse the river before climbing the stairs all the way to the attic. She set her bag down on Mildred Manning's table, which disposed me at once to like her, and then took something from within that made me startle. It was one of Edward's sketchbooks. I would have known it anywhere. The shock was almost physical. More than anything, I wanted to grab her by the wrists and implore her to tell me everything: who she is and how she came by Edward's book. She had mentioned James William Stratton, a company called Stratton, Cadwell & Co., and a collection of archives. Is that where the sketchbook has been stored all of this time? But how on earth could that be? The two men did not know each other; as far as I'm aware, they never even met.

After turning through the pages of the sketchbook—quickly, as if she had done so many times before and knew precisely what she was searching for—she stopped at an illustration and studied it closely; she then went to the window overlooking the back meadow and stood on tiptoe, craning her neck to see.

The sketchbook was still open on the table and I rushed to it.

It was the one that Edward used over the summer of 1862. I had sat beside him while he made those very lines on that piece of cotton paper: studies for the painting he had planned, something he had been thinking about for years. On the following pages, I knew, were his sketches of the clearing in the woods and the fairy mound and a stone croft by the river, and at the bottom corner of one, in loose, scratched lines, the heart he had penned, and the ship on the wide sea, as we spoke excitedly of our plans.

I wanted nothing more than to be able to turn those pages, to see the other drawings, to *touch* the memory of those days. But alas, after much experimentation over the years, I have had to accept that my abilities in that respect are limited. I can make a door slam or a window rattle, I can yank the loosened skirt of a nasty schoolgirl, but when it comes to finer manipulations—the pulling of a thread or the turning of a page—I do not have the necessary control.

I need to know what brought her to the house today. Is she simply an art lover or is there more to it than that? It is remarkable enough that after so many years I should have at once a visitor mention the name Ada Lovegrove and now another speak of James Stratton; but for the latter then to produce Edward's sketchbook from the summer of 1862 is uncanny. I cannot help but think that there is unseen mischief at work.

My young man Jack was curious, too, in his own way, for when she went back downstairs and ducked her head around the door into the malthouse kitchen to call out, "Thank you," he looked up over the top of the blackened dish that he was scraping into the sink and said, "Found what you were looking for?"

There came then the most infuriating of non-answers. "You've been very kind," she said. "Thanks so much for letting me in on a Friday."

Not so much as a hint as to her purpose.

"Are you staying nearby?" he asked as she started down the hallway towards the front door. "Or heading back to London now?"

"I have a room booked at the Swan—the pub down the road. Just for the weekend."

I shifted closer and concentrated all of my might on sending him my message. *Invite her to stay. Invite her to come back.*

"Feel free to drop in anytime," he said, a look of brief confusion settling on his face. "I'm here every day."

"I might just do that."

It was, as they say (when they must because they've been denied their heart's desire), better than a kick in the teeth.

Her visit was brief, but the disturbance sat in the house all afternoon. It left me flummoxed and excited, and so while Jack got on with his inspection of the house—he is in the hallway on the first floor now, running his hand lightly along the wall—I retreated to my spot at the bend of the stairs, from which I distracted myself by ruminating on the old days.

———

Mostly, I thought of Pale Joe and the morning that we met.

For while I was a good thief, I was not above making mistakes.

Ordinarily they were inconsequential and easily resolved: I chose to target the wrong person, I was forced to give a policeman the slip, I picked a wallet only to find it as empty as a fool's promise. On one occasion, though, when I was twelve years old, I made a mistake with more far-reaching consequences.

It was one of those London mornings when the sun does not rise as much as the fog changes color, from black to pewter to a yellow-tinged gunmetal grey. The air was thick with factory smog and the oily smell rising from the river; it had been thus for days and I had suffered a poor week's takings. There were simply fewer fine ladies willing to ride alone in London when the sullen fogs came in.

That morning I had taken Little Girl Passenger on the omnibus that ran between Regent's Park and Holborn, in the hope that I might find the wife or daughter of a lawyer returning from her morning stroll around the park. The plan was sound, but my technique was not, for I was distracted by a conversation I'd had with Mrs. Mack the night before.

Although she was of an optimistic disposition, Mrs. Mack had an image to uphold and was thus never happier than when she had a gripe in her mouth. One of her frequent laments, owing to the expense of keeping me in fine dresses, was that I grew like a weed: "No sooner do I finish letting out the seams or dropping the hems, then I have to go back and start all over again!" This time, however, she had not left the comment there: "The Captain and I have been saying it might be time we made some changes to your work. You're getting too old to be Little Girl Lost. Won't be long and those Helpful Gentlemen are going to be getting other ideas about how they might like to 'help' a pretty girl like you. More so, how you might be able to help them."

I didn't want to make changes to my work, and I was quite sure that I didn't like Mrs. Mack's insinuation as to the sort of "help" I might be able to render the gentlemen. I had started to perceive a change in the way the barflies at the Anchor and Whistle looked at me when I was sent in to drag the Captain home for dinner, and I knew enough to realize that it had more than a bit to do with the "nice little pair of buds" that Mrs. Mack had noted when she was measuring me up for recent alterations.

Martin, too, had begun to observe me more closely. He lingered in the hallway outside the room where I slept, and when I dressed in the mornings, where light should spill through the keyhole, it was dark instead. I was finding it almost impossible to escape his watch. It had always been a part of his role within his mother's enterprise to keep an overseeing eye on things—to make sure that none of us kids mistakenly dragged home trouble in the evenings—but this was different.

And so, as I rode the omnibus that morning, as I slipped my hand into the pocket of the lady beside me and felt her purse beneath my fingertips, I was not concentrating as I should have been; I was turning over Mrs. Mack's worrying pronouncement, probing it for implications, and wondering for the umpteenth time why my father still had not sent for me. Every month or so, Jeremiah would arrive to collect from Mrs. Mack the money to be forwarded on to America, and Mrs. Mack would read me my father's most recent letter. But whenever I asked whether he had instructed me to purchase a ticket to America, she told me no, that it was not yet time.

Thus, I was careless, and the first I knew that the lady was intending to leave the omnibus was when I felt the tug against my hand as she stood up, taking her pocket with her and my arm with it. And then, the cry of "Why, you little thief!"

Over the years I had prepared myself for this precise scenario. I had been through it many times in my head. I should have feigned innocence, widened my eyes and pretended that it was all a mistake, perhaps even produced some pitiable tears. But I was caught unawares. I hesitated a fraction too long. All that I could hear was Mrs. Mack's voice reminding me that accusing is proving where power sits in judgment. Against this lady with her fancy hat, fine manners, and wounded delicacy, I was nothing.

The driver was moving up the aisle towards me; a gentleman, two seats ahead, was on his feet. I glanced over my shoulder and saw that there was a relatively clear path towards the rear door, and so I ran.

I was a good runner, but in a stroke of bad luck a newly minted policeman doing rounds nearby heard the commotion, saw me take flight, and with a jolt of lusty enthusiasm began to give chase. "Stop! Thief!" he yelled, wielding his baton above his head.

It was not the first time that I had been pursued by a policeman, but on this particular morning the fog had driven me too far north to be able to rely on any of my friends to help my flight. As Lily Millington had warned, to risk capture at my age was to flirt with a one-way ticket to the workhouse, so I had no choice but to run as hard as I could towards the safety of Covent Garden.

My heart pounded as I pelted down Red Lion Square. The policeman was carrying more weight than he might, but was nonetheless a grown man and faster than I was. High Holborn was teeming with traffic and my spirits lifted; I could duck and weave between vehicles and that way escape him. But alas, when I reached the other side and shot a look over my shoulder, he was still there, even closer than before.

I slipped down a narrow alleyway and immediately realized my folly: on the other side was Lincoln's Inn Fields, with its wide green plain offering nowhere to hide. I was all out of options, he was almost upon me, and then I glimpsed a slender lane that ran behind the imposing row of rendered houses, a ladder snaking up the brick back of the nearest one.

With a surge of elation, I gambled that I would be faster than the policeman if I were to move the chase off the ground.

I began to climb, step by step, as quickly as I could. The ladder shook beneath my grip as my pursuer clambered after me, his heavy boots clanging on the metal rungs. Higher and higher I went, past one, two, three rows of windows. And when I had gone as high as the ladder would take me, I scrambled off and onto the slate tiles of the rooftop.

I picked my way along the guttering, arms out wide to keep my balance, and when one house gave way to the next, I climbed over the partitions between them and shimmied past the chimneys. I had been correct in my assumption that I would have an advantage at height, for although he was still behind me, I had gained a small amount of breathing space.

But my relief was short-lived. I was already well along the row of houses, and once I reached the other side, there was nowhere further for me to go.

Just as the dire realization was dawning, I saw it! One of the windows in the rooftop dormer was pushed halfway open in its sash. I didn't think twice: I forced it higher still and slipped beneath.

I fell hard to the floor, but there was not a spare second to admit injury. I scurried to fit under the wide sill, pressing myself against the wall in a tight crouch. My pulse was roaring such that I was sure the policeman would be able to hear it. I needed to silence it so that I could hear him pass, for only then would I know that it was safe to climb out again and start making my way home.

It had been such a blessed relief to find the window open that I hadn't given a single moment's thought as to what sort of room I was leaping into. Now, though, as I began to catch my breath, I turned my head to take stock and saw that I was in the bedroom of a child. Which was not a disaster in itself, except that the child in question was in current occupation of the bed and looking directly at me.

He was the palest creature I had ever seen. About my age, with a wan face and hair the color of bleached straw, propped up against enormous white feather pillows, his waxen arms draped limply over the smooth linen sheets. I tried to smile reassuringly and had opened my mouth to speak when I realized that there was nothing I could say or do to make the moment seem normal; what was more, the policeman would be upon us at any minute, and really, it would be best if neither of us were to say anything.

I lifted my finger to my lips to implore the boy to silence, aware that he held my fate in his hands, and then he spoke: "If you come any nearer"—his vowels were so crystal-sharp that they sliced through the room's thick, stale air—"I shall call for my father and you will be on a transport ship to Australia before you can utter even the hint of an apology."

Transportation was about the only thing worse than the workhouse, and I was trying to find the words to explain to him how it came to pass that I had arrived in his room through a rooftop window when I heard another voice: the gruff, embarrassed tones of a man above me at the window saying, "My apologies, sir—Little Master—There was a girl I was chasing, you see: a young girl running away from me."

"A young girl? On the rooftop? Have you gone mad?"

"Not at all, Little Master, she climbed, you see, like a monkey, straight up the ladder—"

"You expect me to believe that a young girl outran you?"

"Well, ah, er . . . yes, sir."

"And you a grown man?"

A slight pause. "Yes, sir."

"Remove yourself from my bedroom window this minute or I shall call out at the top of my lungs. Do you know who my father is?"

"Yes, sir, but I . . . You see, sir, there was a girl . . ."

"This. Minute!"

"Sir. Yes, sir. Very good, sir."

There was a scuffling noise on the roof, followed by the sound of something heavy sliding along tiles, and then a diminishing yelp.

The boy turned his attention to me.

It was my experience that when there was nothing to be said, it was best to say nothing, and so I waited to see which way the wind was going to blow. He regarded me quizzically before saying, finally, "Hello."

"Hello." With the policeman gone, there seemed little point in remaining crouched, and so I stood. It was my first opportunity to look properly at the room and I am not ashamed to say that I was powerless to stop gawping.

I had never seen anything like it. The room was a nursery, with a slanted roofline and shelves lining the walls from floor to ceiling, upon which sat an example of every toy I could have thought to name. Wooden soldiers and skittles, balls and bats and marbles, a remarkable clockwork train engine with carriages containing little dolls, an ark with pairs of each animal under the sun, a set of spinning tops in different sizes, a red and white drum, a jack-in-the-box, and a rocking horse in the corner keeping a cool eye on things. A Punch and Judy set. An elaborate doll's house that stood as tall as I did on its plinth. A spinning hoop and stick that had the shining look of items that had never before been used.

As I conducted my inspection, my eyes alit upon a tray on the foot of his bed. It was covered with the sort of food I had glimpsed through the windows in Mayfair but never even hoped to sample for myself. My stomach became a knot, and perhaps he noticed me staring because he said, "You would be doing me a great favor were you to eat some. They are always trying to feed me, even though I've told them that I'm rarely hungry."

I did not need to be told twice.

The food on the tray was still warm, and I ate it gratefully, perched on the very end of his quilted bed. I was too busy eating to speak, and as he was inclined to do neither, we watched one another warily across the tray.

When I was finished, I patted my mouth with the napkin, the way Mrs. Mack always did, and smiled cautiously. "Why are you in bed?"

"I am not well."

"What's the matter with you?"

"There seems to be a degree of uncertainty in that regard."

"Are you going to die?"

He considered. "It is possible. Although I haven't to this point, which I take as a positive sign."

I nodded in agreement but also encouragement. I did not know this strange, pale boy, but I was glad to think that he was not on death's door.

"But how rude of me," he said. "Forgive me. I don't have many guests." He held out a fine hand. "I was named for my father, of course, but you shall call me just plain Joe. And you are . . . ?"

As I took his hand, I thought of Lily Millington. Inventing a name was by far and away the more sensible thing to do, and I still cannot say why I told him the truth. An irrepressible urge started deep down inside my stomach and then rose, growing in pace and solidity until I could resist it no longer. "I was named for my mother's father," I said. "But my friends call me Birdie."

"And so shall I, for you arrived on my windowsill just like a bird."

"Thank you for lending it to me."

"Not at all. I've often had cause, lying here with nothing much else to look at, to wonder why the builders wasted so much material in making it so wide. I see now that they were wiser than I gave them credit."

He smiled at me, and I smiled back.

On the table beside him was something that I had never seen before. I felt emboldened by his kindness and picked it up. It was a disc with pieces of twine attached to two opposing edges; on one side of the disc was drawn a canary, and on the other side a metal cage. "What is this?"

He indicated that I should hand it to him. "It's called a thaumatrope." He held one of the strings and then rotated the disc so that it wound tightly. Holding both strings, he then pulled them away from one another so that the disc began to spin rapidly. I clapped, delighted, as the bird suddenly flew into the cage.

"Magic," he said.

"An illusion," I corrected.

"Yes. Quite right. It is a trick. But a pretty one."

With a final glance at the thaumatrope, I thanked him for the lunch and told him that I had to go.

"No," he said quickly, shaking his head. "I forbid it."

The response was so unexpected that I could think of nothing to say. It was all I could do not to burst out laughing that this pale bed-ridden boy thought he might be capable of forbidding me anything; it made me sad, too, because in three words he had exposed himself so plainly, both his wishes and his limitations.

Perhaps he also glimpsed the absurdity of his order, for his tone lost its bravado and he continued, almost desperately, "Please. You must stay longer."

"I will be in trouble if I stay out after dark."

"There's plenty of time until sunset—two hours at least."

"But I haven't done my work. I've nothing to show for the day."

Pale Joe was confused by this and asked what sort of work I meant. Did I mean schoolwork, and if so, where were my books and slate and where did I intend to meet my governess? I told him that I did not mean schoolwork, that I had never been to school, and I explained to him about my omnibus route and the gloves and the dresses with the deep pockets.

He listened to this account with widening eyes and then asked me to show him the gloves. I sat closer to him on the edge of the bed, pulled them from my pocket, and arranged them on my lap, acting the part of the little lady in her carriage. "You see that my hands are here," I said, nodding at the gloves, to which he agreed. "And yet," I continued, "what is this?"

He gasped, because without appearing to alter my position I had slipped my actual hand beneath the covers to tickle his knee.

"And that is how it works," I said, jumping off the bed and smoothing my skirts.

"But—that's wonderful," he said, a quick smile spreading across his face, restoring to him, briefly, a welcome look of life. "And you do this every day?"

I was at the window now, surveying the climb back down. "Mostly. Sometimes I just pretend to be lost and then pick the pocket of the gentleman who helps me."

"And the things you take—purses, jewelry—you deliver them home to your mother?"

"My mother is dead."

"An orphan," he said reverently. "I have read books about them."

"No, not an orphan. My father is away for a time, but he is going to send for me as soon as he's settled." I hoisted myself onto the sill.

"Don't go," said the boy. "Not yet."

"I have to."

"Then come again—please. Say you will?"

I hesitated. To agree, I knew, would be foolish: this was not an area that a young girl without a chaperone would go unnoticed for long, and the policeman at the end of the street knew me now. He might not have had a chance to see my face, but he had already given chase, and the next time I might not be so lucky. But then, that food—I'd never tasted anything like it. And those shelves of toys and wonders . . .

"Take this," said Pale Joe, holding the thaumatrope towards me. "It's yours. And next time you come, I promise, I'll show you something far, far better."

And that is how I came to meet Pale Joe and he became my secret, just as surely as I became his.

There has been a shift in the house's temperament. Something of importance has happened while I was thinking of my old friend Pale Joe. Sure enough, Jack is in the hallway, a look upon his face just like the cat that got the cream. It does not take me long to realize why. He is standing in front of the hiding hole, its concealed panel wide-open.

He has gone off now at a trot, back to his room in order to fetch his torch, I imagine. Despite telling Rosalind Wheeler that he would not enter the house before Saturday, I understand curiosity and its demands and have no doubt that he has plans to search every square inch of the hiding hole, every groove within the boards, in the hope that he might find the diamond lurking. He won't. It isn't there. But all truths must not be told at all times. It will do him no harm to search. I rather like him when frustration makes him bearish.

I am going to leave him to it and wait for him in the malthouse. I have other things to think about, like Elodie Winslow's visit. There was something familiar in her bearing when she was here this afternoon. I couldn't place it at first, but I have since realized what it was. When she entered the house, as she walked about its rooms, she let out a sigh that no one else but I would have been able to detect, and I saw upon her face a look of satisfaction that could almost be termed completeness. It reminded me of Edward. It is the same way that he looked when we first came to this house.

But Edward had a reason to feel such strong attachment. He was tethered to this place when just a boy, by his night of terror in the nearby fields. Why is Elodie Winslow here? What is her connection to Birchwood Manor?

I hope that she comes back. I wish it with a fervency that I have not felt in years. I begin to understand at last how it must have been for Pale Joe that first day, when he promised to show me something wonderful if I would only agree to return. One becomes rather desperate for visitors, when one has lost the power to visit.

After Edward, Pale Joe is the person whom I miss most in this limbo of mine. I used to think of him a lot and wonder what became of him, for he was a special person; he had been poorly for some time when I met him and his life of isolation in that room of untouched treasures made him far more interested than most in the world beyond his window. Everything that Pale Joe knew he had learned from books, and thus there was a lot he did not understand about the way things worked. He could not comprehend when I told him about the poky damp rooms that I had shared with my father in the shadow of St. Anne's; the communal privy and the toothless old woman who cleaned it out in exchange for leftover cinders; what happened to Lily Millington perhaps saddest of all. He wanted to know why people would choose to live in such a way and was forever asking me to tell him stories of the London that I knew, the alleyways of Covent Garden, the dark areas of commerce below the bridges along the Thames, the infants with no parents. He wanted to hear especially about the babies who had come to live with Mrs. Mack, and his eyes would fill with tears when I told him of those unlucky little ones who just weren't strong enough for this world.

I wonder what he thought when I disappeared so completely from his life. Did he look for me? Not at first, but eventually, when more time passed than could be explained away with logic? Did he doubt and ask questions, or did he believe the worst? Pale Joe was the same age that I was, born in 1844; if he lived into old age, he would have been eighty-seven years old when Leonard's book was published. Being such an avid reader—we read together often, up there in his attic bedroom, the two of us sitting shoulder to shoulder in his white linen nest—he was always aware of what was being published and when; he was a lover of art, too, a passion acquired from his father, whose house on Lincoln's Inn Fields was filled with Turners. Yes, I feel sure that Pale Joe would have read Leonard's book. What did he make of its theories? I wonder. Did he believe me a faithless jewel thief who fled to a better life in America?

Pale Joe certainly knew me capable of thievery. He knew me better than Edward in some respects. We had met, after all, when I was mid-flight from a policeman, and from the start he had been filled with questions about Mrs. Mack and her enterprise, delighting in my tales of Little Girl Lost and Little Girl Passenger and, as time went on, Theater-Going Lady, encouraging me to tell him my stories, as if they described great feats of derring-do.

Pale Joe knew, too, that I had resolved that if my father did not send for me, I would travel to America and find him. For although Jeremiah delivered regular reports, standing importantly in Mrs. Mack's parlor as she read out letters in which my father described his efforts to remake himself and encouraged me to listen to Mrs. Mack and to do as she bade me, I was always concerned that there was something I was not being told; for if my father's new life was progressing as his letters said, then why did he continue to insist that I should not yet join him?

But later Pale Joe knew that I also loved Edward. Indeed, it was he who saw it first. I can still remember the night, on the evening of the Royal Academy exhibition of 1861, when Edward invited me to see the *La Belle* painting unveiled, and afterwards I went to Pale Joe's window. I have had much time since to reflect upon Pale Joe's words that evening, after I gave him my report. "You are in love," he said, "for that is exactly how love feels. It is the lifting of a mask, the revealing of one's true self to another, and the forced acceptance, the awful awareness, that the other person may never feel the same way."

He was wise about love, Pale Joe, for a boy who rarely left his bower. His mother was always encouraging him to attend Society dances so that he could meet London's eligible young debutantes, and many times, as I bade him farewell, I left him to dress in his black-and-white suit for this dinner or that. I used to think about him as I hurried back along the laneways towards Covent Garden, my pale, elegant friend with his limp and his kind heart, who had grown tall in the five years since we'd met, and handsome; and I pictured the two of us as if from above, going about our parallel lives in the one great city.

I suppose Pale Joe must have met a woman at one of those dances, a fine lady with whom he fell in love as completely as I did with Edward, and who perhaps did not reciprocate, because his words that night were perfect.

He never did have the chance to tell me who she was. The last time that I saw Pale Joe, we were eighteen years old. I had come to his window to let him know that I'd agreed to go with Edward to Birchwood Manor for the summer. I revealed nothing of my plans beyond; I didn't even say a proper farewell. I didn't think I had to, not then. I thought that there would be more time. I suppose people always do.

Jack is back in the malthouse and my house is calm again, catching its breath after a day of unusual activity. It has been a long time since anyone ventured inside the hiding hole.

He is dispirited, but not because he failed to find the stone. Its absence will involve another telephone call to Rosalind Wheeler, which will not be pleasant, for she will not be happy. But the search for the Radcliffe Blue is just a job for Jack; he has no personal connection other than human curiosity driving his quest. His mood is related,

I am certain, to his meeting yesterday with Sarah regarding the two little girls.

I long to know what happened between them. It gives me something to focus on besides my own memories and the endless, aimless stretch of time.

He has put aside Mrs. Wheeler's notes and floor plan and picked up his camera. I have noticed a pattern with Jack. When something upsets him, he takes out his camera and looks through the lens, pointing it at things—anything, it seems—fiddling with the aperture and the focus, and bringing the zoom in close before retracting it again. Sometimes he takes the shot; more often than not, he doesn't. By and by, his equilibrium is restored and the camera goes away.

Today, however, he is not so easily mended. He returns the camera to its bag and then hangs the strap over his shoulder. He intends to go outside to take more photographs.

I am going to wait for him in my favorite corner at the turn of the stairs. I like to look at the Thames between the trees beyond the meadow. The river is quiet up here; only the canal boats go back and forth, dragging after them the faint plume of coal smoke. One can hear the plink of a fishing line being sunk, the skid of a duck coming in to land on the surface, laughter sometimes in the summer if the day is warm enough to swim.

What I said earlier was not entirely truthful, that I have never managed to go as far as the river. There was one time, and one time only. I did not mention it because I still cannot explain it. But on the afternoon that Ada Lovegrove fell from the boat, I was there, in the river, watching as she sank to the bottom.

Edward used to say that the river possessed a primeval memory of everything that had ever happened. It occurs to me that this house is like that, too. It remembers, just as I do. It remembers everything.

———

Such thoughts bring me back to Leonard.

He had been a soldier but was a student by the time he arrived at

Birchwood Manor, working on a dissertation about Edward, his papers spread across the desk in the Mulberry Room downstairs. It was from him that I learned much of what happened after Fanny died. Amongst his research notes were letters and newspaper articles and eventually the police reports, too. What a strange feeling it was to read the name Lily Millington there amongst the others. Thurston Holmes, Felix and Adele Bernard, Frances Brown, Edward, Clare and Lucy Radcliffe.

I saw the policemen as they carried out their investigation into Fanny's death. I watched as they searched the rooms, raking through Adele's clothing and stripping the walls of Felix's darkroom. I was there when the shorter of the two men pocketed a photograph of Clare in her lace slip, tucking it inside the pocket of his straining coat. I was there, too, when they cleared out Edward's studio, taking from it everything they could find that might shed light on me . . .

Leonard had a dog that would sleep on the armchair as he worked; a great big shaggy animal with muddy paws and a long-suffering expression. I like animals: they are often aware of me when people are not; they make me feel appreciated. It is amazing how far a little acknowledgment will go when one has become used to being ignored.

He brought a record player with him and used to play songs late at night, and he kept a glass pipe on the table beside his bed, an object I recognized from the time of my father's nights in the Chinese den in the Limehouse. Occasionally a woman, Kitty, came to visit and he would hide the pipe away.

I watched him sometimes when he slept, just as I watch Jack now. He had military habits, like the old major who was known to Mrs. Mack and the Captain, who could beat a young girl where she stood but wouldn't countenance falling into bed without polishing his boots and lining them up carefully for the next day.

Leonard wasn't violent, but his nightmares were bleak. Neat as a pin, quiet and polite by day, but with dreams of the darkest kind. He would shake in his sleep, and wince, and call out in a voice made raw with fear. "Tom," he used to call. "Tommy."

I used to wonder about Tommy. Leonard cried for him as one might for a lost child.

On the nights when he smoked through the glass pipe and fell into a languorous sleep where Tommy couldn't find him, I sat in the still of the dark house and thought of my father, of how long I waited for him to come back for me.

And when Leonard didn't use the pipe, I stayed with him. I understand despair; and so, on those nights, I knelt and whispered in that young man's ear, "It is all right. Be at peace. Tommy says that he is well."

Tom . . . Tommy . . . I still hear his name on nights when the wind blows strong down the river and the floorboards quiver.

Chapter Thirteen

SUMMER 1928

It was the hottest day so far, and Leonard had determined when he woke that he would swim. He'd taken to strolling along the towpath in the early mornings, and sometimes again in the hovering afternoons that burned on and on before fading suddenly like a limelight being snuffed.

The Thames here had a vastly different character to the wide, muddy tyrant that seethed through London. It was graceful and deft and remarkably light of heart. It skipped over stones and skimmed its banks, water so clear that one could see the reeds swaying deep down on her narrow bed. The river here was a she, he'd decided. For all its sunlit transparency, there were certain spots in which it was suddenly unfathomable.

A long, dry stretch through June had given him ample opportunity to explore, and Leonard had discovered a particularly inviting bend a mile or two upstream before the Lechlade Halfpenny Bridge. A co-op of scrappy children had set up camp for the summer in a field just beyond, but a coppice of birch trees gave the bend its privacy.

He was sitting now with his back against the trunk of a willow, wishing he'd finished the repairs he was planning to make to the old wooden rowboat he'd found in the barn behind the house. The day was perfectly still, and Leonard couldn't think of anything more pleasant than lying in that boat and letting it carry him downstream.

In the distance, a boy of about eleven, with long, skinny legs and knobbly knees, ran from beneath the shadows of one tree towards the trunk of another. He streaked across the sunny clearing circling his arms like a windmill, just for the hell of it, a wide grin lighting his face.

For a split second Leonard could remember the fluid joy of being young and fast and free. "Run with me, Lenny, run!" He still heard it sometimes, when the wind blew a certain way or a bird sailed over-head. "Run with me, Lenny."

The boy hadn't seen Leonard. He and his mates were on a stick-gathering mission, collecting swordlike lengths and carrying them to a particular boy by the calico tent who then inspected the offer-ings, admitting some and shaking his head no to others. To Leonard's adult eyes, there was nothing about that boy that marked him out as the leader. He was a little taller, perhaps, than the others, a bit older, maybe, but children had an instinctive ability to discern power.

Leonard got on well with children. With them there was none of the duplicity that adults relied upon to ease their way. They said what they meant and described what they saw, and when they disagreed, they fought and then made amends. He and Tom had been like that.

A tennis ball soared from nowhere, landing with a soft thud and rolling along the grass towards the river's edge. Dog raced after it be-fore trotting back to drop the gift at his master's feet. Leonard accepted the sodden offering, weighing it in his palm briefly, before hurling it back in the direction from which it had come.

There was some warmth in the sun now. He took off his shirt and trousers and, wearing only his trunks, made his way to the water's edge. He dipped in a toe as a family of ducks drifted by.

Without giving himself time to change his mind, Leonard dived beneath the surface.

The early morning cold of the water made his skin tighten. He kept his eyes open as he swam down, down, down, as deep as he could go, reaching out when he met the bottom to clutch at the silt floor. He held on and started counting. Tom grinned back at him from within the clump of slippery reeds.

Leonard couldn't remember a time before Tom. There'd only been thirteen months between them. Their mother had lost a child prior to Leonard, a girl called June who'd been stricken with scarlet fever in her second year, and she hadn't been about to take the chance that she'd be left short again. He'd heard her confess to his aunt one afternoon over tea that she'd have had ten children if not for the "women's problems" that had stopped her.

"You've 'an heir and a spare,'" the aunt had said with customary pragmatism, "and that's better than naught."

It had occupied Leonard on and off for years, wondering whether he was the "air" and whether that was a good or a bad thing. His mother always hated it when the wind blew at night and rattled the windows in their frames.

Tom was the younger one, but he'd been more physical than Leonard. By the time they were five and four years old, Tom was the taller of the pair. He was broader, too, with strong shoulders—like a swimmer's, their dad used to say with stilted masculine pride—and a charming character, open and easy, that drew people to him. Leonard, by contrast, was more internal. His mother liked to tell them that their personalities had been visible from the moment they were placed as newborns in her arms. "You pulled your little limbs tight against you and tucked your chin into your chest like you were trying to escape the world. Tom, though—he clenched his fists, jutted his chin, and stuck out his bottom lip as if to say, 'Come and get me!'"

Leonard's lungs ached in his chest, but he remained submerged. He met his brother's laughing gaze as a school of minnows swam between them. He kept counting.

Women liked Tom; they always had. He was handsome—even Leonard could see that—but it was something else. He had a way about him. He was funny, and generous, and when he laughed it was like the sky had cracked open and the sun was shining directly on your skin. Leonard, with plenty of time to reflect upon it since, had decided that it was an innate honesty that people responded to in Tom. Even when he was angry or fierce, there was a truthfulness to his emotion that drew people to him.

Leonard's pulse was hammering hot in his ears now. It had expanded to fill his whole skull and he could stand it no longer. He pushed off the bottom and arrowed back through the water towards the glistening top, gasping sharply when he broke the surface. He squinted as the world turned briefly white and then rolled onto his back to catch his breath.

Leonard floated star shaped, the sun pleasingly hot on his stomach. Ninety-three seconds. He was still well short of Tom's record, snatched during the summer of 1913, but he would try again tomorrow. A lark was singing nearby and Leonard closed his eyes. Water lapped gently. The boys whooped gleefully in the distance, mad on summer.

Leonard swam slowly back to the bank. It was another day, just like the one before.

Hora pars vitae. His Latin teacher had made them write it out in lines. *Every hour is a part of life.*

Serius est quam cogitas, said the sundial in France. A modest construction in the garden of a small church where Leonard's unit had collapsed, spent, during a muddy retreat. *It's later than you think.*

"Come on, Dog." The hound leapt to his feet and Leonard noted again the animal's remarkable gift for optimism. He'd shown up on Leonard's first night at Birchwood Manor, almost a month ago now, and they'd adopted one another by unspoken mutual agreement. Hard to know what sort of dog he was: large, brownish, a strong, hairy tail with a mind of its own.

They walked back towards the house, Leonard's shirt damp where it pressed against his skin. A pair of red-tailed kites was hovering like a magic act in the air above a wheat field, and Leonard had a sudden flashback to the front. An enormous ruined mansion that they'd stayed at one night in France, collapsed on one side but intact on the other. There'd been a clock in the black-and-white hallway, a grandfather clock that tocked even louder at night, counting down the minutes, though to what he was never sure; there never seemed to be an end.

One of the men had found a violin upstairs, in a dusty room of books and peacetime pleasures, and he carried it down to the garden and started playing, a haunting piece that Leonard vaguely knew. War by its nature was surreal: events so shocking that they could never become normal; further shock when inevitably they did. Day after day of dissonance as the old reality and the new sat side by side, as men who'd only months before been printers and shoemakers and clerks found themselves loading bullets into guns and dodging rats in water-logged trenches.

To Leonard's mind there had been no irony so great in the whole four-year stretch as that afternoon spent listening to violin music in a summery garden, while less than a mile away shells exploded and men lay dying. There had been falcons circling in the distant sky then: peregrine falcons, high above the action. They were unmoved by what was happening in the fields below. The mud and blood and slaughter, the senseless waste. They had the long memory of birds; they had seen it all before.

Humans could look back across time now, too. All it had taken was a war. Another irony, that the very aerial photography developed to help bombers cause maximum destruction was now being deployed by cartographers to reveal wondrous geographical preservation on the earth below.

Wars were useful like that, apparently. Leonard's old school friend Anthony Baxter had told him so over a pint some months back. Necessity was the mother of invention, he'd said, and there was nothing so motivating as the need to survive. Anthony worked in manu-facturing—some sort of new material replacing glass. There was a lot of money to be made, he'd continued, his cheeks flushed with ale and greed, if a fellow allowed himself to think creatively.

Leonard despised money. That is, he despised the quest to pos-sess it. In his view, the only positive to be drawn from the war was the realization of how little a man actually needed to survive. How little the rest of it mattered. All of those abandoned grandfather clocks; people who simply closed the doors on their mansions and fled with their families in search of safety. What was real, he knew now, was the soil beneath a man's feet. The earth, the natural world, from which could be derived every necessity, and on which were preserved the imprints of every man, woman, and child that had ever lived.

Before he came to Birchwood Manor, Leonard had purchased a couple of Ordnance Survey maps from Stanfords on the Long Acre, taking in the spread of Oxfordshire, Wiltshire, and Berkshire. One could make out Roman roads etched into the chalk by millennia-old footfalls, crop circles where ditched enclosures once stood, parallel ridges made by medieval plows. Stretching back further still, the capillary networks of Neolithic mortuary enclosures could be seen; marks left during the last ice age.

The earth was the ultimate museum, recording and presenting a narrative of time, and this area, the Ridgeway—the chalk of the Salisbury Plain, the Cerne Abbas Giant, the Uffington White Horse—was particularly tractable. Chalk was more resistant to slumping than clay; it had a better memory. Leonard knew chalk. It had been one of his jobs in France to tunnel under the battlefield; he'd trained at Larkhill in Wiltshire, learned how to build listening posts and sit for hours with a stethoscope pressed against the cold earth. And then, pitching in with the New Zealanders, he'd dug the real thing beneath the city of Arras. Weeks on end in the dark, candles for light and a bucket turned brazier through the coldest stretch of winter.

Leonard knew chalk.

Britain was an ancient isle, a place of ghosts, and every acre could lay claim to being a landscape of legacy, but this part was particularly rich. Layers of human habitation could be glimpsed within the same parcel of land: prehistoric, Iron Age, medieval, and now Great War tunneling practice, too. The Thames snaked its way across the middle of the map, rising as a series of trickling headsprings in the Cotswolds and widening as it progressed. Tucked within a fork made by a slender tributary was the village of Birchwood. Not too far away, on a ridge there ran a track, straighter than nature usually drew, a ley line. Leonard had read Alfred Watkins, and the account given by William Henry Black to the British Archaeological Association in Hereford, speculating that such "grand geometrical lines" linked Neolithic monuments all over Britain and Western Europe. They were the old paths, forged thousands of years ago, magical, powerful, sacred.

The mysterious and mystical past was what had drawn Edward Radcliffe and the others to the area during the summer of 1862. It had also led, in part, to Radcliffe's initial purchase of the house. Leonard had read the manifesto many times, and also the letters Radcliffe wrote to his friend and fellow artist Thurston Holmes. Unlike Radcliffe, who had drifted into relative obscurity after his fiancée died, his professional memory upheld only by a core group of devoted enthusiasts, Holmes had continued to paint and enjoy public life well into his seventies. He had died only recently, leaving his correspondence and journals to posterity, and Leonard had made a number of trips to the University of York, spending weeks combing through them for anything that might cast new light on Edward Radcliffe's connection to the house at Birchwood.

In a letter sent in January 1861, Radcliffe had written:

> *I have bought a house. A rather charming house, which although not grand is of elegant proportions. It sits like a humble, dignified bird, within its own bend of the river, on the edge of the woods, by a small but perfectly formed village. And Thurston, there is more. I will not commit it to paper here, but will wait until next we meet, saying only that there is something else within the house that draws me, something old and essential and not entirely of this world. It has called to me for a long time, you see, for my new house and I are not strangers.*

Radcliffe had not elaborated then and there, and although Leonard knew from further research that he'd lived in the area for a time as a boy, there was some mystery as to precisely what had led him to the house, and when: Radcliffe had made veiled references on a couple of occasions to a boyhood experience that was both "life-changing" and "haunting," but thus far Leonard had not been able to ascertain its true nature. Whatever the case, something had happened; Radcliffe was not willing to discuss it; and the event had played an important part in his obsession with—and possession of—Birchwood Manor. In December 1860 he'd sold every painting he had and made an agreement with a benefactor to provide six paintings in exchange for the final two hundred pounds necessary. Armed with the purchase amount, he'd signed the contract and, at last, Birchwood Manor and its surrounding acres were his.

Dog let out a small bark of anticipation and Leonard followed his gaze. He had been expecting to see a cluster of ducks or geese, but instead there was a couple walking towards them, a man and a woman. Lovers, that much was clear.

As Leonard watched, the man laughed at something the woman had said; the hearty noise cut through the other morning sounds and earned him a sharp elbow to the ribs.

The woman was smiling, and Leonard found himself smiling faintly, too, as he observed them. They were so shiny and unbroken, the pair of them, their outlines so clear. They walked as if they had a perfect right to be in the world; as if they didn't doubt for a second that they belonged right here and now.

Leonard knew himself by comparison to be thin and transparent, and his deficiency made him shy. He didn't know that he could face a cheery "Good morning" exchange; he wasn't sure that he'd be able to summon the words or whether a simple nod would suffice. He had never been particularly easy in social situations, even before the war hollowed him out.

There was a stick on the ground, a lovely piece of blond wood, and Leonard picked it up, weighing it in his hand.

"Hey, Dog, come on, boy, fetch."

Leonard hurled the stick across the meadow and Dog set off in delighted pursuit, the man and woman forgotten.

Turning his back on the river, Leonard followed. The peaks of Birchwood Manor's twin gables were visible above the top of the willows lining the Hafodsted Brook, and Leonard noticed that one of the attic windows was catching the sun so that its glass panes looked to be alight.

When Leonard went up to Oxford as an eighteen-year-old, he hadn't imagined for a second that he would end up focusing his research on Radcliffe and a four-hundred-year-old house in a sleepy corner of the country. But then, a lot of what had happened in the intervening fifteen years went beyond the scope of Leonard's youthful imagination. Truth be told, in 1913 he hadn't imagined much of anything with respect to his academic studies. He'd gone up to Oxford because he was an intelligent boy from a certain class; there'd been little more to it than that. He'd opted to read history at Christ Church College because he liked the lawn and the grand stone building that overlooked the meadow. It was during a first-year introductory class that he met Professor Harris and discovered modern art.

What had been a random choice transformed rapidly into a passion. Leonard had been ablaze with the courage and effect of Marcel Duchamp's *Nude Descending a Staircase, No. 2*, the splintering confrontation of Picasso's *Les Demoiselles d'Avignon*; he'd read Marinetti late into the night, and traveled down to London to see the Umberto Boccioni exhibition at the Doré Gallery. The irony of the ready-made, Duchamp's bicycle wheel upon its stool, was a revelation, and Leonard was infused with optimism. He craved innovation, worshipped speed and invention, embraced new ideas about space and time and their representation; he felt as if he'd crested a giant wave and was gliding at its top into the future.

But 1914 rolled on and one night his brother came to visit him at the college. They had plans to dine in town, but Tom suggested a walk first on the meadow. It was summer and warm, and the light lingered, and Tom became nostalgic, talking rapidly about the past, their childhood, so that Leonard knew at once that something was afoot. Then, as they sat down at the restaurant table:

"I've enlisted."

With those two words, the war that had been brewing in the mastheads of newspapers was suddenly in the room with them.

Leonard hadn't wanted to go. Unlike Tom, he didn't seek adventure—not of that kind. He'd had to struggle to feel even a tickle of duty. What business was it of his if a trigger-happy madman in Sarajevo took a disliking to an Austrian archduke in a feathered hat? Leonard had resisted saying as much to anyone, not least his mother and father, who were tearfully proud of Tom's new uniform, but he couldn't help but think it was a terrible inconvenience that war should start right when he'd discovered his passion.

But.

He figured.

How long could it last?

It would be a brief interruption, a new experience that would only feed his ability to perceive the world from different standpoints; he would be able to study mechanization and modernity up close . . .

No point dwelling on the hows and wherefores. Tom was going to France and Leonard had gone, too.

Five years later, he returned to a country and a world that he no longer knew.

CHAPTER FOURTEEN

LONDON after the war had been a shock. History had the last laugh and Leonard was confronted with change and progress on a scale he could never have anticipated. Not just the world, but also the people in it. Large-faced people he didn't recognize loomed, all of them eager to dance and to celebrate, to laugh like goats, to shed their long hair and old-fashioned ways, and anything else that might tie them to the past and the long misery of war.

Leonard took a bedsit at the top of a building near the Holloway Road. There was a pig in the small back garden and a train tunnel deep in the bowels of the earth beneath. He'd spotted the pig when he made his inspection, but hadn't known about the trains until after he'd paid his first month in full and was sitting with a glass of ale and a cigarette at the small wooden desk beside his bed. It was right on dusk—always a fidgety time for Leonard, when even the light could not be trusted—and he'd thought the place was being shelled, that there'd been a terrible mistake and the war wasn't over at all; but it had only been the train. In his panic, he'd knocked his beer off the desk and earned a sharp rap of the broom end against his floor from the woman in the room beneath.

Leonard had tried to move with the times, but rather than being footloose and fancy-free he'd found himself merely unrooted. Everyone was drinking too much, but where others were made merry, Leonard became maudlin. He would be invited to a club at night and arrive with the best of intentions: he'd wear a new suit and school himself to stay upbeat, to listen and to nod, even to smile sometimes.

213

Invariably, though, at some point in the evening, having allowed himself to be drawn into conversation, Leonard would hear himself speaking of the friends he'd lost, the way they still came to him in the stillness of the bedsit, or in the mirror when he was shaving, sometimes even in the half-light of the evening street, where he'd hear the tread of their boots behind him.

In the clatter of the club, he would find the other people at his table staring at him askance when he spoke like that, turning their backs in wounded delicacy, as if they couldn't understand why he'd set out to ruin their fun. Even when he wasn't speaking of his lost friends, Leonard lacked the silvery flint of frivolous conversation. He was too earnest. Too straight. The world was a bubble now, thin and glistening, and everyone else had found their way inside. But Leonard was too heavy for the bubble. He was a man out of time: too old to be one of the spirited young people and too young to fit in with the hopeless drunkards who lined the river. He felt a connection to nothing and to nobody.

One afternoon, standing on the Charing Cross Bridge as the boats and the people went back and forth, he had a chance encounter with his old professor, who was on his way to the National Gallery. Professor Harris had invited Leonard to join him and then spoken amiably about art and life and people they had both once known, as Leonard listened and nodded, turning the anecdotes over in his mind like vaguely diverting relics. When they rounded the corner into the Renaissance rooms, and the professor suggested that Leonard might think about resuming his studies, the words were as a foreign language. Even if Leonard could have seen his way back to the disconcertingly beautiful buildings of Oxford, modernism was dead: Boccioni had been killed in 1916 and French critics were agitating now for a "return to order." All of the youth and vitality of the movement had ebbed away with Leonard's own, and lay buried now amidst the bones and mud.

But he needed to do something. London was too fast and too loud, and an urgency grew within Leonard to escape. He felt it building like the pressure before a thunderstorm: his eardrums hurt with it; his legs became restless. He woke at night in a sweat as the night trains shuddered his bedhead and the thin painted woman in the room below slammed her door after a rowdy customer. The fine black wings of panic enwrapped his throat and he prayed that they would squeeze harder and finish the job. He found himself tracing the paths in his mind that he had taken as a child—that he and Tom had taken together, over the brick wall at the bottom of the garden, through the shrubbery, along the lane that dwindled to nothing as it crossed the meadow towards the woods. "Run with me, Lenny." He heard it more and more often, but when he turned he saw only old men in bars, and young boys on street corners, and mean, skinny alley cats that followed him with their glass eyes.

Before his lease was ended, he slipped two months' rent into the glass on the desk and left his bedsit, left London on one of the trains that rattled past the little windows of other people's lives. His own family's house was smaller than he remembered, more down-at-heel, but it smelled the same and that was no bad thing. His mother reopened his boyhood bedroom, but she didn't do anything about the empty bed on the far wall. Countless conversations hung in the corners, silent by day but loud at night, so that Leonard sat bolt upright sometimes and turned on the lamp, certain that he'd catch his brother grinning at him from the other bed. He could hear the springs beneath its mattress creaking in the dark as the memory of his brother shifted in sleep.

Their old toys and books were still on the shelf—the set of wooden soldiers, the spinning top, the well-worn box of Snakes and Ladders; and Leonard reread H. G. Wells's *The Time Machine*. It had been his favorite story when he was thirteen; Tom's, too. Their dreams had all been of the future then, the two of them fantasizing about climbing through time to see what wonders lay ahead. Now, though, Leonard found himself always looking backwards. Sometimes he simply sat with the book in his hands, marveling at its solidity and shape. What a dignified object was a book, almost noble in its purpose.

Some nights he took down the game of Snakes and Ladders. They'd always played with the same counters. Leonard's a perfectly rounded grey stone he'd found when their mother and father took them to the seaside at Salcombe; Tom's a silver coin, a tuppence given to him one day by an old man he'd helped after a fall in the street. They'd been religious about their lucky counters, each insisting that his was the finer, but Leonard could remember being envious of Tom's, because nine times out of ten times his brother won the game. Tom had always been the luckier of the two. Except, of course, the one time it had mattered.

One day in early 1924, Leonard's legs were especially restless. He packed some water in his kitbag and went out for a walk as he often did, but when darkness began to drop, he didn't turn around and head back towards the house, he kept walking. He didn't know where he was going and he didn't care. He slept eventually where he fell, in an open field, the half-moon gleaming above him in the cloudless sky. And when a lark at first light woke him, he gathered his things and set off again. He walked from one side of Dorset to the other and on into Devon, finding and following the paths of Dartmoor, communing with its ghosts. He began to notice how many different shades of green there were, layers of foliage in the trees above him, the way strands of grass faded to white as they neared the earth.

A beard grew and his skin browned. He gained blisters on his heels and toes that hardened so that his feet were those of another man, a man he preferred. He became expert at selecting a stick to walk with. He learned how to lay a fire and grew calluses on his fingers. He took work where he could get it: odd jobs that required no commitment and forged no connection, and when he finished the task he took his meager pay and walked on again. He met people sometimes, strangers on the same path, and they exchanged a nod or even a wave. On rare occasions he spoke to a fellow traveler in a country pub, surprising himself at the sound of his own voice.

It was at one such pub that he saw his first photograph of England taken from the air. It was lunchtime on a Saturday and the pub was full; a man was sitting alone at one of the wooden tables out front, a dusty black bicycle leaning beside him and a leather cycling cap still on his head. He was poring over a large printed photograph, taking notes, and hadn't noticed at first that Leonard was observing him. He scowled when he saw, moving instinctively to cover his work with his arm, looking for all the world like he might have been about to snap at Leonard, but then something in his expression changed and Leonard knew that he'd been recognized. Not that they knew one another; they'd never met before. But they were all of them branded in some way after where they'd been, the things they'd seen and done.

The man's name was Crawford and he'd served in the Royal Flying Corps. He'd been employed afterwards by the Ordnance Survey and was now traveling the counties of Wiltshire and Dorset, plotting the location of archaeological sites; he'd already identified several that were previously unknown. Leonard had always preferred to listen than to talk, and he drew comfort from the things that Crawford told him. They confirmed for Leonard a number of the vague, unformed notions he'd been feeling about time and its malleability. Crawford's photographs brought together time and space in a single image, showed the past coexisting with the present; and Leonard realized that he felt a greater connection to the ancient people who'd tracked the very paths across the land that he followed now than he did with the bright young things dancing the nights away in London. He was aware as he walked of belonging; in an essential way he knew himself to be of the earth, and with each footstep he drew further solidity from it. *Belonging.* The word lodged in his mind, and when he resumed his travels that afternoon he found his feet moving to the rhythm of its syllables.

It was late that day, when Leonard was deciding where to set up camp for the evening, that a thought had come to him, a distant memory from his first-year history course at Oxford, a paper that he'd read about a Victorian movement, which included an artist called Edward Radcliffe. Although there were a number of artists in the self-termed Magenta Brotherhood, Radcliffe had been memorable due to the tragic story attached to him: the murder of his young fiancée and his subsequent spiral into decline. Even so, the group had not interested Leonard at the time: he'd been bored by the Victorians. He'd resented their certainties and scoffed at their fusty black lace and cluttered hallways. Like all modernists, like all children, he had sought to define himself in defiance of the looming granite stature of the Establishment.

But Professor Harris's Introduction to the History of Art had been thorough and thus they'd been required to read the paper. It had referenced at one point a "manifesto" penned in 1861 by Edward Radcliffe and titled, "The Art of Belonging," in which the artist exulted about the connection he perceived between human beings and places; places and art. "The land does not forget," Leonard could remember reading. "Place is a doorway through which one steps across time." The paper had gone on to mention a particular house that had obsessed the artist and in which he believed he had found his own "belonging." To eighteen-year-old Leonard, Radcliffe's musings about place, the past, and belonging had seemed extraneous and dull. Now, though, a decade later, he couldn't get the words out of his head.

When Leonard eventually made it back to his parents' house, he was thinner than before, and hairier; his skin had weathered and his clothes had become worn. He'd expected his mother to recoil or shriek in horror at his deterioration, and to order him upstairs to wash. She did none of those things. She opened the door and, after a split second of surprise, dropped her tea towel to the floor, wrapping her arms so tightly around him that he thought his ribs might crush.

She ushered him inside, wordlessly, to his father's chair and fetched a bucket of warm, soapy water. She took off his old boots and the socks that had molded to his skin, and began to wash his feet. It was something he couldn't remember her doing before, not since he was a very small child, and silent tears appeared on her cheeks. Her head bowed and Leonard was aware, as if for the first time, of her greying hair, its changed texture. Over her shoulder, a collection of family photographs stood side by side on the lace-cloaked table: Tom and Leonard in their sharp army kits, as little boys in shorts and caps, as babies in crocheted bonnets. Various uniforms across time. The water was so warm, the kindness so pure and unexpected, and Leonard so out of practice at receiving such things that he realized he was crying, too.

They had a cup of tea together later and his mother asked what he'd been doing these past months.

"Walking," said Leonard.

"Walking," she repeated. "And did you enjoy yourself?"

Leonard told her that he had.

A little nervously, she said, "I had a caller the other day. Someone you used to know."

It turned out Leonard's professor had tracked him down using the records of his old college. Professor Harris had entered one of Leonard's papers in a competition at the university and he'd been awarded a small stipend, enough to buy a new pair of walking boots and a couple of maps at Stanfords. With the change, he'd bought a train ticket. Leonard had come to feel a kinship with Radcliffe during his walkabout and headed now to York to read Thurston Holmes's papers. It seemed to him that something must have happened to cause a young man—only twenty years old at the time—to write with such enthusiasm about place and belonging, to make him fall so wholeheartedly in love with a house. Surely only a man who knew himself to be an outsider would think along such lines.

He hadn't had much luck. The Holmes archive contained many letters from Radcliffe, but there were none from the period in which Leonard was interested. Exceedingly frustrating, but curious, too. Throughout 1859, 1860, and into 1861, Radcliffe and Holmes had corresponded regularly, their lengthy, conversational letters making it clear that the two men saw a lot of one another and that each found his thinking and his art stimulated by the other. But Radcliffe was reticent to write further about the house and then, after a brief, rather curt letter in which he requested the return of a borrowed paint set in

January 1862, there appeared to have been only occasional, perfunctory exchanges between them.

It was possible of course that there was no mystery: that the two men had simply drifted apart, or else that they'd continued corresponding, but the more fulsome letters had been lost to a winter fire, a poor filing system, a feverish session of spring cleaning. There was no way of knowing and Leonard didn't spend too much time then wondering. Whatever the case, evidently in mid-1862 they had been close enough to go away together for the summer, with the other members of the Magenta Brotherhood—Felix and Adele Bernard—and Edward's sister, Clare, who was modeling for Thurston Holmes, to Edward Radcliffe's house at Birchwood.

And although Leonard hadn't found precisely what he'd come looking for, he didn't leave the archives empty-handed. He'd discovered a doorway, and on the other side was a group of young people from over half a century before who'd reached through time and taken him back with them.

It was Edward Radcliffe whose charisma leapt most vividly from the pages of the letters. His energy and openness, his willingness to engage with life and everything it offered, the inclusiveness of his art, its readiness to grow and transmute and capture experiences, was clear. Each line in each letter pulsed with youth, possibility, and sensuality, and Leonard could picture the state of blissful domestic dishabille in which Radcliffe lived, his perch on the edge of artistic poverty, just as surely as if he were there. He understood their intimacy and ease, the camaraderie that others found both cliquish and alluring; they were a true brotherhood. It was the same way Leonard had felt about Tom, almost proprietorial, as if they were made of the same stuff, and therefore they were the same person. It allowed them to fight and wrestle and then to laugh it off as they lay on the ground panting, for one to lean across and slap a mosquito on the other's leg just as he would his own. Leonard perceived, too, the way the men, like brothers, had been stimulated by competition, each working feverishly to create works that would leave an indelible mark on the

Establishment. Each seeking to attract the praise of John Ruskin, the glowing review of Charles Dickens, the patronage of a gentleman with deep pockets.

It was intoxicating stuff, and reading the young men's letters, the joyful flowering of creativity and their attempts to put their thoughts and ideas into words, seemed to reanimate some deep, forgotten part of Leonard. After he left the library in York, he kept reading and walking and thinking, wondering about the purpose of art, the importance of place, the fluidity of time, and Edward Radcliffe slipped further and deeper under his skin, so that one day he found himself back at the university, knocking on Professor Harris's door.

The long barn near the house came into sight and Dog raced ahead, straight through the cool flowing water of the Hafodsted Brook, anticipating the breakfast he assumed would be coming his way when they made it back. For an interloper, he had a lot of faith in the kindness of strangers. Not that they were strangers anymore.

Leonard's shirt was almost dry now, as he left the sunlit field and made his way over the fallen log. He crossed the grass to arrive at the dusty coach way that ran along the stone wall surrounding the front garden of the house. Hard to imagine that this must once have been a busy thoroughfare where carriages arrived and glossy horses hoofed impatiently, anxious for a drink and a rest after the long journey from London. Today it was just Leonard, Dog, and the hum of early morning bee song.

The iron gate was hanging off the latch, just as he'd left it, its powder-green paint faded to the color of lavender leaves. Tangled jasmine tendrils grew along the nubbly stone wall and over the arch, tiny pink and white flowers still falling in sprays, their fragrance heady.

Leonard pinched himself as he did each time he approached the house. Birchwood Manor, Edward Radcliffe's pride and joy. It really had been a piece of extraordinary good luck. Almost immediately after his doctoral candidacy had been accepted, Leonard had found himself, for once, the right man in the right place at precisely the right time: a woman named Lucy Radcliffe had approached the Art Historians' Association and announced that she was considering leaving them a significant gift. The house had come to Miss Radcliffe after her brother's death and she had lived in it ever since. Now, though, only a couple of years off eighty, she had decided to find herself a place with fewer staircases and corners, and wished to endow the house as part of a legacy in her brother's name. She envisaged it as a place where students pursuing the same interests might go to work; a locus for artists exploring notions of truth and beauty, of light and place and home. Her solicitor had suggested that before she commit to the plan, she give it a test run.

Leonard had read about the new Residential Scholarship in *Cherwell* and begun working immediately on an application. Some months after submitting his letter and résumé, he'd received word that the award was his: a handwritten reply arrived, inviting him to take up residence at Birchwood Manor for a three-month period during the summer of 1928. He'd flinched, briefly, at the cited lack of electricity and necessary reliance on candles and lamplight, but had shaken away thoughts of the gloomy chalk tunnels in France, telling himself that it would be summer and he would have no need to face the dark. He would live by nature's clock. *Ad occasum tendimus omnes,* he had read once on a grey, pitted gravestone in Dorset. *We are traveling each towards his sunset.*

Leonard had arrived with a predisposition to love the place, but the reality, in what he'd observed to be a very rare occurrence in life, was infinitely better than the imagining. He had approached that day from the village rather than the river, down the winding country lane that tapered as it neared the house and became the Thames Path, leaving the row of cottages on the village outskirts behind so that one was alone for a time amidst fields dotted with bored cows and curious calves.

The first sign of the house itself had been the wall, eight feet high, and the twin gables of the grey slate roof just visible beyond. Leonard noted with satisfaction the way the slates mimicked nature, just as Radcliffe had written in his letters to Holmes: tiny, neat rectangles at the peak, gaining size as they fell towards the guttering, just like feathers grading along the wing. Here, then, was Radcliffe's dignified bird, roosting in its own river bend.

He'd found the key in a small, deep hollow behind a loose stone in the wall, just as the letter of acceptance said he would. There'd been no one else around that day, and Leonard had wondered briefly who had put the silver key in this most particular hiding place.

When he turned the handle of the gate, he stood, transfixed, as it opened like the cover of a book onto a scene that seemed too perfect to be real. An effusive garden grew between the flagstone path and the house, foxgloves waving brightly in the breeze, daisies and violets chattering over the edges of the paving stones. The jasmine that covered the garden wall continued its spread across the front of the house, surrounding the multipaned windows to tangle with the voracious red flowers of the honeysuckle creeper as it clambered over the roof of the entry alcove. The garden was alive with insects and birds, which made the house seem still and silent, like a Sleeping Beauty house. Leonard had felt, as he took his first step onto the path, as if he were walking back through time; he could almost see Radcliffe and his friends with their paints and easels set up on the lawn beyond the blackberry bramble . . .

This morning, though, Leonard did not have time to picture ghosts from the past. When he reached the gate, there was a very real person standing by the front door, leaning casually against one of the posts supporting the alcove roof. She was wearing his shirt, he noticed, and little else, smoking a cigarette as she gazed towards the Japanese maple tree against the far wall.

She must have heard him, for she turned and her features rearranged themselves. A slight smile straightened her bow lips and she raised a neat hand in greeting.

He returned the gesture. "I thought you were due in London by midday."

"Trying to get rid of me?" She closed one eye as she drew on her cigarette. "Ah, that's right. You're expecting company. Your old lady friend. Want me out of the way before she comes? Wouldn't be surprised if that's one of the house rules: no guests overnight."

"She's not coming here. We're meeting at her place."

"Should I be jealous?" She laughed, but the sound made Leonard sad.

Kitty wasn't jealous, she was kidding; she kidded a lot. Kitty didn't love Leonard and he never let himself think that she did, not even on those nights when she clung to him so tightly that it hurt.

He gave her a kiss on the cheek as he reached the door and she returned it with a small unguarded smile. They'd known each other for a long time; since they were kids, she sixteen to his seventeen. The Easter Fair of 1913. She'd been wearing a pale blue dress, he remembered, and carrying a small satin purse. A ribbon had come loose from somewhere and fallen to the ground. She hadn't realized and no one else had seen; after a moment's hesitation Leonard had reached down to pick it up for her. They'd all been kids back then.

"Stay for breakfast?" he asked. "Dog has his heart set on eggs."

She followed him into the kitchen, which was dark after the glaring morning light outside. "Too nervous to eat. I'll have a cup of tea, though, just to see me through."

Leonard fetched the matches from the tin on the shelf behind the cooker.

"I don't know how you can stay here by yourself."

"It's peaceful." Leonard lit the tricky burner and scrambled some eggs while the kettle was boiling.

"Tell me again where it happened, Lenny?"

Leonard sighed. He wished he'd never told her about Frances Brown. He wasn't sure what had come over him, only that it was so unusual to be asked about his work, and being here at Birchwood Manor had made it all so much more real to him. Kitty had lit up when he mentioned the jewel thief who'd crept into the house one day and shot Radcliffe's fiancée dead.

"Murder?" she'd gasped. "How awful!" Now she said, "I had a look in the drawing room, but I couldn't see any sign."

Leonard had no desire to speak of murder or its markers again; not now, not with Kitty. "Could you pass me the butter?"

Kitty handed it to him. "Was there a big police investigation? How did the thief disappear without a trace? Wouldn't a diamond as rare as that have been recognized when it resurfaced?"

"You know as much as I do, Kit."

Truthfully, Leonard was curious about the Radcliffe Blue. It was right what Kitty had said: the gem within the pendant was so valuable and rare that it would have been recognized instantly by anyone in the jewelry trade; to keep its discovery and sale a secret would have taken an enormous amount of subterfuge. And gemstones didn't simply disappear: even if it had been cut down into smaller diamonds, they were somewhere. Moreover, popular wisdom had it that it was the theft of the Blue that led to the shooting of Radcliffe's fiancée, and the death of Fanny Brown that had in turn broken Radcliffe's spirit and tipped him into a long, spiraling decline, all of which interested Leonard very much, not least because he was beginning to develop doubts about the theory.

As Leonard cooked, Kitty fell to fiddling with the other items on the wooden table in the center of the room. After a time she disappeared, returning, bag in hand, as Leonard was loading everything onto the tray to take it outside.

They sat together at the iron table and chairs beneath the crab apple tree.

Kitty was dressed now in her own clothing. A smart suit that made her look older than she was. She had a job interview, a typist's position at an insurance agency in Holborn. She was going to walk to Lechlade, where she'd arranged for one of her father's friends to collect her in his motorcar.

She would have to move to London if she got the job. Leonard hoped that she did. It was her fourth interview in as many weeks.

"... not your old lady friend, perhaps, but there is someone else."

Leonard glanced up; Kitty's nerves had made her talkative and he hadn't been listening.

"I know you've met someone. You've been distracted—more so than usual. So . . . who is she, Lenny?"

"What's that?"

"A woman. I heard you last night, talking in your sleep."

Leonard felt his face grow hot.

"You're blushing."

"I'm not."

"You're being evasive."

"I'm busy, that's all."

"If you say so." Kitty took out her cigarette case and lit one. She exhaled smoke and then waved her right hand through it absently. Leonard noticed the fine gold ring she wore catching the light. "Do you ever wish you could see into the future?"

"No."

"Never?"

Dog nudged Leonard's knee and then dropped a ball at his feet. The last time he'd looked, Dog hadn't owned a ball. One of those kids by the river was going to be disappointed later.

Leonard picked it up and lobbed it into the distance, watching as Dog bounded through the wildflowers and bracken towards the bank of the Hafodsted Brook.

There was no one else—not in the way Kitty meant it—and yet Leonard couldn't deny that something strange was happening to him. In the month since he'd arrived at Birchwood he'd been having the most vivid dreams. They'd been intense from the outset, vibrant concoctions about painting and pigments, and nature and beauty, in which he'd woken with a split-second certainty that he'd glimpsed important answers to the deepest questions of life while he was gone. And then, at some point, the dreams had begun to change, and he'd started to see a woman in his sleep. Not just any woman but one of the models from Radcliffe's paintings. In his dreams she spoke to him;

she told him things as if he were a composite of Radcliffe and himself, things he couldn't always remember when he woke.

It was being here, of course, in the very place that Radcliffe had invested with so much of his own passion and creativity, a place that he had immortalized in his writings; it was only natural that Leonard, already of an obsessive bent, should find himself slipping beneath the skin of the other man, seeing the world through Radcliffe's eyes, particularly when he surrendered each night to sleep.

He would never tell Kitty, though: he could just imagine how that conversation would go: "Well, Kitty, it seems that I've fallen in love with a woman called Lily Millington. I've never met her or spoken with her. She is most likely dead, if not extraordinarily old; she may well be an international diamond thief. But I can't stop thinking about her and at night she comes to me when I'm sleeping." Leonard knew exactly what Kitty would say to that. She'd tell him that he wasn't dreaming, he was hallucinating, and that it was high time he stopped.

Kitty made no secret of her feelings about the pipe. It didn't matter how often Leonard explained that opium was the only way he knew to dull the nightly terrors: the cold, wet trenches, the smell and the noise, the ear-shattering explosions that pulled at a man's skull as he watched, helpless, while his friends, his brother, ran through the smoke and mud towards their end. If the woman from the painting pushed Tom out of the way at night . . . well, where was the harm in that?

Kitty was standing now, her bag over her shoulder, and Leonard felt bad suddenly, because she had come all this way, and even though he hadn't asked or expected her to do so, they were bonded, the two of them, and she was his responsibility.

"Shall I walk you into Lechlade?"

"Don't bother. I'll let you know how I get on."

"Are you sure?"

"Always."

"Well, all right, good lu—"

"Don't say it."

"Break a leg, then."

She smiled at him, but the smile didn't reach her eyes. They were filled with unsaid things.

He watched her as she started along the coach way towards the barn.

In a minute or two she would reach the lane that led through the village to the Lechlade Road. She would disappear from sight, until the next time.

He told himself to do it now, for both of their sakes, to break it off once and for all. He told himself that he would be setting her free; it was wrong what he was doing, holding on to her like this. "Kitty?"

She turned back, an eyebrow lifted in response.

Leonard swallowed his courage. "You'll be great," he said. "Break two legs."

CHAPTER FIFTEEN

THE meeting that afternoon with Leonard's "old lady friend" had been arranged for four o'clock, or "teatime," as she'd insisted on calling it. Her manner had smacked of a privileged childhood in which "teatime" meant cucumber sandwiches and Battenberg cake and was as natural a marker of daily life as sunrise and sunset.

After spending the rest of the day poring over his notes to ensure that he had a clear list of questions to take with him, Leonard set off well ahead of time, partly because he was excited and partly because he wanted to walk the long way past the village churchyard at the end of the lane.

Leonard had stumbled upon the headstone quite by accident a couple of weeks before. He'd been returning from a long walk across country, and Dog had raced ahead as they neared the village road, ducking beneath a gap at the bottom of the picket fence to nose about in the ivy that grew like ocean spray between the graves. Leonard had followed him into the churchyard, drawn by the modest beauty of the stone building nestled amidst greenery.

There was a smaller creeper-clad structure on the southern edge with a marble bench beneath it, and Leonard had sat there for a time contemplating the pleasing form of the twelfth-century church as he waited for Dog to finish exploring. The headstone, as chance would have it, had been right in front of him, and the familiar name—Edward Julius Radcliffe—chiseled in a plain elegant font, had leapt out.

Leonard had taken to stopping in at some point most days. As far as resting places went, he had decided, it was a good one. Quiet and beautiful, close to the home Radcliffe had once loved. There would be enormous solace in that.

He glanced at his wristwatch now as the churchyard came into view. It was only three thirty; still plenty of time to duck inside for a few minutes before circling back and making his way to the cottage on the other side of the village. "The village" was an overstatement, after all: Birchwood was little more than three quiet streets diverging from a triangular green.

He tracked the familiar path to Radcliffe's grave and sat on the marble bench. Dog, who had followed him, sniffed at the few spots around the edge of the grave where the ground was slightly disturbed. Finding nothing to interest him further, he cocked his head in the direction of a noise in the underbrush before darting off to investigate.

On Radcliffe's headstone, in smaller text beneath his name, was written, *Here lieth one who sought truth and light and saw beauty in all things, 1842-1882.* Leonard found himself staring as he often did at the dash between the dates. Within that lichen-laced mark there lay the entire life of a man: his childhood, his loves, his losses and fears, all reduced to a single chiseled line on a piece of stone in a quiet churchyard at the end of a country lane. Leonard wasn't sure whether the thought was comforting or distressing; his opinion changed, depending on the day.

Tom had been buried in a cemetery in France, near a village he had never set foot in alive. Leonard had seen the letter sent to their mother and father and had marveled at the way Tom's commanding officer made things sound so brave and honorable, death in duty a terrible but noble sacrifice. He supposed it was all down to practice. Lord knew, those officers had written an awful lot of letters. They'd become expert at ensuring they betrayed not a hint of the chaos or horror, and certainly no suggestion of waste. Incredible how little official waste there was in war, how few mistakes.

Leonard had read the letter twice when his mother showed it to him. She'd drawn great comfort from it, but beneath its smooth words of gentle consolation, Leonard could hear the ill choir shouting out in pain and fear, calling for their mothers, their boyhoods, their homes. There was nowhere farther from home than the battlefield, and no more wretched homesickness than that of the soldier facing death.

Leonard had been sitting in this very spot the other day, thinking of Tom and Kitty and Edward Radcliffe, when he first met his "old lady friend." It was late in the afternoon and he'd noticed her at once because she'd been the only other person in the churchyard. She'd arrived with a small posy of flowers and had brought them over to lay on Radcliffe's grave. Leonard had watched with interest, wondering whether she'd known the man himself or was simply an admirer of his art.

Her face was lined with age, and her hair, white and very fine, was pulled back into a bun at the nape of her neck. She was dressed in the sort of clothing one might wear to go on an African safari. She'd stood very still, leaning on a delicate silver-handled cane, her shoulders hunched in silent communion. There'd been a reverence to her posture, which seemed to Leonard to go beyond that of an admirer. After a time, when she reached down to shake loose a weed from the stones around the grave, Leonard had known for certain that she must be a relative or friend.

The opportunity to speak with someone who had known Edward Radcliffe was tantalizing. Fresh material was the research student's holy grail, particularly in the case of historical subjects, where the chance of stumbling across anything new was generally next to nil.

He had approached carefully so as not to startle her, and when he was close enough to be heard said, "Good morning."

She'd looked up swiftly, her movements and manner that of a wary bird.

"I didn't mean to disturb you," he went on quickly. "I'm new to the village. I'm staying in the house on the river bend."

She stood straighter and appraised him over the top of her fine wire spectacles. "Tell me, Mr. Gilbert, what do you think of Birchwood Manor?"

It was Leonard's turn to be surprised: she knew his name. But then, the village was small, and he had it on good authority that news traveled quickly in such circumstances. He told her he thought very highly of Birchwood Manor; that he'd read a lot about it before he arrived, but the reality had far surpassed his imaginings.

She listened, blinking occasionally, but otherwise giving no indication that she approved or disapproved of what he was saying. When he stopped speaking she said only "It was a school once, did you know? A school for girls."

"I'd heard that."

"It was a terrible shame what happened. It was going to be revolutionary. A new way of educating young women. Edward used to say that education was the key to salvation."

"Edward Radcliffe?"

"Who else?"

"You knew him."

Her eyes narrowed slightly. "I did."

It took every ounce of restraint Leonard could rally to sound casual. "I'm a research student up at Oxford. I'm working on a thesis about Radcliffe and this village, the house, and his art. I wonder whether you'd mind speaking with me?"

"I had thought that's what we were doing, Mr. Gilbert."

"We are, of course—"

"You meant that you would like to speak with me about Edward, to *interview* me."

"I've had to rely to this point largely on letters from the archives and accounts written by his friends, you see, people like Thurston Holmes—"

"Pah!'

Leonard flinched at her vehemence.

"Of all the self-aggrandizing weasels! I shouldn't rely upon a word that fell from his pen."

Her attention had been caught by another weed and she was loosening it now with the end of her cane. "I don't like talking," she said between stabs. "I don't like it at all." She reached to pluck the weed from the rubble, shaking it fiercely to rid the roots of dirt before throwing it into the bushes. "I can see, though, Mr. Gilbert, that I am going to have to speak with you, lest you publish more lies. There have been enough of those over the years."

Leonard had started to thank her, but she'd waved her hand with imperious impatience.

"Yes, yes, you may save all that for later. I am doing this against my better judgment, but I shall see you at teatime on Thursday." She gave him her address, and Leonard was on the cusp of saying good-bye when he realized that he hadn't even asked her name. "Why, Mr. Gilbert," she said, with a frown, "whatever is the matter with you? My name is Lucy, of course; Lucy Radcliffe."

He should have guessed. Lucy Radcliffe—the younger sister who had inherited her brother's beloved house; who had loved him too well to allow it to be sold to someone who might not care for it as he had done; Leonard's landlady. Leonard had gone home directly after their meeting, bursting through the front door into the late afternoon dim of the house, heading straight to the mahogany desk in the room with the mulberry fruit-and-leaf wallpaper, across which he'd spread his research. He'd had to sort through hundreds of pages of handwritten notes, quotes he'd jotted down in libraries and private houses over the years, from letters and journals; ideas he'd scribbled and then circled, attached to diagrams and arrows.

He found what he was looking for late that night when the lantern had burned for long enough that the room smelled like kerosene. Amongst notes he'd taken from a collection of documents kept in the private collection of a family in Shropshire was a series of letters exchanged between Edward and his youngest sister while he was at boarding school. They had come to rest in this place, in a trove of other old family correspondence, through a series of marital twists and turns stemming from the middle Radcliffe child, Clare.

The letters had seemed unimportant to Leonard at the time; they hadn't concerned the house or Radcliffe's art; they were personal letters between siblings, one nine years older than the other; he'd only copied out their contents because the family had intimated that his visit was an inconvenience and he wouldn't be permitted a second look at their papers. But as he reread the exchanges—funny anecdotes, enchanting and frightening fairy stories, childish gossip about family members—and viewed them in the context of the old woman he'd just met, unsteady on her feet and yet still walking across the village to lay fresh flowers on her brother's grave fifty years after his death, he saw another side to Edward Radcliffe.

All of this time, Leonard had been focused on Radcliffe the artist, the spirited thinker, the writer of the manifesto. But the long, engaging letters of a boy who was miserable at school to an earnest little sister who begged—rather precociously for a five-year-old, it seemed to Leonard—for books about "how the stars were born" and "whether it is possible to travel through time," had added a new aspect to the man. Furthermore, they'd hinted at a mystery Leonard had thus far been unable to resolve. For both Lucy and Edward referred on more than one occasion to "the Night of the Following"—always capitalized—and "the house with the light," the context making it clear that they were speaking about something that had happened to Edward.

At the archives in York, Leonard had puzzled over the letter Edward wrote to Thurston Holmes in 1861 announcing his purchase of Birchwood Manor and admitting that he was no stranger to the house; now he was beginning to think that the two sets of correspondence were linked. Both made allusions to a mysterious event from the past, and Leonard had a feeling that whatever had happened on "the Night of the Following" had led to Radcliffe's obsession with Birchwood Manor. It was one of the foremost questions on the list of those he intended to ask Lucy at their meeting.

Leonard stood and lit a cigarette. The ground was still rough from where she'd plucked at the weeds the other day, and he smoothed over the spot with his foot. As he returned the lighter to his pocket, his fingertips grazed the cool edge of Tom's lucky tuppence. He had never stood at the end of his own brother's grave. He hadn't seen the point; he knew Tom wasn't there. Where was he? Leonard wondered. Where had they all gone? It seemed impossible that it could all just end like that. Impossible that so many young men's hopes and dreams and bodies could be buried in the earth and the earth remain unchanged. Such an almighty transfer of energy and matter must surely have affected the world's balance at an essential—an elemental—level: all of those people who had once been, suddenly gone.

A pair of birds swooped from one of the boughs of an enormous oak to perch at the top of the steeple, and Leonard whistled for Dog. They left the churchyard together, circling back towards the pitted stone plinth known locally as "the crossroads."

The triangle-shaped green was just beyond, a large oak at its center and an elegant two-story pub called the Swan on one of the corners opposite. A woman was out on the pavement sweeping around a bench beneath the window. She lifted a hand to wave at Leonard and he returned the gesture. He took the narrowest of the three roads, passing the memorial hall building to arrive at a row of terraced cottages. Lucy Radcliffe had told him number six, which was the furthest one along.

The cottages were of pale honey-cultured stone. Each had a central gable with chimneys on either side and pretty bargeboards rising to its peak. Matching sash windows were set into each of the two levels, and an entrance portico with a roof pitched to match the gable stood above the front door. The door itself was painted a pale lilac blue. Unlike the front gardens of the other cottages, which were overflowing with a perfect chaos of English summer flowers, number six contained a number of notably more exotic species: a bird-of-paradise, and others that Leonard couldn't name and knew he hadn't seen before.

A cat meowed from a patch of sunlit gravel stones before standing and arching and pouring itself through the door, which Leonard saw now was on the latch. She was expecting him.

He felt unusually nervous and didn't cross the road at once. He allowed himself another cigarette as he went over the list of talking points he'd prepared. He reminded himself not to set his expectations too high; that there was no guarantee that she would hold the answers he sought; that even if she did, there was no certainty she would share them with him. She had been very clear on that front, saying to him as she left the churchyard, "I have two conditions, Mr. Gilbert. The first is that I will speak only if you promise strict anonymity: I have no interest in seeing my name in print. The second is that I can give you one hour, but no more."

With a deep breath, Leonard unlatched the rusted metal gate and closed it carefully behind him.

He didn't feel comfortable simply pushing the door open and arriving inside with no announcement, so he knocked lightly and called, "Hello? Miss Radcliffe?"

"Yes?" came a distracted voice from inside.

"It's Leonard Gilbert. From Birchwood Manor."

"Well, for goodness' sake, Leonard Gilbert from Birchwood Manor. Come in, won't you?"

Chapter Sixteen

THE cottage was pleasantly dark inside, and it took a moment for his gaze to arrive at Lucy Radcliffe in the midst of all her treasures. She had been expecting him only a minute before, but clearly had more important things to do than to sit in readiness. She was engrossed in her reading, posed as still as marble in a mustard-cultured armchair, a tiny figure in profile to him, a journal in her hand, her back curved as she peered through a magnifying glass at the folded page. A lamp was positioned on a small half-moon table beside her, and the light it cast was yellow and diffuse. Underneath it, a teapot sat beside two cups.

"Miss Radcliffe," he said.

"Whatever do you think, Mr. Gilbert?" She did not look up from her journal. "It appears that the universe is expanding."

"Is it?" Leonard took off his hat. He couldn't see a hook on which to hang it, so he held it in two hands before him.

"It says so right here. A Belgian man—a priest, if you can believe it—has proposed that the universe is expanding at a constant rate. Unless my French is rusty, and I don't think that it is, he's even calculated the rate of expansion. You know what this means, of course."

"I'm not sure that I do."

Her cane was leaning against the table beside her, and Lucy began now to pace across the worn Persian rug. "If one is to accept that the universe is expanding at a constant rate, then it follows that it has been doing so since its beginning. Since its *beginning*, Mr. Gilbert." She stood very still, her head capped neatly by her white hair. "A beginning. Not Adam and Eve, I don't mean that. I mean a *moment*, some

237

sort of *action* or *event* that started it all off. Space and time, matter and energy. A single atom that somehow"—she flexed open the fingers of one hand—"exploded. Good God." Her bright, quick eyes met his. "We might be on the verge of understanding the very birth of the stars, Mr. Gilbert—the *stars*."

The only natural light in the room came from the small front window of the house, and it graced the surface of her face, which was a study in wonder. It was beautiful and engaged, and Leonard could see in it the young girl she must once have been.

Before his very eyes, though, her expression faltered. The light drained from her features and her skin appeared to sag. She wore no powder, and her weathered complexion was that of a woman who had spent her life outdoors, the lines on her face telling a hundred stories. "Oh, but it is the worst thing about getting old, Mr. Gilbert. Time. There isn't enough of it left. There is simply too much to know and too few hours in which to know it. Some nights that terrible fact keeps me from sleeping—I close my eyes and hear my pulse ticking away the seconds—and so, I sit up in my bed and I read instead. I read and write notes and memorize, and then I start on something new. And yet it is in vain, for my time will end. What wonders am I going to miss?"

Leonard didn't have much in the way of consolation to offer. It wasn't that he didn't understand her regrets, only that he'd seen too many die who hadn't had a quarter of the time that she'd been given.

"I know what you are thinking, Mr. Gilbert. You needn't say it. I sound like a selfish and irascible old woman, and by God I am. But I have been this way for too long now to think of changing. And you are not here to discuss my regrets. Come, sit down. The tea is brewed, and I'm sure I have a scone or two tucked away somewhere."

Leonard opened by reiterating his gratitude that she had selected his application for the residency at Birchwood Manor, telling her how much he loved staying in the house, and how gratifying it was to have the opportunity to get to know a place about which he had read and thought so much. "It's helping enormously with my work," he said. "I feel close to your brother at Birchwood Manor."

"I understand the proposition, Mr. Gilbert; many wouldn't, but I do. And I agree. My brother is a part of the house in a way that most people cannot appreciate. The house was a part of him, too: he fell in love with Birchwood Manor long before he bought it."

"I'd gathered as much. He wrote a letter to Thurston Holmes in which he told him about the purchase and intimated that he'd known the house for some time. He didn't go into detail, though, as to how."

"No, well, he wouldn't have. Thurston Holmes was a talented enough technician, but unfortunately for all concerned he was a vain-glorious prig. Tea?"

"Please."

As tea gurgled from the spout she continued: "Thurston had none of the sensitivity required of a true artist; Edward would never have willingly told him about the night that he discovered Birchwood Manor."

"But he told you?"

She regarded him, her head tilted in a way that brought to mind a teacher Leonard hadn't thought of in years; rather, the parakeet that the teacher had kept in a golden cage in his classroom. "You have a brother, Mr. Gilbert. I remember reading it in your application."

"I had a brother. Tom. He died in the war."

"I'm sorry to hear that. You were close, I think."

"We were."

"Edward was nine years older than I, but circumstances had thrown us together when we were young. My earliest and fondest memories are of Edward telling me stories. If you are to understand my brother, Mr. Gilbert, you must stop seeing him as a painter and start seeing him instead as a storyteller. It was his greatest gift. He knew how to communicate, how to make people feel and see and be-lieve. The medium in which he chose to express himself was irrel-evant. It is no easy feat to invent a whole world, but Edward could do that. A setting, a narrative, characters who live and breathe—he was able to make the story come to life in someone else's mind. Have you ever considered the logistics of that, Mr. Gilbert? The transfer of an *idea*? And, of course, a story is not a single idea; it is thousands of ideas, all working together in concert."

What she said was true. As an artist, Edward Radcliffe could transport people, so that they were no longer simply spectators of his work but participants, coconspirators in the realization of the world that he sought to create.

"I have an excellent memory, Mr. Gilbert. Too good, it has sometimes seemed to me. I can remember being a tiny thing; my father was still alive, and we all lived in the house in Hampstead. My sister Clare was five years older than I was and used to grow impatient playing with me, but Edward would keep us both spellbound with his tales. They were often terrifying, but always electric. Some of the happiest moments of my life were spent listening as he wove his story. But one day everything changed in our household and a terrible darkness descended."

Leonard had read about the death of Edward's father, killed when he was run down by a carriage in Mayfair late one night. "How old were you when your father died?"

"My father?" She frowned, but the gesture was soon swept aside by a delighted laugh. "Oh, Mr. Gilbert, dear me, no. I barely remember the man. No, no, I meant when Edward was sent away to boarding school. It was dreadful for all of us, but nightmarish for him. He was twelve years old and hated every minute of it. For a boy whose imagination worked as Edward's did, whose temper was unguarded and whose passions were dazzling, who didn't enjoy cricket or rugby or rowing but preferred to bury himself in ancient books about alchemy and astronomy, a school like Lechmere was a poor fit."

Leonard understood. He'd attended a similar school when he was a boy. He was still trying to slip free of its yoke. "Was it while he was at school that Edward came across the house?"

"Mr. Gilbert, really. Lechmere was miles away, up near the Lakes, I hardly think that Edward would have had the opportunity to stumble upon Birchwood Manor whilst at school. No, it was when he was fourteen years old and home for the holidays. Our parents traveled frequently, so that summer, home was the estate belonging to my grandparents. Beechworth, it's called; not far from here. Our grandfather saw too much of our mother in Edward—a wildness of spirit, a disregard for convention—and decided it was his duty to beat it out of him so that Edward might be forced to take on the 'proper' Radcliffe form. My brother reacted by doing everything that he could to antagonize the old man. He used to steal his whisky and took to climbing from the window after we'd been sent to bed, taking long walks across the night-darkened fields, returning with esoteric signs and symbols drawn upon his body in charcoal, with mud on his face and clothing, with stones and sticks and river weed in his pockets. He was quite ungovernable." Her face was full of admiration, before a grim cast replaced it. "One night, though, he did not come home. I woke and his bed was empty, and when he finally reappeared, he was pale and very quiet. It took him days to tell me what had happened."

Leonard was alert with anticipation. After all of the hints as to an event in Radcliffe's past that had driven his obsession with Birchwood Manor, it seemed that answers were finally in reach.

Lucy was watching him closely and he suspected that not much passed beneath her notice. She took a long sip of tea. "Do you believe in ghosts, Mr. Gilbert?"

Leonard flinched at the unexpected question. "I believe that a person can find himself haunted."

Her eyes were still fixed upon him and, at length, she smiled. Leonard had the disquieting sense that she could see inside his soul. "Yes," she said, "just so. A person can be haunted. And my brother certainly was. Something followed him home that night and he could never shake it off."

The Night of the Following. This, then, was what the young Lucy and Edward had been referencing in their letters. "What sort of something?"

"Edward headed out that night with the intention of raising a ghost. He had found a book in the school library, an ancient book, filled with old ideas and incantations. Being Edward, he couldn't wait to put them into practice, but in the end he didn't get a chance to try. Something happened to him in the woods. He read everything that he could afterwards and came to the conclusion that he had been followed by the Black Dog."

"A spirit?" Vague memories returned to Leonard from childhood: sinister creatures of folklore said to be found in ancient places where the two worlds met. "Like in *The Hound of the Baskervilles*?"

"The 'what' is not important, Mr. Gilbert. All that matters is that he feared for his life, and as he fled across the fields he saw a light in the attic window of a house on the horizon. He ran towards it and found the front door open to him and a fire in the hearth."

"And that house was Birchwood Manor," Leonard said softly.

"Edward said that as soon as he set foot inside he knew that he was safe."

"The people who lived in the house took care of him?"

"Mr. Gilbert, you are missing the point entirely."

"But I thought—"

"I take it your research has included the history of Birchwood Manor?"

Leonard confessed that it had not; that it hadn't occurred to him that the house's past, prior to Edward's purchase of it, was remotely relevant.

Lucy lifted her eyebrows with the same mix of disappointment and surprise that he might have expected had he handed her his notebook and asked her to write his thesis for him. "The house as you see it today was built in the sixteenth century. It was designed by a man called Nicholas Owen with the intention of providing safety to Catholic priests. But there was a reason that they chose to build in that spot, Mr. Gilbert, for the land on which Birchwood Manor stands is of course much older than the house. It has its own history. Has nobody told you yet about the Eldritch Children?"

Movement at the corner of his vision made Leonard startle. He glanced into the darkest recess of the room and saw that the cat who had slipped through the door earlier was stretching now, shiny eyes turned on Leonard.

"It is an old local folktale, Mr. Gilbert, about three fairy children who many years ago crossed between the worlds. They emerged from the woods one day into the fields where the local farmers were burning stubble and were taken in by an elderly couple. From the start, there was something uncanny about them. They spoke a strange language, they left no footprints behind them when they walked, and it is said that at times their skin appeared almost to glow.

"They were tolerated at first, but as things began to go wrong in the village—a failed crop, the stillbirth of a baby, the drowning of the butcher's son—people started to look to the three strange children in their midst. Eventually, when the well ran dry, the villagers demanded that the couple hand them over. They refused and were banished from the village.

"The family set up instead in a small stone croft by the river, and for a time they lived in peace. But when an illness came to the village, a mob was formed, and one night, with torches lit, they marched upon the croft. The couple and the children clung together, surrounded, their fates seemingly inevitable. But just as the villagers began to close in, there came the eerie sound of a horn on the wind and a woman appeared from nowhere, a magnificent woman with long, gleaming hair and luminous skin.

"The Fairy Queen had come to claim her children. And when she did, she cast a protection spell upon the house and land of the old couple in gratitude to them for protecting the prince and princesses of fairyland.

"The bend of the river upon which Birchwood Manor now stands has been recognized ever since amongst locals as a place of safety. It is even said that there are those who can still see the fairy enchantment—that it appears to a lucky few as a light, high up in the attic window of the house."

Leonard wanted to ask whether Lucy, with all of her evident learning and scientific reason, really believed that it was true—

whether she thought that Edward had seen a light in the attic that night and that the house had protected him—but no matter how he rearranged the words in his mind, the question seemed impolite and certainly impolitic. Thankfully, Lucy seemed to have anticipated his line of thinking.

"I believe in science, Mr. Gilbert. But one of my first loves was natural history. The earth is ancient and it is vast and there is much that we do not yet comprehend. I refuse to accept that science and magic are opposed; they are both valid attempts to understand the way that our world works. And I have seen things, Mr. Gilbert; I have dug things up from the earth and held them in my hand and felt things that our science cannot yet explain. The story of the Eldritch Children is a folktale. I have no more reason to believe it than I do to believe that Arthur was a king who pulled a sword from a stone or that dragons once soared across our skies. But my brother told me that he saw a light that night in the attic of Birchwood Manor and that the house protected him, and I know he spoke the truth."

Leonard did not doubt her faith, but he also understood psychology; the abiding sovereignty of the elder sibling. When he and Tom were younger, Leonard had been aware that no matter how often he tricked his brother or told him an untruth, Tom would trust him again the next time. Lucy had been much younger than Edward. She had adored him and he had disappeared from her life. She might be seventy-nine and impregnable now, but where Edward was concerned, a part of her would always be that young girl.

Nonetheless, Leonard jotted down a note about the Eldritch Children. Frankly, the veracity of the story was of secondary importance as far as Leonard's dissertation was concerned. It was enough that Radcliffe had been haunted by an idea, that he believed the house to possess certain properties, and fascinating to be able to tie them to a particular local folktale. Aware that time was ticking, he drew a line under the note and moved on to the next subject. "I wonder, Miss Radcliffe, if we could speak now about the summer of 1862."

She took up a walnut cigarette box from the table and offered one to Leonard. He accepted and waited while she deftly teased a flame from the silver lighter. She lit her own and exhaled, waving her hand through the smoke. "I expect you would like me to say that the summer of 1862 feels like yesterday. Well, it doesn't. It feels like a different country. Strange, isn't it. When I think of Edward telling me stories as a child, I can smell the moist muddy air of our attic in Hampstead. But to think back to that summer is like looking through a telescope at a distant star: I see myself from the outside only."

"You were here then? At Birchwood Manor?"

"I was thirteen years old. My mother was going to the Continent to stay with friends and had proposed to send me to my grandparents at Beechworth. Edward invited me to accompany him and the others instead. I was excited to be within their orbit."

"What was it like?"

"It was summer, and hot, and the first couple of weeks were spent as you might imagine: boating, picnicking, painting, and walking. They all sat up late into the night telling stories and arguing over the scientific, artistic, and philosophical theories of the day."

"But then?"

Her gaze met his directly. "As you know, Mr. Gilbert, it all fell apart."

"Edward's fiancée was killed."

"Fanny Brown, yes."

"And the intruder stole the Radcliffe Blue pendant."

"You've done your research."

"There were a number of articles in the Newspaper Library."

"I should expect so. Fanny Brown's death was widely reported."

"And yet, from what I saw, it appeared that there was even more speculation as to the whereabouts of the Radcliffe Blue diamond."

"Poor Fanny. She was a nice enough girl, but prone to being overshadowed—in life and, as you point out, in death. I hope you are not asking me to account for the obsessions of the tabloid-reading public, Mr. Gilbert?"

"Not at all. In fact, I'm far more interested in the reactions of the people who knew Frances Brown. While the rest of the world appears to have been fascinated by the events, I noticed that the correspondence of Edward's friends and colleagues, of Thurston Holmes, and Felix and Adele Bernard, is all but silent on the matter. It's almost as if it didn't happen."

Did he imagine the slight flicker of recognition in her eyes?

"It was a terrible day, Mr. Gilbert. I shouldn't think it would come as a surprise that those unfortunate enough to bear witness would choose not to dwell on it afterwards."

She regarded him steadily over her cigarette. What she said was reasonable, but Leonard couldn't shake the feeling that there was more to it than that. There was something *unnatural* about their reticence. It wasn't simply an absence of conversation about the day in question; to read the letters of the others immediately afterwards, it was as if Edward Radcliffe and Frances Brown had never existed. And it wasn't until after Edward Radcliffe's death that his ghost crept back into the correspondence of Thurston Holmes.

There was something he was missing about the friendship between the two of them, and not just after Frances Brown was killed. Leonard thought back to his visit to the Holmes archive in York: he had noticed an earlier change in tenor in the letters between the two young men. The long, unrestrained conversations discussing art, philosophy, and life that they had exchanged frequently after they met in 1858 had dried up in early 1862, becoming brief, perfunctory, and formal. Something had happened between them, he was sure of it.

Lucy frowned when he asked that very question, before saying, "I do remember Edward coming home hot under the collar one morning—it must have been around then, because it was before his second exhibition. His knuckles were grazed and his shirt was torn."

"He'd been in a fight?"

"He didn't tell me the details, but I saw Thurston Holmes later that week and he had a big purple bruise around his eye."

"What did they fight over?"

"I don't know, and I didn't give it much thought at the time. They were often at odds, even when they were good friends. Thurston was competitive and vain. A bull, a peacock, a rooster—take your pick. He could be charming and generous, and as the older of the two he introduced Edward to a number of influential people. He was proud of Edward, I think. He enjoyed the kudos of having such a dynamic, talented young friend. They attracted a lot of attention when they were together, the way they dressed, their loose shirts and scarfs, their wild hair and free attitudes. But Thurston Holmes was the sort of person who needed to be the friend on top. He did not take it well when Edward began to receive more acclaim than he did. Have you ever noticed, Mr. Gilbert, that it's friends like that who have a habit of becoming one's most fiercely committed adversaries?"

Leonard made a note of this insight into the friendship between the two artists. The firmness with which it was imparted explained his invitation here today. Lucy had told him in the graveyard that Holmes's accounts of Edward could not be trusted; that she would have to set the record straight "lest you publish more lies." And here it was: she had wanted Leonard to know that Holmes had an agenda, that he was a jealous friend eager to elevate himself.

But Leonard wasn't convinced that professional envy alone explained the falling-out between the two men. Radcliffe's star was on the rise during 1861 and 1862, but the exhibition that made his name hadn't taken place until April of the latter year, and correspondence between the men had cooled much earlier than that. Leonard suspected that there had been something else at play and he had a good idea of what it might have been. "Edward started using a new model in mid-1861, didn't he?" He feigned nonchalance, but even as he broached the subject, an echo of his recent dreams assailed him and he felt his face warm; he couldn't meet Lucy's gaze, pretending to focus on his notes instead. "Lily Millington? I think that was her name?"

Despite his best intentions, he had betrayed himself, for there was a suspicious note to Lucy's voice when she said, "Why do you ask?"

"From what I've read, the Magenta Brotherhood were a tight-knit group. They shared their ideas and influences, their secrets, their houses, even their models. Both Edward and Thurston Holmes painted Diana Barker, and all three of them painted Adele Winterson. But Lily Millington appears only in Edward's paintings. It struck me as unusual and I wondered why. I could only think of two possibilities: either the others hadn't wished to paint her, or Edward had objected to sharing."

Taking her cane, Lucy stood and slowly crossed the rug to stop near the window overlooking the street. Light was still filtering in through the glass, but it had shifted since Leonard arrived, and her profile was now in shadow. "That intersection up there where the lanes meet is called the crossroads. A medieval cross used to stand at its center. It was lost during the Reformation, when Elizabeth's men stormed through the region, destroying the trappings of Catholicism, the churches, and the religious art—the priests, too, when they could catch them. Now only the base of the cross remains. And its name, of course, passed through time. It is remarkable, is it not, Mr. Gilbert, that a name, a simple word, is all that remains of such traumatic historical events. Things that happened right here to real people at another point in time. I think about the past every time I walk through the crossroads. I think about the church, and the priests who hid, and the soldiers who came to find and kill them. I think about guilt and forgiveness. Do you ever concern yourself with such matters?"

She was being evasive, avoiding his question about Lily Millington. Yet, not for the first time, Leonard had the sneaking sense that she could somehow see inside him. "Sometimes," he said. The word stuck in his throat and he coughed to clear it.

"Yes, I should imagine one would, having been to war. I don't usually go in for advice giving, Mr. Gilbert, but I have lived a long time and I have learned that one must forgive oneself the past or else the journey into the future becomes unbearable."

Leonard felt a wash of shame-tinged surprise. It was a lucky guess, that's all. She didn't know his past. As she'd said, most men who had been to war had seen and done things that they would just as soon forget. He refused to let himself be thrown. Nonetheless, his voice was shakier than he'd have liked when he continued: "I have an extract from a letter that Edward wrote to your cousin Hamish in August 1861. I wonder if I could read it to you, Miss Radcliffe?"

She did not turn back towards him, but neither did she try to stop him. Leonard began to read: "*I have found her, a woman of such striking beauty that my hand aches to put pen to paper. I long to capture all that I see and feel when I look upon her face, and yet at once I cannot bear to start. For how can I hope to do her justice? There is a nobility to her bearing, not of birth perhaps but of nature. She does not primp and appeal; indeed, it is her very openness, the way she has of meeting one's attention rather than averting her eyes. There is a sureness—a pride even—to the set of her lips, that is breathtaking. She is breathtaking. Now that I have seen her, anyone else would be an imposter. She is truth; truth is beauty; and beauty is divine.*"

"Yes," she said softly. "That's Edward. I would know his voice anywhere." She turned and came slowly back to her chair to sit down, and Leonard was surprised to notice a sheen of moisture on her cheeks. "I remember the night that he met her. He had been at the theater and he came home in a daze. We all knew something was afoot. He told us everything in a rush, and then he went straight to his studio in the back corner of our mother's garden and started to sketch. He worked compulsively and did not stop for days. He didn't eat or sleep or speak to anyone. He filled pages and pages of his notebook with her image."

"He was in love with her."

"I was going to tell you, Mr. Gilbert, that my brother was an obsessive person. That he always behaved that way when he met a new model, or discovered a new technique, or had a new idea. And it would have been true." Her hand fluttered onto the armrest of the chair. "And false. For it was different with Lily Millington, and everyone could see it from the start. I could see it, Thurston saw it, and poor old Fanny Brown saw it, too. Edward loved Lily Millington with a madness that boded ill, and that summer, here at Birchwood, it all came to a head."

"So, Lily Millington *was* here. I thought she must have been, but there's no mention of her. Not in anyone's letters or diaries, and not in the newspapers either."

"Have you read the police reports, Mr. Gilbert? I expect they keep such things."

"Are you saying that they'll tell a different story?"

"Mr. Gilbert, my dear man, you were a soldier in the Great War. You know better than most that the account served up by the papers for public consumption often bears little relation to the truth. Fanny's father was a powerful man. He was very keen that there should be no suggestion in the press that his daughter had been supplanted in Edward's affections."

Connections were lighting up in Leonard's mind. Edward had loved Lily Millington. It wasn't the death of Frances Brown that broke his heart and sent him spiraling out of control, it was the loss of Lily. But what had happened to her? "If she and Edward were in love, why did he end up alone? How did he lose her?" Lucy had suggested that the police reports would refer specifically to Lily Millington's presence at Birchwood Manor on the night of the robbery and murder . . . Suddenly Leonard realized: "Lily Millington was involved in the robbery. She betrayed him—that's what drove Edward mad."

A dark look came upon Lucy's face and Leonard was immediately doused with regret. In the moment of comprehension, he had forgotten that it was her brother they were discussing. He had sounded almost gleeful. "Miss Radcliffe, I'm sorry," he said, "how insensitive of me."

"Not at all. But I am growing tired, Mr. Gilbert."

Leonard glanced at the clock and saw, with a sinking heart, that he had overstayed his invitation. "Of course. I won't take up any more of your time. I'll seek out the police reports as you suggest. I'm certain they'll shed further light upon the subject."

"There are very few certainties in this world, Mr. Gilbert, but I will tell you something I know: the truth depends on who it is that's telling the story."

Chapter Seventeen

As he strolled back through the village, along the quiet road with its ragged verge, Leonard pondered Lucy Radcliffe. He was confident that he had never met a woman—another person—quite like her. It was clear that she was very bright. Age had not dimmed her fascination for all areas of intellectual inquiry; her interests were wide and varied; her ability to retain and process complex information evidently remarkable. She had been wry, too, and self-critical. He had liked her.

He had also felt sorry for her. He had asked, as he was packing up to leave, about her school, and a look of deep regret had come upon her face. "I had such high hopes, Mr. Gilbert, but it was too soon. I knew that compromise would be necessary; that in order to attract sufficient students I would have to concede to certain parental expectations. I had thought I would be able to honor my promise to shape the girls into 'young ladies' whilst also instilling in them a love of learning." She had smiled. "I don't think I flatter myself that there were some whom I started along a road they might otherwise not have found. But there was rather more singing and sewing than I'd envisaged."

As she spoke about the school and its students, it had occurred to Leonard that the house bore very little sign of them. All indication that schoolgirls had once filed through the halls en route to class had been erased, and one would be hard-pressed to imagine Birchwood Manor anything other than a nineteenth-century artist's country home. In fact, with all of Radcliffe's furnishings and fittings still in place, entering the house felt to Leonard like stepping back in time.

When he'd said as much to Lucy, she mused in reply, "A logical impossibility, of course, time travel: How can one ever be in two places 'at the same time'? The phrase itself is a paradox. In this universe, at any rate . . ." Not wanting to be drawn into another scientific debate, Leonard had asked how long the school had been closed. "Oh, decades now. It died with the Queen, in 1901. There was an accident, a most unfortunate event, a couple of years before. A young girl drowned in the river during a school picnic, and one by one the other students were withdrawn. With no new enrollments to take their place, well . . . one had little choice but to accept the reality. The death of a student is never good for business."

Lucy had a frankness that appealed to Leonard. She was forthcoming and interesting, and yet, as he reflected on the conversation, he had a distinct feeling that she'd shared nothing more with him than she'd intended. There was only one moment in their interview when he'd sensed that the mask had slipped. Something niggled at Leonard in the way she had described the events of 1862. It struck him now that she'd sounded almost guilty when she spoke of Frances Brown's death and her brother's consequent decline. There had been that odd crossroads tangent, too, in which she'd reflected on guilt and the need to forgive oneself, impressing upon Leonard his need to do the same.

But Lucy Radcliffe had been a child in 1862 and, from the way she'd told it, a spectator rather than a participant in the summertime antics of her brother's brilliant and beautiful friends. There had been a robbery, a priceless gem had been stolen, and Frances Brown had been killed in the process. Lily Millington, the model with whom Edward Radcliffe had been in love, had disappeared. Apparently, police reports from the time would suggest that she'd acted with the thief. Lucy's beloved brother had never recovered. Leonard could understand Lucy suffering grief and a feeling of general regret, but not guilt. She had no more pulled the trigger that killed Miss Brown than Leonard had been responsible for the piece of flying shrapnel that killed Tom.

Do you believe in ghosts, Mr. Gilbert?

Leonard had thought carefully before answering. *I believe that a person can find himself haunted.* Now, as he contemplated her evident but irrational guilt, Leonard realized suddenly what she'd meant: that, despite her talk of folktales and mysterious spirit lights in windows, she hadn't been speaking about spooks in the shadows after all. She had been asking whether Leonard was haunted by Tom in the same way that she was haunted by Edward. She had recognized in him a kindred spirit, a fellow sufferer: the guilt of the sibling survivor.

As he passed the Swan, and Dog appeared from somewhere to fall into panting step beside him, Leonard took a small rectangular card from his pocket and thumbed its well-worn edge. He'd met the woman who gave it to him at a party several years before, back when he was still living in London in the bedsit above the train line. She'd been set up in the corner of a room at the back of the house, sitting behind a round table with a purple velvet cloth covering it and some sort of board game laid out across its top. The sight of her, with a brightly beaded scarf wrapped around her head, had been enough to make him stare. And then there were the five party guests sitting at the table with her, all of them holding hands around the circle, their eyes closed as they listened to her muttering. Leonard had stopped and leaned against the doorway, watching through the haze of smoke.

All of a sudden, the woman's eyes had snapped open and fixed on him. "You," she'd said, pointing a long red talon as the others at the table turned to take him in. "There's someone here for you."

He'd ignored her then, but her words and the intensity of her stare had stayed with him, and later, when he found himself leaving the party at the same time she did, he'd offered to carry her awkwardly shaped carpet bag down the four flights of stairs. When they reached the ground and he bade her good night, she'd taken the card from her pocket and handed it to him.

"You're lost," she'd said in a calm, cool voice.

"What?"

"You've lost your way."

"I'm fine, thank you very much." Leonard had started down the road, shoving the card deep into his pocket, shaking off the strange, unpleasant feeling the woman had given him.

"He's been trying to find you." The woman's voice, louder now, followed him down the street.

It was only when Leonard reached the next streetlight and read the card that her words made sense.

Madame Mina Waters
Spiritualist
Apartment 2B
16 Neal's Yard
Covent Garden
London.

He'd confided the conversation with Madame Mina to Kitty soon after it happened. She'd laughed and said that London was full of crackpots looking to exploit their victims' loss for profit. But Leonard told her that she was being too cynical. "She knew about Tom," he insisted. "She knew I'd lost someone."

"Oh, God, look around: *everyone's* lost someone."

"You didn't see the way she stared at me."

"Was it anything like this?" She crossed her eyes and pulled a face, then smiled and reached across the sheet to grab her discarded stockings, tossing them at him in fun.

Leonard shook them away. He wasn't in the mood. "She told me he's been trying to find me. She told me I was lost."

"Ah, Lenny." All the sport was gone now; she sounded only tired. "Aren't we all?"

Leonard wondered now how Kitty had got on with her interview in London. She had looked smart when she left that morning; she'd done something different with her hair. He wished he'd remembered to comment. Kitty wore her cynicism well, but Leonard had known her before the war and he could see all the stitches that were holding the costume together.

As he passed the church and started down the empty lane towards Birchwood Manor, Leonard picked up a handful of gravel from the verge on the side of the road. He weighed the small stones in his palm before letting them sift through his parted fingers as he walked. One, he noticed as it fell, was clear and round, a perfectly smooth piece of quartz.

The first time Leonard and Kitty slept together was on a mild October night in 1916. He was home on leave and had spent the afternoon in his mother's drawing room drinking tea from a china cup as his mother's friends tut-tutted alternately, and with equal verve, about the war and the politics of the upcoming village Christmas Fair.

There'd been a knock at the door, and his mother's parlor maid Rose had announced Miss Barker's arrival. Kitty had come with a box of scarves for the war effort, and when Mother invited her to stay for tea, she had said that she couldn't: there was a dance on at the church hall and she was in charge of refreshments.

It was Mother who suggested that Leonard ought to attend the dance. It had been the last thing he'd imagined doing that evening, but anything was preferable to remaining in the drawing room as the merits of serving mulled wine next to sherry were weighed, and so he'd leapt to his feet and said, "I'll fetch my coat."

As they walked along the village street together in the creeping dark, Kitty had asked after Tom.

Everyone asked after Tom, so Leonard had a ready answer. "You know Tom," he'd said. "Nothing makes a dent in his swagger."

Kitty had smiled then and Leonard had wondered why he'd never noticed that dimple in her left cheek before.

He danced a lot that night. There was something of a man shortage in the village, and thus he was bemused (and pleased) to find himself in high demand. Girls who'd never noticed him were now lining up to dance.

It was getting late when he glanced over and spotted Kitty at the cloth-covered table on the edge of the dance floor. She'd been busy all night serving cucumber sandwiches and slices of Victoria sponge, and her hair was coming loose from its fastenings. The song was ending when she caught his eye and waved, and Leonard excused himself from his partner.

"Well, Miss Barker," he said as he reached her, "a resounding success, I should say."

"You should say correctly. We raised far more than I dared hope, and all of it for the war effort. My only regret is that I haven't danced all evening."

"That is regrettable indeed. Surely it wouldn't be right for you to call it a night without at least one foxtrot?"

That dimple again when she smiled.

His hand rested in the small of her back as they danced, and he was aware of the smoothness of her dress, the fine gold chain around her neck, the way her hair shone.

He offered to walk her home and they spoke easily and naturally. She was relieved that the dance had gone well; she'd been worried.

The night had come in a little cooler, and Leonard offered her his coat.

She asked about the front and he found that it was easier to talk about it in the dark. He spoke and she listened, and when he'd said as much as he was able, he told her that it seemed like a bad dream when he was back here, walking with her, and she said that in that case she wouldn't ask any more. They started reminiscing instead about the Easter Fair of 1913, the day they met, and Kitty reminded him that they'd walked up to the top of the hill behind the village, the three of them—Kitty, Leonard, and Tom—and sat against the massive oak tree with its view over the whole of southern England.

"I said that we could see all the way to France, remember?"

said Kitty. "And you corrected me. You said, 'That's not France, it's Guernsey.'"

"What a prig I was."

"You were not."

"I absolutely was."

"Well, maybe a little priggish."

"Hey!"

She laughed and took his hand and said, "Let's climb the hill now."

"In the dark?"

"Why not?"

They ran together up the hill, and Leonard had a fleeting realization that it was the first time in over a year that he'd run without an attendant fear for his life; the thought, the feeling, the freedom was exhilarating.

In the darkness beneath the tree at the top of the hill above their village, Kitty's face had been lit by the silver moon, and Leonard had lifted a finger to trace a line from the top of her nose, ever so lightly, all the way down until he reached her lips. He hadn't been able to help himself. She was perfect, a marvel.

Neither of them spoke. Kitty, still wearing his coat around her shoulders, knelt across him and began to unbutton his shirt. She slipped her hand beneath the cotton and held it flat against his heart. He brought his hand to cup her face, his thumb grazing her cheek, and she leaned into his touch. He pulled her towards him and they kissed, and in that moment the die was cast.

Afterwards, they dressed in silence and sat together beneath the tree. He offered her one of his cigarettes and she smoked it before saying matter-of-factly, "Tom can never know."

Leonard had nodded agreement, for of course Tom must never know.

"It was a mistake."

"Yes."

"This blasted war."

"It was my fault."

"No. It wasn't. But I love him, Leonard. I always have."

"I know."

He'd taken her hand then and squeezed it, for he did know. He knew, too, that he also loved Tom.

They saw one another twice again before he returned to the front, but only in passing and always in the presence of other people. And it was strange, because in those moments he knew that it was true, that Tom need never know and that they would be able to go on as if nothing had happened.

It wasn't until he returned to the front a week later, and the weight of the place descended, that he began to turn things over in his mind, always arriving at the same question—a boy's question, small and needy, which filled him with self-loathing as it grazed his consciousness: Why did his brother seem so often to come out on top?

Tom was one of the first men Leonard saw when he reached the trenches, his dirt-smeared face erupting in a grin as he cocked his tin hat. "Welcome back, Lenny. Did you miss me?"

It was about half an hour later, as they shared a mug of trench tea, that Tom asked after Kitty.

"I only saw her once or twice."

"She mentioned in her letter. Good stuff. I don't suppose you and she had any special conversations?"

"What are you talking about?"

"Nothing private?"

"Don't be stupid. We hardly spoke."

"I see leave has done nothing to improve your mood. I just meant"—his brother couldn't keep the smile from his face—"Kitty and I are engaged to be married. I was sure she wouldn't be able to resist telling you. We promised that we wouldn't tell anyone until after the war—her father, you know."

Tom looked so pleased with himself, so boyishly happy, that Leonard couldn't help but give him a great big slapping hug. "Congratulations, Tom, I'm really pleased for you both."

Three days later his brother was dead. Killed by a piece of flying shrapnel. Killed by loss of blood in the long, dark hours after the shrapnel hit, lying out in no-man's-land as Leonard listened from the trenches. (*Help me, Lenny, help me.*) All they managed to salvage from him, from Tom of the garden wall, Tom the breath-holding champion, Tom the boy most likely, was a cologne-scented letter from Kitty and a dirty old silver tuppence.

No, Lucy Radcliffe's talk of guilt and self-forgiveness had been kindly meant, but whatever similarities she thought she had perceived between them, she'd been mistaken. Life was complicated; people made mistakes, certainly. But they were different. Their guilt with respect to their dead siblings was not the same.

Kitty had started writing to him in France after Tom's death, and Leonard back to her, and when the war was over and he returned to England, she had come to see him one night in his bedsit in London. She brought a bottle of gin and Leonard helped her to drink it and they talked about Tom and they both cried. Leonard had presumed when she left that that would be the end of it. Somehow, though, Tom's death had tied them together. They were two moons bound in orbit around his memory.

In the beginning, Leonard told himself he was looking after Kitty for his brother, and perhaps if that night in 1916 hadn't happened he might have believed it. The truth, though, was more complicated and less honorable and he couldn't hide from it for long. Both he and Kitty knew it was their disloyalty that night that had brought on Tom's death. He was aware that it wasn't entirely rational, but that didn't make it any less true. Lucy Radcliffe was right, though: a person couldn't go on indefinitely under the weight of so much guilt. They needed to justify their action's devastating effect, and so they agreed, without discussion, to believe that what had happened between them that night on the hill was love.

They stayed together. Bound by grief and guilt. Hating the reason for their bond, yet unable each to let the other go.

They didn't speak about Tom anymore, not directly. But he was always with them. He was in the fine gold band with its pretty little diamond that Kitty wore on her right hand; he was in the way she looked at Leonard sometimes with faint surprise, as if she'd expected to see someone else; he was in every dark corner of every room, every atom of sunlit air outside.

Yes, Leonard believed in ghosts all right.

Leonard had reached the gate to Birchwood Manor and he went through it. The sun was getting lower in the sky, and the shadows had started to lengthen across the lawn. As he glanced towards the front garden wall, Leonard stopped in his tracks. There, reclining in the sunny patch beneath the Japanese maple tree, he saw a woman, fast asleep. For a split second, he thought that it was Kitty, that she'd decided not to go to London after all.

Leonard wondered for a moment if he was hallucinating, but then he realized that it wasn't Kitty at all. It was the woman from the river that morning: one half of the couple he'd gone out of his way to avoid meeting.

Now he found himself unable to look away. A pair of brogue shoes sat neatly beside her sleeping body, and her bare feet in the grass seemed to Leonard in that moment the most erotic sight. He lit a cigarette. It was her unguardedness, he supposed, that drew him to her. Her materialization here, today, in this place.

As he watched, she woke and stretched, and the most beatific expression came upon her face. The way she was looking at the house sparked a distant recognition in Leonard. Purity, simplicity, love. It made him want to cry as he hadn't since he was a small boy. For all of the loss and the ugly mess and the awareness that, no matter how he willed it, he could never go back and make it so that the horror hadn't happened; that whatever else he did in life, the fact of the war and his brother's death and the wasted years since would always be a part of his story.

And then "I'm sorry," she called out, for she had seen him. "I didn't mean to trespass. I lost my way."

Her voice was like a bell, pure and unsullied, and he wanted to run over and take her by the shoulders and warn her, to tell her that life could be brutal, that it could be relentless and cold and wearying.

He wanted to tell her that it was all meaningless, that good people died too young, for no good reason, and that the world was filled with people who would seek to do her harm, and that there was no way of telling what was around the corner or even if there was any corner ahead at all.

And yet—

As he looked at her, and she looked at the house, something in the way the leaves of the maple caught the sun and illuminated the woman beneath it made his heart ache and expand, and he realized that he wanted to tell her, too, that by some strange twist it was the very meaningless of life that made it all so beautiful and rare and wonderful. That for all its savagery—*because* of its savagery—war had brightened every color. That without the darkness one would never notice the stars.

All of this he wanted to say, but the words caught in his throat, and instead he lifted his hand to wave, a silly gesture that she didn't see, because by now she'd looked away.

He went inside the house and from the kitchen window watched as she gathered her bag and, with a final dazzling smile up at the house, disappeared into the sunlit haze. He didn't know her. He would never see her again. And yet he wished he could have told her that he'd lost his way, too. He'd lost his way, but hope still fluttered in and out of focus like a bird, singing that if he kept putting one foot in front of the other, he might just make it home.

VII

My father once told me that when he saw my mother in the window of her family home, it was as if his entire life to that point had been led in the half-light. Upon meeting her, he said, every color, every fragrance, every sensation that the world had to offer, was brighter, sharper, more truthful.

I was a child and took this story for the fairy tale that it sounded, but my father's words came back to me on the night that I met Edward.

It was not love at first sight. Such claims make a mockery of love.

It was a presentiment. An inexplicable awareness that something important had happened. Some moments are like that: they shine like gold in a prospector's pan.

I said that I was born twice, once to my father and mother, and a second time when I woke up in the house of Mrs. Mack, above the shop selling birds and cages on Little White Lion Street.

That is the truth. But it is not the whole truth. For there was a third part to my life's story.

I was born again, outside the Theatre Royal in Drury Lane, on a warm evening in 1861 when I was a month from turning seventeen years old. The very same age that my mother was when I was born for the first time, that starlit night in the narrow house in Fulham on the banks of the river Thames.

—

Mrs. Mack had been right, of course, when she said that the days of Little Girl Lost and Little Girl Passenger were numbered, and so a new scheme had been hatched, a new costume procured, a new persona put

262

on like a second skin. It was simple enough: the theater foyer was a hive of activity. The ladies' dresses were bright and generous, the men's reserve loosened by whisky and expectation; there were any number of opportunities for a woman with quick fingers to relieve a gentleman of his valuables.

The only problem was Martin. I was no longer a green child, but he refused to relinquish the minder's role he'd been assigned. He badgered Mrs. Mack, filled her head with extravagant ways in which I might come to harm or even—I had heard him whispering when he thought I wasn't listening—be "turned against them"; and then he proposed an arrangement by which he might insinuate himself into my work. I argued that he was overcomplicating matters, that I preferred to work alone, but at every turn he was there, watching with a grating proprietary air.

That night, though, I had given him the slip. The show had finished and I'd made my way quickly across the foyer and out through a side exit, arriving in an alley that ran away from the theater. It had been a good night: the deep pocket of my dress was heavy, and I was glad. The most recent letter from my father had advised that, after a number of unfortunate setbacks, the clock-making enterprise he had established in New York was almost solvent. I was hopeful that a fruitful summer would occasion his permission for me to set sail for America. It had been over nine years since he'd left me with Mrs. Mack.

I was alone in the alley, wondering whether I ought to walk the shortcut home through the narrow laneways or follow instead the crowded Strand so that I might add one or two more wallets to my haul, and it was in that moment of indecision that Edward appeared through the same door by which I had left, catching me without my mask.

It was like the swift clarity that comes with the lifting fog. I felt alert, suddenly filled with anticipation, and yet at once unsurprised, for how could the night have ended without our meeting?

He came towards me, and when he reached out to brush my

cheek, his touch was as light as if I were one of the treasures in Pale Joe's father's collection. His eyes studied mine.

I could not say how long we stood like that—seconds, minutes—time had slipped its bounds.

Only when Martin appeared and uttered a cry of, "Stop! Thief!" was the spell broken. I blinked and stepped away.

Martin launched into his practiced ruse, but I was impatient, suddenly, with its shabbiness. No, I said firmly, this man was not a thief.

No, indeed, said Edward, he was a painter and he wished to paint my portrait.

Martin began to stammer—nonsense about young ladies, his "sister," respectability; but Edward took no heed. He spoke of his family, promising that he and his mother would come to my home and meet my parents: reassure them that he was a gentleman of fine character and that an association with him would not tarnish my reputation.

The proposal was wholly unexpected, the suggestion of parents and a home so very quaint, and I confess to being much taken with the idea of myself as the sort of young lady whose modesty might require such protection.

I agreed, and when upon leaving he asked me my name, aware that Martin was watching, I told him the first thing that came to mind: "Lily," I said. "My name is Lily Millington."

—

Mrs. Mack, always able to smell a profit, was inspired to immediate action. She began at once the process of turning her parlor into the picture of domestic gentility. One of the newer children, Effie Granger, who was eleven years old but big for her age, was outfitted in a maid's black-and-white uniform, snatched by Martin from a drying line in Chelsea, and given a quick and brutal course in the basics of service. Martin and the Captain were instructed in the roles of upstanding brother and father, and Mrs. Mack began a process of embodiment as she turned herself into a Doting Mother Fallen on Hard Times with a commitment that would have put the actresses down on Drury Lane to shame.

When the auspicious day arrived, the younger ones were tucked away upstairs, under strict instruction not to so much as twitch the lace curtains with their spying if they knew what was good for them, and the rest of us waited downstairs nervously for the doorbell to ring.

Edward and his mother, a woman Mrs. Mack described later as being of Continental looks and manners, were shown inside, the latter unable to resist a curious glance around as she unpinned her hat. Whatever she thought of "Mr. and Mrs. Millington" and their household, her son was her pride and joy, and in him she had invested all of her artistic aspirations; if he believed that Miss Millington was what he needed to complete his vision, then Miss Millington would be his. And if that meant drinking tea from the pot of a strange couple in Covent Garden, then she was more than willing to do it.

During the meeting I sat upon one end of the sofa—a position I was rarely granted—with Edward at the other, Mrs. Mack intoning, in what I can only suppose she imagined a decorous manner, as to my goodness and virtue. "A proper Christian girl, my Lily. Innocent as the day."

"I am very glad to hear it," said Mrs. Radcliffe, with a charming smile. "And so she shall remain. My late husband's father is the Earl of Beechworth, and my son is a gentleman of most noble character. You have my word that he will take the utmost care of your daughter, returning her to you in the condition that she arrives."

"Harrumph," said the Captain, who had been schooled in the role of Reluctant Paterfamilias. ("When in doubt," Mrs. Mack had said, "grunt. And whatever you do, don't remove that leg.")

Permission was eventually won and a price agreed, the payment of which, Mrs. Mack declared, would make her feel comfortable that her daughter's virtue would remain intact.

And then, as I finally allowed myself to meet Edward's gaze, a date was agreed on which the initial sitting would take place.

His studio was at the back of his mother's garden, behind her house in Hampstead, and on the first day he took my hand to help me down the slippery path. "Cherry blossoms," he said. "Beautiful but deadly."

I had no experience with painters, having learned all that I knew of art from Pale Joe's books and the walls of his father's house. And so, when Edward opened the door, I had little idea what to expect.

The room was small, with a Persian rug on the floor and an easel upon it facing a plain but elegant chair. The ceiling was made of glass, but the walls were wooden and painted white; along two of them ran a purpose-built bench with shelves beneath, filled with wide drawers. The top was covered with tiny jars containing pigments, bottles of assorted liquids, and pots of brushes in every size.

Edward went first to light the furnace in the far corner. He did not want me to get cold, he said; I was to tell him if I became uncomfortable. He helped me to remove my cloak, and when his fingers brushed my neck I felt my skin heat. He indicated that I should sit upon the chair; he would be working on studies today. I noticed then that the wall at the back of the room was already covered with a haphazard array of pen and ink sketches.

Here, now, in this strange betwixt-and-between existence that I lead, I can see but no longer be seen. I did not understand before how fundamental an act it is to exchange glances, to look into the eyes of another human being. I did not understand, either, how rare it is to be afforded the opportunity to devote one's entire attention to another person without fear of being caught.

While Edward studied me, I studied him.

I became addicted to his focus. And I learned, too, the power of being watched. If I were to move my chin, even a little, I would see the change reflected in his face. The slight narrowing of his eyes as he took in the new spill of light.

I will tell you something else I know: it is hard not to fall in love with a handsome man who pays you his complete attention.

There was no clock inside the studio. There was no time. Working together, day after day, the world beyond its walls dissolved. There was Edward and there was me, and even those boundaries came to blur within the strange envelopment of our endeavor.

Sometimes he asked me questions about myself that came from nowhere to disrupt the dense quiet of the room, and I answered as best I could whilst he listened and painted, concentration making a faint line appear between his brows. At first I was able to skirt the truth, but as the weeks wore on, I began to fear that he could see through my shadows and embellishments. More than that, I felt a new and troublesome urge to lay myself bare.

And so I steered the conversation on to safer subjects like art and science and the sorts of things that Pale Joe and I discussed, about life and time. This surprised him, for he smiled, a slight quizzical frown, and stopped what he was doing, considering me over the top of his canvas. These topics were of great interest to him, too, he said eventually, and he told me then about an essay he had written recently about the connection between places and people, the way certain landscapes were more potent than others, speaking to the present about the happenings of the past.

Edward was like no one I had met before. When he spoke, it was impossible not to listen. He was wholly committed to whatever it was that he was doing or feeling or expressing at the time. I found myself thinking of him when we weren't together, remembering a sentiment that he'd expressed, the way he'd thrown his head back and laughed freely at an anecdote I'd told him, and yearning to make him laugh like that again. I could no longer remember what I used to think about before I knew him. He was the music that gets inside a person's head and changes the rhythm of their pulse; the inexplicable urge that drives a person to act against their better judgment.

We were never disturbed, except briefly, on occasion, by the arrival of a hot teapot. Sometimes it was his mother who brought the tray, eager to glance over her shoulder and to gauge Edward's progress. Other days it was the maid. And one morning, after I had been meeting Edward daily for a week or two, when the knock came at the door and he called out, "Yes," it was opened by a young girl of about twelve years old, holding her tray very carefully.

She had a nervousness that immediately endeared her to me. Her face was not pretty, but I glimpsed strength in the set of her chin that made me feel that she should not be underestimated; she was curious, too, her eyes darting around the room from Edward to me to the sketches on the wall. Curiosity was a trait with which I identified and which, in truth, had always seemed to me a prerequisite for life. What purpose could a person find in the long trudge ahead, if they hadn't curiosities to light the way? I knew at once who she must be, and sure enough:

"My littlest sister," said Edward, with a smile, "Lucy. And, Lucy, this is Lily Millington, 'La Belle.'"

———

I had known Edward for six months when the *La Belle* painting debuted at the Royal Academy in November 1861. I had been told to arrive at seven, and Mrs. Mack was eager to ensure that I had a dress befitting the occasion. For a woman of such blowsy self-confidence, she was almost endearingly impressed by celebrity, even more so if it brought with it the prospect of ongoing income. "This is it," she said, fastening the pearl buttons that ran all the way up my back to the nape of my neck. "Play your cards right, my girl, and this could be the start of something magnificent." She nodded then towards the collection of *cartes de visite* on her mantel, members of the royal family and other well-known and distinguished persons. "You could be on your way to being one of *them*."

Martin, predictably, did not share her enthusiasm. He had resented the time that I'd spent as Edward's model, seeming to take my absence during the days as a personal slight. I heard him some nights in Mrs. Mack's parlor, complaining about the diminished returns, and when those arguments failed to sway her—the payment for my modeling services was more than equal to the earnings from my thievery— he insisted that it was a "risk" to let me get "too close to the quarry." But it was Mrs. Mack who ruled the roost in the rooms above the bird shop. I had been invited to an exhibition at the Royal Academy, one of the brightest, most important events on the London social scene, and so, tailed by Martin, I was dispatched.

I arrived to find a mass of people, men in shiny black top hats and long evening jackets, and women in exquisite silk dresses, filling the great room. Their eyes brushed over me as I made my way through the thick, warm sea. The air was very close and it thrummed with rapid conversation broken occasionally by barks of laughter.

I was beginning to give up hope that I would find Edward when suddenly his face came into focus before me. "You're here," he said. "I waited at the other entrance, but I missed you."

As he took my hand I felt a hot rush of electric energy surge through me. It was novel to see him like this, in public, having spent the past six months cloistered away in his studio. We had spoken about so many things, and I knew by now so much about him, yet here, surrounded by all these other laughing people, he was out of context. The new setting, familiar to him but foreign to me, rendered him a different person from the one I knew.

He led me through the crowd to where the painting was hanging. I had glimpsed it in the studio, but nothing could have prepared me for the way it would look upon the wall, magnified by virtue of its display. His eyes searched mine. "What do you think?"

I was at an unusual loss for words. The painting was extraordinary. The colors were lush and my skin looked luminous, as if it would be warm to the touch. He had painted me at the center of the canvas, my hair flowing in ripples, my eyes direct and my expression as if I had just given a confidence that would not be repeated. And yet, there was something more underlying the image. Edward had captured in this beautiful face—far more beautiful than my own real face—a vulnerability that rendered the whole exquisite.

But my speechlessness was about more than the image itself. *La Belle* is a time capsule. Beneath the brushstrokes and the pigments lies every word, every glance, that Edward and I exchanged; she bears a record of every time he laughed, that he came to touch my face, shifting it ever so carefully towards the light. Each thought that he had is recorded, each instance that our minds met in that isolated studio in the corner of the garden. Within La Belle's face there lie one thousand secrets, which together tell a story, known only to Edward and me. To see her hanging on the wall in that room of noisy strangers was overwhelming.

Edward was still waiting for my answer and I said, "She's . . ."

He squeezed my hand. "Isn't she?"

Edward excused himself then, for he had spotted Mr. Ruskin, and told me that he would be back immediately.

I continued to look at the painting and was aware that a tall, handsome man had come to stand close by. "What do you think?" he said, and at first I thought that he was speaking to me. I was struggling to find words when another woman answered. She was on his other side, pretty and petite, with honey-brown hair and a small mouth.

"The painting is wonderful, as always," she said. "I do wonder, though, why he insists on choosing his models from the gutter."

The man laughed. "You know Edward. He has always been of a perverse nature."

"She cheapens it. Look at the way she stares directly at us; no shame, no class . . . And those lips! I said as much to Mr. Ruskin."

"And what did he reply?"

"He was inclined to agree, although he did say that he assumed Edward had intended to make that very point. Something about contrast, the innocence of the setting, the boldness of the woman."

Every cell in my body retracted. I wished nothing more than that I might disappear. It had been a grave mistake to have come; I saw that now. Martin had been right. I had become caught up in the energy that surrounded Edward. I had allowed my guard to drop. I had thought us partners in a great endeavor. I had been unthinkably stupid.

My cheeks burned with embarrassment, and I longed to escape. I glanced behind me to see how easily I could get to the door. The room was overflowing with guests, one pressed up hard against the next, and the air was cloying, thick with cigar smoke and cologne.

"Lily." Edward was back, his face warm with excitement. But then: "What is it?" as his gaze raked mine. "What's happened?"

"There you are, Edward!" said the tall, handsome man. "I was wondering where you'd got to—we were just admiring *La Belle*."

Edward shot me a final glance of encouragement before meeting the grin of his friend, who was now slapping him on the shoulder. He placed his hand gently in the small of my back and ushered me forward. "Lily Millington," he said, "this is Thurston Holmes, one of the Magenta Brotherhood and my good friend."

Thurston took my hand and brushed it with his lips. "So, this is the famous Miss Millington about whom we've heard so much." His eyes met mine and I read within them unmistakable interest. One did not grow up in the shady laneways of Covent Garden and the dank streets around the Thames without learning to recognize that look. "It is a pleasure finally to make your acquaintance. About time he shared you with us."

The honey-haired woman beside him held out her cold little hand then and said, "I see that I shall have to introduce myself. My name is Miss Frances Brown. Soon to be Mrs. Edward Radcliffe."

———

As soon as I noticed Edward in deep conversation with another guest, I gave a vague excuse to no one in particular and extricated myself, making my way through the crowd until I reached the door.

It was a relief to escape the room, and yet as I slipped quickly into the dark folds of the cool night, I could not help but feel that I had stepped through more than one doorway. I had left behind an alluring world of creativity and light, and was now returned to the dim, bleak alleyways of my past.

I was in just such an alley, thinking just such a thought, when I felt a grip on my wrist. I turned, expecting to see Martin, who had been lurking all night in the middle of Trafalgar Square, but it was Edward's friend from the exhibition, Thurston Holmes. I could hear the clatter of noise on the Strand, but aside from a vagrant slumped in a gutter we were alone.

"Miss Millington," he said. "You left so suddenly. I was concerned that you were unwell."

"I'm fine, thank you. The room was so hot—I needed air."

"It can be overwhelming, I expect, when one is unused to the attention. But I fear it is not safe for a young lady by herself out here. There are dangers in the night."

"Thank you for your concern."

"Perhaps I could take you somewhere for some refreshment. I have rooms nearby and a very understanding landlady."

I could see at once the sort of refreshment he desired. "No, thank you. I don't wish to detain you from your evening."

He came closer then and laid one hand upon my waist, sliding it around my back and pulling me towards him. With his other hand, he took two gold coins from his pocket, holding them up between his fingers. "I promise to make it worth your while."

I met his eyes and did not look away. "As I said, Mr. Holmes, I would prefer to get some air."

"As you wish." He took off his top hat and gave a quick nod. "Good night, Miss Millington. Until we meet again."

The interaction was unpleasant, and yet I had matters of more importance on my mind. I had no wish to return yet to Mrs. Mack, and so, with care not to attract Martin's attention, I went instead to the only place that I could think to go.

—

If Pale Joe was surprised to see me, his reaction was mild: he set the bookmark on his page and closed the cover. We had spoken with much anticipation about the unveiling of the painting, and he turned now to receive my triumphant story. Instead, as soon as I opened my mouth to speak, I began to cry—I who had not cried since the first morning that I woke up at Mrs. Mack's house without my father.

"What is it?" he said with some alarm. "What has happened? Has somebody hurt you?"

I told him no, that it was nothing like that. That I was not even certain myself why I was crying.

"Then you must start at the beginning and describe everything. That way, maybe *I* will be able to tell you why you are crying."

So I did. I told him first about the painting: the way I had stood before it and felt shy of myself. The way the image that Edward had created in that glass-roofed studio of his was so much *more* than I was. That it was radiant; that it swept away all of the petty concerns of daily life; that it captured vulnerability and hope and the woman beneath the artifice.

"Then you are crying because the beauty of the artwork overwhelmed you."

To which I shook my head, because I knew that was not it.

I told him then about the tall, handsome man who had come to stand beside me, and the pretty woman with her honey-colored hair and neat mouth, and the things that they had said and the way that they had laughed.

Pale Joe sighed then and nodded. "You are crying because the woman said unkind things about you."

To which I shook my head again, because I had never cared for the good opinion of those I did not know.

I told him then that as I had listened to them I had become vividly conscious of the gaudy dress that Mrs. Mack had procured for me. That I had at first thought it extraordinary—the crushed velvet fabric, the delicate trim of lace around the décolletage—but that I had realized, suddenly, that it was garish and overbright.

Pale Joe frowned. "I know you are not crying because you wished for a different dress."

I agreed with him that the dress was not the matter; rather, that in that particular room, I had realized *myself* to be garish and overbright, and I had become overwhelmed with sudden anger at Edward. I had trusted him, but he had betrayed me, had he not? He had made me feel at home in his company, in his world, flattered me with his absolute attention—those deep, dark, watchful eyes, the clench of his jawline when he concentrated, the hint of need—for surely I had not

273

imagined it?—only to embarrass me in a room filled with people who were not like me at all; who could see at once that I was not like them. When he invited me to attend as his guest, I had thought— Well, I had misunderstood. And of *course* there was a fiancée, that pretty woman with neat features and fine clothing. He should have told me, allowed me to prepare, to arrive on proper terms. He had tricked me and I never wanted to see him again.

Pale Joe was looking at me with a fond, sad expression, and I knew what he was going to say. That the charge was unfair. That I had been a fool and the mistake was all mine, for Edward owed me nothing. I had been engaged and paid to perform a task: to pose as his model for a painting he wished to exhibit at the Royal Academy.

But Pale Joe said none of those things. Instead he put his arms around me and said, "My poor Birdie. You are crying because you are in love."

After leaving Pale Joe, I hurried through the dark streets of Covent Garden, thick with ruddy-cheeked men spilling out of supper clubs and drunken songs drifting upstairs from basement rooms, cigar smoke mingling with the leftover smells of animals and rotting fruit.

My long skirts shushed along the cobblestones, and as I turned into Little White Lion Street, I glanced skyward and glimpsed the hazy moon between buildings; not the stars, though, for the grey smog of London sat too heavy. I let myself in the front door of the shop selling birds and cages, careful not to wake the winged creatures asleep beneath their shrouds, and then tiptoed up the stairs. As I passed the doorway to the kitchen, a voice from the dark said, "Well, well, look what the cat dragged in."

I saw then that Martin was sitting at the table, a gin bottle open in front of him. A dull wedge of moonlight fell through the crooked window, and one side of his face disappeared into shadow.

"Think you're clever, don't you, giving me the runaround? I lost a night waiting for you. I couldn't work the theater alone, so I wasted my time under Nelson's bloody Column watching the toffs come and go. What am I going to tell Ma and the Captain when they want to know why I haven't brought home the coin what they was promised, eh?"

"I have never asked you to wait for me, Martin, and I would be very pleased if you would promise not to do so anymore."

"Oh, you'd be *pleased*, would you?" He laughed, but the sound was parched. "You'd be pleased indeed. Aren't you the proper little lady now." He pushed his chair back suddenly and came to where I was standing in the doorway. He took my face by the chin and I felt his breath, warm on my neck, as he said, "You know the very first thing my ma said to me when you came to live with us? She sent me upstairs where you was sleeping and she said, 'Go and have a look at your pretty new sister, Martin. She's going to need a close eye kept on her. You mark my words, we're going to have to watch her close.' And my ma was right. I see the way they look at you, those men. I know what they're thinking."

I was too tired for a petty argument and one that we'd already had a number of times before. I was eager to get upstairs where I could be alone in my bedroom to reflect on the things that Pale Joe had said. Martin was leering at me and I felt repulsed, but I was sorry for him, too, for he was a man whose palette was empty of color. The boundaries of his life had been drawn narrow when he was a boy and they had never been extended. As his grip continued firm on my face, I said softly, "You need not worry, Martin. The painting is finished now. I am home. The world has been set to rights."

Perhaps he had been expecting me to argue, for he swallowed whatever it was that he had been preparing to say next. He blinked slowly and then nodded. "Well, don't you forget it," he said. "Don't you forget that you belong here with us. You're not one of them, no matter what my ma might tell you when she's sniffing after artists' gold. That's just for show, right? You'll get hurt if you forget it, and you'll only have yourself to blame."

He let go of me at last and I made myself smile. But as I turned to leave, he reached out to grab my wrist, pulling me back fast towards him. "You look pretty in that dress. You're a beautiful woman now. All grown up."

There was menace in his tone, and I could imagine that a young woman accosted in such a way on the street would feel terror shoot up her spine as she met the scrutiny of his gaze, his curled lip, his thinly veiled intentions; and well might she be advised to react thusly. But I had known Martin for a long time. He would never harm me while his mother was alive. I was far too valuable to her enterprise. And so, "I'm tired, Martin," I said. "It's very late. I have much work to catch up on tomorrow and I need to go to bed now. Ma wouldn't want either of us too tired for a proper day's work tomorrow."

At the mention of Mrs. Mack, his grip loosened, and I took the opportunity to pull myself free and hurry upstairs. I left the tallow candle unlit as I stripped immediately from my velvet dress, and when I draped it from the hook on the back of the door, I made sure to flare out the skirt to cover the keyhole.

I lay awake that night, turning over the things that Pale Joe had said to me, reliving every minute of time that I had spent with Edward in his studio.

"Does he love you, too?" Pale Joe had asked.

"I think not," I had replied. "For he is engaged to be married."

Pale Joe had smiled patiently at that. "You have known him for some months now. You have spoken to him many times. He has told you about his life, his loves, his passions and pursuits. And yet tonight you learned for the first time that he is engaged to be married."

"Yes."

"Birdie, if I were engaged to be married to the woman whom I love, then I would talk about her to the man who puts down grit during snowstorms. I would sing her name at every opportunity to every willing set of ears this side of Moscow. I cannot tell you with any certainty what he feels for you, but I can tell you that he does not love the woman that you met tonight."

———

It was just after dawn when I heard the knock on the door downstairs. The streets of Covent Garden were already busy with carts and barrows and women with baskets of fruits on their heads trudging towards the market, and I assumed it was the local watchman. He and Mrs. Mack had an understanding, such that when he was performing his daily patrol of the streets, rattling out the half-hour marks so that people could tell the time, he would stop to bang the knocker of our door to signal wake-up time.

The noise was softer than usual, though, and when it sounded for a second time, I rose from my bed and pulled the curtain aside to peer down through the window.

It was not the watchman in his slouch hat and greatcoat at the door. It was Edward, still dressed in his coat and scarf from the night before. My heart leapt, and after a split second of indecision I opened the window and called down to him in a half whisper: "What are you doing?"

He stepped backwards, looking up to see where my voice was coming from, and was almost hit by a flower cart being pushed down the street. "Lily," he said, his face brightening when he saw me. "Lily, come down."

"What are you doing here?"

"Come down, I must speak with you."

"But the sun has barely risen."

"I realize, but I cannot make it rise any faster. I have been standing here all night. I have drunk more coffee from that stall on the corner than a man should ever drink, but I cannot wait any longer." He placed one hand across his heart and said, "Come down, Lily, or else I will be forced to climb up to you."

I nodded quickly and started dressing, my fingers overzealous with anticipation so that I fumbled each button and put a tear in my stockings. There was no time to neaten or pin my hair; I hurried down the stairs, eager to reach him before anyone else did.

I undid the latch and pulled open the door and in that moment, as we faced each other from either side of a threshold, I knew that what Pale Joe had said was true. There was so much that I wanted him to know. I wanted to tell him about my father and Mrs. Mack and Little Girl Lost and Pale Joe. I wanted to tell him that I loved him and that everything up until that point had been time but a pencil sketch, preliminary and pale, in anticipation of our meeting. I wanted to tell him my true name.

But there were too many words to find, and I did not know where to start, and then Mrs. Mack was beside me, her housecoat tied crookedly around her generous middle, the creases of sleep still pressed into her cheek. "What's all this about? What on earth are you doing here at this hour?"

"Good morning, Mrs. Millington," said Edward. "I apologize for interrupting your day."

"It's not even light yet."

"I realize, Mrs. Millington, but it is urgent. I must impress upon you my deepest admiration for your daughter. The painting of *La Belle* sold last night and I wish to speak to you about painting Miss Millington again."

"I'm afraid I can't spare her," said Mrs. Mack with a sniff. "I rely on my daughter here. Without her I have to pay my maid to do extra, and although I'm an honorable lady, Mr. Radcliffe, I am not wealthy."

"I will make sure to compensate you, Mrs. Millington. My next painting is likely to take longer. I propose to pay your daughter double what I did last time."

"Double?"

"If that sounds acceptable to you."

Mrs. Mack was not the type to turn down an offer of coin, but there was no one with a better nose for value. "I don't think double will do. No, I don't think that will do at all. Perhaps if you were to suggest three times the price . . . ?"

Martin, I noticed then, had come downstairs and was watching proceedings from the darkened doorway that led into the shop.

"Mrs. Millington," said Edward, his eyes now firmly on mine, "your daughter is my muse, my destiny. I will pay you whatever you think fair."

"Well, then. At four times the price I'd say we have ourselves a deal."

"Agreed." He risked a smile at me then. "Do you need to collect anything from here?"

"Nothing."

I said good-bye to Mrs. Mack, and then he took my hand and started leading me north through the streets of the Seven Dials. We did not speak at once, but something between us had changed. Rather, something that had been there all along had finally been acknowledged.

As we left Covent Garden, and Edward turned to look at me over his shoulder, I knew that there would be no going back from here.

———

Jack has returned and it is just as well; the bones of the past are seductive and I am at risk of picking over them all night long.

Oh, I remember love.

It has been a long time since Jack set out with his camera and his melancholy mood. Dusk has fallen and the purple noises of night are upon us.

Inside the malthouse, he connects his camera to the computer and the photographs import at a rapid speed. I can see them all. He has been busy: the churchyard again, the woods, the meadow, the crossroads in the village, others that are all texture and color, their subjects not immediately identifiable. None of the river, I note.

The shower is on now; his clothes are in a pile on the floor; the bathroom is filling with steam. I imagine he is starting to wonder about dinner.

Jack does not go straight to the kitchen, though. After his shower, with the towel still low around his hips, he picks up his phone and rocks it back and forth, considering. I watch him from the end of the bed, wondering whether he is going to disappoint Rosalind Wheeler with his report about the hiding place and the still-missing diamond.

With an exhalation that lowers his shoulders a full inch, he starts to dial and then waits with the phone at his ear. He is tapping his lips lightly with his fingertips, a thoughtful nervous habit.

"Sarah, it's me."

Oh, good! Much better than a progress report.

"Listen, you were wrong yesterday. I'm not going to change my mind. I'm not going to turn around and go back home. I want to know them—I *need* to know them." Them. The girls, the twins. His and Sarah's. (One thing is certain: society has changed. Back in my day it would have been the woman shut out of her children's lives if she dared to break company with their father.)

Sarah is speaking now, and she is no doubt reminding him that parenting is not about *his* needs, because he says, "I know; that's not what I meant. I should have said that I think they need me, too. They need a dad, Sar; at least, they will one day."

Further silence. And from the raised tone of her voice at the other end of the line, evident even from where I sit, she does not agree.

"Yes," he says, "yes, I know. I was a terrible husband . . . Yes, you're right, and that's on me. But it's been a long time, Sar—seven years. I'm a whole new set of cells . . . No, I'm not trying to be funny, I mean it. I've made changes. I even have a hobby. Remember that old camera—"

She is speaking again and he nods and makes occasional listening noises, eyes on the corner of the room where the walls meet the ceiling, tracing the line of the joist with his gaze as he waits for her to finish.

Some of the wind has left his sails when he says, "Look, Sar, I'm just asking you to give me a chance. A visit every so often—the opportunity to take them to Legoland or Harry Potter World or wherever it is they want to go. You can draw the boundaries however you see fit. I just want a chance."

The call ends without a resolution. He drops the phone onto the bed and rubs the back of his neck and then he goes slowly to the bathroom and takes up the photo of the girls.

We are of one mind tonight, he and I. Each of us separated from the people we love; each of us wading through memories of the past, seeking resolution.

All human beings crave connection, even the shy: it is too frightening for them to think themselves alone. The world, the universe—existence—is simply too big. Thank God, they cannot glimpse how much bigger it is than they think. I wonder about Lucy sometimes—what she would have made of it all.

In the kitchenette, Jack eats beans in sauce straight from the tin. He makes no attempt to heat them. And when the phone rings again, he hurries back in to check the screen but is disappointed. He doesn't answer the call.

They all have a story, the ones to whom I am drawn.

Each one is different from those who came before, but there has been something at the heart of each visitor, a loss that ties them together. I have come to understand that loss leaves a hole in a person and that holes like to be filled. It is the natural order.

They are always the ones most likely to hear me when I speak . . . and, every so often, when I get really lucky, one of them answers me back.

CHAPTER EIGHTEEN

SUMMER 1940

THEY found the matches in an old green tin on a shelf behind the stovetop. It was Freddy who spied them, leaping from foot to foot with lusty enthusiasm and declaring himself the winner. Such gleeful celebrations sent Tip into another weary round of tears, and Juliet cursed quietly as she struggled to light the burner beneath the kettle. "Come, now," she said as at last the match flared. "Spilt milk, Tippy, love. It doesn't matter." She turned to Freddy, who was still larking. "Really, Red. You're four years older than he is."

Freddy, preternaturally unperturbed, continued to dance as Juliet mopped Tip's face.

"I want to go home," said Tip.

Juliet opened her mouth to reply, but Beatrice beat her to it. "Well, you can't," she called from the other room, "because there's nothing left. There is no 'home.'"

Juliet held on to the last threads of her frayed patience. She had been jolly all the way from London, but it seemed further jolliness would be required. Addressing her daughter's adolescent acerbity—which had arrived at least a year too early, surely?—would have to wait. She leaned closer to Tip's alarmingly blotched face, aware with sudden pressing anxiety of his short breaths and sparrow shoulders. "Come and help me with the supper," she said. "I might even find you a little square of chocolate if I look hard enough."

The welcome basket had been a kind touch. Mrs. Hammett,

the publican's wife, had arranged it: a fresh loaf of bread, a wedge of cheese, and a stick of butter. Strawberries and gooseberries in a muslin cloth, a pint of creamy milk, and beneath it all—what joy!—a small block of chocolate.

As Tip took his square and retreated like a stray cat in search of a quiet place to lick his wounds, Juliet made a plate of cheese sandwiches for them all to share. She'd never been much good in the kitchen—when she met Alan she'd been able to boil an egg and the intervening years had not added much to her repertoire—but there was a certain therapy to it: slice the bread, scrape the butter, lay out the cheese, repeat.

She glanced as she did so at the handwritten card that had come with the basket. Mrs. Hammett's steady pen, wishing them welcome and extending an invitation to dinner at the Swan in the village on Friday night. Bea had been the one to remove the card from its envelope and was so taken with the idea of seeing the place where her parents had spent their honeymoon that it would have been unwise to say no. Strange to go back, though, especially without Alan. Twelve years now since they'd stayed in that tiny room with its pale, yellow-striped wallpaper, its leadlight window and view across the fields towards the river. There'd been a beautiful pair of teasel pods in a cracked vase on the chimney hearth, she remembered, and gorse that made the room smell of coconuts.

The kettle shrilled and Juliet called out to Bea to put her recorder aside and make the tea.

Huffing and flouncing ensued, but eventually a pot of tea arrived at the table where the rest of them had gathered to eat the sandwiches.

Juliet was tired. They all were. They'd spent the entire day on a packed train crawling west from London. Their provisions had been gone before they reached Reading; the journey afterwards had been exceedingly long.

Poor little Tip, beside her at the table, had deep, dark bags beneath his eyes and had hardly touched his sandwich. He'd slumped, cheek resting in the palm of his hand.

Juliet leaned close enough that she could smell the oiliness of his little-boy scalp. "How are you holding up, Tippy Toes?"

He opened his mouth as if about to speak but yawned instead.

"Time to visit Mrs. Marvel's garden party?"

He nodded slowly, his curtain of straight hair shifting back and forwards.

"Come on, then," she said. "Let's get you to bed."

He was asleep before she'd even started to describe the garden in her story. They were still on the path, about to reach the gate, when his weight settled against her and Juliet knew that she'd lost him.

She allowed herself to close her eyes, matching her breathing to his, relishing the solidity of his small, warm body; the simple fact of him; his fluttering exhalations tickling her cheek.

A light breeze drifted through the open window and she could easily have fallen asleep herself if not for the sporadic punctuations of gleeful laughter and noisy thumps emanating from downstairs. Juliet managed to ignore them until the fun degenerated, predictably enough, into a spat of sibling discord, and she was forced to disentangle herself from Tip and make her way back down to the kitchen. She dispatched the older two to bed and, alone at last, took stock.

The representative from the AHA who'd given her the key had done so with an air of defensive apology. The house hadn't been lived in for at least a year, not since the war started. Someone had made an effort to tidy things up, but there were certain telltale signs. The fireplace, for instance, had a significant amount of foliage protruding from its chimney, and the noises that fell from its dark cavern when she tugged at the tendrils made it clear that something was in habitation. It was summer, though, so Juliet reckoned it a problem for another time. Besides, as the AHA fellow had blustered when a swallow flew at them from the top of the pantry, there was a war on and it didn't do to make a fuss.

Upstairs, the bathroom was basic, but the rings in the tub could be cleaned, as could the moldy floor tiles. Mrs. Hammett had mentioned to Juliet on the phone that although the old woman who'd owned the house had loved it dearly, she hadn't had a lot to spend on it towards the end. And she'd been "very picky about tenants," so for long stretches of time the house had stood empty. Yes, they had some work ahead of them, that much was certain, but the occupation would be useful. It would encourage the children to feel at home, give them a sense of possession and belonging.

They were all asleep now, despite the brightness of the long summer evening, and Juliet leaned against the doorway to the larger bedroom at the back of the house. The frown that had set up on Bea's face some months before was gone. Her arms, long and slender, lay beside her atop the sheet. When she was born, the nurse had unfurled those arms and legs and declared her a runner, but Juliet had taken one look at the fine, pale fingers—spellbindingly perfect—and known that her daughter would be a musician.

Juliet had a flash of memory, the two of them holding hands as they crossed Russell Square. Bea, at four, talking earnestly, her eyes wide, her expression avid, as she made elegant, fawn-like leaps to keep up. She'd been a lovely child—engaged and engaging, quiet, but not shy. This intense changeling who had taken her place was a stranger.

Freddy, by contrast, was reassuringly familiar. His chest was bare and broad, and his shirt had been flung inside out onto the floor beside his bed. He lay with legs akimbo, as if he'd been wrestling the sheets. There was no hope in straightening them and Juliet didn't try. Unlike Bea, he'd been scarlet and compact when born. "Good God, you've given birth to a small red man," Alan had said, peering wonderingly at the bundle in Juliet's arms. "A very *angry* little red man." Thus had Freddy been known as Red ever since. His passions had not subsided. He had only to feel in order for those feelings to be known. He was dramatic, charming, fun, and funny. He was hard work; sunshine in human form; thunderous.

Juliet stood at last above little Tip, curled up now in a nest of pillows on the floor beside his bed, as was his recent habit. His sweaty head had cast a damp ring on the white pillowcase, and fine blond hair was pasted slick on either side of his ear. (All of her children ran hot. It came from Alan's side.)

Juliet lifted the sheet and draped it across Tip's narrow chest. She tucked it gently on either side and smoothed the center, hesitating for a moment with her flattened palm over his heart.

Was it only because he was her youngest that Juliet worried especially about Tip? Or was it something else—an innate, gossamer frailty she sensed in him; the fear that she could not protect him, that she would not be able to mend him if he broke.

"Don't slide down the rabbit hole," the Alan in her mind said cheerily. "The way down's a breeze, but climbing back's a battle."

And he was right. She was being maudlin. Tip was fine. He was perfectly fine.

With a final glance at her sleeping three, Juliet pulled the door behind her.

The room she'd taken for herself was the smaller one in the middle. She'd always liked small spaces—something to do with the womb, no doubt. There was no desk as such, but a walnut dressing table beneath the window that Juliet had requisitioned for her typewriter. The arrangement wasn't fancy but it was serviceable, and what more did she need?

Juliet sat on the end of the iron-framed bed with its faded patchwork quilt. There was a painting on the other wall, a deep wooded grove with a neon rhododendron in its foreground. The frame was suspended from a nail by a piece of rusty wire that seemed unequal to the task. Something made scurrying noises in the ceiling cavity above and the painting moved lightly against the wall.

Stillness and silence returned and Juliet released a breath that she hadn't realized she'd been holding. She had longed for the children to go to sleep, finally to have some time for herself; now, though, she missed the certainty of their noise, their essential confidence. The house was quiet. It was unfamiliar. Juliet was quite alone.

She opened her suitcase beside her. The leather was worn at the corners, but it was a faithful friend, harking back to her days in repertory theater, and she was glad to have it. Her fingers traced a thoughtful line between two small piles of folded dresses and blouses, and she considered unpacking.

Instead, she dug out the slender bottle from where it was wedged beneath the clothing and took it downstairs.

Fetching a glass tumbler from the kitchen, she headed outside.

The air in the walled garden was warm, the light bluish. It was one of those long summer evenings when the day becomes fixed in transition.

There was a gate in the stone wall leading out to the dusty strip that the man from the AHA had called "the coach way." Juliet followed the path and spied a garden table set up in the gap between two willows on the grassy knoll. Beyond it, a strip of water tripped cheerfully in the gully. Not as wide as the river; a tributary, she supposed. She set the glass down on the table's iron top and poured the whisky carefully, eyeing the midline. When she reached it, she dropped another generous slug.

"Bottoms up," she said to the dusk.

That initial long slow sip was a balm. Juliet's eyes closed and for the first time in hours she let her thoughts settle on Alan.

She wondered what he'd think if he knew that she and the children were here. He'd liked this place well enough, but not as she had. Her affection for the small Thames-side village, more specifically the twin-gabled house on its edge, had always amused him. He'd called her a romantic, emphasizing the capital *R*.

Perhaps she was. She certainly wasn't the lowercase sort. Even with Alan away in France, Juliet had resisted the urge to shower him with ostentatious declarations of love. There was no need—he *knew* how she felt—and to allow absence and war to induce hyperbole, to trick her into a sentimentality she'd have been embarrassed to employ if they were speaking face-to-face, was to admit a lack of faith. Did she love him more because Britain was at war with Germany? Had she loved him less when he was whistling in the kitchen, apron round his middle as he fried their fish for dinner?

No. Stubbornly, resolutely, certainly, no.

And so, instead of reams of wartime promises and affirmations, they honored one another by sticking to the truth.

The most recent letter she'd received was in her pocket, but Juliet didn't take it out now. Instead, she collected the whisky bottle and followed the grassy track towards the river.

Alan's letter had become a totem of sorts, an integral part of this journey that she'd embarked upon. She'd had it with her in the shelter that night, tucked inside the copy of *David Copperfield* she'd been rereading. While the old duck from number thirty-four clacked her knitting needles and hummed "We'll Meet Again" and the four Whitfield boys tripped over people's feet and honked like geese, Juliet had read again Alan's account of the scene at Dunkirk, heavily redacted, but striking nonetheless. He'd described the men on the beach, and the journey to make it that far; the villagers they'd passed on their way, small children and elderly women with bowed legs, wagons piled high with suitcases and birdcages and knitted blankets. All of them fleeing the misery and destruction, but with nowhere safe to run.

"I came across a young boy with a bleeding leg," he'd written. "He was sitting on a broken fence, and the look in his eyes conveyed that awful point beyond panic, the terrible acceptance that this was now his lot. I asked him his name, and whether he needed help, where his family were, and after a time he answered me in soft French. He didn't know, he said, he didn't know. The poor lad couldn't walk and his cheeks were stained with tears and I couldn't just leave him there, all alone. He reminded me of Tip. Older, but with the same seriousness of spirit as our little one. He hopped on my back in the end, with no complaint or query, and I carried him to the beach."

Juliet reached the wooden jetty, and even through the twilight she could see that it had deteriorated in the twelve years since she and Alan had sat on its end drinking tea from Mrs. Hammett's thermos. She closed her eyes briefly and let the noise of the river surround her. Its constancy was heartening: no matter what else was happening in the world, regardless of human folly or individual torment, the river kept flowing.

She opened her eyes and let her gaze roam across the dense copse of trees beyond, hunkered down for the night. She wouldn't go beyond this point. The children would be frightened if they woke and found her gone.

Turning to look back in the direction from which she'd come, above the soft curved darkness of the Birchwood Manor garden, she could just make out a silhouette of sharper lines, the rise of the twin gables and punctuating columns of the eight chimneys.

She sat herself against the trunk of a nearby willow, positioning the whisky bottle in a clump of grass at her feet.

Juliet felt a wave of excitement, dampened almost at once by the circumstances that had brought her here.

The idea to come back to this place, twelve years after she'd discovered it, had arrived fully formed. They'd clambered from the shelter at the sound of the all clear, and Juliet's thoughts had been on other things.

The smell was the first indication that things were awry—smoke and smolder, dust and unhappiness—and then they'd emerged into the haze and an uncanny brightness. It had taken a moment to realize that their house was gone and that dawn streamed now through a gap in the row of terraces.

Juliet hadn't realized that she'd dropped her bag until she saw her things on the ground at her feet amongst the rubble. The pages of *David Copperfield* were fluttering where the volume had landed open, the old postcard she'd been using as a bookmark lying beside it. Later, there would be a thousand small details to organize and worry about, but in that moment, as she reached to retrieve the postcard and the picture of the Swan on its front came into focus, and her children's panicked voices piped in and out of earshot, and the immensity of what was happening to them rose like a hot cloud around her, there'd been only one cool thought.

A feeling so strong had risen from that place where memories are stored, and with it an idea that hadn't then seemed crazy at all but clear and certain. Juliet had known simply that she had to get the children to safety. The imperative had been instinctive, animal; it was all that she could focus on, and the sepia image on the postcard, a gift from Alan, a reminder of their honeymoon, had made it seem that he was standing beside her, holding her hand. And the relief, after missing him so long, after worrying and wondering while he was far away, unreachable, unable to help, had been overwhelming. As she picked her way across the rubble to take Tip's hand, she'd felt a surge of exhilaration, because she'd known exactly what she must do next.

It had occurred to her afterwards that the flash of certainty might actually have been a symptom of madness, brought on by shock, but over the following days, as they slept on the floors of friends and acquired a motley collection of new essentials, she'd settled on the idea. The school was closed and children were leaving London in droves. But Juliet couldn't imagine sending her three off alone. It was possible that the older two might have leapt at the chance of adventure—Bea especially relishing the independence and opportunity to live with anyone but her mother—but not Tip, not her little bird.

It had taken days after the bombing before he'd let her out of his sight, watching her every move with wide, worried eyes so that Juliet's jaw ached by evening with the effort of having to keep a bright face on things. Finally, though, with much love and the clever deployment of new rocks for his collection, she'd been able to reassure him sufficiently to earn an hour or so to herself.

She'd left the three of them with Alan's best friend, Jeremy, a playwright of some note upon whose Bloomsbury floor they were currently sleeping, and had used the phone box on Gower Street to telephone the Swan; Mrs. Hammett herself had picked up at the faraway end of the whistling line. The older woman had remembered her with genuine delight when Juliet explained about the honeymoon, and promised to ask around the village when she mentioned her intention to bring her children to the country. The following day, when Juliet telephoned back, Mrs. Hammett had told her that there was one house vacant and available to lease. "A bit run-down, but you could do worse. There's no electricity, but with the blackout I suppose that's neither here nor there. The rent is fair and there's nothing else for love nor money, what with the evacuees taking up every spare room this side of London."

Juliet had asked where it was in relation to the Swan, and when Mrs. Hammett described the location, she'd felt a thrill up her spine. She'd known exactly which house; she hadn't needed to think it through. She'd told Mrs. Hammett that they'd take it and made brief arrangements to wire a deposit of the first month's rent to the group that was handling the lease. She replaced the receiver and stood for a moment inside the phone box. Beyond the glass, the fast-moving clouds of the morning had gathered and darkened, and people were walking faster than usual, arms folded across their bodies, heads down against the sudden chill.

Until that point Juliet had kept her plans to herself. It wouldn't have taken much to talk her out of it and she hadn't wanted that to happen. But now, having come this far, there were certain things that would need to be done. Mr. Tallisker, for one, would have to be told. He was her boss, the editor at the newspaper where she worked, and her absence would therefore be noticed.

She went straight to the offices on Fleet Street, arriving minutes after the rain began to fall. In the bathroom on the first floor she did what she could with her damp hair, fluffing her blouse back and forwards in an attempt to dry it. Her face was drawn, she noticed, and pale. In lieu of lipstick she gave her lips a pinch, rubbed them together, smiled at her reflection. The effect was unconvincing.

Sure enough: "Good God," said Mr. Tallisker when his secretary had left them. "Things *are* grim." He gathered his eyebrows as she told him what she intended to do, leaning back in his leather chair, arms crossed. "Birchwood," he said at last, from the other side of the vast paper-strewn desk. "Berkshire, is it?"

"Yes."

"Not a lot of theater."

"No, but I plan to come back to London every fortnight—every week if necessary—and file my reviews that way."

He made a noise that did not signal encouragement, and Juliet felt her imagined future slipping away. His voice when he spoke again was unreadable. "I was sorry to hear about things."

"Thank you."

"Bloody bombers."

"Yes."

"Bloody war." He picked up his pen and dropped it repeatedly, incendiary-style, against the wooden surface of his desk. Beyond the crooked blinds, half drawn against the dusty window, a fly was batting its death throes.

A clock ticked.

Someone in the hallway laughed.

Finally, with a rapidity and deftness that belied his generous size, Mr. Tallisker tossed the pen aside and took up a cigarette in its stead. "Birchwood," he said finally, on a current of smoke. "It could work."

"I'll make it work. I can be back in London—"

"No." He swatted the suggestion aside. "Not London. Not theater."

"Sir?"

The cigarette became a pointer. "Londoners are brave, Jules, but they're tired. They need an escape and most of them aren't going to get it. Theater's all well and good, but sunny village life? That's the stuff. That's the story people want to hear."

"Mr. Tallisker, I—"

"A weekly column." He swept his hands out to either side as if suspending a banner: " 'Letters from the Laneway.' The sort of thing you might write home to Mother. Stories of your life, your children, the people you meet. Anecdotes about sunshine and hens laying eggs and village japes."

"Japes?"

"Farmers and housewives and vicars, neighbors and gossip."

"Gossip?"

"The funnier the better."

Juliet frowned now as she readjusted her back against the rough bark of the tree. She wasn't funny, at least not in print, not for the benefit of strangers. Acerbic at times—barbed, she'd been told—but funny was not her métier. However, Mr. Tallisker had been unmoved, and thus had the Faustian pact been made. The chance to get away, to come to this place, in exchange for . . . what? "Why, your integrity, of course," the Alan in her mind supplied, a light smile playing on his lips. "Only your integrity."

Juliet glanced down. The blouse she was wearing was not her own and it wore like an apology. Kind of the volunteers to find them clothes, of course; remarkable the way such groups popped up to meet the needs du jour. She remembered a trip to Italy some years before, when she and Alan had emerged from St. Peter's to find it raining, and suddenly the Gypsies who'd been selling hats and sunglasses only an hour before were laden with umbrellas.

A shiver rippled through her at the memory, or perhaps its cause was simpler than that. The last of the day's light was dissolving and the night would be cool. In this place, the warmth went with the light. Juliet and Alan had been surprised when they came here on honeymoon by the night air on their skin, in that small square room above the pub, with its lemon-striped wallpaper and a window seat for one that they'd managed to share. They'd been different people back then, other versions of themselves: lighter, leaner, with fewer layers of life to see through.

Juliet glanced at her watch, but it was too dark to read. She didn't need to see the hour to know that it was time to be getting back to the house.

Palm against the tree trunk, she pushed herself to a standing position.

Her head swooned; the whisky bottle was lighter now than she'd realized, and Juliet took a moment to regain her balance.

As she did, something in the distance caught her eye. It was the house, but there was a faint show of light inside, right up high in one of the gables—the attic, perhaps.

Juliet blinked and shook her head. She must have imagined it. Birchwood Manor had no electricity and she hadn't been upstairs to leave a lamp.

Sure enough, when she looked again, the light was gone.

CHAPTER NINETEEN

THEY rose next morning with the sun. Juliet lay in bed listening as the children ran excitedly from room to room, exclaiming at the light, the birdsong, the garden, tripping over themselves to get outside. Her head was a whisky mud and she feigned sleep for as long as she could. Only when she sensed a looming presence on the other side of her eyelids did she finally admit to being awake. It was Freddy, right above her, proximity rendering his face—already generous of feature—unusually large.

Now it widened into a delighted gap-toothed grin. Freckles danced, dark eyes shone. Already, somehow, he had crumbs around his mouth.

"She's awake," he shouted, and Juliet winced. "Come *on*, Mummy, we *must* go down to the river."

The river. That's right. Juliet turned her head by degrees and saw a shock of blue-glass sky through the gap between the curtains. Freddy was tugging her arm now and she managed a nod and a brave, meager smile. It was sufficient to send him scampering from the room with an excited whoop.

Impossible to explain to Red, whose faith in the world's never-ending supply of good times was absolute, but Juliet wasn't on holiday; she had a meeting with the local arm of the Women's Voluntary Services lined up at eleven, in the hope of uncovering an angle for her first "Letters from the Laneway" column. Nevertheless, the single benefit of being woken at such an ungodly hour—for, really, one had to look on the bright side—was the unexpectedly long stretch of hours remaining until duty called.

Juliet threw on a spotted cotton blouse because it was close to hand, belted a pair of trousers, and ran her fingers through her hair. A brief trip to the bathroom to splash water on her face, and she was ready. Rough, but she would do. Downstairs, she gathered Mrs. Hammett's basket with its bread and cheese, and they left the house, following the same flagstone path that she had taken the night before.

Tip, in a pair of faded dungarees at least an inch too short, propelled himself forward like a windup doll, his short legs racing as he chased his brother and sister across the grass towards the track that met the river. Beatrice had stopped by the big old stone barn at the top of the coach way and was holding out her arms. Tip leapt into them when he was close enough, and she slid him around so that he could clamber onto her back. What it was to be the youngest of three—what luck to be born into a jumbly, rowdy group of bigger people and be simply adored.

A huddle of geese retreated in alarm as the children barreled past them, Red laughing with glee for the simple joy that he was running with the sun on his skin and the breeze in his hair. They looked quite unlike her children, and Juliet was struck again by the contrast between this place and London, the only home her three had ever known. It was the world they came from, to which their father so resolutely belonged. She remembered the first time she'd seen him, a tall, lean Londoner with a wooden pipe that he'd been frowning around in a most pretentious manner. She'd thought him arrogant then—talented but impossibly self-assured; pompous, even, with his mannered way of speaking and his opinions on just about everything. It had taken time and the unfortunate business with the revolving door at Claridge's for her to see through his irony to the beating heart beneath.

She'd caught up with the children now, and they took turns climbing over the ivy-covered wooden stile before setting off westwards along the river's edge. There was a red canalboat moored against the bank, and it reminded Juliet, vaguely, that there was a lock or weir nearby. She made a mental note to take the children exploring one day. It was the sort of thing Alan would suggest if he were here; he'd say how marvelous it was for them to see the lock in action.

A salty man with a beard and a peaked cap nodded at them from the rear deck of the longboat, and Juliet nodded back. Yes, she thought, this was the right thing to do, to come here to Birchwood Manor. They would all do better here; the change of scene would be a balm after the dreadful things that they'd been through.

While the boys tripped on ahead, Bea had fallen into step beside her. "When you came here on honeymoon, did you and Daddy walk this way along the river?"

"We did."

"Is this the way to the jetty?"

"It is."

"My jetty."

Juliet smiled. "Yes."

"Why did you come here?"

She looked sideways at her daughter.

"To this village," explained Beatrice. "On your honeymoon. Don't people usually go to the seaside?"

"Oh, I see. I don't know. It's hard to remember now."

"Maybe someone told you about it?"

"Maybe." Juliet frowned, thinking. Strange that she remembered so many of the details from back then, yet others were completely gone. Bea was right: it was most likely that someone—the friend of a friend—had given them the suggestion, possibly even the name of the pub itself. That's how things tended to happen in the theater. A conversation in the dressing room, or at a backstage script rehearsal, or, perhaps most likely, over an after-show pint at Berardo's.

Whatever the case, they'd reserved the little room at the Swan by telephone and traveled down from London on the afternoon following their wedding lunch. Juliet had lost her favorite pen somewhere between Reading and Swindon—and this is what she meant by some memories sticking like films, for she remembered the train ride vividly. The last thing in her journal had been a hastily sketched note about a West Highland terrier she'd been watching on the floor across the aisle. Alan, who'd always loved dogs, had been chatting with the owner, a man wearing a green cravat, who'd talked at length about poor Mr. Percival's diabetes and the insulin shots required to keep him well. Juliet had been making notes, as was her habit, because the man was interesting to her and belonged, she was certain, in a play she was planning to write. But then she'd been overcome with a wave of nausea, and there'd been a dash to the loo, and Alan's surprised concern to deal with, and the arrival into Swindon—and in all the bluster her pen had been forgotten.

Juliet kicked at a small rounded stone and watched as it skittered along the grass and disappeared into the water. They were almost at the jetty. By the clear light of day, she could see how decrepit it had become in the intervening twelve years. She and Alan had sat together on its end, their toes trailing in the water; Juliet wasn't sure she'd trust it to hold even her weight anymore.

"Is this the one?"

"And only."

"Tell me again what he said."

"He was delighted. He said that at long last he was going to have the little girl he'd always wished for."

"He did not."

"He did."

"You're making it up."

"I'm not."

"What was the weather like?"

"Sunny."

"What were you eating?"

"Scones."

"How did he know I was going to be a girl?"

"Ah . . ." Juliet smiled. "You've become cleverer since the last time I told you the story."

Beatrice lowered her chin to hide her pleasure, and Juliet fought the urge to embrace her prickly little child-woman while she still could. The gesture, she knew, would not be appreciated.

They walked on and Beatrice picked a dandelion, blowing gently to send spores of fluff startling in all directions. The effect was so elemental and dreamlike that Juliet had an urge to do the same herself. She spotted a full head and plucked it by the stem.

Beatrice said, "What did Daddy say when you told him we were moving here?"

Juliet considered the question; she had always promised herself that she would be truthful with her children. "I haven't told him yet."

"What do you think he'll say?"

That she'd clearly gone mad? That they were city kids, just like their dad? That she'd always been a romantic . . . ? A familiar, half-forgotten trill rang out above, and Juliet stopped sharply, reaching out to alert Bea, too. "Listen!"

"What is it?"

"*Shhh* . . . a skylark."

They stood silently for a few seconds, Beatrice squinting at the blue sky, scanning for the distant, hovering bird, Juliet watching her daughter's face. Bea's features took on a particularly Alan cast when she concentrated: the slight furrow above her aquiline nose, the heavy knitted brow.

"There!" Bea pointed, eyes widening. The skylark had appeared, shooting towards the ground like one of Herr Hitler's incendiaries. "Hey, Red, Tippy, look."

The boys spun around, attention following their sister's finger towards the diving bird.

Hard to imagine that this leggy eleven-and-a-half-year-old was the new life that had caused such commotion in this very spot all those years ago.

After the episode on the train, Juliet had managed to mollify Alan. She'd pleaded too much rich food at lunch, the motion of the carriage, that she'd been focusing on her notebook instead of looking out the window, but Juliet had known that she was going to have to tell him the truth soon.

Mrs. Hammett at the Swan had torpedoed that time with her well-meaning query on their first morning. "And when are you due?" she'd said with a beaming smile as she arranged the milk jug on the breakfast table. Juliet's expression must have painted a clear enough picture, for the publican's wife had tapped her nose and given a wink and promised that the secret was safe with her.

They'd found the jetty later that day, when Mrs. Hammett sent them off with a picnic basket—"Part of the honeymoon package"—and Juliet had broken the news over a thermos of tea and a rather good scone.

"A baby?" Alan's confused glance had dropped from her eyes to her waist. "In there, you mean? Now?"

"Presumably."

"Goodness."

"Quite."

It had to be said, he'd taken it well. Even Juliet had found herself beginning to relax a little, his easy acceptance bringing solidity to the flimsy picture of this new future she'd been trying to imagine since the nurse confirmed her fears. But then:

"I'll get work somewhere."

"What?"

"There are things I can do, you know."

"I do know. You're the best Macbeth this side of Edinburgh."

"Real work, Jules. In the day, I mean, like a normal person. Work that pays."

"Pays?"

"So you can stay at home, raise the baby, be a mother. I can . . . sell shoes."

She wasn't precisely sure what she'd said next, only that the thermos had fallen over and the tea had scalded her thigh, and then she was somehow on her feet at the end of the jetty, gesticulating wildly and explaining that she had no intention of staying home, that he couldn't make her, that she'd take the child out with her if she must, that it would learn to be happy that way, that they'd manage. Needless to say, this wasn't the version of the story they told Beatrice.

Juliet had heard herself as if from outside—she'd felt articulate and certain—and then Alan had reached for her and said, "For goodness' sake, Juliet, sit down!" and she'd considered it, moving a step closer, before he added the fatal "You have to be careful in your condition." And then she'd felt his words like a stranglehold, and her breaths had shortened, and she'd known that she simply had to get away, from here, from him, to find clear air.

She'd stormed along the river in the opposite direction from which they'd arrived, ignoring his calls to come back, and heading instead towards a copse of trees on the horizon.

Juliet didn't cry, not as a rule; she hadn't since she was six years old, when her father died and her mother told her they were leaving London to live with Granny in Sheffield. Now, though, the heat of her anger, her frustration that Alan could possibly see things so wrong-headedly—that he should think she was going to give up her work, stay home each day while he went out to make a living as a . . . a what? a shoe salesman?—caused everything to spin away from her, as if she were being pulled apart like wisps of smoke on the breeze.

Before she knew it, Juliet had reached the trees and, seized by a sudden urge to disappear from sight, plowed directly into the grove. There was a narrow path of flattened grass, the sort made by repeated footfalls, and it was leading away from the river. She'd supposed that it would bring her full circle to arrive on the other side of the village, back near the Swan, but Juliet had never been great with directions. Deeper and deeper she went, her thoughts thundering, and when she finally reemerged into the sunlit day, she hadn't been on the edge of the village at all. She'd no idea whatsoever where she was. To add insult to injury, she'd been hit with a wave of nausea so strong she'd needed to grab the nearest tree and be sick—

"Wheeeeee!"

Juliet jumped as Red soared towards her, arms outstretched. "Mummy, I'm a Spitfire and you're a Junker."

On instinct, she swerved her body to avoid collision.

"Mummy," he said, crossly, "that's not very patriotic of you."

"Sorry, Red," she began, but her apology was lost in his wake as he zoomed away.

Bea, she noticed, was already well ahead, almost at the copse of trees.

Juliet was disappointed: the jetty had been part of their family story for over a decade, and she'd looked forward to bringing her daughter back here one day to see it. She wasn't sure what she'd expected—not reverence, not really, but something.

"Are you sad, Mummy?"

Tip was next to her, looking up with his searching eyes.

Juliet smiled. "With you in the room? Never."

"We're not in a room."

"No. You're quite right. Silly me."

He slipped his small hand into hers and together they started walking again towards the others. It never ceased to amaze Juliet how perfectly the hands of her children fit within her own and how warming she found the simple gesture.

On the other side of the river, a field of barley glimmered yellow. It was hard to believe, as the Thames tripped freshly and bees sought clover in the grass, that a war was being fought. There were signs in the village, of course: the street names were all gone, windows were crisscrossed with tape, and Juliet had seen a poster on a phone box reminding passersby that they should all be digging for victory. They'd even covered the Uffington White Horse, lest it prove useful to enemy pilots seeking the way home. But here, now, on this gentle bend of the river, it seemed almost impossible to believe.

Tip let out a small sigh beside her and it occurred to Juliet that he was quieter than usual. The dark smudges from the night before were still under his eyes, too.

"Sleep all right, little mouse?"

A nod.

"It's always a bit tricky in a new bed."

"Is it?"

"Yes, but only at first."

He seemed to think about this. "Is it tricky for you, too, Mummy?"

"Oh, yes. Because I'm a big person, and everything is always tricky for us."

"But only at first?"

"Yes."

Tip seemed to take some relief at this, which was sweet but also a little disconcerting. Juliet hadn't supposed her comfort played much on his mind. She glanced at her older two striding away into the distance. She was quite sure neither one of them had ever inquired as to whether she'd slept well at night.

"A Pooh-stick!" Tip slipped his hand free and picked up a slim silver branch, almost hidden in the grass.

"Oh, yes. What a find. Isn't it lovely?"

"Very smooth."

"It's willow, I think. Maybe birch."

"I'm going to see if it floats."

"Careful not to go too close to the river's edge," she said, ruffling his hair.

"I know. I won't. It's deep in there."

"It certainly is."

"That's where the girl drowned."

Juliet was taken aback. "Darling, no."

"Yes, Mummy."

"I'm sure that's not true."

"It is. She fell from a boat."

"Who did? How do you know?"

"Birdie told me." And then he smiled his worrying, solemn little boy smile and, with a quicksilver change of heart, ran off instead to where his brother and sister were fighting over a pair of long sticks, brandishing his own victoriously above his head.

Juliet watched him go.

She caught herself biting a snag from her fingernail.

She didn't know what was more alarming: his talk of dead girls or the fact that the news had been delivered to him by a feathered friend.

"He just has a vivid imagination," came Alan's voice in her head.

"He's talking to birds," Juliet replied beneath her breath.

She rubbed her eyes, her forehead, her temple. Her head was still thumping from the night before, and she'd have given anything to curl up and go back to sleep for a few more hours; a few more days.

With a long, slow sigh, she decided to set the worry aside. There would be time to ruminate later. Tip had caught up to the others and he was laughing now as Red chased him around the field, glancing over his shoulder in raptures of delight while his brother pretended to hunt him. Just like a normal boy. ("He *is* a normal boy," said Alan.)

Juliet looked at her watch and saw that it was almost eight. Giving her shoulders a light shake, she headed towards the children, who were all waiting for her now by the copse.

When she reached them, she waved her arm, signaling that they should follow her into the trees; and as they continued their gamboling game of swords and knights, Juliet thought again of Alan and the day twelve years before when she'd stormed away from him and followed this path for the first time . . .

She wasn't in the center of the village, that much was clear; she was, instead, standing on the edge of a field with big round hay bales set at intervals across it. Beyond, on the far side of a second field, was a stone barn; further yet she could make out the pitch of a roof. A twin-gabled roof possessing an embarrassment of chimneys.

With a sigh, because the sun was very high and very hot, and the initial fire of her rage had reduced to a pile of smoldering coals that now sat uncomfortably in her belly, Juliet started trudging through the grass towards it.

To think that Alan could so misunderstand her; that he could imagine, even for a second, that she would give up her job. Writing wasn't something she did; it was who she was. How could he not realize that, the man with whom she'd pledged to spend her life, into whose ear she'd whispered her deepest secrets?

She had made a mistake. It was all so obvious. Marriage was a mistake, and now there was going to be a baby, hers and Alan's, and it would be small and helpless and probably noisy, not welcome in theaters, and she was going to end up just like her mother after all, a woman whose grand dreams had withered to form a net that contained her.

Perhaps it was not too late to have the whole thing canceled? It had only been a day. Barely twenty-four little hours. Maybe there was still time, if they went straight back to London this afternoon, to catch up with the official who'd married them and beg back the certificate before he even had time to file it with the register office. It would be as if it had never happened.

Sensing, perhaps, the precariousness of its future, the tiny life inside her sent another wave of nausea: *Here I am!*

And it was right. It *was* here. He or she, a little person, was growing, and one day in the not-too-distant future would be born. Being unmarried to Alan would not change that fact.

Juliet reached the end of the first field and opened a simple wooden gate to enter the next. She was thirsty; she wished she'd thought to bring the thermos with her.

Halfway across the second field she drew level with the barn. The large double doors were open and as she passed them she glimpsed inside a large farm machine—a thresher; the word came to her—and above, strung from the rafters, a wooden rowboat with a distinct look of neglect about it.

As Juliet neared the edge of the field, the yellow crop made a dramatic transition to the vibrant, juicy green of an English country garden in summer. The garden was at the rear of the twin-gabled house, and while most of the fence line was concealed by an abundant blackthorn hedge, there was a hinged gate through which Juliet could see a gravel courtyard with a chestnut tree at its center. Surrounding it were raised beds from which tumbled a profusion of foliage and cheerful flowers.

She skirted along the hedge until she reached the corner of the field and hit a dirt road. Faced with the choice to turn right and head back in the direction from which she'd come, Juliet turned left. The blackthorn hedge continued along the boundary of the garden before abutting a stone wall that became the side of the house. Just past the house was another gate, this one decorative iron with an arched top.

On the other side of the gate, a flagstone path led to the front door of the elegant house, and Juliet stopped to drink in its pleasing shape and details. She had always had an eye for beauty, especially that of an architectural nature. Sometimes, on weekends, she and Alan had taken the train to the country or borrowed a car from a friend and puttered around the winding lanes of the smallest villages. Juliet had a notebook into which she made quick notes about rooflines she liked or paving patterns that charmed her. The hobby had made Alan laugh fondly and call her "Lady Tessellated," because she'd made the mistake of drawing his attention to the tile pattern one too many times.

This house was of lichen-colored stone and stood two stories high. The roof—also stone, but a shade or two darker—was deeply satisfying. The slates at the peak were small, gaining in size with each course as they lowered towards the eaves. Sunlight made them appear dappled and shifting like the scales of a slow-moving fish. There was a window in each of the gables, and Juliet pressed lightly against the gate to observe them more closely; for a second she thought she saw movement behind one of them, but there was nothing there, just the shadow of a passing bird.

As she studied the house, the gate pushed open beneath her hands like an invitation.

With barely a hesitation, Juliet stepped down onto the flagstone path and was suffused immediately with a sense of deep contentment. It was a beautiful garden: the proportions, the plants, the feeling of enclosure granted by the surrounding stone wall. The fragrance, too, was heady: a hint of late-blooming jasmine mingled with lavender and honeysuckle. Birds flitted in the gaps between leaves, and bees and butterflies hovered over flowers in the ample garden beds.

The gate through which she'd come was the side entrance, Juliet saw now, for another, larger path led away from the house towards a solid wooden gate set into the stones of the front wall. The wider path was lined on either side by standard roses wearing soft pink petals, and at its end was a large Japanese maple tree that had grown to reach across the front entrance.

The lawn was a deep bright green, and without thinking twice Juliet took off her shoes and stepped forwards onto it. The grass was cool and soft between her toes. Heavenly—that was the word.

There was a particularly inviting patch of dappled shade on the grass beneath the Japanese maple tree, and Juliet went to sit down. She was trespassing, of course, but surely no one in possession of a house and garden like this one could be anything but charming.

The sun was warm and the breeze light and Juliet yawned widely. She had been struck by a wave of weariness so intense that she had no choice but to surrender to it. It had been happening a lot lately, at the most inopportune times—ever since she'd found out about the baby.

Using her cardigan as a pillow, she lay on her back, her head turned to face the house. She told herself that she would just take a few minutes to rest, but the sun was delicious on her feet, and before she knew it, her eyelids had turned to lead.

When she woke, it took Juliet a moment to remember where she was. She'd slept so soundly: deep and dreamless, in a way she hadn't for weeks.

She sat up and stretched. And that's when she noticed that she was no longer alone.

There was a man standing at the corner of the house near the gate. He was older than she was. Not by much, not in terms of years, but she could tell at once that his soul weighed heavy. He had been a soldier; there was no mistaking it. They still wore uniforms, those poor, broken men. They would always be a generation unto themselves.

He was looking at her, his expression serious but not stern.

"I'm sorry," Juliet called out. "I didn't mean to trespass. I lost my way."

He didn't say anything for a moment, and then answered with a simple wave of his hand. From the gesture, Juliet understood that all was well; that he didn't consider her a menace; that he understood the lure of this garden, this house, the magic it cast, and the helplessness a passerby might feel when called on a hot day by the cool, shady patch of grass beneath the maple tree.

Without the exchange of another word or glance, the man disappeared inside the house, the door closing behind him. Juliet watched him go and then let her gaze fall to her shoes on the grass. She noticed the creep of the shadows since she'd arrived and glanced at her watch. It had been over four hours since she'd left Alan at the jetty.

Juliet slipped on her shoes and laced them up, and then she pushed herself to standing.

She knew she had to leave; she still wasn't even sure where she was in relation to the village; and yet, it was a wrench. She felt a pain in her chest as if something were physically restraining her. She stood in the middle of the smooth lawn, staring up at the house, and an odd suffusion of light made everything seem so clear.

Love—that's what she felt, an odd, strong, general love that seemed to flow from everything she saw and heard: the sunlit leaves, the dark hollows beneath the trees, the stones of the house, the birds that called as they flew overhead. And in its glow, she glimpsed momentarily what religious people must surely feel at church: the sense of being bathed in the light of certainty that comes with being known from the inside out, from belonging somewhere and to someone. It was simple. It was luminous, and beautiful, and true.

Alan was waiting for her when she found her way back to the Swan. Juliet hurried up the stairs, two by two, bursting through the door to their room, her face warm with the day's heat, her day's revelation.

He was standing by the leadlight window with its crooked glimpse of the river, his pose stiff and self-conscious, as if he'd assumed it only when he heard her coming, a performance of readiness. His expression was wary and it took a moment for Juliet to remember why: the argument on the jetty, the fire of her withdrawal.

"Before you say anything," Alan started, "I want you to know that I never meant to suggest—"

Juliet was shaking her head. "It doesn't matter, don't you see? None of it matters anymore."

"What is it? What's happened?"

It was all inside her—the clarity, the illumination—but she couldn't find the words to explain, only the golden energy that had infused her and that she could no longer contain. She hurried to him, passionate, impatient, seizing his face between her palms and kissing him so that any animosity between them, any lingering guardedness, fell away. When he opened his mouth to speak, surprised, she shook her head and pressed a finger to his lips. There were no words. Words would only spoil things.

This moment.

Now.

CHAPTER TWENTY

THE garden was more or less as Juliet remembered it. A little wilder, but then Mrs. Hammett had mentioned that the woman who'd owned the house when Juliet first stumbled upon it had been forced to hand over the reins in recent years. "Ninety years old, she was, when she died last summer." The gardener still came once a month, but he was slapdash, and, she'd added with a moue of disdain, an out-of-towner. Mrs. Hammett said that Lucy would turn in her grave if she could see how hard he'd pruned back the roses over the winter.

Juliet, picturing the perfection of the garden in 1928, asked whether Lucy had still lived in the house back then, but Mrs. Hammett said that no, it was around that time she'd started her "arrangement" with the Art Historians' Association and moved into the little place around the corner. "One of the stable cottages in the row. You might have seen them? Fewer stairs, Lucy used to say. Fewer memories, methinks is what she meant."

"She had bad memories of Birchwood?"

"Oh, no, I didn't mean that. She loved that place. You're too young to understand, I expect, but when one gets old, *all* memories have a weight, even the happy ones."

Juliet was perfectly familiar with the heaviness of time, but she hadn't wished to get into all of that with Mrs. Hammett.

The arrangement with the AHA, from what she understood, allowed the house to be granted to students as part of a scholarship scheme. The man who'd handed over the key on the night that they arrived from London had pushed his spectacles back up the bridge of his nose and said, "It's not the most modern of houses. We usually accommodate individuals, not families, and not for long stretches of time. There's no electricity, I'm afraid, but—well, the war . . . I'm sure everything else will be in order—" And then the bird had launched itself from above the pantry, straight at their heads, and he'd become defensive, and Juliet had thanked him for coming and walked him to the exit, and they'd breathed parallel sighs of relief as he scurried along the path and she closed the door behind him. And then she'd turned around and been met by the faces of three small displaced people waiting for their dinner.

Since then, they'd settled into a good routine. It had been four days now, each one clear and bright, and they'd become used to early mornings in the garden. Bea had taken to climbing the stone wall that ran around the house, setting up in the sunniest spot, legs crossed, to play her recorder, while Red, who was worryingly less deft but not to be outdone, carried his arsenal of carefully selected sticks onto the thinnest part of the wall to practice jousting. Juliet continued to point out that there were perfectly lovely patches of grass on which they could be playing, but her suggestions fell on deaf ears. Tip, thank goodness, was not interested in scaling the heights. He seemed content to sit in whichever concealed patch of undergrowth he favored that day, lining up the set of toy soldiers that a kind lady at the local Women's Voluntary Service meeting had sent home with Juliet.

Home. Strange to think how quickly the word had slipped into her thoughts about Birchwood. It was one of those words of multiple meanings: the perfunctory description accorded the building in which one currently resides, but also the warm, rounded name used to describe the place from which ultimate comfort and safety is derived. Home was Alan's voice at the end of a long, hard day; his arms around her; the known quantity of his love for her and hers for him.

God, she missed him.

Along with the children, work proved a welcome distraction. Juliet had met the women of the local WVS group as planned at eleven on Monday. Their meetings were conducted in the village hall, across the green from the Swan, and she'd arrived to the strains of what sounded like a lively dance in progress—music and laughter, chatter and singing. She'd stopped on the stairs and wondered for a moment whether she had the wrong address, but when she poked her head around the door, Mrs. Hammett had waved and called her over to where the group was sitting on a circle of chairs in the center of the room. The hall was strung with Union Jack flags, and posters of Churchill puffed and glowered from each wall.

Juliet had arrived with a list of questions, but she'd soon turned over a page in her notebook and started taking shorthand summaries of the free-ranging conversation instead. For all that she'd sat up late the night before planning her articles, her imagination, it turned out, was no match for the reality of these women, whose eccentricities, charm, and wisdom made her laugh with them and ache for them. Marjorie Stubbs provided a remarkable insight into the trials and tribulations of backyard pig farming; Milly Macklemore offered a revelatory perspective on the many uses of stockings with holes; and Imogen Stephens had everybody reaching for their handkerchiefs when she told of the recent return of her daughter's pilot fiancé, who had been missing and presumed dead.

And although the other women evidently knew each other well, many of them mothers and daughters, aunts and nieces, friends since childhood, they welcomed Juliet into the group with enormous generosity. They were as intrigued and amused, it seemed, at gaining a Londoner's approach to life and the strange times in which they found themselves as Juliet was by their experiences. By the time she left the meeting, promising to come back for the next, Juliet had learned enough to keep readers of the newspaper engaged until the year 2000. If the war was going to be won, she had decided as she made the short walk back to Birchwood Manor, it was going to be won in part from rooms like that one, all over the country, where steadfast, ingenious women kept their collective chins up and refused to give in.

And so, in their spirit, Juliet had spent much of the past three days at her typewriter beneath the window in her bedroom. For all that it was not the most comfortable place to work—the dressing table upon which she'd positioned her typewriter was pretty but not ideal when one had legs to accommodate—Juliet liked it very much. Tendrils of fragrant honeysuckle and clematis reached through the open window to clutch at the curtain fastenings, and the view over the orchard towards the village, in particular the churchyard at the end of the lane, was restorative. The stone church was very old, and the grounds around it, though small, were beautiful; lots of tumbling ivy and mossy headstones. Juliet hadn't had a chance yet to visit, but it was on her list of things to do.

Sometimes, when the day was simply too glorious to spend indoors, Juliet took her notebook into the garden. There she worked in the shade, lying on her stomach with her head resting on her palm as she alternated between scribbling notes and chewing on her pencil, all the while carrying out secret observations of the children. They seemed to be adjusting well enough: there was laughter and playing, their appetites were good, they fought and wrestled and thumped and drove her slightly mad as they always had.

Juliet was determined to remain strong for them. She was the pilot of her family's little plane, and no matter the indecision she felt, the questions that suffocated her when she turned off the lamp at night and lay awake in the slow-passing dark, the worry that she would make the wrong choice and in so doing ruin them, it was her responsibility to make them feel safe and secure the next day. The responsibility was that much heavier without Alan. It wasn't easy being the only grown-up.

Most of the time she managed to keep a cheerful face on things, but there had been that one unfortunate moment on Wednesday evening. She had thought the children were all outside in the meadow behind the back garden and had been sitting at her desk trying to finish the article for Mr. Tallisker before dinner. Since the meeting on Monday she'd become convinced of her editor's wisdom: the diverse and fascinating ladies of the Birchwood and Lechlade branches of the

WVS had provided invaluable inspiration, and Juliet was determined to do them justice.

She'd been writing about Imogen Stephens's daughter, describing the moment in which the young woman glanced through the kitchen window and saw that the man she loved, whom she'd been told to give up for dead, was walking up the garden path towards her. Juliet's fingers had been tapping faster than the hammers of the typewriter could manage; she had been right there with her subject as she threw off her apron and ran to the door, as she warned herself not to believe her eyes, as she hesitated, unwilling to prove herself wrong, and then heard the key turn in the lock. And as Imogen's daughter fell into her lover's arms, Juliet's own heart had overwhelmed her: the months of worry and waiting, her weariness and all the change; just for a minute she had let down her defenses.

"Mum?" The voice had come from behind her, and then closer. "Mummy? Are you crying?"

Juliet, her elbows on her dressing table, her face in her hands, had frozen in mid-sob. She'd caught her breath as quietly as she could and said, "Don't be silly."

"What are you doing, then?"

"Thinking, of course. Why? How do *you* do it?" And then she'd turned around and smiled and tossed a pencil lightly at her daughter, and said, "Funny Bear! Have you ever known me to cry?"

And then there was Tip. He was a concern, but then he always had been. Juliet was still trying to decide whether there was anything new to worry about. She just *loved* him so much—not more than the others, but differently. And he had been taking himself off alone quite often. ("Great," said the Alan in her mind. "He's self-directed. Best way to be. He's creative, you'll see, he'll be an artist when he grows up.") But along with the games that he was playing, lining up the little soldiers and then knocking them down again, taking them on secret missions in the garden and the quiet pockets of the house, Juliet was pretty sure she'd seen him talking when there was no one else around. She'd scoured the trees for birds, but he seemed to do the same thing inside, too. There was a warm spot on the stairs that he appeared to like especially, and once or twice Juliet had caught herself lurking around the corner, watching.

One day, when he was kneeling beneath an apple tree in the back garden, she'd crept up softly and sat beside him. "Who are you talking to?" she'd said with an attempt at ease that sounded strained even to her own ears.

"Birdie."

Juliet glanced up at the leaves. "Is the birdie up there, love?"

Tip was staring at her as if she'd lost her mind.

"Or has it flown away already? Maybe Mummy scared it?"

"Birdie doesn't fly."

"No?"

He shook his head. "She walks, just like you and me."

"I see." A ground-bound bird. They existed. Sort of. "Does she sing, too?"

"Sometimes."

"And where did you meet this Birdie? Was she in a tree?"

Tip frowned slightly at his soldiers as if making sense of the question, and then shrugged towards the house.

"Inside the house?"

He nodded without shifting his attention.

"What was she doing there?"

"She lives there. And in the garden sometimes."

"I see."

He looked up sharply. "Can you? Can you see her, Mummy?"

Juliet hadn't known how to answer. She'd considered agreeing with him that, yes, she, too, could see his imaginary friend; but while she was willing to accept that he'd invented a companion to provide comfort at a time of great change, feeding the delusion seemed to cross a line. "No, darling," she said. "Birdie is your friend, not Mummy's."

"She likes you, though, Mummy. She told me so."

Juliet's heart hurt. "That's lovely, darling. I'm glad."

"She wants to help you. She said that I should help you."

Juliet could resist no longer. She took the little man in her arms and hugged him tight, aware of his frail limbs within her embrace, how small and warm he was, how far he had to go in life and how dependent he was on her—*her*, for God's sake, poor lad.

"Are you crying, Mummy?"

Damn it! Again! "No, darling."

"I can feel you shaking."

"You're right. But they're not sad tears. I'm a very lucky mummy to have a little boy like you."

Later that night, when the children were fast asleep, their faces returned by slumber to younger, poutier versions of themselves, Juliet had slipped out into the cooling air and taken a walk along the river, stopping again at the jetty so she could sit for a time and look back at the house.

She'd poured a glass of whisky and swallowed it straight.

She could still remember the rage she'd felt that day in 1928 when she told Alan that she was pregnant.

But what she'd thought then had been fury at Alan's failure to understand her, she perceived now had not been fury at all, but fear. A sudden, emptying sense of aloneness that had felt an awful lot like childish abandonment. Which probably explained why she'd behaved like a child, stropping off like that.

Oh, to go back and do it all again, to live it again. That day. The next. The one after. The arrival of Bea in their lives, and then Red, and then Tip. All three growing up and away from her now.

Juliet topped up her drink. There was no going back. Time only moved in one direction. And it didn't stop. It never stopped moving, not even to let a person think. The only way back was in one's memories.

When she'd returned to their room at the Swan that day, after they'd kissed and made up, the two of them had lain together on the little bed with its pretty iron rails, Alan's hands either side of her face, his eyes searching hers, and he'd promised solemnly never again to insult her by suggesting that she work less.

And Juliet, with a kiss to the tip of his nose, had promised never again to stop him from giving up acting if he wished to sell shoes instead.

First thing Friday morning, Juliet read through her "Letters from the Laneway" article for a final time and then wired it to Mr. Tallisker. She'd given the piece a provisional title: "Women's War Rooms: or, An Afternoon with the Ministry of Defence" and crossed her fingers that her editor would agree to keep it.

Pleased with how the article had turned out, Juliet decided to take a morning's break from her typewriter and, at the insistence of the older children, while Tip was playing with his soldiers in the garden, went with them to the barn in the back field. There was something they were desperate to show her.

"Look! It's a boat."

"Well, well," said Juliet, with a laugh.

She explained to the children that she'd glimpsed a little wooden rowboat strung from those very rafters twelve years before.

"The same one?"

"I should think so."

Red, who had already scurried up the loft ladder, was hanging from it now by one arm in a state of alarming excitement. "Can we get it down, Mummy? Say we can, please!"

"Careful, Red."

"We know how to row," said Bea. "And besides, the river's not too deep here."

Tip came to mind, tales of drowned girls; dangers.

"Please, Mummy, please!"

"Red," said Juliet sharply. "You'll fall and end up in plaster and that will be the summer over for you."

Naturally he didn't heed her warning but started bouncing on the ladder's rung.

"Get down, Red," said Bea with a scowl of reproof. "How is Mummy supposed to look if you're blocking the ladder."

As Red scurried back to the ground, Juliet considered the boat from below. Alan was just behind her shoulder, his voice soft in her ear, reminding her that cosseting them would only lead to troubles down the line: "You'll turn them into awful frightened people if you're too protective, and then what will we do? We'll be stuck with them! Dithering and worrying and spoiling our fun for the rest of our lives."

"Well," said Juliet, at length, "I suppose if we can untie it, and if it's seaworthy, there's no reason that the two of you shouldn't carry it down to the river."

Great elation ensued, Red leaping against Bea's fine frame, foisting a hug on her, as Juliet took his place on the ladder. The boat, she discovered, was suspended via a system of ropes and pulleys which, though a bit rusted, still did the job. She released the rope from the hook on the rafter where it was fastened, let its end slip free and drop, and then followed it to the ground, where she began winching the boat down.

Juliet had been quietly confident, having glimpsed the boat twelve years before, that it would prove too derelict for use; but, although it was filled with spiderwebs and a thick cloak of dust, a careful inspection of the base yielded nothing of concern. The boat was bone-dry, no sign of wood rot; it appeared that someone, at some point, had done some careful repair work.

Juliet was sweeping her fingertips along a join where the wooden edge met the base when something caught her eye. It glinted in the beam of sunlight.

"Well, Mummy?" Red was tugging at her shirt. "Can we take it down to the river? Can we, *please*?"

It was stuck down deep within the groove between pieces of timber, but Juliet managed to wedge it clear. "What is it?" said Bea, standing on tiptoes to peer over Juliet's shoulder.

"A coin. An old coin. A tuppence, I think."

"Valuable?"

"I shouldn't think so." She rubbed the surface with her thumb. "But pretty, isn't it?"

"Who cares?" Red was leaping from foot to foot. "Can we launch her, Mummy? Can we?"

Suppressing all residual maternal worries and what-ifs, Juliet awarded the little vessel a clean bill of health and helped them carry it as far as the field's edge before standing back to watch as they teetered, one on either side of the awkward load, into the distance.

Tip was still in the front garden when Juliet returned. Sunshine filtered through gaps between the leaves of the maple tree, finding flecks of silver and gold in his soft, straight hair. He had the wooden soldiers out again and was playing an elaborate game, a mighty collection of sticks, stones, feathers, and assorted items of interest arranged into a circular pattern.

He was chattering away, she noticed, and as she drew closer he laughed. The bell tinkle made the day, the sun—the future—brighter, until the moment he tilted his head and it became clear that he was listening to something Juliet couldn't hear. From light to shadow in an instant.

"Something funny, Tippy Toes?" she said, coming to sit beside him.

He nodded and picked up one of his feathers, twisting it back and forth between his fingertips.

Juliet swept a piece of dried leaf from his knee. "Tell me—I love jokes."

"It wasn't a joke."

"No?"

"It was just Birdie."

Juliet had been expecting this; nonetheless her stomach tightened. He continued, "She makes me laugh."

Juliet kept her sigh to herself and said, "Well, now, that's good, Tippy. If you're going to spend time with people, it's important to choose people who can make you laugh."

"Does Daddy make you laugh, Mummy?"

"More than anyone. Except perhaps you three."

"Birdie says—" He stopped short.

"What is it, Tippy? What does she say?"

He shook his head, focusing his attention on the stone he was turning over in his lap.

Juliet tried another tack. "Is Birdie with us now, Tip?"

A nod.

"Right here? Sitting on the ground?"

Another nod.

"What does she look like?"

"She has long hair."

"Does she?"

He lifted his gaze slightly to look straight ahead of him. "It's red. Her dress is long, too."

Juliet followed his glance and sat up straighter, forcing a broad smile onto her face. "Hello there, Birdie," she said. "It's lovely to meet you at last. I'm Juliet, Tip's mummy, and I've been meaning to thank you. Tippy told me that you said he should help me, and I just wanted to let you know what a good boy he's been. Helping with the washing up at night, folding clothes with me when the other two are behaving like wild things. I really couldn't be prouder."

Tip's little hand crept into hers and Juliet gave it a squeeze.

"Being a parent's a breeze," came Alan's cheerful voice on the wind. "No more difficult than flying a plane with a blindfold on and holes in your wings."

CHAPTER TWENTY-ONE

At six o'clock on Friday evening, the four of them set off together, down the lane towards the village. For children wearing the hand-me-downs of strangers, they had scrubbed up pretty well and, by six thirty, having stopped to admire a number of long-lashed cows in a field along the way, and to allow Tip to collect a couple of stones that had caught his attention, they crossed the triangular green to arrive at the Swan.

Mrs. Hammett had said to come in through the main entrance, but to turn right instead of left, into the dining room rather than the pub.

She was already there, drinking cocktails with a tall woman of around fifty years old who was wearing the most wonderful tortoise-shell-framed glasses that Juliet had ever seen. They both turned when Juliet and the children burst through the door, and Mrs. Hammett said, "Welcome, all! Come on in, I'm so glad you could make it."

"Sorry we're late." Juliet nodded fondly in Tip's direction. "There were important stones to be gathered along the way."

The woman with the glasses said, "A boy after my own heart," her accent betraying a hint of America.

The children stood relatively still to deliver the introductions Juliet had schooled them in along the walk, and then she ushered them back out to the entrance hall, where a pair of leather armchairs seemed to offer the perfect repository while they waited for dinner to be served.

"Mrs. Wright," said Mrs. Hammett, when Juliet returned, "this is Dr. Lovegrove. Dr. Lovegrove is staying with us in the accommoda-

320

tions upstairs—another return visitor to the village. Nineteen forty must be the year for it!"

Dr. Lovegrove held out a hand. "A pleasure to meet you," she said, "and please, call me Ada."

"Thank you, Ada. And I'm Juliet."

"Mrs. Hammett has just been telling me that you and your children have moved into Birchwood Manor."

"We arrived on Sunday evening."

"I went to school in that house, many years ago."

"I had heard it was a school, once upon a time."

"Once upon a time indeed. It closed decades ago, soon after I left. It was one of the last bastions of the old ideas about girls and their education. Plenty of sewing, singing, and, as I remember it, quite a lot of balancing books on our heads when we should have been reading them."

"Now, now," said Mrs. Hammett. "Lucy did her best. And it doesn't seem to have done you any harm, Doctor."

Ada laughed. "That's true. And you're right about Lucy. I had so hoped to see her again."

"Such a shame."

"I only have myself to blame. I left it too long. Age catches up with us all, even Lucy, it would seem. In a funny way, I have the school at Birchwood, for all its oddities, to thank for the direction of my adult life. I'm an archaeologist," she explained to Juliet. "A professor at New York University. But before all that I was a very keen member of the Natural History Society at Miss Radcliffe's school. Lucy—Miss Radcliffe—was a real enthusiast. I've met professors with a less keen instinct: she'd amassed a wonderful collection of fossils and finds. Her specimen room was a veritable trove. It was only small—but then, of course, you'll know which one I mean, at the top of the stairs on the first floor."

"That's my room now," said Juliet with a smile.

"Then you can picture how crowded it was with shelves lining the walls and objects covering every available surface."

"I can," said Juliet, retrieving her notebook, which was never far from hand. "And I love the notion that a single house has had so many different incarnations; in fact, it's given me an idea."

She jotted down a note, explaining as she did so about "Letters from the Laneway," to which description Mrs. Hammett couldn't resist adding, "My ladies and I are already featured, Dr. Lovegrove—the debut article, no less! You will make sure we have copies, won't you, Mrs. Wright?"

"I've instructed my editor especially, Mrs. Hammett. They'll be in the post on Monday morning."

"Wonderful! The ladies are so excited. Now, if you write about Lucy, you'll have to remember to mention that she was the sister of Edward Radcliffe."

Juliet frowned lightly; the name was vaguely familiar.

"The artist. One of those Magenta Brotherhood they talk about. He died young, so he isn't as famous as the others, but it was he who bought the house there on the river. Something of a scandal, there was. He and his friends were staying at the house one summer—a long time ago, back when my mother was just a girl, but she remembered it to her dying day. A beautiful young heiress was killed. She and Radcliffe were supposed to be married, but after she died, his heart was broken and he never returned to the house. It came to Lucy in his will."

The door opened and Mr. Hammett arrived, fresh from his duties behind the bar, shepherding in a young kitchen maid with an anxious expression on her face and a tray of steaming plates in her hands. "Ah," said Mrs. Hammett, beaming, "dinner is served. Just you wait to see what our cook can do with a steamed sausage roll!"

What their cook could do, it turned out, was nothing short of a miracle. Steamed end cuts had never been among Juliet's favorites, but served beneath a gravy of better-not-to-ask, the roll proved delicious. Equally pleasing, the children brought their most charming selves to the table, replying to every question with answers that were engaging if perhaps a little frank for some tastes, even returning a few interesting queries of their own. Tip had managed to stick his little fingers in the waxy pools of each candle, leaving a smattering of small fossilized prints, but they remembered to say thank you when they were finished, no one blew his or her nose on the tablecloth, and when Bea asked whether they might please be excused to continue their game of cards in the entrance hall, Juliet was glad to say yes.

"Are your children enjoying Birchwood Manor?" Ada asked as Mrs. Hammett's poor kitchen maid worried over the pouring of tea and coffee. "It must be quite a change after London."

"Thankfully the change seems to agree with them."

"But of course: the country offers so much for children," said Mrs. Hammett. "It would be a strange child indeed who didn't delight in our part of the world."

Ada laughed. "I was always a strange child."

"You didn't enjoy it here?"

"Eventually. Not at first. I was born in India and very happy there until I was packed off to school. I was not disposed to like it and I didn't: I found the countryside insipid and polite. Unfamiliar, to put it in the best light."

"How long did you spend at the school?"

"Just over two years. It closed when I was ten and I was sent on to a bigger school outside Oxford."

"There was a terrible accident," said Mrs. Hammett. "A girl drowned during a summer picnic. The school only lasted a few years after that." She frowned at Ada. "Then, Dr. Lovegrove, you must have been there when it happened."

"I was," said Ada, taking her glasses off to clean a lens.

"Did you know the girl?"

"Not well. She was older than I was."

The other two women continued to talk, but Juliet had fallen to thinking of Tip. He had told her that a girl drowned in the river and now she wondered whether he'd heard something in the village to that effect. But he had mentioned the fact to her on their first morning at

Birchwood, so there hadn't been time for any of that. It was possible, she supposed, that the nervy young man from the AHA had whispered to him about it. Now that she thought about it, there'd been something a bit sly-looking about him.

But then, Tip might merely have been voicing his own deepest fears. Wasn't she always warning him—especially him—to be careful? Alan would say he'd told her so: she was turning them into scaredy-cats with her maternal worry. And perhaps Tip had simply made a good guess: people drowned in rivers; it was a safe bet that over time someone had drowned at just about any point along the Thames. She was only finding things to worry about, because she always worried about Tip.

"Mrs. Wright?"

Juliet blinked. "I'm sorry, Mrs. Hammett. I was a million miles away."

"Everything's all right, I hope? Would you like some more coffee?"

Juliet slid her cup across the table with a smile and, as so often happened when one had been struggling with a prevailing worry alone, found herself explaining to the other women about Tip and his imaginary friend.

"The poor little mite," said Mrs. Hammett. "Not surprising after all the changes. He'll come good, you'll see. One of these days you'll realize that he hasn't mentioned his 'friend' in a week."

"Perhaps you're right," said Juliet. "I never had one myself, you see, and it just seems such a remarkable thing to conjure an entire person from thin air."

"Does his imaginary friend make him do naughty things?"

"No, thank goodness, Mrs. Hammett. I'm pleased to say that she's been rather a good influence."

"Small mercies!" said their host, with a clap. "Is she with us tonight? I've never had an imaginary guest."

"Happily, no. She stayed in for the night."

"Well, that's something. Perhaps it's a good sign that he only needs her sometimes?"

"Perhaps. Although he did say that he'd asked her to come. Apparently, she told him she couldn't walk that far."

"An invalid? How intriguing. Has he told you any other details about the child?"

"She's not a child, to begin with. She's a lady. I don't know what that says about me, that he's chosen to create an adult woman to spend time with."

"Perhaps she's another version of you," said Mrs. Hammett.

"No, not so. From what he tells me, she's almost my direct opposite. Long red hair, a long white dress. He's been quite specific in his description."

Ada, who had been quiet to this point, said, "Have you considered that he is being truthful?"

There was a momentary silence, and then: "Why, Dr. Lovegrove," said Mrs. Hammett, with a nervous laugh, "you *are* a tease. But Mrs. Wright is worried."

"Oh, I shouldn't worry," said Ada. "I'm sure it means nothing more than that your little boy is a creative spirit who's invented his own way to cope with the changes in his life."

"You sound like my husband," said Juliet with a smile. "And no doubt you're right."

As Mrs. Hammett began to talk about seeing what had happened to the pudding, Ada excused herself to "take some fresh air," and Juliet took the opportunity to check on the children. Red and Bea were easy enough to find, ensconced as they were within the pleasantly dim space beneath the stairs, engaged in a boisterous round of gin rummy.

Juliet scanned the hallway for Tip. "Where's your brother?"

Neither looked up from their fan of cards.

"Don't know."

"Somewhere."

Juliet stood for a moment with her hand on the post at the bottom of the stairs, surveying the hall. As her gaze swept up the carpeted flight, for a split second she saw Alan standing at the top, that infernal pipe in his mouth.

It was the same staircase she'd raced up that day to find him waiting for her inside the room, armed and ready to resume their argument.

She couldn't resist climbing it now.

The banister felt familiar beneath her hand, and Juliet closed her eyes as she neared the top, imagining herself back to that instant in time. An echo of the memory charged the air around her. Alan was so close, she could *smell* him. But when she opened her eyes, he, with his smile of lopsided irony, was gone.

The first-floor landing was exactly as she remembered. Clean and neat, with little details that showed care if not au courant artistry. Fresh flowers in the porcelain vase on the hall table, small framed paintings of local landmarks along the wall, imprints from the carpet sweeper on the mottled runner. There was the same smell, too, of laundry soap and wood polish and, underlying it, the faint, comforting hint of day-old ale.

No sign, though, of a small fleet-footed boy.

As she came back down, Juliet heard a familiar voice drifting in from outside the pub. She had noticed a bench seat beneath the window when they arrived, and went closer now, leaning to peer through the crack in the blackout curtains and over the edge of the sill. There he was, some of his prized sticks and stones in hand, and beside him Ada, the two of them deep in conversation.

Juliet smiled to herself and stepped back quietly, careful not to disturb them. Whatever it was they were discussing, Tip's face was interested and engaged.

"There you are, Mrs. Wright."

It was Mrs. Hammett, bustling behind the kitchen maid, who was struggling beneath another heavily laden tray. "Ready for some pudding? I'm pleased to say it's eggless sponge with strawberry jelly!"

On Sunday morning, for the first time since they'd arrived, Juliet woke before the children. Her legs were as restless as her mind, so she threw on some clothing and headed out for a walk. She didn't go to the river, following the lane back into the village instead. As she neared the corner with the church, she noticed that people were filing in for the early service. Mrs. Hammett saw her and waved, and Juliet smiled back.

The children were at home, so she didn't go inside but listened for a time from the bench beneath the porch as the minister spoke about loss and love and the indomitable human spirit when it walked hand in hand with God. It was a thoughtful sermon and he a fine speaker, but Juliet feared there would be many more sermons like that before the war was over.

Her gaze roamed the pretty churchyard. It was a peaceful place. Lots of spilling ivy and slumbering souls. Headstones that told of age and youth and death's blind justice. A forlorn, beautiful angel bowed her head over an open book, her stone hair, darkened with age, tumbling onto the cold page. There was a quality to the silence in such places that inspired reverence.

To strains of Elgar's "Nimrod," Juliet wandered the perimeter observing the mottled headstones and contemplating the names and dates, the loving messages of eternity and rest. How remarkable that the human race valued the lives of its individual members sufficiently to commemorate each one's brief time on the ancient earth; and yet, at once, could engage in slaughter of the most meaningless and general kind.

At the bottom of the churchyard, Juliet stopped in front of a grave bearing a familiar name. *Lucy Eliza Radcliffe, 1849-1939.* Beside it was an older headstone belonging to the brother Mrs. Hammett had mentioned at dinner, Edward. Written beneath Lucy's name were the words, *"All past is present,"* a phrase that gave Juliet pause, for it was somehow out of step with the usual sentiments expressed.

Past, present, future—what did any of it mean, anyway? One could aim to do their best with the circumstances dealt them in the time given. That was all.

Juliet left the churchyard, walking back along the grass-lined laneway towards the Thames Path and home. The rising sun had burned off any hint of overnight cool, and the sky was clarifying to a spectacular blue. There would be more requests for boating today, that much was clear. Perhaps they would all have lunch by the river.

The house had the look of wakeful inhabitants even from a distance: strange the way one could somehow tell. Sure enough, even before Juliet had reached the coach way, she was met with the sound of Bea's recorder.

Mrs. Hammett had sent them home with four lovely hens' eggs, and Juliet was looking forward to soft-boiling them; she even planned to use real butter on the soldiers. First, though, she ducked upstairs to put her hat back in her room. She looked in on the children on the way and found Bea sitting cross-legged on her bed like a snake charmer, playing her recorder. Freddy was lying across his mattress on his back, his head touching the ground. He appeared to be holding his breath. There was no sign of Tip.

"Where's your brother?" she said.

Beatrice lifted her shoulders without missing a note.

Red, on a hot exhalation: "Upstairs?"

There was an unmistakable air of altercation in the room, and Juliet knew better than to get involved. Fights between siblings, she had learned, were like smoke on the wind: blinding one moment, gone the next.

"Breakfast in ten minutes" was her retreating statement.

She tossed her hat onto her bed and ducked her head around the corner of the old sitting room at the end of the hall. They hadn't been using the room as a matter of course; it was filled with sheet-draped furniture and rather dusty, but such places were a lure for children.

Tip wasn't there, either, but Red had thought he might be in the attic. She jogged up the stairs, calling his name as she went. "Breakfast, Tip love. Come and help me make the soldiers?"

Nothing.

"Tip?" She searched each corner of the various attic rooms and then stood at the window that overlooked the field towards the river.

The river.

Tip was not a wanderer. He was timid by nature; he wouldn't have gone that far without her.

She was not calmed. He was a child. He was distractible. Children drowned in rivers.

"Tip!" Juliet's voice was unmistakably worried now, and she started quickly down the stairs. She almost missed the muffled "Mummy!" as she hurried along the hall.

Juliet stopped and listened. It was not easy to hear over her own panic. "Tip?"

"In here."

It was as if the wall were speaking: as if it had eaten Tip and he were now trapped within its skin.

And then, before her eyes, a crack appeared in the surface and a panel was revealed.

It was a hidden door, and behind it Tip was smiling at her.

Juliet grabbed him and pressed him hard against her chest; she knew she must be hurting him, but she couldn't help herself. "Tippy. Oh, Tippy, my love."

"I was hiding."

"I see that."

"Ada told me how to find the hidey-hole."

"Did she?"

He nodded. "The other night. It's a secret."

"And a jolly good one. Thank you for sharing it with me." Remarkable how calm she could make her voice sound when her heart was still pummeling her ribs. Juliet was faint. "Sit with me a minute, Tippy Toes?"

She lifted him down and the sliding door shut seamlessly behind him.

"Ada liked my stones. She said that she used to collect stones, too, and fossils. And now she's an arkay—"

"—ologist. An archaeologist."

"Yes," he agreed. "One of those."

Juliet took Tip with her to the top step and sat him on her lap. She had her arms around him and her cheek resting on the top of his warm head. Of all of her children, Tip was the most willing to accept these occasional bouts of excessive parental love. Only when she felt that she was straining even his unending patience did she say, "Right. Breakfast. And time, I think, to find out what your brother and sister are fighting about."

"Bea said that Daddy wouldn't be able to find us here when he comes home."

"Did she?"

"And Red said that Daddy was a magician and that he could find us no matter where we were."

"I see."

"And I came upstairs because I didn't want to tell them."

"Tell them what?"

"That Daddy isn't coming home."

Juliet felt light-headed. "What do you mean?"

He didn't answer but instead reached his little hand up to press lightly on her cheek. His small heart-shaped face was solemn and Juliet could see at once that he knew.

She was aware of the letter in her pocket, the last that she'd received from Alan. She had carried it with her everywhere since it had arrived. That was the only reason she still had it. The black-rimmed telegram from the War Office that had arrived the same day was gone now. Juliet had planned to burn it herself, but in the end she hadn't needed to. One of Hitler's men had taken care of things for her, dropping his bomb when he was directly above Queen's Head Street, Islington, destroying their house and everything in it.

She had meant to tell the children. Of course she had. The problem was—and Juliet had thought of little else—there was simply no acceptable way to tell her children that their wonderful, funny, forgetful, silly father had been killed.

"Mummy?" Tip slipped his hand into Juliet's. "What will happen now?"

There was a lot that Juliet would have liked to say. It was one of those occasions that came rarely, in which a parent recognized that what she said next would remain with her child forever. She so wanted to be equal to it. She was a writer, and yet the right words would not come. Every explanation that she considered and discarded put another beat of silence between the perfect moment for response and the moment that she was now in. Life really was a great big pot of glue, just like Alan had always said. A jar of flour and water in which they were all just trying to tread water as elegantly as they could.

"I'm not entirely sure, Tippy," she said, which was neither reassuring nor wise, but truthful, which was at least something. "But I do know that we're going to be all right."

She knew what he would ask next: he would ask her *how* she knew. And what on earth could she say to that? Because she just did? Because they had to be? Because this was her plane, she was flying it, and blindfolded or not she was damn well going to make sure that they got home safely?

In the end, she was spared having to answer, because she was wrong: he didn't ask her that at all. With a faith that made Juliet want to curl up and weep, he took her at her word and moved on to a different subject entirely:

"Birdie says that even inside the darkest box there are pinpricks of light."

Juliet was suddenly bone weary. "Does she, darling?"

Tip nodded earnestly. "And it's true, Mummy. I saw them inside the hidey-hole. You can only see them from inside. I was frightened at first when I closed the panel, but I didn't need to be, because there were hundreds of little lights in there, twinkling in the dark."

VIII

It is Saturday and the tourists have arrived. I am in the small room where Fanny's portrait hangs upon the wall. Or, as I prefer to think of it, Juliet's bedroom. Fanny, after all, slept here only one night. I used to sit with Juliet while she was working at her typewriter, her papers spread out across the dressing table beneath the window. I was with her, too, late in the evening, after the children were asleep, when she would take out Alan's letter. Not to read; she didn't often do that. She just used to hold it in her hand as she sat and looked, unseeing, through the open window, into the long, dark night.

This is also the room where Ada was brought, after being pulled half-drowned from the river. Back then it was a trove of fossils and specimens next door to Lucy's bedroom, the walls lined with shelves floor to ceiling. Lucy insisted on taking over Ada's care herself, instructing the nurse on how to do her job until the nurse eventually refused to do it any longer. There was not a lot of space to move after the bed was carried back in, but Lucy managed to fit a wooden chair in one corner and would sit there in the evenings for hours at a time, watching the sleeping child.

It was touching to see how caring Lucy was; little Lucy who had found so few people in her life, after Edward, to be close to. She made certain that the bed was warmed each night with a brass pan filled with coals, and she allowed Ada to keep the kitten, despite that Thornfield woman's evident disapproval.

One of today's tourists has gone to stand by the window, craning to see over the wall and into the orchard so that the morning sun bleaches her face. It reminds me of the day after the picnic, when

Ada was well enough to be propped up against her pillows, and light spilled through the panes of glass in four neat rectangles to fall across the foot of her bed.

Lucy brought in the breakfast tray, and as she was setting it down on the dressing table, Ada, pale against the linen sheets, said, "I fell into the river."

"You did."

"I cannot swim."

"No, that much is clear."

Ada did not speak again for a time. I could see, though, that there was more on her mind, and, sure enough, "Miss Radcliffe?" she said eventually.

"Yes, child?"

"Someone else was in the water with me."

"Yes." Lucy sat on the edge of the bed and took up Ada's hand. "I am sorry to have to tell you, but May Hawkins fell into the river, too. She did not fare as well as you: she could not swim, either, and she drowned."

Ada listened to this and then, her voice almost a whisper: "It was not May Hawkins who I saw."

I waited then, wondering how much more she would tell Lucy; whether she would trust her with the truth of what had happened on the riverbed.

But she spoke no more about the "other person," saying instead, "There was a blue light. And I reached out to grab it and it wasn't a light at all. It was a stone, a shining stone." She opened her hand then and revealed within her palm the Radcliffe Blue, snatched from where it had been waiting amidst the river stones. "I saw it shining and I held on to it, because I knew that it would save me. And it did—my very own amulet found me, right when I needed it, and it protected me from harm. Just like you said it would."

The weather is fine and clear today and so it is busy at the house, a constant stream of tourists, with bookings for lunch at one of the nearby pubs. They shuffle through in small groups and I cannot bear to hear the guide tell yet another cluster to close their eyes in "Fanny's bedroom" and "smell the ghostly hint of Miss Brown's favorite rose cologne"; and so I have left and am making my way down to the malt-house, where Jack is trying to keep a low profile. Earlier this morning I saw, amongst the papers that he'd printed from Mrs. Wheeler's recent email, a letter from Lucy to Ada, written in March 1939. Alas, the body of the letter was covered and I have not yet been able to see what it says. I am hopeful that by now he might have moved the other papers aside so I can have a proper read.

In the hall downstairs, a group has gathered around the land-scape painting that hangs upon the southern wall. It is the first work that Edward ever had accepted by the Royal Academy, one of the paintings referred to collectively as the "Upper Thames works," a view taken directly from the top window of this house. The vista itself is a pretty one, overlooking the river: a stretch of fields, a dense area of woodlands and beyond that the distant mountains; in Edward's hands, though, the pastoral scene is transmuted via shades of magenta and deepest grey into an image of disconcerting beauty. The painting was heralded as signifying a shift from representational paintings to "art of atmosphere."

It is a bewitching piece, and the tourists today say all of the same things that they always do. Things like "Wonderful colors," and "Moody, isn't it?" and "Look at that technique!" But few of them ever purchase poster copies from the shop.

One of Edward's gifts was an ability to take his own emotions and, through choice of pigment and brushstroke, render them visually with uncompromising fluency by the force of his own need to communicate and be understood. People do not purchase copies of *View from the Attic Window* to hang above their sofa because it is a painting fueled by fear, and despite its beauty—without even know-ing the story behind its creation—they sense its menace.

The landscape depicted in the painting impressed itself upon Ed-ward when he was fourteen years old. Fourteen is a fragile age, a time of changing perceptions and emotional transition, and Edward was a boy of particularly intense feelings. His was always a compulsive nature. I never knew him to be halfhearted about anything, and in his childhood he had enjoyed a series of obsessive interests and pursuits, each "the one" until the next arrived. He was consumed with stories of fairyland and theories of the occult sciences, and had, for some time, been determined to raise a ghost. The idea had come to him from his illicit reading at school; hours spent poring by candlelight over ancient treatises found deep in the vaults of the library.

It was at this time that Edward's parents embarked upon an art-collecting jaunt to the Far East, which took them away from England for the next year. Thus, when the summer holidays arrived, he was sent not to the house in London where he had grown up but to his grandfather's estate instead. Wiltshire is an old and enchanted county, and Edward used to say that when the full moon rose high and silver, the ancient magic could still be felt. Although he resented his parents' abandonment of him, and the despotic grandfather who must be borne, his fascination with spirits and fairy lore was further fed by his removal to the old chalk country.

He thought carefully about where to go to raise his spirit, and considered several nearby churchyards before a conversation with his grandfather's gardener convinced him instead to follow the River Cole until it met the Thames. There was a spot, the old man said, a clearing in a woods, not far from there, where the river turned sharply back upon itself, in which fairies and ghosts still walked amongst the living. The gardener's grandmother had been born in the north during the chime hour and knew such things, and it was she who had told him of the secret place.

Edward confided the events of that evening on a drizzly London night when we were together in his candlelit studio. I have remembered the occasion of the telling so many times since that I can hear his voice now, as if he were standing right beside me. I can recount the story of that night in the woods as if I had been there with him when it happened.

After walking for some hours, he found the river bend and ventured into the woods, leaving chalk flints that he had collected earlier that day as markers to guide him home. He arrived in the clearing just as the moon was rising to the center of the sky.

The night was clear and warm and he had worn only the lightest of clothing, but as he crouched behind a fallen log he felt a brush of something very cold against his skin. He shook the sensation away, thinking little of it then, for there were far more interesting things happening to occupy his thoughts.

A beam of moonlight had just illuminated the clearing, and Edward felt the pull of premonition. Something, he knew, was about to happen. A strange wind blew, and the surrounding trees rattled their leaves like fine pieces of silver. Edward had a sense that there were eyes hidden in the foliage, watching the empty clearing, just as he was. Waiting, waiting . . .

And then, suddenly, it was dark.

He glanced skyward, wondering if a cloud had come from nowhere to blot out the moon. And as he did so, he was gripped by a sickening claw of terror.

His blood was as ice and, without knowing why, he turned and fled back through the woods, picking his way from one piece of chalk to the next until he emerged on the edge of the field.

He continued, he thought, in the general direction of his grandparents' house. There was something behind him, chasing him—he could hear it over his own ragged breaths—but when he threw a glance over his shoulders, there was nothing there.

His every nerve was alight. His skin rippled cold as if it sought to leave his body.

He ran and he ran, the landscape dark and unfamiliar around him as he leapt over fences, broke through brambly hedgerows, and pounded across fields.

All the while, the creature followed, and just when Edward thought that he could run no further, he glimpsed a house on the horizon, a light visible from a window at its top, like a lighthouse in a storm, signaling the way to safety.

Heart thumping in his chest, he headed towards it, scaling the stone wall and leaping to the ground to land in a moon-silvered garden. A path of flagstones led to the front door. It was not locked and he opened it, hurrying inside and pushing the door closed behind him. He slid the bolt across.

Edward climbed the stairs on instinct, moving higher and higher, away from whatever it was that had pursued him through the fields. He did not stop until he reached the very top, the attic, and there was nowhere else to go.

He went straight to the window, scanning the nocturnal landscape.

And there he stayed, watchful and alert, taking in every detail of the view until at last dawn broke incrementally, miraculously, and the world was once again restored to normal.

Edward confessed to me that for all of the tales of mystery and horror that he had read and heard and invented for his sisters, the night in the clearing of the woods, when he fled for his life and sought refuge in this house, was his first experience of true fear. It changed him, he said: terror opened up something inside him that could never be properly sealed.

I know now exactly what he meant. True fear is indelible; the sensation does not recede, even when the cause is long forgotten. It is a new way of seeing the world: the opening of a door that can never be closed again.

So when I look at Edward's *View from the Attic Window*, I do not associate it with the fields outside Birchwood Manor, even though the likeness is uncanny; it makes me think instead of small dark spaces, and stale air, and the way a person's throat craves and burns when struggling to find the very air for their next breath.

The tourists may not purchase posters of *View from the Attic Window* for their walls, but they do buy copies of *La Belle*.

I suppose I should be flattered, to think that my face stares out from above so many sofas. It is petty of me to care, but *La Belle* outsells any of the other posters available in the gift shop, including the works of Thurston Holmes. I have come to understand that people relish the hint of infamy that comes from hanging a jewel thief—and possible murderess—upon their pretty wall.

Some of them, having read Leonard's book, compare *La Belle* to the *Portrait of Miss Frances Brown on the Occasion of Her Eighteenth Birthday* and say things like "Of course, you can see that he was really in love with his model."

It is a strange thing to hang upon the walls of so many people whom I do not know, over one hundred and fifty years after I met Edward Radcliffe and sat for him in that tiny studio at the bottom of his mother's garden.

To have one's portrait painted is among the most intimate of experiences. To feel the weight of another person's full attention and meet it eye to eye.

I found it overwhelming enough when Edward finished and it came time for the painting to leave the studio and take its place on the Academy's wall. And that was well before it was possible for infinite copies to be made and sold and framed; for my face, as interpreted by Edward in the latter half of 1861, to appear on shopping bags and tea towels and key rings and mugs and the cover of financial year diaries in the twenty-first century.

I wonder what Felix, with his lapel button of Abraham Lincoln and his wild predictions for the future, would make of all this. It is just as he said: the camera is ubiquitous. They all carry one now. Even as I watch, they traipse through the rooms of the house, pointing their devices at this chair or those tiles. Experiencing the world at one remove, through the windows of their phones, making images for later so that they do not need to bother seeing or feeling things now.

It was different after Edward came for me at Mrs. Mack's house on Little White Lion Street. Without discussing it, we each assumed a new permanence to our relationship that had been absent before. Edward began another painting titled, *Sleeping Beauty*; but where once he had been the painter and I his model, now we were something else. Work bled into life, and life into work. We became inseparable.

The first weeks of 1862 were bitterly cold, but the furnace in his studio kept us warm. I remember looking up at the glass roof misting over, the grey sky glowering beyond, as I lay upon the bed of velvet cushions he'd assembled for a bower. My hair he spread around me, long strands over my shoulders, across my décolletage.

We spent all day together and much of the night. And when, finally, he put his brushes away, he would take me back to the Seven Dials only to collect me again at daybreak. There was no longer any barrier to our conversation, and like a needle in the most adept of hands it wove together the various threads of our lives, so that he and I became tied by the stories we shared with one another. I told him the truth about my mother and father, the workshop with its wonders, the trips to Greenwich, the tin in which I'd tried to capture light; I spoke to him of Pale Joe and our unlikely friendship; Mrs. Mack and the Captain; Little Girl Lost and my pair of white kid gloves. I trusted him with my real name.

Edward's friends noticed his absence. He had always been subject to periods of obsessive work and retreat, leaving London for weeks at a time on creative travels that his family knew affectionately as his "faraways"; but evidently his complete withdrawal in early 1862 was different. He did not pause in his endeavors even to write and send a letter; neither did he attend any of the weekly meetings of the Magenta Brotherhood in the public bar at The Queen's Larder.

It was March, and *Sleeping Beauty* was all but finished by the time he introduced me to the others. We met at the home of Felix and Adele Bernard on Tottenham Court Road; a house with a plain brick facade that concealed rooms of great bohemian dishabille. The walls were painted in burgundy and deepest blue, cluttered with enormous framed oil paintings and photographic prints. What seemed like hundreds of tiny flames flickered atop elaborate candelabras, casting shadows across the walls, and the air was thick with smoke and impassioned conversation.

"So, *you're* the one," said Thurston Holmes, his eyes not leaving mine, when Edward introduced us again, and he lifted my hand to his lips, just as he had done at the Royal Academy. Once again I felt the same churn of warning deep down in the pit of my stomach.

I was not then frightened of many things. Growing up in the Seven Dials had cured me of most fears, but Thurston Holmes unnerved me. He was a man used to getting his own way, a man who wanted for nothing material but obsessed over that which he could not have. He possessed streaks of cruelty, both casual and calculated, and was expert at their deployment. I saw him slight Adele Bernard one night with a caustic comment about one of her early photographic efforts, and then sit back, a smile on the edge of his lips, enjoying the scene as sport.

Thurston was interested in me insofar as I presented a challenge: a treasure he could take away from Edward. I knew this at the time, but I confess I did not understand then to what lengths he would go, how willing he would be to prove to inflict unhappiness on others for his own amusement.

I reflect sometimes on how much of what happened the summer of 1862 might have been averted had I gone with Thurston that evening in November after the exhibition at the Royal Academy, or paid him a well-placed compliment. But we all make choices, for better and for worse, and I had made mine. I continued to refuse his requests to paint me; I made sure that we were never alone together; I avoided his lingering attentions. For the most part he was discreet, preferring to needle me in secret. Only once did he push things too far with Edward; what he said I do not know, but he paid for it with a purple eye that lasted into the next week.

Mrs. Mack, meanwhile, was kept happy by frequent payments for my services as a model, and Martin was left with little choice but to grudgingly accept the turn events had taken. He continued to voice his disapproval whenever he saw an opportunity, and there were times when we would leave Edward's studio at night and a hint of movement in my peripheral vision would alert me to his presence on the other side of the street. But I could live with Martin's misguided attentions so long as he kept them at a distance.

Edward's mother, for her part, encouraged our ongoing association. *Sleeping Beauty* was exhibited to wide acclaim in April 1862 and a hover of prospective patrons descended; she entertained dreams of Royal Academy glory and wild commercial success, but she was worried, too; for while Edward's usual habit was to move on immediately to a new subject, he had not yet begun another painting. After the exhibition, he alternated instead between bouts of distraction, in which a faraway expression cast a glaze across his features, and periods of feverish scribbling in his notebook. Motivated by the quality of his recent work and her own reliance on his future, she urged him down to the studio day and night, plying me with cake and tea as if she feared that only by such morsels could I be kept from vanishing back to the place from which I had come.

As for Fanny, aside from a brief nod of aloof acknowledgment at the exhibition of *Sleeping Beauty*, I saw her only once, when she and her mother came to tea with Mrs. Radcliffe and were walked down the garden path to observe the artist at work. They stood inside the door, behind Edward's shoulder, Fanny preening and posing in a new satin dress. "Goodness," she said, "aren't the colors pretty?"—at which Edward met my eyes, and within his own I saw a smile of such warmth and longing that it took my breath away.

Will you believe me if I say that in all of those months Edward and I did not ever discuss Fanny? Neither did we consciously avoid the subject. It seems hopelessly naive to say it now, but Fanny simply was not on our minds. There was so much else to talk about, and she did not seem important. Lovers are ever selfish.

It is one of my greatest regrets, to which I return over and again in my ruminations, wondering how I could have been so foolish: my failure to understand how unwilling Fanny would be to let Edward go. I was blinded, as was he, by the knowledge that for us there was no choice: we had to be together. Neither of us could contemplate the possibility that others could not see and would not accept this basic truth.

She has come back!

Elodie Winslow, the archivist from London, keeper of James Stratton's memory and Edward's sketchbook.

I see her at the entrance kiosk, trying to buy a ticket to enter the house and garden. There is some sort of bother: I can tell by the air of polite frustration on her face as she gestures towards her watch. One glance at my clock in the Mulberry Room and I know what the matter is.

Sure enough, when I arrive at her side it is in time to hear her say, "I *would* have arrived earlier, but I had another appointment. I came here immediately afterwards, but my taxi was stuck behind a piece of farm machinery and the lanes are so narrow he couldn't get past."

"Be that as it may," says the volunteer, whose badge announces that he is called Roger Westbury, "we only allow a fixed number of visitors in, and the last allotment for today is full. You'll have to come again next weekend."

"But I won't be here. I have to go back to London."

"I'm sorry to hear that, but I'm sure you understand. We have to protect the house. We can't have too many people traipsing through at once."

Elodie looks towards the stone wall surrounding the house, the gables rising above it. There is an expression of utter longing on her face, and I vow to make certain that Roger Westbury has a particularly uncomfortable winter. She turns back to him and says, "I suppose it's okay to buy a cup of tea in the café?"

"Of course. The café is just behind us, over there in the long barn near the Hafodsted Brook. The gift shop is beside it. You might like to pick up a nice bag or a poster for your wall."

Elodie starts towards the barn, and when she is halfway there, without a hint of duplicity, she turns right instead of left and slips past the open wrought iron gate and into the walled garden of the house.

She is wandering along the paths now and I am following her. There is something different in her attitude today. She does not take out Edward's sketchbook, and she does not wear the mooning expression of completeness on her face that she did yesterday. She is frowning slightly, and I have the distinct impression that she is looking for something specific. She is not here just to admire the roses.

In fact, she is avoiding the prettiest parts of the garden and tracing the outer border where the walls are covered with rampant ivy and other creepers. She stops and digs around in her handbag and I wait to see whether she will pull out the sketchbook.

She withdraws a photograph instead. A color photograph of a man and woman sitting together outdoors in a grove of abundant greenery.

Elodie is holding the photograph up, comparing it with the garden walls behind, but evidently she is not pleased with the comparison, because she lowers her hand to her side and continues on the path, following it around the corner of the house and past the chestnut tree at the back. She is nearing Jack's rooms now, and I am determined that she should not be allowed to go without my learning more. I see her glance towards the kitchen where yesterday she saw Jack scraping his pie dish. She is in two minds; I recognize the signs. She just needs a little encouragement and I am only too happy to provide it.

Go on, I urge her. *What have you got to lose? He might even let you look inside the house again.*

Elodie goes to the door of the malt house and knocks on the door.

Jack, meanwhile, who has been keeping odd hours of an evening and sleeping poorly, is napping and does not even stir.

But I refuse to see her leave, so I kneel down close beside him and blow with all of my might into his ear. He sits bolt upright and shivers, just in time to hear the second knock.

He staggers over and pulls open the door.

"Hello again," she says. There is no hiding the fact that he has just got himself out of bed, and she adds, "I'm sorry to disturb you. Do you live here?"

"Temporarily."

He gives no further explanation and she is too polite to ask.

"I'm sorry to bother you again, but you were so kind yesterday. I wondered if you'd mind letting me look inside the house again."

"It's open now." He nods towards the back door, indicating the other tourists who have just been disgorged.

"Yes, but your colleague on the ticket desk pointed out that I was too late today to be sold a ticket for the last entry period."

"Did he? What a pedant."

She smiles, surprised. "Yes, well, I thought so, too. But you seem less . . . pedantic."

"Look, I'd let you in anytime, but I can't tonight. My . . . colleague . . . informed me earlier that he's sticking around to supervise some repairs. Worse luck, he expects to be back tomorrow morning to oversee the return of the furniture to its proper place."

"Oh."

"If you come back at midday they should be done."

"Midday." She nods thoughtfully. "I have another appointment at eleven, but I could come straight after that."

"Great."

"Great." She smiles again; she is nervous of him. "Well, thanks. I might just go and enjoy the garden for a little longer now. Until they kick me out."

"Take your time," he says. "I wouldn't let them do that."

———

It is almost six o'clock. The last of the day's visitors are being ushered to the gate when Jack finds her sitting on a garden seat against the stone wall that separates the lawn from the orchard. He has split a beer into two small glasses and hands one to her. "I told my colleague that my cousin had dropped in to say hello."

"Thank you."

"You looked like you could use a little longer." He sits on the grass. "Cheers."

"Cheers." She smiles and takes a sip of the beer. Neither one speaks for a while and I am deciding which of them to press when she says, "This is a beautiful place. I knew it would be."

Jack doesn't answer and after a time she continues.

"I'm not always so . . ." She lifts her shoulders. "It's been a strange day. I had a meeting earlier and I've been reflecting on it. I go back to London tomorrow afternoon and I don't feel like I've done what I hoped to do while I was here."

I want Jack to probe further, to ask her what it is that she hoped to do, but he resists my urging and in this instance he is right, because she fills the silence without being asked. "I was given this recently," she says, handing him a photograph.

"Nice," he says. "Someone you know?"

"My mother. Lauren Adler."

Jack shakes his head, uncertain.

"She was a cellist, pretty famous."

"And he's your dad?"

"No. He was American, a violinist. They'd been playing to-gether, a concert in Bath, and were driving back to London when they stopped for lunch. I had hoped that I might find the spot where they were sitting."

He hands back the photograph. "They had lunch here?"

"I think so. I'm trying to find that out for sure. My grand-mother lived in this house for a few years from when she was eleven; she and her family had to evacuate out of London after their house was bombed in the Blitz. Grandma Bea isn't alive anymore, but her brother—my great-uncle—told me that in the week before this photo was taken my mother came to see him, eager to know the address of this house."

"Why?"

"I think that's what I'm trying to work out. We have this family story—a fairy story, really—that's been passed down the line. I only

Kate Morton

found out the other day that it was set in a real house. My great-uncle told me that he had a friend here, a local person, who told him the tale when he was a boy. He told my mum and she told me. The story is special to us; the house is special, too. Even now, today, sitting here, I feel a strange sort of possessive feeling. I can understand why my mother wanted to come here, but why then? What was it that made her go and see my uncle Tip and then come here that day?"

So. She is Tip's great-niece, and little Tip is still alive, and he remembered the story that I told him. If I had a heart, it would be warmed. I feel the ripples, too, of other memories shifting when she speaks about her mother, the cellist, and the photograph of the two young people in the ivy. I remember them. I remember everything. Memories like the jewels in the kaleidoscope that Pale Joe kept upon his toy shelf: discrete gems that shift into new positions when they're put together, creating different but related patterns every time.

Elodie is looking at the photograph again. "My mother died just after this was taken."

"I'm sorry."

"It was a long time ago."

"I'm still sorry. Grief doesn't have a time limit, I've found."

"No, and I'm lucky to have it. The photographer who took it is famous now, but she wasn't back then. She was staying around here and came across them by chance. She didn't know who they were when she took the shot. She just liked the way they looked."

"It's a great photograph."

"I was sure that if I explored every inch of the garden, I'd turn a corner at some point and see it in front of me—the very spot—and that then maybe I'd somehow know what my mother was thinking that day. Why she was so eager to get the address. Why she was here."

The unspoken words "with him" drift into the cooling air and disappear.

Elodie's phone rings then, an unnatural, jarring noise; she glances at the screen but does not take the call.

346

"I'm sorry," she says with a quick shake of her head. "I'm not usually so . . . expansive."

"Hey. What are cousins for?"

Elodie smiles and finishes her beer. She hands him the glass and tells him that she'll see him tomorrow.

"I'm Jack, by the way," he says.

"Elodie."

And then she tucks the photograph back into her bag and leaves.

Jack has been reflective ever since she left. The carpenter was here all evening, clattering carelessly with his hammer and nails, and after an hour or two of being unable to settle to anything, Jack went through to the house and asked if he could help. It turns out he is handy. The carpenter was happy to have an assistant and they worked together without saying much of consequence for the next two hours. I like that he has added something material to the house that will remain when he is long gone.

Jack ate toast with butter for dinner and then telephoned his father in Australia. There was no anniversary this time on which to hang the call, and conversation for the first five minutes was stilted. Just as I thought things were winding up, Jack said, "Do you remember how good he was at climbing, Dad? Remember that time Tiger got stuck up the mango tree, and he climbed all the way up after him and brought him down?"

Who is "he" and why does Jack look so sad when he speaks about him? Why does his voice constrict and some slight shift in his bearing make him seem like a lonely child?

These are the sorts of wonderings that occupy me.

He is asleep now. The house is quiet. I am the only presence shifting in these rooms, and so I have come up to Juliet's bedroom, where Fanny's likeness hangs.

In her new green dress, the young woman gazes at the painter. The portrait catches her forever as she was in the spring that she met

347

Edward. She stands within an elaborate room decorated in her father's style. The gaping sash window beside her is open, and such is Edward's eye for detail, his skill, that one can feel the freshness of the air against her right forearm. Damask curtains fall on either side of the glass in rich shades of burgundy and cream, framing a timeless rural view.

But it is the light, the light, always the light, that makes his paintings sing.

Critics argued that the depiction of Fanny was more than just a portrait—that it was a comment on the juxtaposition of youth and timelessness, of society and the natural world.

Edward was drawn to allusion and it is possible that he had all of these oppositions in mind when he set up at his easel. It is certainly true that the painting served a double purpose. For the view through the window, of a summer field yellowed by heat, is unremarkable in every way until one notices in the distance—almost disappeared behind a copse of trees—a railway engine pulling four carriages.

This was no accident. The painting of Fanny in the green velvet dress was commissioned by her father on the occasion of her eighteenth birthday, and the engine was no doubt an attempt to appeal to him. Edward's mother would have urged such flattery; her ambitions for her son were naked, and Richard Brown was one of the "railway kings," a man who had made his fortune in steel production and was happily poised to enlarge his business at the precise moment the railway lines were spreading across the face of Britain.

Mr. Brown adored his daughter. I read his interview in the police reports that Leonard obtained when he was working on his thesis. He was distraught after Fanny's death and determined that her legacy should not be tarnished by any talk of a broken engagement and certainly not of another woman in Edward's personal life. Fanny's father was a powerful man. Until Leonard started his digging, Mr. Brown had managed to cut my page completely from history's book. To such lengths would a father go for his beloved child.

Parents and children. The simplest relationship in the world and yet the most complex. One generation passes to the next a suitcase filled with jumbled jigsaw pieces from countless puzzles collected over time and says, "See what you can make out of these."

To that end, I have been thinking about Elodie. There is something in her nature that reminds me of Pale Joe. I noticed it when she first arrived yesterday: the way she introduced herself to Jack, the way she answered his questions. She is thoughtful and considered in her responses, listening carefully to what he says—partly, one can tell, because she wants to do justice to what he is telling her or asking, but also, I think, because she is slightly worried at all times that she will not be equal to the task. Pale Joe was like that, too. In his case it was a consequence of having a father like his. I expect that it was common in those families of primogeniture, where sons were named for fathers and expected to grow up to fit into a mold; to step into the old man's shoes and continue the dynasty.

Pale Joe was proud of his father: he was an important man in government and political circles, and a dedicated collector, too. Many a time when I was visiting the attic room and his family were out, Pale Joe would invite me to explore the grand house overlooking Lincoln's Inn Fields. And what a place of wonders it was! His father had traveled the world and brought back all manner of antiquities: a tiger stood beside an Egyptian sarcophagus, which lay beneath a bronze mask rescued from Pompeii, which sneered beside an assortment of miniature Japanese sculptures. There were ancient Greek friezes and Italian Renaissance paintings, too, and a number of Turners and Hogarths—even a collection of medieval manuscripts including a copy of *The Canterbury Tales* thought to predate that in the Earl of Ellesmere's library. Occasionally, when his father was hosting a great man of science or art, Pale Joe and I would sneak downstairs to listen at the door to the lecture being given.

The house had been remodeled to accommodate long corridors that Pale Joe called "the galleries," supported by columns and arches between which the enormous walls were covered with framed artwork and shelves filled with treasures. Sometimes over the years, when Pale Joe and I were having too much fun to countenance my leaving to complete my day's work, he would bid me to sneak quietly down into the house and find a small curiosity that I could pocket and present to Mrs. Mack as my picking for the day. One might imagine that I felt some guilt over the thievery of such rare and precious artifacts, but as Pale Joe pointed out, many of them had been stolen already from their original possessors, long before I helped them on their way.

I ache to know what happened to Pale Joe. Did he marry the lady to whom he alluded that night in his attic when he spoke of unrequited love? Did he find a way to win her heart and make her see that she would find no kinder man than he? I would give anything to know. I would also like to learn what he became; into which avenue he funneled his great energy, interest, and care. For Pale Joe was proud of his father, but he worried about filling the big man's shoes. Make no mistake: Pale Joe let me steal from his father's collection in part because he wanted me to stay longer with him, and in part because he had a rather modern disdain for the accumulation of possessions and wealth; but there was another reason, too. Pale Joe allowed me to pinch small items from his father's shelves for the same reason that he refused to use, when young, his father's name: it pleased him to chip away a little at the statue's feet.

Pale Joe, Ada, Juliet, Tip . . . Mrs. Mack used to have a lot to say about one's birds coming home to roost, and she was not talking of chickens or curses. There was a man who used to turn up regularly to buy pigeons from the bird and cage shop downstairs at Little White Lion Street. He ran a messenger service: his birds were sent afar and then dispatched, when necessary, with an urgent note, for a pigeon will always fly home. When Mrs. Mack talked about birds returning to roost, she meant that if one sends enough opportunities out into the world, eventually they come back.

And so. My birds are coming home to roost, and I feel myself being drawn inexorably towards the nexus of my story. It all happens so quickly from here.

CHAPTER TWENTY-TWO

SUMMER 2017

ELODIE'S room at the Swan was on the first floor at the far end of
the hallway. There was a leadlight window, with a box seat for one
that provided a glimpsed view of the Thames, and she was sitting
with a pile of books and papers beside her, eating the sandwich she'd
bought at lunchtime but had decided would do just as well for dinner. It did not pass beneath Elodie's attention that it had been one
week exactly since she'd sat in the window of her own flat in London,
wearing her mother's veil and watching the same river heave silently
towards the sea.

A lot had happened since then. Ergo, she was ensconced in a
room of her own in the tiny village of Birchwood, having been to the
house itself not once but twice since she'd arrived in town yesterday
afternoon. Today had presented something of a frustration: as she was
being led around Penelope's friend's elaborate conversion in Southrop, admiring politely the boundless soft furnishings in every shade
of tasteful grey, Elodie had been longing to get back to the house. She
had extricated herself as soon as possible with a promise to return
tomorrow at eleven, telephoned a local taxi, and then had to bite her
hand to stop herself from crying tears of frustration as they traveled
ten miles per hour behind the ambling piece of farm machinery.

She hadn't made it back to Birchwood Manor before closing time,
but she had at least been able to gain access to the garden. Thank God
for Jack, who clearly didn't work for the museum but apparently had

351

some function there. She had met him yesterday when she'd arrived off the train from London and walked down to the house. He'd let her in, and as soon as she stepped across the threshold, she'd been overcome with certainty that for the first time in a long time she was exactly where she was supposed to be. Elodie had felt a strange sense of being drawn further inside, as if the house itself had invited her; which was a ridiculous thing to think, let alone say, and no doubt an imagining created in order to justify an entry that was almost certainly not authorized.

As Elodie finished the sandwich, her phone rang and Alastair's name appeared on the screen. She didn't pick up, letting it ring out instead. He would only be calling to tell her again how upset Penelope was and to ask her to reconsider the wedding music. When Elodie had first told him, there'd been silence at the other end of the line, so that she'd thought, at first, the connection had been lost. And then, "Are you joking?" he'd said.

Joking? "No, I—"

"Listen." He'd made a small choked noise of laughter, as if he were sure there'd been a simple misunderstanding that they would soon sort out. "I really don't think you can back out now. It isn't fair."

"Fair?"

"On Mother. She's very invested in playing the videos. She's told all of her friends. It would crush her, and for what?"

"I just . . . don't feel comfortable with it."

"Well, we're certainly not going to find a better performer." Noise had come from his end of the line, and Elodie had heard him say to someone else "Be there in a minute" before he returned to the call. "Look, I've got to go. Let's leave this for now and we'll talk about it when I'm back in London, okay?"

And before Elodie could tell him that, no, actually, it wasn't okay—she had made a decision and there was nothing further to talk about—he'd gone.

Now, alone in the quiet hotel room, Elodie was aware of a constricted feeling that had spread across her chest. Possibly she was simply tired and overwhelmed. She would have liked to talk to someone who'd agree that's all it was and tell her everything was fine, but Pippa was the obvious choice, and Elodie had a strong suspicion that Pippa would *not* tell her what she wanted to hear. And where would that leave her? In a mess, an enormous mess, and Elodie did not like messes. Her entire life had been an exercise in avoiding, sorting, and eradicating them completely.

So she put Alastair out of mind and took up the articles instead. Tip had turned up out of nowhere with them on Thursday. He'd been standing outside her flat beside his old blue bicycle when she arrived home from work. He'd had a canvas satchel over one shoulder, which he took off and handed to her. "My mother's pieces," he'd said with a nod. "The ones she wrote when we were living at Birchwood."

Inside the satchel was a tattered cardboard folder containing typewritten pages and a large collection of newspaper clippings. The byline belonged to Juliet Wright, Elodie's great-grandmother. "Letters from the Laneway," she'd read.

"My mum wrote them during the war. They came to your Grandma Bea after Juliet died, and then to me. Seemed like it might be the right time to pass them on to you."

Elodie had been overwhelmed by the gesture. She remembered her great-grandmother vaguely: there had been a visit to a very old woman in a nursing home when Elodie was around five. Her abiding memory was a head of paper-white hair. She asked Tip what Juliet had been like.

"Wonderful. She was smart and funny—acerbic at times, but never with us. She looked like Lauren Bacall, if Lauren Bacall had been a 1940s journalist in London and not a Hollywood star. She always wore trousers. She loved my dad. She loved Bea, Red, and me."

"She never married again?"

"No. But she had a lot of friends. People who'd known him—theater people. And she was a fierce correspondent, always writing and receiving letters. That's how I think of her now, sitting at her writing desk, scribbling away."

Elodie had invited him upstairs for a cup of tea; she had a list of questions that had formed since she'd been to see him at his studio at the weekend, particularly after Pippa had given her Caroline's photograph. She showed it to him, explained when and where it had been taken, and watched closely, trying to read his expression.

"Do you recognize the place that they're sitting?"

He shook his head. "There's not a lot of detail. Could be anywhere."

Elodie had been sure that he was obfuscating. She'd said, "I think she went to Birchwood Manor with him on the way home to London. The house was special to her and it seems that he was, too."

Tip had avoided her eyes, handing the photograph back. "You should ask your dad about it."

"And break his heart in the process? You know he can't say her name without weeping."

"He loved her. And she loved him. They were best friends, the two of them."

"But she betrayed him."

"You don't know that."

"I'm not a child, Tip."

"Then you've seen enough to understand that life is complicated. Things aren't always what they seem."

His words had echoed eerily the comment her father had made on the subject all those years ago when he said that life was long, that being human wasn't easy.

They'd changed the subject, but Tip reprised it when he was leaving, saying again that she should speak to her father. He'd said it firmly, almost like an instruction. "He might surprise you."

Elodie wasn't so sure about that, but she certainly intended to pay Tip another visit when she got back to London. She had refrained on Thursday from asking him again about the woman in white, feeling that she'd pushed the friendship far enough for one day; but this morning, over breakfast, when she was reading Juliet's articles, something had struck her as odd.

She riffled through the folder now to find the particular article. Most of the "Letters from the Laneway" pieces were stories about people in the local community, others about her own family. Some were touching, others very sad, a few were laugh-out-loud funny. Juliet was the sort of writer who did not ever completely disappear from the page; each turn of phrase was distinctly her own.

At one point, in an article about the family's decision to adopt a homeless dog, she had written, "There are five of us living in our house. Me, my three children, and a flame-haired figment in a white dress, created by my son's imagination and so vivid to him that we must consult her on every family decision. Her name is Birdie and thankfully she shares my son's affection for dogs, although she has specified that she would prefer an older dog with a settled temperament. It is a sentiment, happily, with which I fully concur, and so both she and Mr. Rufus, our newly arrived arthritic nine-year-old hound, are welcome to remain part of the family for as long as they so choose."

Elodie read the lines again now. Juliet was writing about her son's imaginary friend, but the description was uncannily similar to the woman in the photograph, Edward Radcliffe's model; Juliet also wrote that her son had called the "figment" Birdie. The letter that Elodie had found behind the mount of the framed photograph of Radcliffe's model was addressed to James Stratton and signed from "BB."

While Elodie didn't think for a second that Tip's childhood imaginary friend was going to prove a profitable avenue of inquiry, having now read Leonard Gilbert's book twice since Pippa gave it to her, she had started to wonder whether there might not be another explanation. Whether perhaps her great-uncle, as a boy, had seen a picture of the woman, when he was a child, maybe even the lost painting itself. Edward's book contained preliminary sketches that suggested he was about to start on a new work featuring his model, "Lily Millington." What if the lost painting had been at Birchwood Manor all this time, and Tip had discovered it there as a boy?

There was no point ringing him to ask—he didn't like the telephone, and besides, the last number she had for him was so outdated, it was a digit short—but she would be going to see him again at his studio as soon as possible.

Elodie yawned and climbed down from the window seat, taking Leonard's book with her and hopping into bed. In lieu of the house itself, the book was a close second. Leonard's own love for Birchwood Manor was tangible, even as he wrote about Edward Radcliffe's consuming passion for the place.

There was a photograph of the house inside the book, taken in 1928 during the summer that Leonard Gilbert had been in residence. The property had been neater back then; the trees smaller, the exposure of the photograph blown out so that the sky looked smaller, too. There were earlier photographs as well: images from the summer of 1862, when Edward Radcliffe and his artist friends had been in residence. They didn't look like the usual Victorian portraits. The people in them gazed at Elodie across time and made her feel strange, as if they were watching her. She had felt like that at the house, too—had turned around a couple of times expecting to see Jack behind her.

She read for a while, dipping into the chapter that outlined Lily Millington's supposed role in the theft of the Radcliffe Blue diamond. Elodie had found a later article, published by Leonard Gilbert in 1938, in which he walked his theory back, based on further interviews with his "anonymous source." But it wasn't often cited, probably because it didn't offer much new to scholarship beyond further uncertainty.

Elodie didn't know a lot about jewelry; she would be hard pressed to spot the difference between a priceless diamond and a glass pretender. Her attention went now to her own hand lying across the page of Leonard's book. After Alastair had slipped the diamond solitaire on her finger, he'd told her she could never take it off. Elodie had thought he was being romantic until he said, "A diamond that size? Far too expensive to insure."

It worried her daily, the value of the engagement ring. Sometimes, despite what Alastair had said, she took it off before work and left it at home; the claws snagged on her cotton archival gloves, and she was terrified that if she removed it at her desk, it might drop into one of the boxes and never be seen again. She'd agonized over where to hide it before deciding on her childhood charm box, where it could nestle in amongst the cheerful little girl treasures. There was an irony to the choice, and it seemed like the perfect dissemblance to hide the diamond in plain sight.

Elodie switched off the bedside lamp, and as she watched the minutes on the digital clock change with interminable slowness, her mind went to the reception venue in Southrop. She didn't think she could face another round tomorrow of inane chatter about "the happiest day" of her life. She had a train to catch at four in the afternoon: what if she were held up again, looking through pictures of different place settings, and missed her chance to see inside the house? No, it was impossible. Elodie decided that she would risk Penelope's displeasure and cancel the appointment first thing.

She fell asleep, at last, to the noise of the nearby river, and dreamed of Leonard and Juliet, Edward and Lily Millington, and at one stage even the mysterious Jack, whose purpose at the house was still in question; who had intuited her need to see inside; who had been kind about her mother's death. And to whom, though she would never admit it when awake, she found herself inexplicably drawn.

CHAPTER TWENTY-THREE

THERE had been a change in the wind over the last half hour. It was still not midday, but the sky was darkening and Jack had a feeling it was going to rain later. He was standing on the edge of the meadow and picked up his camera, looking through the viewfinder at the distant water's edge. It was a powerful zoom, and he was able to zero in on the tops of some reeds that grew along the bank. He sharpened the focus and in his concentration the noise of the river disappeared.

Jack didn't take the photo. The temporary silence was enough.

He had known there was a river; in the brief that he'd been given, there'd been a map of the property. But he hadn't realized he would hear it at night when he closed his eyes to go to sleep.

The river was placid up here. Jack had been talking to a fellow with a narrow boat who told him there was a strong pull after storms. He'd gone along with the story, but he didn't really believe it: there were too many locks and weirs that ran the length of the Thames for it to flow with wildness. The river might have been violent once upon a time, but it had long since been shackled and tamed.

Jack knew a bit about water. There had been a creek across the road from their house when he was growing up. It had run dry much of the time, and then when the rains finally came it would fill in a matter of hours. It would rush and tumble, angry and hungry, roaring day and night.

He and his brother Ben used to take an inflatable raft out to ride the short-lived rapids, knowing full well that in a matter of days the creek would be returned to its usual stagnant dribble.

Their dad had always warned them about the raft and about kids who went into drainpipes when the floods came. But Ben and Jack only rolled their eyes at each other and made sure to blow up the raft *after* they'd sneaked it out of the garage and across the road. They weren't worried about the creek. They knew how to handle themselves in water. Until they didn't, that is. Until the flood that happened in the summer when Ben was eleven and Jack was nine.

In the distance, the sky lit up golden, and a low disgruntlement of thunder rolled softly down the river towards him. Jack checked his watch and saw that it was almost midday. The atmosphere was eerie: that strange unearthly twilight that always settled before a storm.

He turned around and started back towards the house. The carpenter had left a light on, he noticed as he crossed the meadow: he could see it up in the attic window, and Jack reminded himself to turn it off when he opened the house for Elodie.

She was waiting for him when he reached the coach way and the iron gate came into sight. She lifted her hand to wave and then she smiled and Jack felt the same frisson of interest that he'd felt the evening before.

He blamed it on the house. He'd been sleeping poorly, and not just because of the god-awful mattress on that bed in the malt house. He'd been having weird dreams ever since he arrived, and although it wasn't the sort of thing he'd have brought up in the local pub, there was a strange feeling in the house, as if he were being watched.

You are, you fool, he told himself. *By the mice.*

But it didn't feel like mice. The sense of being watched reminded Jack of the early days of being in love, when the most ordinary of glances was loaded with meaning. When half a smile from a particular woman could cause a stirring deep down low within his belly.

He gave himself a stern word about overcomplicating his life. He was here to convince Sarah that he should be given another chance to know their girls. That was it. And possibly to find a lost diamond. If it existed. Which it most likely didn't.

She had a suitcase with her, Jack saw as he got closer. "Moving in?" he called.

A blush came immediately to her cheeks. He liked the way she blushed. "I'm on my way back to London."

"Where did you park?"

"I'm going by train. I'm due at the station in about four hours."

"You'll be wanting to see inside, then." He cocked his head towards the gate. "Come on in. I'll open up the house."

Jack was supposed to be packing to leave, but after letting Elodie into the house, he'd decided to work through Rosalind Wheeler's paperwork one last time. Just in case he found something he'd previously missed. Rosalind Wheeler was not a particularly pleasant person, the search seemed hopeless, but she'd hired him to do a job, and Jack didn't like letting people down.

It was one of the things that Sarah used to say to him towards the end: "You have to stop trying to be everybody's hero, Jack. It's not going to bring Ben back." He'd hated it when she said that sort of thing, but he saw now that she'd been right. His entire career, his entire adult life, he'd spent chasing something he could do that would erase the photos that had turned up in all the papers after the flood: the big one of Jack, his eyes wide and frightened, a heated blanket around his shoulders, being loaded into a waiting ambulance. And the smaller school photo of Ben that Dad had insisted on having taken earlier that year, Ben's hair combed carefully from one side, neater than it ever looked in real life. Their roles had been assigned by those newspaper articles and set as hard as a concrete slab: Jack, the boy who was saved. And Ben, the boy hero who'd said to his rescuer, "Take my little brother first," before being washed away.

Jack glanced back towards the door. It had been half an hour since he'd let Elodie into the house, and he was distracted. She'd stood to one side as he switched off the alarm and loosened the lock, and when he pushed the door open, she'd thanked him and been about to step across the threshold, when she hesitated and said, "You don't work for the museum, do you?"

"No."

"Are you a student?"

"I'm a detective."

"With the police?"

"Used to be. Not anymore."

He hadn't offered anything further—it didn't seem necessary to volunteer that the change of vocation was in response to a marriage breakdown—and she hadn't asked. After a moment of silence, she'd nodded thoughtfully and then disappeared inside Birchwood Manor.

The whole time that she had been in there, Jack had been fighting an almost irresistible urge to follow her. No matter how many times he returned to the first page of the notes, he found his thoughts wandering, speculating as to what she was doing, where she was right at that minute, which room she was exploring. At one point he'd even stood up and gone to the door of the house before he realized what he was doing.

Jack decided to make a cup of tea, just to have a task to see through to its end, and was dunking the tea bag violently when he sensed her behind him.

He guessed she was about to say good-bye and so, before she could, he said, "Cuppa? I've just boiled the kettle."

"Why not?" She sounded surprised, whether by the invitation or her acceptance of it, he couldn't tell. "A little bit of milk, please, and no sugar, please."

Jack took out a second mug, careful to find a nice one that didn't have tannin stains around the base. When the two mugs of tea were ready, he carried them over to where she was standing now, on the stone-paved path that ran around the house.

She thanked him and said, "There's not much that smells better than a storm brewing."

Jack agreed and they sat together on the edge of the path.

"So," she said, after she'd taken a first sip, "what's a detective doing picking locks at a museum?"

"I was hired by someone to look for something."

"Like a treasure hunter? With a map and everything? X marks the spot?"

"Something like that. But without the X. That's what's making it all a bit tedious."

"And what is it that you're looking for?"

He hesitated, thinking of the nondisclosure contract Rosalind Wheeler had made him sign. Jack didn't mind breaking rules, but he didn't like breaking promises. He *did* like Elodie, though, and he had the strongest sense that he should tell her. "You realize," he said, "that the woman who hired me could kill me for telling you."

"I'm intrigued."

"And yet, not worried for my life, I see."

"What if I promise not to tell a soul. I never break a promise."

Forget Rosalind Wheeler: the urge was going to kill him first. "I'm looking for a stone. A blue diamond."

Her eyes widened. "Not the Radcliffe Blue?"

"The what?"

She opened her backpack and pulled out an old book with yellowing pages.

"*Edward Radcliffe: His Life and Loves*," Jack read the cover aloud. "I've seen his name in the churchyard."

"This used to be his house and the Radcliffe Blue, as the name suggests, belonged to his family."

"I've never heard it called that. My client said the diamond belonged to her grandmother, a woman called Ada Lovegrove."

Elodie shook her head, the name evidently unfamiliar. "Edward Radcliffe took the Blue from his family's safe in 1862 so his model, Lily Millington, could wear it in a painting. The story goes that she stole it and ran away to America, breaking Radcliffe's heart in the process." Elodie turned carefully through the pages until she reached a color plate near the center. She pointed to a painting called *La Belle* and said, "That's her—that's Lily Millington. Edward Radcliffe's model and the woman he loved."

Looking at the painting, Jack felt an enormous pull of familiarity, and then he realized that, of course, he'd seen the painting many times before, for it was printed on at least half of the bags that he'd seen tourists carrying with them when they left the museum gift shop on Saturdays.

Elodie handed him another photograph, taken reverently from her bag. This was the same subject as in the painting, but here, perhaps because it was a photograph, she looked like a woman instead of a goddess. She was beautiful, but beyond that there was something attractive in the directness with which she stared at the photographer. Jack felt a strange stirring, almost as if he were looking at a picture of someone he knew. Someone he cared for deeply. "Where did you get this?"

The urgency of his tone had clearly surprised her, and a slight frown of interest tugged at her eyebrows. "At work. It was in a picture frame that belonged to James Stratton, the man whose archives I keep."

James Stratton was no one to Jack, and yet the question had formed and was out of his mouth before he even knew that he was going to ask it. "Tell me about him. What did he do? How did he come to have archives worth keeping?"

She considered a moment. "No one ever asks me about James Stratton."

"I'm interested." And he was, although he couldn't have said quite why, keenly interested.

She remained quizzical but pleased. "He was a businessman, very successful—he came from a family of huge wealth and importance—but he was also a social reformer."

"How do you mean?"

"He fronted a number of those Victorian committees aimed at improving the lives of the poor, and he actually managed to make a difference. He was well-connected, articulate, patient, and determined. He was kind and giving. He was instrumental in getting the Poor Laws repealed, providing housing and protecting the lives of poor and abandoned children. He worked at every level—lobbying members of

Parliament, rallying wealthy businessmen to make donations, even working on the streets, handing out food to those who couldn't afford it. He dedicated his life to helping others."

"He sounds heroic."

"He was."

Jack felt the pinch of another question. "What would make someone from a life of privilege take up the cause in such a dedicated way?"

"He formed an unlikely friendship in his childhood with a little girl who lived in unsavory circumstances."

"How did that happen?"

"For a long time, no one knew. He doesn't mention any of the details in his diaries. We only knew there was a friendship at all because of a couple of speeches he gave in later life where he alluded to the relationship."

"And now?"

Elodie was clearly excited by whatever she was going to tell him next, and Jack couldn't help notice how her eyes brightened when she smiled. "I found something the other day. You're the first person I've told. I didn't know what it was initially, but as I read it, I realized." She reached again into her backpack and slid a clear plastic file out of a folder. Inside was a letter written on fine paper, clearly old, creases revealing that it had spent much of its lifetime folded and pressed.

Jack began to read:

> My dearest, one and only, J,
>
> What I have to tell you now is my deepest secret. I am going away for a time to America and I do not know how long I will be gone. I have told no one else, for reasons that will be evident to you. But I approach the journey with great excitement and hope.
>
> I cannot say more now, but you are not to worry—I will write again when it is safe to do so.
>
> Oh, but I will miss you, my dearest friend! How grateful I am for the day that I climbed through your window, the

policeman on my tail, and you gave me the thaumatrope.
Which of us could have imagined then what lay ahead?

   My dearest Joe, I have enclosed a photograph—some-
thing for you to remember me by. I will miss you more than
anything I can imagine missing, and as you know I would
not say such a thing lightly.

      Until we meet again, then, I remain,
      Your most grateful and ever-loving, BB

He looked up. "She calls him Joe. Not James."

"A lot of people did. He never used his real name except for official purposes."

"And what about the 'BB'? What does that stand for?"

Elodie shook her head. "That I don't know. But whatever it stands
for, I think the woman who wrote that letter, James Stratton's childhood friend, grew up to be the woman in the photograph, Edward
Radcliffe's model."

"What makes you so sure?"

"For one thing, I found the letter sealed within the back of the
frame that held the photo. For another, Leonard Gilbert revealed that
Lily Millington wasn't the model's real name. And for a third—"

"I like this theory. It's tight."

"I had this other problem. I'd discovered recently that Edward
Radcliffe came to see James Stratton in 1867. Not only that, he left his
precious satchel and sketchbook in Stratton's care for safekeeping. The
two men weren't connected in any way that I knew of, and at the time
I had no idea what the tie between them could be."

"But now you think it's her."

"I *know* it's her. I've never been so certain of anything. I feel it. Do
you know?"

Jack nodded. He did know.

"Whoever she is. She's the key."

Jack was looking at the photograph. "I don't reckon she did it.
Steal the diamond, I mean. In fact, I'm sure of it."

"Based on what? A photo?"

Jack wondered how to explain the sudden certainty that had overcome him as he stared at the photograph, the woman meeting his gaze. He was almost sick with it. Thankfully, he was spared having to answer, as Elodie continued, "I don't think she did, either. And neither did Leonard Gilbert, as it turns out. I had a feeling when I was reading his book that his heart wasn't in it, and then I found a second article that he published in 1938 where he said that he'd asked his source outright whether she believed that Lily Millington had participated in the robbery and she told him she knew for a fact that she hadn't."

"So it's possible that the diamond really is still here, like my client's grandmother told her?"

"Well, anything's possible, I guess, although it's been a very long time. What exactly did she tell you?"

"She said that her grandmother had lost something precious and there was good reason to believe that it was on an estate in England."

"Her grandmother told her this?"

"In a manner of speaking. She suffered a stroke, and when she started to recover, her words came back to her all in a rush and she started talking about her life, her childhood, her past, with a great sense of urgency. She spoke about a diamond that was precious to her, that she'd left at the house where she went to school. It was all a bit piecemeal, I gather, but after her grandmother died, my client came across a number of items in her effects that she's convinced were her grandmother's way of telling her where to look for it."

"Why hadn't the grandmother come to retrieve the diamond herself? It sounds a bit dubious to me."

Jack agreed. "And I haven't turned up any treasure yet. Her grandmother definitely had a connection to this place, though. When she died, she left a significant legacy to the group who run the museum: it enabled them to set it up. That's why my client was able to organize permission for me to stay here."

"What did she tell them?"

"That I'm a photojournalist, here for a fortnight working on an assignment."

"So she doesn't mind bending the truth."

Jack smiled, thinking back to Rosalind Wheeler's terrier manner. "I have no doubt that she believes every word of what she told me. And to be fair, there was one piece of evidence that seemed to support the theory." He reached into his pocket and produced his copy of the letter Rosalind Wheeler had emailed the other day. "It's from Lucy Radcliffe, who must have been—"

"Edward's sister."

"Right. Written to my client's grandmother in 1939."

Elodie skimmed it and then read a paragraph aloud.

> *I was most disturbed by your letter. I don't care what you saw in the newspaper or how it made you feel. I insist that you don't do as you say. Come and visit me, by all means, but you're not to bring it with you. I don't want it. I never want to see it again. It caused great upset for my family and for me. It is yours. It came to you, remember, against all odds, and I wanted you to have it. Think of it as a gift, if you must.*

She looked up. "This doesn't actually mention a diamond."

"No."

"They could have been talking about anything."

He agreed.

"Do you know what she saw in the paper?"

"Something to do with the Blue, perhaps?"

"Perhaps, and we could probably find out, but for now we're only guessing. Did you mean it when you said you had a map?"

Jack, noting and liking her use of the word "we," told her he'd be back in a minute and went to fetch the map from the end of his bed inside the malt house. He brought it out to the path and handed it to her. "My client put this together based on Ada Lovegrove's effects and the things she said after her stroke."

Elodie opened it out and frowned with concentration; moments later she smiled and gave a soft laugh. "Oh, Jack," she said, "I'm sorry to be the one to tell you, but this isn't a treasure map. It's the map from a children's story."

"Which story?"

"Remember the one I mentioned to you yesterday? The story that my great-uncle heard when he was here as a boy in the war, that he told to my mum, who then told it to me?"

"Yes?"

"The places on this map—the clearing in the woods, the fairy mound, the Crofters' river bend—they're all from the story." Elodie smiled gently and handed the folded map back to him. "Your client's grandmother had a stroke; maybe it was all just a case of her child-hood rushing back upon her?" She lifted her shoulders apologetically. "I'm afraid I don't have anything more helpful to offer. It *is* fascinating, though, to think that your client's grandmother knows my family's story."

"Somehow I don't think my client is going to be as happy with the coincidence as she was hoping to be when I brought her back a diamond."

"Sorry about that."

"Not your fault. I'm sure you didn't mean to shatter an old lady's dreams."

She smiled. "On that note . . ." And she started reloading her backpack.

"You've still got a couple of hours before your train leaves."

"Yes, but I should get going. I've already taken up enough of your time. You're busy."

"You're right. After I master this map, I thought I'd look for the doorway to Narnia in the back of that wardrobe upstairs."

She laughed and Jack felt it like a personal victory.

"You know," he said, pushing his luck, "I was thinking about you last night."

She blushed again. "Really?"

"Do you still have that photograph on you, the one of your mum, from yesterday?"

Elodie was suddenly serious. "Do you think you might know where it was taken?"

"It's worth another look. I've spent a fair bit of time combing through the garden on my hunt for the door to fairyland, you know."

She passed him the photograph and one side of her mouth tightened slightly—an endearing sign that despite all odds she still hoped that he may actually be able to help her.

And Jack *wanted* to be able to help her. (*You have to stop trying to be everybody's hero, Jack.*)

He had been stalling when he asked to see the photo—he'd hoped to stop her from leaving so soon—but as he looked at it, as he took in the ivy and the hint of a structure and the way the light fell, the answer came to him as clearly as if he'd just been told.

"Jack?" she said. "What is it?"

He smiled and gave the photo back. "Up for a little walk?"

Elodie walked beside him through the churchyard and stopped when they reached the far corner. He glanced at her, gave a little smile of encouragement, and then wandered away slowly, pretending interest in the other graves.

She let out a held breath, for he had been right. It was the scene from the photograph. Elodie could tell at once that this was where the picture had been taken. It had changed very little despite twenty-five years having passed.

Elodie had expected to feel sad. Even a little bit resentful.

But she didn't. This was a beautiful, peaceful place, and she was glad to think that a young woman whose life was cut suddenly short had spent her last hours in it.

For the first time ever, as she stood in the grove of ivy, surrounded by the hum of cemetery stillness, Elodie saw clearly that she and her mother were two different women. That she did not have to remain the smaller handprint within the larger one forever. Lauren had been talented and beautiful and a tremendous success, but it occurred to Elodie that the biggest difference between them was none of those things. It was their approach to life: where Lauren had lived fearlessly, Elodie always guarded against failure.

It struck her now that maybe she needed to let go a bit more often. To try and, yes, occasionally to fail. To accept that life is messy and sometimes mistakes are made; that sometimes they're not even really mistakes, because life isn't linear, and it comprises countless small and large decisions every day.

Which wasn't to say that loyalty wasn't important, because Elodie believed strenuously that it was; only—maybe, just maybe—things weren't as black-and-white as she had always believed. As her father and Tip kept trying to tell her, life was long; being a human wasn't easy.

And who was she to judge, anyway? Elodie had spent most of yesterday at a wedding reception venue, nodding politely while well-intentioned women bamboozled her with talk of various types of bon-bonnières and why she didn't "want to go that way," as all the while she'd been longing to get back to Birchwood Manor and to an Austra-lian man who seemed to think she would believe he was employed by the museum.

She had wondered yesterday, when she first showed him Caro-line's photograph, why she was oversharing in such an uncharacter-istic way. She had convinced herself that it was simply a result of her weariness and the emotion of the day. It had seemed a reasonable the-ory, and she had almost believed it until today, when he came around the corner from the meadow.

"Are you okay?" he asked, appearing now at her side.

"I am more okay than I thought I would be."

He smiled. "Then, judging by that sky, I reckon we probably ought to think about getting out of here."

The first rain—big, fat drenching drops—fell as they were leaving the churchyard, and Jack said, "I never imagined that it would rain like this in England."

"Are you kidding? Rain is what we do best."

He laughed, and she felt a jolt of something very pleasant. His arms were wet and she was overcome with an irresistible urge, a need, to reach out and touch his bare skin.

Without a word, and although it made no sense, she took his hand and together they started running back towards the house.

IX

It is raining and they have come inside. Not a light shower but the beginning of a storm. I have been watching it build out there all afternoon, beyond the head of the river, over the distant mountains. There have been many storms in my time at Birchwood Manor. I have become used to the changed, charged atmosphere as air is drawn towards the front.

But this storm feels different.

It feels like something is going to happen.

I am restless and infused with anticipation. My thoughts skip from here to there, picking through the stream of recent conversation, turning over this stone and then that one.

I have been thinking about Lucy, who suffered so terribly after Edward's death. It gladdens me to learn that she told Leonard at last that I was not a faithless lover; I care little for the opinions of those I did not know, but Leonard mattered to me and I am relieved he knew the truth.

I have been thinking of Pale Joe, too. For so long, I craved to know what became of him—how pleased I am, how proud, to hear of what he achieved; that he took his kindness and influence, and his steely sense of justice, and put them to work. But, oh, how cruel it is to have fallen from his life when I did!

And I have been thinking of Edward, as always, and that stormy night spent here, in this house, so many years ago.

I miss Edward most on stormy nights.

It was his idea that we should come here for the summer, to his house, his beloved twin-gabled house on the river, before traveling on

372

to America. He told me his plan on the evening of his twenty-second birthday, as candlelight danced across the night-darkened walls of his studio.

"I have something for you," he said, to which I laughed, because it was his birthday and not mine. "Yours is next month," he said, waving away my halfhearted protest, "that's near enough. Besides, we do not need reasons to surprise one another, you and I."

I insisted nonetheless that I should be allowed to give him my gift first, and held my breath as he began to unwrap the brown paper.

For a decade I had been doing just as Lily Millington advised: keeping a small portion of my spoils each week in a hidden place. At first, I did not know what I was saving for, only that Lily had told me to do it, and in truth it did not matter, for there is a security to be gained from saving that transcends purpose. As I got older, though, and my father's letters continued to counsel patience, I made myself a promise: if he did not send for me by my eighteenth birthday, I would buy myself a ticket to America and travel there alone to find him.

I would be eighteen in June 1862 and had saved almost enough for a single ticket; but since I'd met Edward, my thoughts for the future had shifted. When I saw Pale Joe in April, I asked him where one should go to procure a leather gift of the highest quality, and he sent me to his father's supplier, Mr. Simms on Bond Street. It was there, in that shop which smelled of spice and mystery, that I placed my order.

Edward's face when he unwrapped the satchel was worth every ill-gotten, squirreled-away, secret penny. He ran his fingertips over the leather, taking in the fine stitching, the embossed initials, and then he opened it and slipped his sketchbook inside. It fitted, as I had hoped it would, like a hand into a glove. Immediately, he put the strap over his shoulder, and from that day, until the last, I did not see him without the satchel that Mr. Simms had made to my instructions.

He moved closer then to where I was standing by the bench of art supplies, his proximity causing my breath to catch, and from the pocket of his coat he took an envelope. "And now," he said, softly, "the first half of my gift to you."

How well he knew me, how well he loved me, for within the envelope lay two tickets on a ship making the Atlantic crossing in August.

"But, Edward," I said, "the cost—"

He shook his head. "*Sleeping Beauty* was beloved. The exhibition was a great success, and it is all down to you."

"I did little!"

"No," he said, suddenly serious, "I could not paint without you now. I won't."

The tickets were made out in the name of Mr. and Mrs. Radcliffe. "You will never have to," I promised.

"And when we're in America, we will find your father."

My mind was racing, planning ahead, picking a pattern through the bright new possibilities, considering the best way to extricate myself from Mrs. Mack and the Captain, to avoid letting Martin know until the last, when it came to an abrupt stop. "But, Edward," I said, "what about Fanny?"

A slight frown line appeared between his eyes. "I will let her down gently. She will be all right. She is young, and pretty, and wealthy; she will have other suitors begging for the chance to marry her. She will understand in time. It is another good reason for us to go to America: the kindest thing for Fanny. It will allow distance for the dust to settle, for her to spin whatever story she prefers."

Edward never said a word that he did not believe with all his heart, and of this, too, I know he was convinced. He took my hand in his and kissed it, and when he smiled at me, such was his power of persuasion, I believed that what he said was true.

"And now," he said, his smile widening as he took from the bench a large parcel, "the second half of your gift."

With his free hand, he led me to the cushions on the floor and placed the present—surprisingly heavy—upon my lap. He watched keenly, almost jittery with anticipation, as I started to unwrap it.

When I reached the last layer of paper, there, within the shroud, was the most beautiful wall clock that I had ever seen. The box casing and face were both made of finely crafted wood, with Roman numerals inlaid in gold, and delicate hands with tapered arrows.

I brushed the palm of my hand across the smooth surface, the luster cast by a nearby candle picking out the grain of the wood. I was overwhelmed by the gift. Living with Mrs. Mack, I had not acquired a single possession of my own, let alone an object of such beauty. But the clock was precious beyond its material value. Its bestowal was Edward's way of demonstrating that he knew me, that he understood who I really was.

"Do you like it?" he said.

"I love it."

"And I love you." He kissed me, but as he withdrew his brows shifted. "What is it? You look as if you've just been handed trouble."

And that is precisely how I felt. Almost as soon as I had received the clock, my thrill was replaced by a great covetous need to protect the precious gift; there was no way could I take it near the Seven Dials without Mrs. Mack putting a price upon it. "I think that I should hang it here," I said.

"I have another idea. In fact, there is something important that I must talk to you about."

Edward had mentioned the house by the river before, and I had observed the way his expression changed, a look of longing coming upon his face, which would have made me envious had we been speaking of another woman. But as he told me now of his need that I should see his house, there was something else underlying his features: a vulnerability that made me want to take him in my arms and soothe whatever distant trial such talk evoked. "I have an idea for my next painting," he said at last.

"Tell me."

And that is when he relayed to me what had happened to him when he was fourteen years old: the night in the woods, the light in the window, his certainty that he had been saved by the house. When I asked him how a house could save a boy, he told me the ancient folktale of the Eldritch Children that he had learned from his grandfather's gardener, about the queen of the fairies, who left the land on the bend of the river blessed and any house that stood upon it lit.

"Your house," I whispered.

"And yours now, too. Where we shall hang your clock so that it can keep count of the days, the weeks, the months, until we return. In fact"—he smiled—"I thought we would invite everyone to Birchwood for the summer, before we leave for America. It will be a way of saying good-bye, although they will not know it. What do you say?"

What could I say but yes?

There was a knock at the door then, and Edward called out, "Yes?"

It was his littlest sister, Lucy, whose glance swept the room in an instant, taking in Edward and me, the new satchel on his shoulder, the paper wrapping on the floor, the clock. Not the tickets, though, for at some point, though I did not see it happen, Edward had managed to conceal them.

I had noticed before, the way she watched. Always observing, taking mental notes. It got on the nerves of some—Edward's other sister, Clare, had little time for Lucy—but there was something about her that reminded me of Lily Millington, the real Lily: an intelligence that made me fond. Edward, too, adored her, and was forever feeding her hungry mind with books.

"What do you say, Lucy?" he said now, with a grin. "How do you fancy spending summer in the country? At a house on the river—perhaps even a little boat?"

"At . . . *the* house?" Her face lit up even as she darted a look in my direction. I noted the invisible emphasis upon the words, as if they were a secret.

Edward laughed. "The very same."

"But what if Mother—"

"Don't you worry about Mother. I'll take care of everything."

And when Lucy smiled at him, a look of rapture came upon her face that changed her features completely.

———

I remember everything.

Time no longer binds me; my experience of time is no longer bound. Past, present, and future are one. I can slow memories down. I can experience their events again in a flash.

But the months of 1862 are different. They gather speed, no matter what I do to stop them, rolling like a coin let go at the top of a hill, picking up pace as they hurtle towards the end.

When Edward told me about the Night of the Following, the trees of Hampstead wore only the merest of buds. The branches were all but bare and the sky was low and grey; yet, once the tale was told, the summer of Birchwood Manor was already upon us.

Part Three

THE SUMMER OF
BIRCHWOOD MANOR

CHAPTER TWENTY-FOUR

Iᴛ was Lucy's first time on a train and for the half hour since they'd left the station she had sat very still, trying to decide whether or not she could feel the velocity impacting on her organs. Edward had laughed when she asked if he was worried, and Lucy had pretended she was joking. "Our organs are safe from the railways," he'd said, taking her hand and giving it a squeeze. "It's the well-being of the countryside we should be concerned about."

"Better not let Fanny hear you say that." This was Clare, who had a habit of listening in. Edward frowned when she said it but didn't answer. Fanny's father's role in encouraging the spread of train lines across the surface of Britain did not sit well with Edward, who believed that nature should be valued for itself, and not in terms of the resources it yielded to those inclined to exploitation. It was not an entirely easy opinion to hold—as Thurston enjoyed pointing out—for a man who intended to marry into railway money. Mother's friend, Mr. John Ruskin, went a step further, warning that the push of the railway lines into every hidden corner of the globe was a human folly. "A fool always wants to shorten space and time," he had announced when he was leaving the house in Hampstead the other day. "A wise man wants to lengthen both."

By and by, Lucy stopped thinking about her organs, and the vandalism of the countryside, and found herself becoming distracted instead by the sheer marvel of it all. At one point, another train traveling in the same direction swept onto an adjoining line, and when she looked across and into the other carriage, it appeared stationary beside her. There was a man sitting adjacent and their eyes met, and Lucy fell to thinking about time and motion and speed, and began to glimpse the possibility that they weren't actually moving at all—that it was the earth instead that had started to spin rapidly beneath them. Her knowledge of the fixed laws of physics suddenly loosened and her mind exploded with possibilities.

She was overcome with a fierce desire to share her ideas, but when she glanced across the carriage table to where Felix Bernard and his wife Adele were sitting, her excitement fizzled flat. Lucy knew Adele a little, because before she had married Felix, she used to come to the house to model for Edward. She was in four of his paintings, and for a time had been one of his favorites. Lately she had ambitions to be a photographer herself. Adele and Felix had argued about something at Paddington station and were now at odds, Adele pretending engrossment in the *English Woman's Journal*, Felix properly engrossed by the inspection he was carrying out of his new camera.

Across the aisle, Clare was making eyes at Thurston, a common enough state of affairs ever since he'd asked her to model for his new painting. Everybody said that Thurston was very handsome, but he reminded Lucy, with his strutting gait and heavy thighs, of one of Grandfather's prize racehorses. He was not returning Clare's attentions but was focused instead on Edward and his current model, Lily Millington. Lucy followed his gaze. She could understand why they drew his attention. There was something about the way they were together, as if unaware of everybody else in the carriage, that made Lucy want to watch them, too.

Finding no one available with whom to share her thoughts, Lucy kept them to herself. She decided it was probably for the best. She was eager to make a good impression on Edward's friends, and Clare said that such pronouncements, about energy and matter and space and time, made her sound as if she belonged in Bedlam. (Edward, of course, said the opposite. He said that she had a good brain and that it was important she should use it. What hubris it was, he said, that mankind should think to halve the powers of the human race by ignoring the minds and words of the female half of it.)

Lucy had pleaded with Mother that she might have a governess or, better yet, be sent to school, but Mother had only looked at her concernedly, felt her forehead for fever, and told her that she was a strange little thing and would do well to put such foolish thoughts aside. Once, she had even called Lucy in to see Mr. Ruskin, who was having tea in the parlor, and Lucy had been made to stand by the door as he instructed her gently that a woman's intellect was not for "invention or creation," but for "sweet ordering, arrangement, and decision."

Thank God for Edward, who kept her well supplied with books, she had thought. Lucy was currently reading a new one, *The Chemical History of a Candle*, which contained six of the Christmas lectures for young people that Michael Faraday had given at the Royal Institution. It offered an interesting enough description of candle flames and combustion, carbon particles and the luminescent zone, and it was a gift from Edward, so Lucy was determined to appreciate each word; but, truth be told, it was a little basic. She'd had it on her lap since they left Paddington, but couldn't bring herself to open it now, letting her thoughts rest instead upon the summer ahead.

Four whole weeks at Birchwood Manor with Edward as chaperone! Ever since Mother had said that, yes, she could go, Lucy had been counting down the days, crossing them off on the calendar in her bedroom. She had it on good authority that other mothers might have minded their thirteen-year-old daughter spending the summer in company with a group of artists and their models, but Bettina Radcliffe was utterly unlike any of the other mothers that Lucy knew. She was a "bohemian," according to their grandparents, and since Father died had become expert at attaching herself to the travel plans of others. She was spending July on a tour of the Amalfi Coast, ending in Naples, where her friends, the Potters, had set up house. Far from worrying that Lucy might be morally corrupted, Mother had been exceedingly grateful to Edward when he suggested that his youngest sister should join him and his friends at Birchwood Manor for the summer, as it meant she would be spared having to endure the grudging largesse of the grandparents. "Which is one less thing to worry about," she'd said airily, before returning excitedly to her packing.

There was another reason that Edward wanted Lucy there over the summer. She was the first person he had told when he bought the house. It was January 1861, and he had been away on one of his "faraways" for three weeks, four days, and two hours. Lucy had been reading *On the Origin of Species* again, lying across the bed in her room with its dormer window overhanging the street in their house in Hampstead. Suddenly she heard her brother's familiar rhythm on the pavement below. Lucy knew everybody's footfall: the drag of the heavy man who brought the milk, the *tick-tick-cough* of the frail, phlegmy chimney sweep, Clare's trivial scuttle, and Mother's spindle-sharp heels. But her favorite sound was the purpose and promise of Edward's booted tread.

Lucy hadn't needed to look through the window for confirmation. She tossed aside her book, flew down all four flights of stairs and across the hall, leaping into Edward's arms just as he crossed the threshold into the house. At twelve, Lucy had been too old, really, for such behavior, but she was small for her age and Edward was easily able to catch her. Lucy adored Edward and had done so since she was a tiny baby in her crib. She hated it when he went away, leaving her with none but Clare and Mother for company. He was only ever gone for a month or so at a time, but without him the days dragged, and the list of things that she'd been keeping in her head to tell him grew as long as her leg.

As soon as she reached his arms, she started her report, each word tripping over the one before it in her rush to account for everything that had happened since he'd left. Usually, when he had been away from home, Edward listened avidly to her stories before presenting her with the latest treasure he had procured on her behalf; always a book, and always an indulgence of her love for science, history, and mathematics. This time, however, he had held his finger to her lips to silence her and said that her report must wait, for it was his turn to speak: he had done something incredible, he said, and he needed to share it with her at once.

Lucy had been intrigued but equally gratified. Clare and Mother were in the house, yet it was she, Lucy, who had been chosen. Edward's attention was like a light being shone, and Lucy basked in its warmth. She went downstairs with him to the kitchen, the one place they could always be sure the others wouldn't bother them, and it was there, as they sat together at Cook's waxed and worn table, that Edward told her about the house he had bought. Twin gables, a country garden, the river, and the copse of trees. The description was familiar, even before he said, "It's the one, Lucy, the very one from the Night of the Following."

Lucy had drawn breath then, stars of memory prickling her skin. She had known exactly which house he meant. The Night of the Following was a legend between the two of them. Lucy had only been five years old when it happened, but the night was seared onto her memory. She would never forget how strange he was when he finally returned the next morning with his hair all tangled and his eyes wild. It had taken a full day before he would speak about it, but he had told her in the end, the two of them sitting inside the ancient wardrobe in the attic at Beechworth. Lucy was the only person Edward had ever confided in about the Night of the Following; he had trusted her with his greatest secret and it had become an emblem of the bond between them.

"Are you going to live there?" she said, her mind skipping immediately to the possibility that she might lose him to the countryside.

He laughed and brushed his hand through his dark hair. "I've no plans yet beyond possession. They will say it was a madness, Lucy, a madness, and they'll be right. But I know you understand, I had to have it. The house has been calling to me since the night I first saw it; now, at last, I've answered."

❧

Across the aisle, as Lily Millington laughed at something that Edward had said, Lucy regarded her brother's current model. She was beautiful, but Lucy suspected that she might not have realized quite *how* beautiful without Edward's guidance. That was his gift; everybody said so. He was able to see things that others did not, and then, through his art, alter his spectator's perceptions so that they could not help but see as well. In the last of his *Academy Notes*, Mr. Ruskin had called this the "Radcliffe sensory swindle."

As Lucy watched, Edward brushed a gleaming strand of Lily's red hair from her face. He tucked it behind her ear and the model smiled. It was the sort of smile that hinted at previous conversations, and Lucy felt something unexpected and shivery rise up inside her.

The first time that Lucy saw Lily Millington, she had been little more than a haze of fiery red in the glass house at the bottom of the garden. It had been May 1861 and Lucy, a bit shortsighted, had thought at first that she was looking at the leaves of a potted Japanese maple tree through the glass. Edward had a fondness for exotic plants and was forever visiting Mr. Romano on the corner of Willow Road, making sketches of the Italian man's daughters in exchange for samples of the newest plants brought back from the Americas or even the Antipodes. It was one of their many shared passions, for Lucy, too, delighted in these living, breathing visitors from faraway places, wondrous glimpses into parts of the globe quite unlike their own.

It was only when Mother told Lucy to take *two* cups of tea down the path on a tray that she realized that Edward had a model in the studio. Her curiosity had been aroused immediately, for she knew who this must be. One could not live within the same house as Edward and fail to partake in the great peaks and troughs of his passions.

Some months before, he had fallen into a slump from which it seemed he would not resurrect himself. He had been painting Adele, but had reached a point where he had exhausted the inspiration to be drawn from her small, neat features. "It isn't that her face isn't pleasing," he had explained to Lucy, pacing back and forth in the studio as she sat upon the rosewood chair by the furnace. "It's only that the space between her pretty ears is vacant."

Edward had a theory about beauty. He said that the turn of the nose, the cheekbones and lips, the color of the eyes and the way that the hairs curled at the nape of the neck, were all well and good, but that what made a person radiate, whether as oil on canvas or as an albumen print on paper, was intelligence. "I don't mean the ability to explain the workings of the internal combustion engine, or to conduct a lesson on how the telegraph sends a message from here to there; I mean that some people have a light inside them, a facility for inquiry and interest and engagement, that cannot be fabricated and cannot be counterfeited by the artist, no matter his or her skill."

One morning, though, Edward had arrived home with the dawn, an agitation in his step. The household had barely roused when he threw open the door, but as always the house itself registered his arrival. The stillness of the entrance hall, ever sensitive to his presence, began to reverberate as he tossed his coat onto the hook, and when Lucy, Clare, and Mother appeared in their nightdresses at the top of the stairs, he held his arms out and declared, with a joyous smile spread wide across his face, that he had found her, the one that he'd been looking for.

There was much relief all round as they gathered at the breakfast table to hear his story.

The fates, he began, in their infinite wisdom, had put her in his path at Drury Lane. He had spent the evening at the theater with Thurston Holmes, and it was there, in the crowded, smoky foyer, that he had first caught sight of her. (Lucy would later glean, during a wine-infused dispute between Edward and Thurston on another matter entirely, that it was Thurston who had noticed the fine-limbed, red-haired beauty; he who had observed the way the light caught her hair and rendered her skin alabaster; who had realized that she looked exactly like the subject of the painting that Edward had been planning. It was Thurston, too, who had pulled on Edward's shirtsleeve, swinging him around, thereby breaking off the conversation he'd been having with a fellow to whom he owed some money, in order that his own eyes might lock upon the woman in the deep-blue dress.)

Edward had been spellbound. In that instant, he said, he saw his painting complete. While Edward was experiencing this revelation, however, the woman had turned to leave. Without a thought as to what he was doing, he began pushing through the crowd, powered by a spirit quite outside himself; he knew only that he had to reach her. He threaded his way across the busy foyer after the woman, slipping through the side exit and into the street. And thank goodness he had, Edward said, glancing around the breakfast table, for when he finally caught up with her in the laneway, he was just in time to rescue her. At the precise moment that Edward was wending his way through the crowds inside the foyer, a man dressed all in black, a man of a most deplorable character, had noticed her alone in the alleyway and hurtled past, ripping an heirloom bracelet from her wrist.

Clare and Mother gasped, and Lucy said, "Did you see him?"

"I was too late. Her brother had already set off after the fellow but did not catch him. He returned just as I came upon her in the alley: he thought at first glance that I was the perpetrator, returned to finish the job, and called, 'Stop! Thief!' But she explained quickly that I was no thief and his demeanor changed at once."

The woman had turned then, Edward said, and moonlight illuminated the features of her face, and he saw that he had been right when he had glimpsed her from afar: she was indeed the one that he'd been waiting for.

"What did you do next?" Lucy asked as the parlor maid brought in a fresh pot of breakfast tea.

"I'm afraid that I have no talent for polite intimations," he said. "I simply told her that I had to paint her."

Clare raised her eyebrows. "And what did she say to that?"

"More importantly," said Mother, "what did her brother say?"

"He was caught by complete surprise. And, in retrospect, I did rather spring it on them. He asked what I meant by saying that I wished to paint her and I explained as best I could. I fear that I wasn't as erudite as I might have been; I was still somewhat dazzled."

"Did you tell him that you had exhibited at the Royal Academy?" said Mother. "Did you tell him that you have Mr. Ruskin's favor? That your grandfather is titled?"

Edward said that he had done all of that and more. He said that he may even have exaggerated their position a little, naming all of the ancient land and titles he had heretofore done his best to ignore; he had even offered to have his own mother, "Lady" Radcliffe, come to call on their parents to reassure them that their daughter would be in good hands. "I felt it was important, Mother, for the brother made a point of saying that they would need to speak with their parents before any commitment was made—that a respectable woman's reputation could be damaged by her employment as a painter's model."

The meeting had been agreed and the parties had said good night.

Edward had walked along the river afterwards, and then through the dark London streets, sketching the woman's face in his mind. He was so enamored with her that he had managed to misplace his wallet as he wandered, and had been forced to walk all the way back to Hampstead.

When Edward's spirits were elevated, no one could avoid being swept into his orbit, and while he related this tale, Lucy, Clare, and Mother had listened avidly. As he reached the end, Mother needed to hear no more. She said that of course she would visit Mr. and Mrs. Millington and vouch for Edward. Her lady's maid was set immediately to repairing the moth holes in her finest dress, and a carriage hired to take her down into London.

A metallic scream, a fog of smoke, and the train began to slow. Lucy put her face up to the open window and saw that they were drawing into a station. The sign read SWINDON, which she knew was where they were disembarking. The platform was patrolled by a punctilious-looking man with a smart uniform and a shiny whistle that he was not timid in using; a number of porters were milling, waiting for arriving passengers.

They alighted from the train, Edward and the other men going straight to the luggage compartments to see about the suitcases and art supplies, all of which (except Lucy's—she refused to be separated from her books) were loaded into a horse-drawn coach and sent on to the village of Birchwood. Lucy had assumed that they would all go by coach, too, but Edward said that the day was too perfect to waste; besides, the house was far better approached from the river than the road.

And he was right, it *was* a glorious day. The sky was a lustrous blue, with a clarity that was rarely seen in London, and the air was tinged with country smells like seeding grasses and the tang of sun-warmed manure.

Edward led the way and he did not stick to the roads, taking them instead through wildflower meadows spotted with yellow kingcups, pink foxgloves, and blue forget-me-nots. Delicate white sprays of cow parsley were everywhere, and at times they came upon a meandering stream and had to look for stepping-stones in order to cross.

It was a long walk, but they did not rush. The four hours passed in a flow, broken up by lunch, and a paddle in the shallows near Lechlade, and a few spots of sketching. The atmosphere was one of frivolity and laughter: Felix had a cloth-wrapped bundle of strawberries which he took from his bag to share; Adele wove wreaths of flowers for all of the women—even Lucy—to wear like crowns; and Thurston disappeared at one stage, only to be found with his hat on his face, fast asleep on the soft green grass beneath a great weeping willow. As the day reached the peak of its heat, Lily Millington, whose long hair fell loose down her back, wrapped it into a shimmering knot and fastened it on the top of her head with Edward's silk neck scarf. The skin revealed at the nape of her neck was smooth and white as a lily and made Lucy look away.

Near the Halfpenny Bridge, they took the steps down to the water's edge and followed the river east, through the cattle-filled meadow and beyond St. John's Lock. By the time they reached the rim of the woods, the sun, though still providing light, had surrendered its heat.

Edward was always talking about light, and Lucy knew that he would say that it had "lost its yellow." The effect was one that Lucy liked. Without the sheen of yellow, the rest of the world seemed blue.

The house, Edward told them, lay on the other side of the woods. He insisted that this was the best way to approach it for the first time, for only when one arrived from the river could the building's true proportions be glimpsed. The explanation was reasonable and the others didn't question it, but Lucy knew that there was more to his thinking than he'd admitted. Inside the woods was the clearing from the Night of the Following. Edward was leading them along the very path he'd taken that night, when he fled through the trees and fields, beneath the watchful silver stars, and finally spotted the light in the attic calling to him.

Within the woods, everyone walked in silent single file. Lucy was aware of the sounds of twigs cracking underfoot and leaves rustling, and odd noises at times in the profuse greenery along the secluded track. The branches of the trees in this pocket were not straight. They grew towards the canopy in wavy ribbons, and their trunks were covered in ferns and lichens; they were oaks, she thought, with hazel and birch among them. The light fell spangled in places and the air seemed alive with anticipation.

When they finally reached the clearing, Lucy could almost hear the leaves breathing.

It wasn't difficult to imagine how frightening this place might become in the dead of night.

Lucy would never forget how Edward had looked all those years ago when he finally made it back to their grandparents' house after the Night of the Following. She glanced ahead, curious to see how he was reacting to being back here now, and was surprised when she saw him reach out to take Lily Millington's hand.

They all continued across the clearing and then wended their way through the woods on the other side.

Finally, the air began to lighten, and with a last scramble up the overgrown bank they emerged into the open.

A wildflower meadow spilled out before them, and beyond it sat a house with twin gables and a splendid display of chimneys.

Edward turned around, a look of joyous triumph on his face, and Lucy found herself smiling, too.

The strange enchantment of the woods had lifted and the others now began to talk excitedly, as if, having seen the house, the thrilling promise of the summer ahead could finally be tasted.

Was it true that there was a rowing boat? they asked. Yes, Edward said, it was inside the field barn over there. He'd had a jetty built especially, down at the river.

How much of the land was his? All of it, he said, as far as the eye could see.

Were there bedrooms overlooking the river? Many—the whole first story was room upon room, and the attic above held more besides.

With a loud call to arms, Thurston began to run and Felix fell in quickly beside him, racing; Clare and Adele linked arms as they started across the meadow. Edward caught Lucy's gaze and winked at her. "Hurry, little sister," he said. "Go and claim the best room for yourself!"

Lucy grinned and nodded and started bounding after the others. She felt free and more alive than usual, aware of the country air on her face and the lingering warmth of the afternoon sun, the joy of sharing this most important moment with Edward. In such spirit, as she reached the other side of the meadow, she turned back to beckon him.

But he wasn't watching after her. He and Lily Millington were walking slowly towards the house, their heads bent close together in deep conversation. Lucy waited to catch his eye; she waved her arm to attract his attention but all to no avail.

At length, she turned around and continued, disappointed, towards the house.

And for the first time since they'd set off from Paddington station early that morning, it occurred to Lucy to wonder where Edward's fiancée, Fanny Brown, was.

Chapter Twenty-Five

Birchwood Manor was one of those places in which the threads of time slackened and came unstrung. Lucy noticed how quickly the others all slipped into a routine, as if they had been at the house forever, and she wondered whether it was a function of the weather—the stretch of summer days that seemed to go on and on—the particular collection of people that Edward had gathered, or maybe even something intrinsic to the house itself. She knew what Edward would say to that. Ever since he'd learned the tale of the Eldritch Children as a boy, he had been convinced that the land within this bend of the river held special properties. Lucy prided herself on being of a rational persuasion, but she had to admit that there was something unusual about the house.

Edward had written ahead to engage a young woman from the village, Emma Stearnes, as a maid of all work, to come in early each morning and then to leave after the evening meal had been prepared. On the first night, when they arrived from the railway, traipsing across the wildflower meadow towards the house, Emma had been waiting for them. She had followed Edward's instructions to the letter and the large iron table in the garden had been covered with a white linen cloth, a tremendous spread laid out upon it. Glass lanterns had been suspended from the lowest branches of the chestnut tree, and as dusk fell, the wicks were lit and the candles began to flicker. Their illumination strengthened with the darkening night, and as the wine flowed, Felix took out his guitar. Adele started to dance while a chorus of robins sang away the last of the day's light, and eventually Edward stood upon the table to recite Keats's "Bright Star."

The house slept like the dead that night, and everyone woke late the next morning in high spirits. They had all been too tired the evening before to investigate properly and now ran from room to room exclaiming over this view or that detail. The house had been built by a master craftsman, Edward said proudly, looking on, delighted, as his friends explored; every feature had been knowingly included. In Edward's view, such attention to detail made the house "truthful" and he loved everything about it: every piece of furniture, every curtain, every whorl in every floorboard, hewn from the nearby woods. His favorite aspect was an engraving above the door in a room with mulberry fruit-and-leaf wallpaper; the room was on the ground floor with large windows set into the back wall that made it seem almost part of the garden it overlooked. The engraving read, TRUTH, BEAUTY, LIGHT, and Edward could not stop staring at it in wonder and saying, "You see, this house was *meant* for me."

Over the coming days, Edward sketched the house relentlessly. He went everywhere with his new leather satchel across his shoulder, and could often be seen sitting amongst the long grasses of the meadow, hat upon his head, staring up at the house with an expression of deep contentment, before returning his attention to his work. Lily Millington, Lucy noted, was always by his side.

Lucy had asked Edward about Fanny's whereabouts. He had taken her on the first morning, leading her along the halls by the hand, to show her the Birchwood Manor library. "I thought of you especially when I saw these shelves," he told her. "Look at this collection, Lucy. Books on every subject you could care to mention. It is up to you now to fill your mind with all of the knowledge that the world and its brightest scholars have acquired and published. There will come a time, I know, when women will have the same opportunities afforded men. How can it not come to pass when women are the smarter and more numerous? Until then, you must take control of your own destiny. Read, remember, think."

Edward did not make such declarations insincerely, and Lucy promised that she would do as he said. "You can trust me," she'd replied solemnly. "I will read every book on every shelf before this summer is over."

He laughed when she said it. "Well, perhaps there's no need to work quite so quickly as that. There'll be other summers. Make sure you leave enough time to enjoy the river and the gardens."

"Of course." And then, because the conversation had reached a natural lull: "Are we expecting Fanny to join us?"

Edward's demeanor did not change, but he said, "No, Fanny isn't coming," and then he moved at once to point out a nook beside the fireplace that he suggested would be perfect for concealed reading. "No one would even know that you were in there, and I have it on good authority that reading when hidden improves the experience immeasurably."

Lucy had let the subject of Fanny drop.

Later, she would wish that she had probed further, asked a few more questions; but in truth she did not much care for Fanny and was glad that she wouldn't be joining them. At the time, Edward's perfunctory, almost dismissive response had said it all. Fanny was a bore. She commandeered Edward's attention and tried to make him someone he was not. As a fiancée, she was far more threatening to Lucy than a model. Models came and went, but marriage was forever. Marriage meant a new house for Edward somewhere else. Lucy couldn't imagine living without her brother, and she couldn't imagine what it would be like for him to have to live with Fanny.

Lucy had no plans for marriage—not unless the perfect person happened along. Her ideal husband, she had decided, would be someone just like herself. Or Edward. And they would be very happy, the two of them, alone together forever.

Edward had been right about the library: it was as if it had been designed and stocked with Lucy in mind. Shelves lined the walls, and unlike the collection at their grandparents' house, which comprised copious religious tracts and pamphlets protecting against the commission of social solecisms, here were *real* books. The previous owners of Birchwood Manor had amassed a tremendous amount of material on all manner of fascinating subjects, and where there were gaps, Edward had sent to London for further titles. Lucy spent every spare moment scaling the sliding ladder, scanning the spines, and planning the summer weeks that stretched ahead—and she had many spare moments to fill, because from the first day that they arrived, she was left to her own devices.

Even as they had carried out their initial explorations of the house, each artist had been focused on finding the perfect place in which to work. There was an added urgency to their quest, for just before they left for Birchwood, Mr. Ruskin had undertaken to support an exhibition of their collective works in the autumn. Each member of the Magenta Brotherhood had a new creation in mind, and the air was thus infused with a blend of creativity, competition, and possibility. Once the rooms had been chosen, each painter fell at once to unpacking the art supplies that had come by coach from the railway station.

Thurston chose the sitting room at the front of the house, because he said that the south-facing window afforded him the perfect light. Lucy tried to stay out of his way, partly because she found Thurston inexplicably disconcerting, and partly because she was embarrassed to have to see her sister's big mooning eyes. Lucy had chanced upon Clare modeling when the door was open and had needed to run through the meadow at full speed afterwards just to rid herself of the uncomfortable creeping sensation. Lucy had glimpsed the painting before she left. It was fine, of course—even if still in its earliest incarnation—for Thurston was a competent technician; but something had struck her as notable. The woman in the painting, though she shared the languid position that Clare was modeling, draped with ennui over the *chaise longue*, had been given lips that belonged unmistakably to Lily Millington.

Felix had commandeered the small enclosure off the paneled drawing room on the ground floor, and when Edward pointed out that it had hardly any light at all, he had agreed eagerly and said that this was the point. Felix, who had heretofore been known for painting moody scenes from myth and legend, now declared an intention to use photography rather than paint to portray the same subjects. "I am going to make an image of Tennyson's Lady of Shalott to rival Mr. Robinson's. Your river is perfect. It even has the willows and aspens on offer. It shall *be* Camelot, you'll see."

Fierce debate had been raging ever since amongst the group as to whether it was possible to render the same artistic effect in the new medium. At dinner one night, Thurston said that photographs were a gimmick. "A cheap trick, all well and good for creating reminders of loved ones, but not for communicating on a serious subject."

At which point Felix had taken a button from his pocket, a small tin badge, and flipped it over in his fingers. "Tell that to Abraham Lincoln," he said. "Tens of thousands of these have been given away. There are people all over the continent of America wearing the man's face—his very image—on their clothing. Once, we wouldn't have known what Lincoln looked like, let alone what he thought. Now he has forty percent of the vote."

"Why didn't his opponents do the same thing?" said Adele.

"They tried, but it was too late. He who acts first wins. But I'll promise you this: we won't see another election in which the candidates don't trade on their image."

Thurston took the tin badge and flipped it like a coin. "I'm not denying that it's a useful political tool," he said, slapping the badge down on the top of one hand. "But you can't tell me that this is art." He lifted his palm to reveal Lincoln's face.

"Not that particular button, no. But think of Roger Fenton's work."

"The Crimean pictures are extraordinary," Edward agreed. "And certainly the communication of a serious subject."

"But not art." Thurston poured the last of the red wine into his glass. "I will allow that photographs are useful tools for reporting news and happenings; for performing as the . . . the . . ."

"The eye of history," Lily Millington proffered.

"Yes, thank you, Lily, the eye of history, but art they are not."

Lucy, sitting quietly at the end of the table, enjoying a second serving of pudding, loved the idea of the photograph as the eye of history. So often in her own reading about the past—and in the digging she had been doing in the woods behind the house, where she had started turning up odd and ancient remnants—she was frustrated by the need to extrapolate and imagine. What a gift it was to future generations that photographs could now record the truth! Lucy had read an article in the *London Review* that referred to the "unimpeachable evidence of the photograph" and said that from now on nothing would happen without photography being used to create—

"A tangible, transferable memory of the occurrence."

Lucy looked up so sharply that a dollop of cream fell from her spoon. It was Lily Millington who had taken the words right out of Lucy's mouth. That is, she had taken the *London Review*'s words right out of Lucy's mind.

"Just so, Lily," Felix was saying, "One day the photographic image will be ubiquitous: cameras will be so small and compact that people will carry them on straps around their necks."

Thurston rolled his eyes. "And their necks will be stronger, too, I suppose, these Amazonian people of the future? Felix, you're making my point with your talk of ubiquity. Having a camera to point does not an artist make. An artist is a man who sees beauty in a sulfuric fog where others see only pollution."

"Or a woman," said Lily Millington.

"Why would anybody see a woman in pollution?" Thurston stopped as he realized what she meant. "Oh. I see. Yes, very good, Lily. Very good. Or a *lady* who sees beauty."

Clare chimed in then with the self-evident observation that there was no color in a photograph, and Felix explained that this simply meant he would have to use light and shadow, framing and composition, to evoke the same emotions, but Lucy was only half listening now.

She couldn't stop looking at Lily Millington. She did not think she had ever heard the other models say anything sensible, let alone show up Thurston Holmes. Lucy had imagined, if she had given it any thought at all, that Edward would exhaust the inspiration he had drawn from Lily Millington, just as he had grown tired of the other models who came before her. But she glimpsed now that Lily Millington was different from the others after all. That she was a different kind of model entirely.

Lily Millington and Edward spent each day squirreled away in the Mulberry Room, where Edward had set up his easel. He was working diligently—Lucy recognized the look of distracted inspiration that came upon his features when he was in the process of creating a painting—but so far he had been unusually circumspect about his planned piece. Lucy had thought at first that this must be an effect of his *contretemps* with Mr. Ruskin after the latter's lack of support the previous year when Edward exhibited the *La Belle* painting. Between Ruskin's appraisal of the work and Mr. Charles Dickens's reporting of it, Edward had been left fuming. (When the review was printed, he had stormed down to his studio in the back garden and set fire to every work penned by Mr. Dickens, along with his prized copy of Mr. Ruskin's *Modern Painters*. Lucy, who had lined up at W. H. Smith & Son every week between December 1860 and August 1861 in order to purchase the latest installment of *Great Expectations*, had to hide her treasured copies of *All the Year Round* lest they, too, should be sacrificed to his fury.)

Now, though, she had begun to wonder if there was something else at play. It was hard to say what it was, exactly, but there was an element of secrecy that surrounded Edward and Lily Millington when they were together. And just the other day, Lucy had approached her brother when he was working in his sketchbook, and as soon as he realized that she was beside him, he'd snapped it shut—not before she'd caught a glimpse, though, of a detailed study of Lily Millington's face.

Edward did not like to be watched when he worked, but it was highly unusual for him to behave with quite so much furtiveness. It seemed particularly unwarranted in this case, because what was there to hide in a study of his model's features? The sketch had been like any of the hundred others that Lucy had already seen on his studio wall—except for the pendant necklace she was wearing. Other than that, it was just the same.

Whatever the case, Edward was much intent upon his work, and so, while the others were busy during the day, and Emma was occupied by her many tasks, Lucy took possession of the library. She had told Edward that she would pace herself, but she had no intention of doing any such thing: each day she chose a clutch of books and then took them outside with her to read. Sometimes she read in the barn, other times beneath the ferns in the garden, and on days when there was too much breeze for Felix to attempt to shoot the Lady of Shalott, when he had stalked about the dawn meadow with a finger lifted to assess the prevailing wind and then returned to the house with his hands thrust deep and disconsolately in his pockets, she would sit in the little rowboat, moored down at Edward's new jetty.

They had been at Birchwood for almost two weeks when she came across a particularly ancient and dusty book, its covers hanging by threads. It had been pushed to the back of the very top library shelf, hidden from view. Lucy paused on the ladder and opened to the book's title page, where it was announced in elaborate font that the book was called *Daemonologie, In Forme of a Dialogue, Divided into three Bookes* and that it had been printed in "Edinbvrgh" by "Robert Walde-grave, Printer to the Kings Mageſtie" in the year 1597. A book on necromancy and ancient black magic, written by the king who had also brought them the plain English Bible, was of more than passing interest to Lucy, and she put it under her arm and climbed down the ladder.

She took a number of books with her that day when she set off for the river, along with her lunch, wrapped in cloth. The morning was hot and clear as glass and the air smelled like drying wheat and secret, muddy underground things. Lucy climbed into the boat and rowed herself upstream. Although it wasn't still enough for Felix to make his photographic exposure, it was not windy, and Lucy planned to let the boat drift slowly back towards Edward's jetty. She stopped rowing as she neared St. John's Lock and took up *On Liberty*. It wasn't until after one o'clock that she finished with John Stuart Mill and opened *Daemonologie*, and she did not get far with King James's explanation as to the reasons for persecuting witches in a Christian society, because beyond the first few pages she discovered that the book had been hollowed out to create a cavity. Inside were a number of sheets of paper, folded and tied with a length of twine. She undid the knot and opened the pages. The first was a letter, very old, dated 1586, and written in such faded scratchy writing that she did not even attempt at once to read it. The other pages were drawings, designs for the house, Lucy realized, remembering that Edward had said that it was built during the reign of Elizabeth.

Lucy was thrilled, not because she had any particular interest in architecture, but because she knew that Edward would be delighted, and anything that earned his pleasure made her glad. As she studied the designs, though, she noticed in them something unusual. There were sketches of what the house would look like, the twin gables, the chimneys, the rooms that Lucy now recognized. But there was an additional layer inscribed on the most transparent of paper, which overlaid the first. When Lucy put it on top and lined them up, she noticed that it showed two additional rooms, both of them tiny. Far too small to be bedrooms, or even antechambers. Neither of them had she come across in her explorations.

She frowned, lifting the fine paper and then replacing it in a slightly different position, trying to get a sense of what the rooms might be. The boat had come to rest by now in a small inlet, its prow nosing into the grassy riverbank, and Lucy folded the floor plan away, taking up the letter in the hope that it might shed some light. It was written by a man called Nicholas Owen, the name vaguely familiar to Lucy—perhaps from something she had read? The writing was of an elaborate historical style, but she managed to pick out some of the words—"protect . . . priests . . . holes . . ."

Lucy gasped as she realized what the floor plan revealed. She had read, of course, about the measures taken against Catholic priests after Queen Elizabeth ascended to the throne. She knew that a great many houses had a secret chamber built into them, whether within the walls or beneath the floors, in order to shelter persecuted priests. But to think that there might be one—maybe even two—here at Birchwood Manor was beyond thrilling. Even more exciting, it seemed probable to Lucy that Edward had no idea about the secret hideaways, for surely, if he had, it would have been one of the first things he'd have told them all. Which meant that she was going to be able to share something wonderful with him about the house that he loved: Edward's "truthful" house had a secret.

Lucy couldn't get the boat back to the jetty quickly enough. She tied it up, gathered her books beneath her arm, and started running towards the house. Although she did not often give herself over to glee, and rarely to singing, she found herself humming one of Mother's favorite dance tunes as she ran and took it up with gusto. Arriving back at the house, she went first to the Mulberry Room, for although Edward did not like to be disturbed while he was working, she was certain that under these circumstances he would make an exception. The room was unattended. A silk cloth had been draped over the canvas and Lucy vacillated briefly before deciding that she didn't have the time to spare. Next, she looked upstairs in the bedroom that he had chosen for himself, overlooking the woods, but there was no sign. She ran along the hallways, peeking into each room that she passed, even braving an eyeful of Clare's longing simper when she checked inside the front sitting room.

In the kitchen she found Emma preparing the evening meal, but when asked after Edward's whereabouts, the maid only lifted her left shoulder before launching into an admonishment of Thurston, who had developed a most unpleasant habit of climbing onto the rooftop of a morning and using the Napoleonic Wars rifle he had brought with him from London to take aim at the birds. "It's a terrible racket," said Emma, "I mean, maybe if he stood a chance of bringing down a duck that I could roast, but his aim's no good, and anyway, he takes shot at the smaller birds what don't make for proper eating." It was a familiar lament and Edward had asked Thurston many times to stop, warning him that he might shoot one of the farmers by mistake and find himself up on charges of murder.

"I'll tell Edward as soon as I find him," said Lucy, in her best attempt at placation. They had formed a bond of sorts, she and Emma, during the course of the fortnight. Lucy had a feeling that the maid had her pegged as the only other "normal" person in the house. As the artists and models flew in and out of the kitchen in loose costumes and with paintbrushes tucked behind their ears, Emma seemed to save all of her head shakings and tut-tuts for Lucy, as if they were kindred spirits caught in a current of madness. Today, though, Lucy could spare Emma only the minimum of attention. "I promise, I'll tell him," she said again, already on the move, skipping sideways and through the front door into the garden.

But Edward was in none of his favorite outdoor places, and Lucy was almost *dying* with frustration when she finally spotted Lily Millington about to leave the garden by the front gate that opened out onto the lane. The sun was catching her hair so that it looked ablaze.

"Lily," she called. At first the model did not appear to hear her, so she called again, louder. "Li-ly."

Lily Millington turned around, and perhaps she had been far away in her thoughts, for her expression was as if she had been surprised by the sound of her own name. "Why hello there, Lucy," she said with a smile.

"I'm looking for Edward. Have you seen him anywhere?"

"He went to the woods. He said he'd gone to see a man about a dog."

"Are you meeting him there?" Lucy had noticed that Lily Millington was wearing walking boots and carrying a bag over her shoulder.

"No, I'm off to the village to see a man about a stamp." She held up an addressed envelope. "Fancy a walk?"

With no chance to tell Edward what she had discovered about the house, Lucy decided that it was better to fill her afternoon with an activity than to wait around, cooling her heels.

They rambled along the laneway, past a church on the corner, and into the village. The small post office was next door to a public house called the Swan.

"I'll wait here," said Lucy, who had seen an interesting stone structure over where the roads crossed and wanted to have a closer look.

Lily did not take long, emerging from the post office with her letter in hand, a stamp now affixed on its corner. Whatever she was posting was heavy enough to require a Two Penny Blue, Lucy noted, and was addressed to someone in London.

Lily slipped it into the post box and they started the short walk back to Birchwood Manor.

Lucy did not have the art of small talk, not like Clare and Mother, and she wondered what one was supposed to say to fill the silence in such a situation. Not that she believed silence needed filling, not generally, only that something about Lily Millington made Lucy wish to appear more grown-up, more clever, more *significant* than usual. For some reason that would require unpicking later, it seemed important that she should appear as more than simply Edward's little sister.

"Lovely weather," she said, causing herself to cringe into her collar.

"Enjoy it while it lasts," said Lily, "it's going to storm tonight."

"How can you tell?"

"I have a rare and wondrous ability to read the future."

Lucy glanced at her.

Lily Millington smiled. "I have an interest in synoptic charts and chanced to see one in a copy of the *Times* on the postmaster's desk."

"You know about weather forecasting?"

"Only what I've heard from Robert FitzRoy."

"You've met Robert FitzRoy?" Friend to Charles Darwin; commander of the HMS *Beagle*; inventor of barometers and the first ever Meteorological Statist to the Board of Trade.

"I've heard him speak. He's the friend of a friend. He's working on a book about weather that sounds very promising."

"Did you ever hear him speak about the sinking of the *Royal Charter* and the creation of the FitzRoy storm barometer?"

"Of course. It's quite remarkable . . ."

As Lily Millington launched into a fascinating account of the theory behind FitzRoy's forecasting charts and the science behind his storm glasses, Lucy listened with an avid ninety-seven percent of her attention. With the other three percent, she wondered whether it was too much to hope that when Edward lost interest in his model, Lucy would be able to keep Lily Millington for herself.

Lily Millington had been right about the storm. The stretch of perfect summer weather came to an abrupt end late that afternoon, sunlight disappearing from the sky as suddenly and surely as if someone had blown out the flame within the world's lamp. Lucy didn't notice, though, for she was already sitting in the dark, secreted within a hidden cavity beneath the skin of Edward's house.

She had spent a most exciting afternoon. After they arrived back from the post office, Lily Millington had decided to walk down to the woods to rendezvous with Edward. Emma, still busy in the kitchen, was happy to report that Thurston, Clare, Adele, and Felix had taken a picnic tea to share by the river and were planning afterwards to swim, and that she herself was ahead of schedule with the dinner preparations and—if there was nothing that Lucy was wanting—was going to "pop back home for an hour or so to put my feet up."

With the house to herself, Lucy knew precisely how she was going to spend her time. The initial thrill of discovery had dissipated, and in its wake lay the realization that it would be a terrible folly to rush now into telling Edward about the priest holes. The floor plans were centuries old; it was entirely possible that the chambers had been sealed up years before, or else that the plans, though mooted, had never been put into place. How embarrassing it would be to make a big announcement only to discover herself in error! Lucy did not like making errors. Far better to investigate the secret hideaways herself first.

Once Emma had been sent packing and Lily Millington was little more than a flame-colored speck on the far side of the meadow, Lucy pulled out the floor plans. The first chamber appeared to form part of the main staircase, which seemed so unlikely that Lucy thought initially that she must have been reading the plan incorrectly. She had climbed the staircase at least a hundred times by now and sat to read more than once on the elegant bentwood chair by the window; aside from a pleasant warmth where the stairs made their turn, Lucy hadn't noticed anything out of the ordinary.

Only when she fetched the magnifying glass from the cedar desk in the library and began to decipher the letter did Lucy find the instruction that she'd been lacking. There was a trick step, the letter said. The first rise after the landing had been constructed so that it tilted, when triggered properly, to reveal the entrance to a small secret chamber. But be warned, continued the letter: for the design of the trapdoor was such that in order to remain discreet, the hidden mechanism could only be triggered from the outside.

It was like something out of one of those newspaper serials for schoolboys and Lucy ran to investigate, pushing aside the chair as she knelt on the floor.

There was nothing visible to suggest that the staircase was anything other than it appeared, and she frowned again at the letter. She studied the description, which included a sketch of a spring-operated latch, and then smiled to herself. Pressing each corner of the wooden rise in turn, she held her breath until finally she heard a small click and noticed that the panel had jutted out of position slightly at the base. She slipped her fingers into the newly revealed crack and lifted, sliding it into a recess beneath the next step. A slim, sly opening was revealed, large enough—just—to fit a man carrying no extra weight.

Lucy only considered for a split second before slipping down into the cavity.

The space was tight: not high enough for her to sit unless her head was bent so far forwards that her chin was touching her chest, and so she lay down flat. The air inside was stale and close; the floor was warm to the touch, and Lucy supposed that the chimney from the kitchen must run at an angle beneath it. She lay very still, listening. It was startlingly quiet. She shuffled sideways and pressed her ear against the wall. Dead, wooden silence. Solid, as if there were layers of bricks on the other side.

Lucy tried to envisage the design of the house, wondering how that could be. As she did, the realization that she was lying in a secret chamber, designed to keep a man concealed from enemies bent on his destruction, with a trapdoor that might ease closed at any moment, leaving her alone in a pitch-black space, drowning in thick, broiling air, no one aware of what she'd found and where she'd gone, began to push in on her from all sides. She felt a sudden panic constricting her lungs, her breaths becoming short and loud, and she scrabbled into a crouched position as quickly as she could, hitting her head on the ceiling of the chamber in her rush to get free.

The second hideaway was in the hallway, and that was where Lucy was now. It was a very different prospect: a concealment within the wainscoting, tucked behind an ingenious recessed sliding panel that could be opened, thankfully, from inside or out. The space inside was not large, but it had a different feeling entirely from the stairwell chamber: there was something comforting about this hiding place. It was not truly dark, for one thing, Lucy noticed, and the chamber's panel was thin enough that she could hear through it.

She had heard when the others returned from the river, laughing as they chased one another through the halls; she had heard, too, when Felix and Adele had their hissed spat about a joke (according to him) that had gone wrong (according to her); and she had heard the first great clap of thunder that rolled up the river and seized the house. Lucy had just decided to climb out of the space, and had her ear pressed close against the panel to make sure there was no one in the hallway to see her appear and discover her secret, when she picked out Edward's footfalls approaching.

She considered emerging into his path and surprising him, and was wondering whether it might not be the perfect way to reveal to him the priest holes, when she heard him say, "Come here, wife."

Lucy stopped still, her hand on the panel.

"What is it, husband?" Lily Millington's voice.

"Closer than that."

"Like this?"

Lucy leaned against the panel, listening. They did not say anything else, but Edward laughed softly. There was an edge of surprise to it, as if he had just been told something unexpected but pleasing, and someone inhaled sharply, and then—

Nothing.

Inside the hiding place, Lucy realized that she was holding her breath.

She released it.

Two seconds later, everything went black and a great rumble of thunder shook the house and the ancient earth beneath it.

The others were already in the dining room by the time Lucy arrived. A candelabrum stood in the middle of the unlaid table, nine long white tapers smoking towards the ceiling. The wind had picked up outside, and although it was summer, the night was cool. Someone had lit a small fire, which flickered and popped in the grate, and Edward and Lily Millington were sitting by it. Lucy went to the mahogany armchair on the other side of the room.

"Well, I'm not frightened of ghosts," Adele was saying, perched beside Clare on the tapestry-covered sofa that ran against the longer wall; it was a topic to which the pair returned frequently. "They are simply poor trapped souls seeking to be set free. I think that we should try some table turning—see if we can invite one in to join us."

"Do you have a talking board with you?"

Adele frowned. "I don't."

Edward had his head bowed close to Lily Millington's and Lucy could see his lips moving as he spoke. Lily Millington was nodding every so often, and as Lucy watched, she reached up to run her fingertips along the edge of his blue silk neck scarf.

"I'm famished," said Thurston, pacing behind the table. "Where on earth is that girl?"

Lucy remembered Emma saying that she was going home to put her feet up. "She planned to be back in time to serve the dinner."

"Then she's late."

"Perhaps the storm has waylaid her." Felix, standing by the rain-streaked window, craned to see something up on the eave. "It's bucketing down. The drain's already overflowing."

Lucy glanced again at Edward and Lily. It was possible, of course, that she had misheard them in the hallway. More likely, though, that she had simply misunderstood. The Magenta Brotherhood were always adopting different pet names for one another. For a time, Adele had been "Puss" because Edward painted her in a scene with a tiger; and Clare had once been "Rosie," after Thurston made an unfortunate miscalculation with his pigments and gave her too much flush in her cheeks.

"Every self-respecting house has a ghost these days."

Clare shrugged. "I haven't seen one yet."

"*Seen?*" said Adele. "Don't be so old-fashioned. Everybody nowadays knows that ghosts are invisible."

"Or translucent." Felix turned back to face them. "As in Mumler's photographs."

And *A Christmas Carol*. Lucy remembered the description of Marley's ghost dragging his chains and padlocks; the way Scrooge could look right through him to the buttons on the back of his coat.

"I suppose we could make a talking board of our own," said Clare. "It's only some letters and a glass."

"That's true—the ghost will do the rest."

"No," said Edward, looking up. "No Ouija board. No table turning."

"Oh, Edward!" Clare pouted. "Don't spoil the fun. Aren't you curious? You might have your very own ghost here at Birchwood, just waiting to introduce herself."

"I don't need a talking board to tell me that there's a presence in this house."

"Whatever do you mean?" said Adele.

"Yes, Edward"—this was Clare, standing now—"what *do* you mean?"

For a split second Lucy thought that he was going to tell them all about the Night of the Following, and her eyes pricked with tears. It was *their* secret.

But he didn't. He told them instead the story of the Eldritch Children, the folktale about the three mysterious children who, according to legend, had long ago appeared in the field by the woods, confusing local farmers with their skin that glowed and their long, gleaming hair.

Lucy could have laughed with relief.

The others listened, spellbound, as Edward brought the tale to life: the village people so eager to blame the strange young outsiders when crops failed and family members sickened. The kind old couple who took the children under their wing, moving them to the safety of a small stone croft within a bend of the river; the angry group that stormed the site one night, their torches lit and their bellies filled with fire. And then, at the last moment, the otherworldly sound of the horn on the wind and the appearance of the luminous Fairy Queen.

"That's what I'm painting for the exhibition. The Fairy Queen, protector of the realm, rescuer of the children, at the very point where the doorway between worlds can be opened." He smiled at Lily Millington. "I've wanted to paint her forever, and now that I've finally found her, I can."

There was much enthusiasm from the others, and then Felix said, "You've just given me the most wonderful idea. It has become abundantly clear over the past fortnight that the day will never come when a breeze does not blow down that river of yours." As if to underline the point, a great gust rattled the glass windowpanes in their frames and made the fire hiss in the grate. "I am ready to retire the Lady of Shalott for a time. I say instead that we stage a photograph, all of us, just as Edward described—the Fairy Queen and her three children."

"But that's four characters and there are only three models here," said Clare. "Are you suggesting that Edward should dress in the part of one?"

"Or Thurston," said Adele with a laugh.

"I mean Lucy, of course."

"But Lucy isn't a model."

"She's even better: she's a genuine child."

Lucy felt her cheeks heat at the prospect that she might be asked to serve as a model in one of Felix's photographs. He had taken images of all of them over the past fortnight, but only for practice and not as proper works of art—not for possible display in Mr. Ruskin's exhibition.

Clare said something, but it was drowned out by a crack of thunder so loud that the house shook. And then: "That settles it," said Felix, and talk fell to costumes: how garlands might be made, whether gauze could be used to help create the effect that the Eldritch Children were glowing.

Thurston moved closer to Edward. "You said that there were ghosts here at Birchwood Manor but then told us a story about a Fairy Queen rescuing her children."

"I did not say that there were ghosts; I said there was a presence, and I haven't reached the end of the story yet."

"Go on, then."

"When the queen arrived to take her children back to fairyland, she was so grateful to the old human couple who had protected them that she cast an enchantment across their home and lands. To this day, it is said that a light can be glimpsed at times in the uppermost window of any house that stands upon this plot of land, the presence of the Eldritch people."

"A light in the window."

"That's what they say."

"Have you ever seen it?"

Edward did not answer at once and Lucy knew then that he was thinking of the Night of the Following.

Thurston pressed: "You wrote to me when you purchased Birchwood Manor and told me that the house had called to you for a long time. I did not know then what you meant, and you said that you would tell me the next time we met. By then, though, you had other things on your mind." His glance swept sideways briefly to land on Lily Millington, who met it directly and without even the glimmer of a smile.

"Is it true, Edward?" said Clare, from the other side of the table. "Did you see a light in the window?"

Edward did not answer at once and Lucy could have kicked Clare hard in the shins for putting him on the spot like that. She could still remember how frightened he'd been after the Night of the Following, his pale skin and the dark shadows beneath his eyes after standing watch all night in the attic, waiting to see whether whatever had followed him would find him in the house.

She tried to catch his eye, to signal to him that she understood, but he was focused on Lily Millington. He was reading her face, as if they were the only two people in the room. "Should I tell them?" he said.

Lily Millington took his hand. "Only if you wish to."

With a slight nod and a smile that made him look younger, he began to speak. "Many years ago, when I was still a boy, I ventured into those woods alone at night and something terrifying—"

Suddenly there came a loud rapping on the front door.

Clare squealed and clutched Adele.

"It must be Emma," said Felix.

"About time," said Thurston.

"But why would Emma knock?" asked Lily Millington. "She never has before."

The knock came again, louder this time, and then the hinge-creaking sound of the front door being pushed wide open.

In the flickering glow of the candles, they all glanced at one another, waiting as footsteps sounded down the passage.

As a flash of lightning silvered the outside world, the door flew open and a gust of wind shot through, throwing shadows with teeth along the walls.

There on the threshold, in the green velvet dress that she had worn to have her portrait painted, stood Edward's fiancée. "So sorry I'm late," Fanny said as thunder growled past her. "I hope I haven't missed anything important?"

CHAPTER TWENTY-SIX

FANNY stepped into the room and began to remove her traveling gloves, and with her came an invisible, but potent, change. Lucy wasn't sure how exactly, but after a stretched moment of suspension, the others all fell at once to action, as if their movements had been choreographed beforehand. Clare and Adele became emphatically involved in a close conversation on the sofa (each keeping one ear carefully tuned to happenings beyond their coterie), Felix returned his attention to the downpipe outside the window, Thurston spoke loudly and generally to the room about his hunger and the difficulty in finding good help these days, and Lily Millington excused herself, muttering something about cheese and bread for supper as she left the room. Edward, meanwhile, went to Fanny and began to help her with her dripping coat.

But Lucy had not received the cue. Instead, she sat lumpen on the armchair, looking left and right for someone to whom she could attach herself. Finding no relief, she stood awkwardly and made a slow blinkered walk towards the door, easing past Fanny, who was saying, "A glass of wine, Edward. Red wine. The journey from London was excruciating."

Lucy found herself heading towards the kitchen. Lily Millington was at Emma's large wooden table cutting slices from a wheel of cheddar. She looked up as Lucy appeared at the doorway.

"Hungry?"

Lucy realized that she *was* hungry. With all of the excitement of the day—the finding of the floor plans, the hunt for Edward, the discovery of the priest holes—she had forgotten all about tea. Now, she took up the serrated bread knife and started slicing thick slabs from the loaf.

Lily had lighted the tallow lamp that Emma preferred to work by, and the greasy beef smell permeated the room. It was not a pleasant odor, but its familiarity on such a night, as the rain continued in sheets outside, and dynamics shifted slyly inside, was welcome and Lucy experienced an unexpected pang of nostalgia.

She felt very young, suddenly, and longed for nothing more than to be a small child again, for whom everything was black and white, and whose bed was even now being prepared by Nanny, a brass warming pan slipped beneath the covers to shoo away the cold and the damp.

"Do you want to see a trick?" Lily Millington did not pause in her cheese-slicing task and Lucy was so far away with her thoughts that she wondered if she might have misheard.

Lily Millington looked up at her then and seemed to stare; she reached across the table, a slight quizzical frown on her brow, and with her outstretched fingers she took something gently from behind Lucy's ear. She opened her hand and a silver coin lay in her palm. "A shilling! Lucky me. I'll have to check you more often."

"How did you do that?"

"Magic."

Lucy's fingers went quickly to the skin behind her ear. "Will you tell me how to do it?"

"I'll think about it," and Lily took a few slices of bread from Lucy's board. "Sandwich?"

She'd made one for herself, too, and now went to sit on the end of the table nearest the front window. "Cook's prerogative," she said, when she noticed Lucy watching. "I see no reason that we should rush back. The others have enough to keep them occupied. They'll not starve."

"Thurston said that he was famished."

"Did he?" Lily Millington took a deep satisfied bite of her sandwich. Lucy went to sit beside Lily Millington on the table end.

Outside, through the window, a rift between clouds revealed a small patch of clear sky above the storm. Within it, a few faraway stars twinkled. "Do you think that we will ever know how the stars were formed?" asked Lucy.

"Yes."

"Really? How can you be so sure?"

"Because a chemist called Bunsen and a physicist named Kirchhoff have worked out how to use the spectrum produced when sunlight passes through a prism to name the chemicals present in the sun."

"And the stars?"

"They say that it follows." Lily Millington was also staring up at the distant sky now, her profile illuminated by the hazy light of the tallow lamp. "My father used to tell me that I was born under a lucky star."

"A lucky star?"

"An old sailor's superstition."

"Your father was a sailor?"

"He was a clockmaker once upon a time, a very good one. He used to repair the collection of a retired sea captain out in Greenwich and it was there that his mind was filled with seafaring superstitions. It was in Greenwich that I first looked through a telescope."

"What did you see?"

"I was very fortunate, for Neptune had just been found. A planet both new and ancient at once."

Lucy wished that her father had been a clockmaker who had taken her with him to the Royal Observatory. "My father died when I was only a child; he had a run-in with a carriage."

Lily Millington turned and smiled at her. "Then let us hope that we have better luck than they did." She inclined her head towards the table. "In the meantime, I suppose it's time to feed the others."

As Lucy finished her sandwich, Lily Millington assembled the rest of the bread and cheese and arranged the supper on a porcelain serving platter.

Yes, Lily Millington was different from the models who had come before her, those pretty faces who reminded Lucy of the leaves that fell from the towering lime trees in autumn—the lushest of green in summer, but lasting only one season before they fell clean away; replaced the following year by a fresh new crop. Lily Millington knew about science and had seen the planet of Neptune through a telescope and there was something inside her that came out in Edward's paintings. Something that had made him tell her about the Night of the Following. Lucy had a feeling she should hate Lily Millington for that, but she didn't.

"Where did you learn to do magic?" she asked.

"I learned from a French street performer in Covent Garden."

"You did not."

"I did."

"As a child?"

"A very young child."

"What were you doing in Covent Garden?"

"Picking pockets, mostly."

Lucy knew then that Lily Millington was teasing. Edward did that, too, when he wanted to end a conversation. As she finished her sandwich, she noticed that the clouds had closed over the gap already and the stars had disappeared.

Edward was just leaving when they arrived back at the dining room, a candle in one hand and Fanny leaning hard against his other side. "Miss Brown is tired after the day's travel," he said with careful politeness. "I'm going to show her to bed."

"Of course," said Lily Millington. "I'll make sure to save you some supper."

"I know you didn't mean it, Edward," Fanny was saying as they made their way slowly along the hallway, her voice more slurred than usual. "I haven't told a soul. You were just confused. It's normal before a wedding."

"Shh, there now—" Edward helped her begin up the stairs— "we'll talk about it tomorrow."

Lucy did not return to the dining room; instead, she watched them disappear and when she considered it safe to do so started up the stairs herself. Edward, she noticed, had taken Fanny into the room beside her own. It was small but pretty, with a four-poster bed and a walnut dressing table under the window.

All was quiet until Lucy heard Fanny notice that the window faced east towards the village churchyard.

"It is just a different type of sleep," Lucy could hear Edward saying, "nothing more than that. Just the long sleep of the dead."

"But Edward." Her voice carried through the open door and down the hall. "It is bad luck to sleep with one's feet facing the dead."

Whatever Edward said by reply he said it too softly to be heard, for the next words came again from Fanny. "Is your room close by? I shall be frightened otherwise."

Lucy changed into her nightgown and went to stand by her own window. The clematis creeper that grew hungrily along the stone wall of the house had woven its way into the room and a sprig of flowers sat upon the damp sill. Lucy picked them one by one, sprinkling the petals over the edge and watching them fall like snow.

She was wondering about Fanny on the other side of the wall, when she heard Edward's voice on the lawn below. "I understand that I have you to thank for this?"

Careful to stay out of sight, Lucy craned to see who else was there. Thurston. The rain had stopped and the chill in the air had lifted. A swollen moon had emerged in the clearing sky, brighter it seemed for the preceding darkness, and Lucy could see both men standing near the wisteria arbor that ran towards the orchard.

"She says that you wrote and told her where to find me."

Thurston had a cigarette between his lips and was holding his Napoleonic Wars rifle, taking careless aim at imagined adversaries in the chestnut tree behind the house. Now, he let its trigger guard roll around his finger like a pantomime villain and held his arms out to the side. "Not at all. I wrote to suggest an appointment and when we met I *told* her where to find you."

"You're a bastard, Thurston."

"What else could I do? The poor girl threw herself upon my mercy."

"Your mercy! You're enjoying this."

"Edward, you wound me. I'm simply being a friend. She begged me to help you see things clearly. She said that you'd lost your mind and behaved most improperly."

"I spoke with her—I wrote to her, too, explaining everything."

"Everything? I highly doubt that. *I don't believe it*, she kept saying, *does he not know who my father is? What he'll do to him? What this would do to me?* And then, *Why would he do it? What reason could he possibly have for breaking his promise?*" Thurston laughed. "No, I don't think you explained *everything*, my dear Edward."

"I told her what she needed to know without hurting her more than was necessary." Edward's voice was low, furious.

"Well, whatever it was you *did* write, it is little more than a pile of ash in her father's fireplace now. She refused to accept it. She told me that she needed to see you herself to put things right. Who was I to refuse? You should be thanking me. It's no secret that your family needs what Fanny offers—" His lips curled in an unkind smile. "Those poor sisters of yours haven't much hope otherwise."

"My sisters are none of your concern."

"I wish you'd tell that to Clare. She goes to such great lengths to make herself my concern. I've a good mind to give her what she needs. She's going to spoil my painting with her damn longing otherwise. I'm more than happy to look after Lily, too, once you and Fanny repair your differences."

The arbor was in the way so Lucy didn't see the first punch thrown, she only saw Thurston staggering backwards onto the lawn, his hand on his jaw and a half-smile of surprise on his face. "Only

419

trying to help, Radcliffe. Fanny might be a bore, but she'll give you a home and allow you to paint. Never know—with time and a bit of luck, she might even learn to turn a blind eye."

Lucy lay in bed afterwards ruminating. The fight between Edward and Thurston had not lasted long and when it was over they had gone their separate ways. Lucy had left the window and slid beneath the cool bedcovers. She'd always enjoyed being alone, but now, as she registered a gnawing sensation deep within her stomach, she realized that she felt lonely. More than lonely, she felt uncertain, which was infinitely worse.

The small bronze clock on Lucy's bedside table said that it was five minutes after midnight, which meant that she had been lying in bed, waiting for sleep to claim her, for over an hour. The house was motionless; the woolly weather outside had calmed. A few night birds had emerged from their hiding spots to perch upon the branches of the moonlit chestnut tree. Lucy could hear them now, clearing their throats. Why, she wondered, did the minutes stretch and the hours become interminable when it was dark?

She sat up.

She was wide-awake and there was no point in pretending otherwise.

Her mind was too busy to sleep. She wanted to understand what was going on. Edward had said that Fanny Brown would not be coming to Birchwood Manor, and yet here she was. Everyone else seemed to know enough to be behaving strangely; Thurston and Edward had even had a fight beneath Lucy's window.

When she was a little girl and her racing thoughts had refused to let her sleep, it was always Edward to whom Lucy had gone. He would tell her a story and answer any question she had; he would calm her down and usually make her laugh. She always felt better when she left him than she had when she'd arrived.

Lucy decided to go and see if he was still awake. It was late, but Edward wouldn't mind. He was a night owl, often working in his studio until long after midnight, the candles burning down towards the necks of the old green bottles that he collected.

She crept into the hallway but saw no light coming from beneath any of the bedroom doors.

Lucy stood very still, straining to hear.

As she listened, a faint noise came from downstairs. The soft, brief scrape of a chair leg moving against the wooden floor.

Lucy smiled to herself. Of course: he would be in the Mulberry Room with his paints and easel. She might have guessed. Edward always said that painting helped to clear his mind—that without it his thoughts would drive him mad.

Lucy tiptoed down the stairs, past the platform that masked the secret chamber, all the way to the ground floor. As she had expected, a faint flicker of candlelight emanated from the room at the end of the hallway.

The door stood slightly ajar and Lucy hesitated when she reached it. Edward did not like to be disturbed when he was working, but surely tonight, after what had happened with Thurston, he would be just as glad for company as she. Carefully, Lucy prodded the door, just enough that she could poke her head in to see whether he was there.

She saw his painting first. Lily Millington's face, stunning, regal, otherworldly, stared back at her, red hair flaming behind. Lily Millington, the Fairy Queen, was luminous.

Lucy noticed then the gem at the hollow of Lily's neck: the same gem that she'd spied when she sneaked an illicit peek at Edward's sketchbook, now depicted in color. Bright iridescent blue. As soon as she saw the startling shade, she knew what it was, for Lucy had heard much about the Radcliffe Blue pendant, even though she'd never seen it in real life. And she wasn't seeing it in "real life" now, she reminded herself, only Edward's imagined rendering of it: a talisman at his Fairy Queen's throat.

There was a noise then from inside the room, and Lucy peeked around the edge of the door; she was about to call out to let Edward know that she was there, when she saw him on the settee and stopped. He was not alone. Edward was above Lily Millington, his damp hair hanging over his face while hers was spread glimmering on the velvet cushion; he wore nothing and neither did she; their skin was candlelit, smooth, and they gazed at one another, the two of them locked within a moment that belonged to them alone.

Lucy managed to withdraw from the room unseen. She fled back along the corridor and up the stairs to her bedroom, where she threw herself onto her bed. She wanted to disappear, to explode like a star into tiny, tiny pieces of dust that burned up and became nothing.

She didn't understand what she was feeling, why she was hurting this way. Tears fell and she hugged her pillow to her chest.

She was embarrassed, she realized. Not for them, for they had been beautiful. No, Lucy was embarrassed for herself. She knew herself, suddenly, to be a child. An awkward clomping girl who was neither beautiful nor desirable, who was clever, certainly, but otherwise ordinary, who was, she saw clearly now, not the first and most special person to anyone.

The way that Edward had looked at Lily Millington, the way that they had looked at one another—he would never look at Lucy like that, and neither should he, neither would she want him to; and yet at the same time, as she pictured his expression, Lucy felt something inside her that had been carefully constructed and important crumble and fall away, because she understood that the time of being children together, brother and sister, was over, and that they were each standing on different sides of a river now.

The next morning Lucy was woken by a tremendous noise, and her first thought was that the storm had returned to rage on for another day. When she cracked her eyes open, though, light spilled in and she saw that it was a bright and brilliant morning. She noticed, too, that she was curled up in a tangle of sheets at the foot of her bed.

The noise came again, and Lucy realized it was Thurston shooting at the birds. Events of the previous day came rushing back upon her.

Lucy had a headache. It happened sometimes when she hadn't slept for long enough, and now she went downstairs to fetch a glass of water. She had hoped to find Emma in the kitchen and to sink down into the woven chair by the cooker, from which she would listen as the maid told mild stories of local happenings and tut-tutted good-naturedly about the louche behavior of the others. But Emma wasn't there; the kitchen was empty and showed no sign that anyone had been in it since Lucy and Lily Millington had made cheese sandwiches the night before.

The night before. Lucy shook her head in an attempt to rid herself of the confusion of what she had seen in Edward's studio. It certainly provided an explanation as to the conversation she'd overheard between Edward and Thurston. So, too, Edward's preference that Fanny Brown not come to Birchwood Manor for the summer. But what did it all mean? What was going to happen?

She filled a glass with water and, when she noticed a line of light creeping across the tiles from beneath the back door, decided to take it outside with her.

Everything was better beneath the big blue sky, and Lucy walked barefooted across the dew-damp grass. When she reached the corner of the house near the croquet lawn, she closed her eyes and tilted her face towards the morning sun. It was only nine o'clock, but already it held the promise of heat to come.

"Good morning, Little Radcliffe." Lucy opened her eyes and saw Thurston sitting on Edward's iron peacock chair, smiling around his cigarette. "Come and sit with Uncle Thurston. I might even let you hold my rifle if you're a very good girl."

Lucy shook her head and stayed where she was.

He laughed, lifting the weapon to take casual aim at a sparrow that had alit briefly on the wisteria arbor. He mimed pulling the trigger.

"You shouldn't shoot the birds."

"There are many things in life one shouldn't do, Lucy. And they're usually the things one most enjoys." He lowered the weapon. "Big day ahead for you."

Lucy did not know what he meant but did not wish to give him

423

the pleasure of hearing her say so. Instead, she eyed him coolly and waited for him to continue.

"Bet you didn't imagine you'd be modeling this summer."

With everything that had happened since, Lucy had forgotten Felix's suggestion of the night before, his determination to make a photographic plate based on the tale of the Eldritch Children.

"Little Lucy the stunner. Have you been practicing your poses?"

"No."

"Good girl. Natural is better. I've tried to tell Clare. The most beautiful people are those who don't care enough to try."

"Is Felix planning to take the photograph today?"

"There was much excited talk of capturing light earlier."

"Where are the others?"

Thurston stood up and used the barrel of his rifle to indicate towards the attic. "Raking through the costume chest." He tucked the weapon under his arm and brushed past Lucy on his way towards the kitchen.

"Emma's not in there."

"So I heard."

Lucy wondered what else he'd heard. She called after him: "Do you know where she is?"

"Ill at home in bed. A messenger came this morning, someone from the village—she won't be in today and we are all to fend for ourselves."

Lucy found the others in the attic, where, just as Thurston had said, they were busy pulling costumes from the large trunk, trying on flowing dresses, cinching them with ribbons at the waist, and talking animatedly about how best to weave garlands for their hair. The novelty of her inclusion made Lucy shy, and she hovered in the corner near the top of the stairs, as she waited to be invited closer.

"We should make sure that they match," Clare was saying to Adele.

"But not exactly. Each of the Eldritch Children would have a different type of magic."

"Would they?"

"We could show it through the use of different flowers. I'll be a rose; you can be a honeysuckle."

"And Lucy?"

"Whatever she likes. I don't know—a daisy, perhaps. Something befitting. Don't you think, darling?"

"Yes, yes, wonderful!" Felix, only half listening, was nonetheless ecstatic in his response. He was by the window, holding a piece of fine gauze up to the light, squinting first one eye and then the other as he considered its effect.

Lily Millington, Lucy noticed, was not present. Neither was Fanny or Edward.

Adele took Clare by the hand and together they brushed past Lucy's corner in a giddy rush. "Come on, slow coach," Clare called back from halfway down the stairs. "You need to make a garland, too."

Some of the roses were a little the worse for wear after the previous night's rain, their delicate petals littering the grass, but there had been such an abundance to start with that the garland makers were still spoiled for choice.

Along the stone wall that bordered the orchard were a number of daisy bushes, and Lucy picked a selection of the pink, white, and yellow flowers, keeping the stems long enough that she was able to sit upon a dry patch of grass afterwards and braid them together. The garland would not keep for long, but Lucy was happy with her progress. She couldn't think that she had ever made such a thing before, and in any other context she would have thought the occupation a frivolous waste of time. But this was different. Lucy had been uncertain about being part of Felix's photograph; now she realized that she was starting to feel excited. She would never have admitted it to anyone else—she wasn't even able to explain the feeling properly to herself—but being part of the photograph made Lucy feel more like a *real person* than she had before.

Lily Millington had joined them in the garden and was sitting quietly to weave her own garland, and Lucy, stealing glances from where she was sitting cross-legged by the daisy bush, noticed that a slight frown pulled at her brows. Thurston, too, had gathered his sketchbook and pens and was now helping Felix to assemble the glass plates and collodion, ready to carry them with the camera and tent to the woods. Only Edward and Fanny were missing, and Lucy wondered whether they were having the "talk" that Edward had promised as he shepherded her up to bed the night before.

Felix said that the light would be best in the middle of the day, when the sun was at its strongest, and everything was geared towards his decree.

For the rest of her life, Lucy would remember the way the others looked, dressed in their garlands and costumes as they made their way through the long meadow grasses towards the woods. Sprays of wildflowers peppered the grass and rustled when the light breeze blew warmly across their tops.

They had passed the barn with the threshing machine inside it and had almost made it as far as the river, when the cry came from behind them: "Wait for me. I want to be in the photograph."

They turned around and saw Fanny stalking towards them. Edward was close on her heels, a stormy look upon his face.

"I want to be in the photograph," she said again, drawing near. "I want to be the Fairy Queen."

Felix, the wooden tripod balanced on his shoulder, shook his head, confused. "I need Lily as the Fairy Queen; it has to be the same as Edward's painting. I want them to stand as companion pieces. How better to demonstrate that photography and painting are on a level? But Fanny can be one of the princesses."

"We're engaged to be married, Edward. I should be the Fairy Queen from your story."

Lily glanced at Edward. "Of course she should."

"I didn't ask you to speak," said Fanny, with a curl of her lip. "You're paid to stand there and look vacant. I was talking to my fiancé."

"Fanny," said Edward, a note of controlled caution in his voice, "I told you—"

"I'm going to lose the perfect light," said Felix, with some desperation. "I need Lily as the Queen, but Fanny, you can be the frontmost child. Clare and Adele, one either side."

"But, Felix—"

"Adele, that's enough. The light!"

"Lucy," said Clare, "give your garland to Fanny so that we can get started."

Within a fraction of a second Lucy took in the faces of Clare, Edward, Lily Millington, Felix, and Fanny, all now staring straight at her, and then without a word she started to run.

"Lucy, wait!"

But Lucy didn't wait. She tossed her garland to the ground and kept running like a little girl, all the way back towards the house.

Lucy did not go to her bedroom, or to the library, or to the kitchen, where she could have had her way with the remaining half of the Victoria sponge that Emma had baked on Friday. Instead she went to Edward's studio in the Mulberry Room. Even as she pushed open the door, she was uncertain as to why she had come, only that it had somehow seemed the *only* place to go. Lucy was fast learning that she knew a lot less about her own motivations than she did about the way the internal combustion engine worked.

Having arrived, she found herself at a loss. She was out of breath from running and embarrassed for fleeing. She felt rejected but at the same time cross with herself for having let the others see her disappointment. And she was tired, very tired. There had been so much excitement and such a lot to comprehend.

When no better option came to mind, she sank to the ground in self-pity and curled up like a cat.

It was approximately two and a half minutes later that her gaze, which had been sweeping generally across the floor of the room, fell upon Edward's leather satchel, leaning against the leg of his easel.

The satchel was new. Lily Millington had given it to him for his birthday and Lucy had been envious when she saw how much he loved it. She had been confused, too, for never before had a model given Edward a gift, let alone a fine, prized gift. She understood more clearly now, after what she'd seen last night.

Lucy decided that she no longer had the necessary commitment required for self-pity. The urge had been replaced by another, stronger impulse: curiosity. She righted herself and went to pick up the satchel.

Lucy undid the buckle and flipped it open. She could see Edward's current sketch pad and his wooden pen holder, and with them something else, something less expected. It was a black velvet box of the same sort that Mother kept on her dressing table in Hampstead to safeguard the pearls and brooches that Father had given her.

She slid the box out of the satchel and with a shiver of nerves lifted the lid. The first things she saw were two pieces of paper. They had been folded together but opened in the space created when the lid lifted. They were *Cunard* tickets for a Mr. and Mrs. Radcliffe, traveling to New York City on the first of August. Lucy was still considering the implications of this discovery when the tickets fell to the ground.

As soon as she saw the large blue gem beneath, Lucy knew that she had expected all along to find the Radcliffe Blue within the jeweler's box. Edward hadn't imagined the diamond onto Lily Millington's neck: he had taken it from the bank's safety deposit box. And without permission, she was sure, for there was no way Grandfather would have allowed such a terrifying breach of protocol.

Lucy lifted the pendant from the box and held it in her palm, draping the fine chain over the top of her hand. She was shaking a little, she noticed.

She glanced back at the painting of Lily Millington.

Lucy was not the type of girl who longed for frills and lace and shiny gems, but over the past two weeks she had become more aware than ever of the distance between herself and beauty.

Now she took the necklace with her to the looking glass above the fireplace.

She stared squarely for a moment at her small, plain face and then, with a slight tightening of her lips, lifted the fine chain and attached it at the nape of her neck.

The pendant, sitting cool against her skin, was heavier than she had imagined it would be.

It was wondrous.

Lucy turned her head this way and that, slowly, observing the way light caught the diamond's facets and threw flecks upon her skin. She inspected each of her profiles in turn, and then every position between, watching the lights dance. *This*, she thought, *is what it is to be adorned.*

She smiled tentatively at the girl in the mirror. The girl smiled back.

And then the girl's smile dropped. In the mirror, behind her, was Lily Millington.

Lily Millington did not bat an eyelid. She neither admonished nor laughed. She merely said, "I've come on Felix's behalf. He insists that you must be in the photograph."

Lucy did not turn around but spoke instead to the mirror. "He doesn't need me, not with Fanny. There are four of you already."

"No, there are four of *you*. I have decided against being in the photograph."

"You're just trying to be kind."

"I make a point of never trying to be kind." Lily Millington was before her now and she looked closely at Lucy, frowning. "What on earth?"

Lucy held her breath, waiting for what she knew must follow. Sure enough, Lily Millington reached out and brushed the side of her neck.

"Well, now, look at that," she said softly, unfurling her fingers to reveal another silver shilling in her palm. "I had a feeling you'd turn out to be a valuable friend."

Lucy felt a sting of tears threaten. There was a part of her that wanted to hug Lily Millington. She reached up to unhook the necklace. "Did you think about whether you're going to tell me how it's done?"

"It's all to do with this part of your hand here," said Lily Millington, pointing at the skin between her thumb and forefinger; "You have to hold the coin firmly, but be careful to keep it concealed."

"How do you get the coin in there without being seen?"

"Well, now, that's the art, isn't it."

They smiled at one another then and a wave of understanding passed between them.

"Now," said Lily Millington, "for the sake of Felix, who is becoming more frantic with each passing minute, I suggest that you get yourself down to the woods at once."

"My garland, I threw it—"

"And I gathered it. It's hanging on the back doorknob."

Lucy glanced down at the Radcliffe Blue pendant, still in her hand. "I should put this away."

"Yes," said Lily Millington, and then, when hurried footsteps sounded suddenly in the hallway, "Oh, dear—Felix, I fear."

But the man when he arrived at the door to the Mulberry Room was not Felix. It was a stranger, someone whom Lucy had never seen before. A man with brown hair and a wet smirk that set Lucy against him from the start. "The front door was unlocked. I didn't think you'd mind."

"What are you doing here?" said Lily Millington in an anguished voice.

"Checking up on you, of course."

Lucy looked from one to the other, waiting for an introduction.

The man was standing in front of Edward's painting now. "Very nice. Very nice indeed. He's good. I'll give him that."

"You must go, Martin. The others will soon be back. If they find you here, it will likely cause a disturbance."

"*Likely cause a disturbance.*" He laughed. "Listen to the hoity-toity lady." His mirthful expression dropped suddenly and he said, "Leave? I don't think so. Not without you." He reached out to touch the canvas and Lucy drew breath at the sacrilege. "That's the Blue? You were right. She's going to be very pleased. Very pleased indeed."

"I said a month."

"You did. But you're a fast worker, one of the best. Who can resist your charms?" He nodded at the painting. "Seems to me like you've got on ahead of time, sister dear."

Sister? Lucy remembered then the story of Edward meeting Lily Millington. The brother who had been with her at the theater, the parents who had needed convincing that their daughter would not be risking her respectability if she were to pose for Edward's painting. Was this horrid man really Lily Millington's brother? Why, then, hadn't she said so? Why hadn't she introduced him to Lucy? And why was Lucy filled now with a sense of dread?

The man noticed the tickets on the floor then and scooped them up. "America, eh? The land of new beginnings. I like the sound of that. Very clever. Very clever indeed. And a travel date so soon."

"Run ahead, Lucy," said Lily Millington. "Go and join the others. Hurry, now. Before anyone else comes up here looking for you."

"I don't want to—"

"Lucy, please."

There was an urgency to Lily Millington's tone, and reluctantly Lucy left the room, but she didn't go back to the woods. She stayed on the other side of the door and listened. Lily Millington's voice was soft, but Lucy could hear her saying, ". . . more time . . . America . . . my father . . ."

The man burst out laughing and said something so quietly that Lucy couldn't hear.

Lily Millington made a noise then, as if she had been hit and was winded, and Lucy was about to charge in to help, when the door flew open and the man—Martin—swept past her, dragging Lily by the wrist behind him, muttering to her, "blue . . . America . . . new beginnings . . ."

Lily Millington saw Lucy and shook her head, indicating that Lucy should make herself scarce.

But Lucy refused. She followed them, down the hallway, and when they reached the drawing room and the man saw her, he laughed and said, "Look out, here comes the cavalry. The little knight in shining armor."

"Lucy, please," said Lily Millington. "You must go."

"Best listen to her." The man grinned. "Little girls who don't know when to leave have a habit of coming to sticky ends."

"*Please*, Lucy." There was a look of fear in Lily's eyes.

But Lucy was overcome, suddenly, with all of the uncertainty of the past few days, the prevailing sense that she was too young to be of any use, that she didn't belong, that decisions were made above and around her but never to include her; and now this man whom she did not know was trying to take Lily Millington away, and without understanding why, Lucy did not want that to happen; and she saw that this was her opportunity to put her foot down on a matter, any matter, that she cared about.

She glimpsed Thurston's rifle, lying on the chair where he'd left it after breakfast that morning, and in one fell swoop she seized it, held it by the barrel, and whacked it as forcefully as she could against the sneering head of the awful stranger.

His hand went to the side of his face in shock and Lucy struck him again and then kicked him hard in the shins.

He stumbled and then tripped over a table leg and fell to the ground. "Quick," said Lucy, pulse drumming in her ears, "he'll be on his feet again soon. We have to hide."

She took Lily Millington by the hand and led her halfway up the stairs. At the landing, she pushed aside the bentwood chair, and as Lily Millington watched, Lucy pressed the wooden rise to reveal the trapdoor. Even in that moment of fearful panic, Lucy managed to feel a jolt of pride at Lily Millington's surprise. "Quick," she said again. "He'll never find you in there."

"How did you—"

"Hurry."

"But you must come in, too. He is not kind, Lucy. He is not a good man. He *will* hurt you. Especially now that he's been bested."

"There isn't room, but there's another one. I'll hide there."

"Is it far?"

Lucy shook her head.

"Then get inside it and don't hop out. Do you hear me? No matter what happens, Lucy, stay hidden. Stay safe until Edward comes to find you."

Lucy promised that she would and then sealed Lily Millington inside the chamber, repositioning the bentwood chair on top.

Without wasting another moment, aware that the man was clambering to his feet in the drawing room below, she ran to the top of the stairs and along the hallway, sliding back the panel and climbing in quickly. She sealed the door behind her, enclosing herself within the dark.

Time passed differently in the hideaway. Lucy heard the man calling out for Lily Millington, and she heard other noises, too, far away. But she wasn't frightened. Her eyes had begun to adjust, and at some point Lucy had noticed that she wasn't alone, and that it wasn't truly dark at all; there were thousands of little lights, the size of pinpricks, twinkling at her from within the fiber of the wooden boards.

As she sat waiting, hugging her knees to her chest, Lucy felt strangely safe in her secret hiding place, and she wondered whether Edward's fairy story might have had some truth to it after all.

X

I still hear his voice sometimes, that whisper in my ear. I still remember the smell of cheese and tobacco from his lunch. "Your father isn't in America, Birdie. He never was. He was trampled by a horse the day that you were supposed to sail. It was Jeremiah what brought you to us. Scooped you off the ground while you were sickly, left your dad for the poorhouse to bury, and brought you to my ma. Your lucky day, it was. Jeremiah's lucky day, too, for he's been on a very good wicket ever since. He said that you were a bright little thing and you've done very well for him, you have. You didn't really think that he was sending all those spoils across the ocean, did you?"

He could not have winded me more surely had he driven his knee hard into my chest. And yet, I did not question what he told me. I did not doubt his claim, not even for a second, for I knew, as soon as he said it, that it was true. It was the only thing that made sense, and everything in my life to date was suddenly brought into sharper focus. Why else would my father fail to send for me? It had been eleven years since I had woken up in the room above the shop selling birds and cages, surrounded by Mrs. Mack and the others. My father was dead. He had been dead all along.

Martin grabbed my wrist then and started pulling me towards the door of the Mulberry Room. He was whispering that it was going to be all right, that he would make it all right, that I wasn't to be sad because he had an idea. We would take the Blue, he and I, and instead of delivering it back to London we would take it ourselves, the diamond and the tickets, too, and sail to America. It was the land of new beginnings, after all, just like it said in the letters that Jeremiah brought for me each month.

He meant, of course, the letters that Mrs. Mack used to read out loud, the news from America, the news from my father, all of it made up. It was a breathtaking deception. But what moral platform did I have from which to beat my breast? I was a petty thief, a pretender, a woman who had taken on an assumed name without a blink of hesitation.

Why, I had deceived Mrs. Mack little more than a fortnight ago, when I told her of my intention to go away with Edward to the country. Mrs. Mack would never have let me go away willingly, not to Birchwood Manor for the summer and not on to America with Edward. Over the years, I had become her most reliable earner, and in my short life, there was one thing I had learned for certain: people become used to riches quickly, and even if they've done nothing themselves to earn the wealth, once it's been had, they consider it their due.

Mrs. Mack believed that she was entitled to everything that I was and that I had, and so, in order that I might leave London with Edward, I told her it was all part of a scheme. I told her that within a month I would return with riches the likes of which they'd never seen.

"What sort of riches?" said Mrs. Mack, never one for generalities.

And because the best deceptions always skirt the truth, I told them about Edward's plans to paint me and his idea to include the priceless Radcliffe Blue.

It was dark in the chamber and very hard to breathe. It was eerily quiet.

I thought about Edward and wondered what was happening with Fanny down by the woods.

I thought about Pale Joe and the letter I had sent him from the village telling him that I was going to America; that he might not hear from me for some time but he was not to worry. And I thought about the photograph that I had enclosed for him "to remember me by," the photograph that Edward had taken with Felix's camera.

I thought of my father and the weight of his hand around mine, the supreme happiness I had felt when I was tiny and we set out together on our railway journeys to visit a broken clock.

And I thought of my mother, who was like sunlight on the surface of my memories, bright and warm but shifting. I remembered being with her one day at the edge of the river that ran behind our house in London. I had dropped a scrap of ribbon I'd been treasuring and was forced to watch, helpless, as the current took it away. I had cried, but my mother had explained to me that it was the nature of the river. The river, she said, is the greatest collector of them all; ancient and indiscriminate, carrying its load on a one-way journey towards the depthless sea. The river owes you no kindness, little Bird, she said, so you must be careful.

I realized that I could hear the river in that pitch-black hole, that I could feel its currents lulling me to sleep . . .

And then I heard something else, a set of footprints heavy on the floorboards above, and a muffled voice: "I have the tickets." It was Martin, right above the trapdoor. "Where have you got to? We just need the Blue and then we can get out of here."

And then there came another noise, a door slamming downstairs, and I knew that someone else was in the house.

Martin ran towards the interruption.

Raised voices, a scream.

And then a gunshot.

Moments later, more shouting—Edward calling out.

I felt about for a latch to release the trapdoor, but no matter where my fingers traced, I could not find one. I could not sit up; I could not turn around. I began to grow frightened, and the more I panicked, the shorter my breaths became, the harder they stuck against the back of my throat. I tried to answer, but my voice was little more than a whisper.

It was hot, so hot.

Edward called out again; he called for me, his voice sharpened with fear. He called for Lucy. He sounded a long way away.

Rapid footprints overhead, lighter than Martin's, coming from the hallway upstairs, and then a tremendous thump that made the floorboards rattle.

Mayhem, but not for me.

———

I was a boat on a gentle tide, the river shifting softly beneath me, and as I closed my eyes another memory came. I was a baby, not yet a year old, lying in a crib in an upstairs room of the little house by the river in Fulham. A warm breeze wafted through the window and brought with it the sounds of morning birds and the secretive smells of lilac and mud. Light was turning circles on the ceiling, in step with the shadows, and I was watching them dance. I reached up to clutch at them, but they slipped through my fingers every time . . .

CHAPTER TWENTY-SEVEN

SPRING, 1882

"A NICE old place. Been a bit neglected inside, but good bones. Let me just get the door open and you can see for yourself what I mean."

Lucy did not do herself or Edward's lawyer the discourtesy of pretending that she had never been inside Birchwood Manor; neither did she volunteer the fact. She said nothing and waited instead for the man to jiggle the key in the lock.

It was a morning in early spring and the air was crisp. Someone had been maintaining the garden—not perfectly, but with sufficient care to stop the tendrils overgrowing the paths. The honeysuckle had a promising layer of buds, and the first jasmine flowers along the wall and around the kitchen window were starting to open. They were late. The laneways of London were already perfumed, but then, as Edward used to say, the city plants were always more precocious than their country cousins.

"There she goes," said Mr. Matthews of Holbert, Matthews & Sons as the lock gave way with a deep, gratifying clunk. "That's got it now."

The door swung open and Lucy felt a roiling sensation deep within the pit of her stomach.

After twenty years of absence, of wondering, of trying *not* to wonder, the moment was finally upon her.

She had received the letter five months before, only days after news of Edward's death in Portugal had finally reached them. She had spent the morning at the museum in Bloomsbury, where she had volunteered to help catalogue the donated collections, and had been home only long enough to sit down to a pot of tea when her maid, Jane, brought in the afternoon post. The letter, written on gold-embossed letterhead, had begun by expressing the writer's deepest sympathies for her loss before moving on to notify her in the second paragraph that she had been named as a beneficiary in the last will and testament of her brother, Edward Julius Radcliffe. In closing, the letter's writer had invited "Miss Radcliffe" to make an appointment at their offices to discuss the matter further.

Lucy had read the letter again, and again tripped over the words, "your brother, Edward Julius Radcliffe." *Your brother.* She wondered whether there were many beneficiaries who needed reminding of their relationship to the deceased.

Lucy had not needed a reminder. While it had been many years since she had seen Edward, and then only a very brief and unsatisfactory meeting in a dingy building in Paris, reminders of him were everywhere. His paintings covered almost every wall of the house; Mother insisted that none should be removed, holding out hope to the last that he would return and take up where he'd left off—that perhaps it was not too late for him to "make a name for himself" as Thurston Holmes and Felix Bernard had done. And so the beautiful faces of Adele and Fanny and Lily Millington stared down at Lucy—in repose, in consideration, in character—watching her every move as she tried to get on. Those eyes that followed a person. Lucy was always careful not to meet them.

When she received the letter from Messrs. Holbert and Matthews, Lucy had written back by return post to make an appointment to meet at noon that Friday; and, as the first flurry of December snow fell lightly outside the window, she found herself sitting on one side of a large somber desk in the Mayfair office of Mr. Matthews Sr., listening as the old lawyer told her that Birchwood Manor—"a farmhouse in a little village near Lechlade-on-Thames"—was now hers.

When the meeting was at a close, he sent her home to Hampstead with a direction that she must let them know when she wished to visit

439

the house so that he could arrange for his son to accompany her to Berkshire. Lucy, with no intention then of visiting Berkshire, had told him that it was far too much to ask. But it was "all part of the service, Miss Radcliffe," Mr. Matthews had said, indicating a large wooden panel on the wall behind him on which in gold cursive lettering was painted:

Holbert, Matthews & Sons
Carrying out the wishes of our clients in death as
indeed in life.

Lucy had left the office, her thoughts in an uncharacteristic swirl.
Birchwood Manor.
What a generous gift; what a double-edged sword.

In the days and weeks that followed, when the nights were at their blackest, Lucy had wondered whether Edward had left her the house because on some level, due perhaps to the deep connection they'd once shared, he had guessed. But no, Lucy was too rational to let such an illogical idea take root. For one thing, there was nothing certain to guess; even Lucy did not know for sure. For another, Edward's thinking had been clear: he had specified within a handwritten letter attached to his will that the house should be used by Lucy to build a school offering education to girls as bright as she had been. Girls who quested for the type of knowledge that was otherwise denied them.

And just as Edward had possessed a gift in life that enabled him to win people over to his way of thinking, in death, too, his words had influence. For although, in the offices of Holbert, Matthews & Sons, Lucy had promised herself that she would sell the house, that she would never again willingly set foot within its walls, almost immediately upon leaving, Edward's vision had seeped into her thoughts and began weakening her better judgment.

Lucy had walked north through Regent's Park and her gaze had alit upon one little girl after another, each obedient beside her nanny and longing, surely, to *do* more, to *see* more, to *know* more than she was currently permitted. Lucy had a vision of herself shepherding a clutch of pink-cheeked girls with questing spirits and excited voices, girls who did not fit within the molds that had been ascribed to them; who longed to learn and improve and grow. Over the coming weeks, she thought of little else: she became obsessed with the idea that everything in her life had led her to this point; that there was nothing more "right" than that she should open a school in the twin-gabled house on the bend of the river.

And so, here she was. It had taken five months to reach this point, but she was ready.

"Do I need to sign something?" she said as the lawyer led her into the kitchen where the square pine table was still in place. Lucy half expected to see Emma Stearnes coming through the narrow parlor door, shaking her head in bemusement at whatever strange behavior she'd witnessed on the other side.

The lawyer looked surprised. "What sort of thing?"

"I'm not certain. I've never been given a house before. I presume there is a deed of title?"

"There is nothing to sign, Miss Radcliffe. The deed, as it were, is done. The papers have been finalized. The house is yours."

"Well, then"—Lucy held out her hand—"I thank you, Mr. Matthews. It has been a pleasure to meet you."

"But, Miss Radcliffe, would you not like me to show you the property?"

"It won't be necessary, Mr. Matthews."

"But having come all this way—"

"I trust that I am able to stay behind today?"

"Well, yes, as I said, the house is yours."

"Then thank you kindly for accompanying me, Mr. Matthews. Now, if you will excuse me, I have much to get on with. There is going to be a school, did you hear? I am going to open a school for promising young ladies."

But Lucy did not get on at once with preparations for the school. There was something more pressing that she had to do first. A task as awful as it was essential. For five months she had turned it over in her mind. Longer than that, to be honest. For almost twenty years now she had been waiting to discover the truth.

She closed the door behind the young Mr. Matthews, whose countenance left little doubt as to his dejection, and watched each step of his retreat from behind the kitchen window. Only when he had cleared the garden path and latched the wooden front gate did Lucy let out the breath that she'd been holding. She turned away from the window and stood for a moment with her back against the glass, surveying the room. Uncanny though it seemed, all was exactly as she remembered. It was as if she had merely stepped out for a walk to the village, become waylaid, and returned two decades later than expected.

The house was quiet, but it did not feel still. Lucy was reminded of a story Edward used to read to her from a book by Charles Perrault, *La Belle au bois dormant*, about a princess cursed to sleep within her castle for a hundred years, the inspiration for his *Sleeping Beauty* painting. Lucy was not a romantic person, but she could almost imagine, as she stood by the kitchen window, that the house knew she was back.

That it had been waiting.

Indeed, Lucy had a most disconcerting sense that she was not alone in the room.

She reminded herself, however—even as the hairs on her forearm tensed—that she was not of a suggestible disposition, and that to begin to fall prey to superstition here and now would be a deeply regrettable slip. Her mind was playing tricks on her; the reason was clear.

Steeling herself to her purpose, she crossed the hallway and started up the central staircase.

The bentwood chair was exactly where she'd last seen it, on the corner of the landing where the stairs made their turn. The chair was angled towards the large glass window overlooking the back garden and beyond it the meadow. Sunlight spilled through the glass and countless motes of dust drifted in unseen currents.

The chair was warm when Lucy sat gently on its edge. The landing itself, too. She remembered now that it had always been so. The last time she had sat here, the house had been filled with laughter and passion; the air had thrummed with creativity.

But not today. It was just Lucy and the house. Her house.

She let the air of the old place settle around her.

Somewhere out there in the great green beyond a dog was barking.

Closer by, in the Mulberry Room downstairs the wall clock was keeping count. Lily Millington's clock, still ticking. Lucy supposed that the lawyer, Mr. Matthews, had made sure that it was wound. She still remembered when Edward had bought it for her: "Lily's father was a clockmaker," he'd announced, whisking the package into the hall in Hampstead, "I saw this on the wall of a fellow in Mayfair and exchanged it for a commission. I'm going to surprise her."

Edward had always been a giver of gifts. He thrilled in the gratification of selecting well. Books for Lucy, a clock for Lily Millington—it was he who had given Thurston the rifle. "A genuine Baker, carried by a member of the 5th Battalion of the 60th Regiment, during the Napoleonic Wars!"

Impossible to believe that she was sitting here now because Edward was dead. That she would never see him again. Somehow she had always supposed that one day he would come home.

They had not seen much of one another after the summer at Birchwood Manor, but Lucy had known that he was out there. Every so often a note would arrive, scratched on the back of a piece of card, usually begging a few pounds to pay a debt that he'd gathered in his travels. Or else word would be passed along the grapevine that someone had seen him in Rome, Vienna, Paris. He was always on the move. He traveled in order to escape his grief, Lucy knew, but she wondered sometimes whether he also believed that by moving fast enough, often enough, he might find Lily Millington again.

For he had never given up hope. No matter the evidence to the contrary, he never could accept that she had been involved in a deception—that she had not loved him with every bit as much devotion as that with which he had loved her.

When they met that last time in Paris, he had said, "She's out there somewhere, Lucy, I know it. I can *feel* it. Can't you?"

Lucy, who had not felt anything of the sort, had merely taken her brother's hand and held it tight.

After climbing into the hallway hideaway, the next thing Lucy had remembered was opening her eyes in a bright room that she did not recognize. She was in a bed, not her own. She was in pain.

Lucy blinked, taking in the yellow-striped wallpaper, the leadlight window, the pale curtains hanging either side. The room smelled faintly of something sweet—honeysuckle, perhaps, and gorse, too. Her throat was parched.

She must have made a sound, for Edward was suddenly beside her, pouring water from a small crystal jug into a glass. He looked terrible, more disheveled than usual, with a drawn face and anxious features. His loose cotton shirt was hanging limply from his shoulders, giving the appearance of clothing that had not been removed in days.

But where was she and how long had she been here?

Lucy was not aware that she had spoken, but as Edward helped her up to drink, he told her that they'd taken rooms for a few days in the public house in the village.

"Which village?"

His eyes studied hers. "Why, the village of Birchwood. Can you really not remember?"

The word was vaguely familiar.

Edward tried to reassure her with an unconvincing smile. "Let me call for the doctor," he said. "He'll want to know that you're awake."

He opened the door and spoke quietly to someone on the other side, but he did not leave the room. He came back to sit on the mattress beside Lucy, encasing her hand in one of his, stroking her forehead lightly with the other.

"Lucy," he said, a look of pain in his eyes, "I have to ask you. I have to ask about Lily. Did you see her? She went back to the house to fetch you, but no one's seen her since."

Lucy's thoughts were swimming. Which house? Why was he asking her about Lily? Did he mean Lily Millington? She was his model, Lucy remembered, the one with the long white dress. "My head," she said, realizing that it ached on one side.

"You poor love. You fell, you've been out cold, and here I am asking you questions. I'm sorry, I just—" He raked a hand through his hair. "She's gone. I can't find her, Lucy, and I'm terribly worried. She wouldn't just leave."

Lucy had a flash of memory then, a gunshot in the dark. It had been loud and there'd been a scream. She'd run and then— Lucy gasped.

"What is it? Did you see something?"

"Fanny!"

Edward's expression darkened. "It was terrible, a terrible thing. Poor Fanny. A man, an intruder—I don't know who he was . . . Fanny ran off and I went after her. I heard the shot when I was near the chestnut tree, and I ran inside, Lucy, but I was too late. Fanny was already . . . and then I saw the back of the man, running from the front door towards the lane."

"Lily Millington knew him."

"What?"

Lucy wasn't sure exactly what she meant, only that she was sure that she was right. There had been a man and Lucy had been frightened, and Lily Millington had been there.

"He came to the house. I saw him. I went back to the house, and the man came, and he and Lily Millington talked."

"What did they say?"

Lucy's thoughts were swimming. Memories, imaginings, dreams, were all as one. Edward had asked her a question and Lucy always liked to give the right answer. And so she closed her eyes and reached into the pot of swirling noise and color. "They spoke about America," she said. "A boat. And something about a Blue."

"Well, well, well . . ."

When Lucy opened her eyes, she discovered that she was no longer alone in the room with Edward. Two other men had come in while she was concentrating on her brother's question. One of the men was wearing a grey suit; he had ginger sideburns and a moustache that curled at the ends, and he was carrying a black bowler hat in his hands. The other was dressed in a deep navy coat with brass buttons down the front and a black belt strapped to his round middle; his hat was on his head and had a silver badge on its front. It was a uniform, and he a policeman, Lucy realized.

As it transpired, they were both policemen. The shorter man in the blue uniform belonged to the Berkshire Constabulary and had been contacted because Birchwood Manor fell within his jurisdiction. The grey-suited fellow was an inspector with the Metropolitan Police in London and had been brought in to render assistance with the investigation at the request of Mr. Brown, Fanny's father, who was wealthy and important.

It was Inspector Wesley of the Metropolitan Police who had spoken, and when Lucy's eyes met his across the room, he said again: "Well, well, well . . . ," adding this time: "Just as I suspected."

What he suspected, as he was to tell her over the coming days—after a thorough search had been carried out and it was discovered that, just as Lucy had suggested, the Radcliffe Blue diamond was missing—was that Lily Millington had been in on the whole thing.

"A mighty deception," he announced through his moustache, his thumbs tucked into the lapels on either side of his coat. "A most scandalous and brazen scheme. The pair of them hatched it well in advance, you see. The first step was for one Miss Lily Millington to win a place as your brother's model, whereby gaining access to the Radcliffe

Blue. The second step, once your brother's trust was won, was for the two of them to make off with the prize. And there it might have ended had Miss Brown not caught them in the act and paid the price with her blameless young life."

Lucy listened to this scenario, trying to take it all in. It was true what she had said to Edward: she *had* heard Lily Millington and the man talking about America and the Blue, and she could remember now *seeing* a pair of boat tickets. She had seen the pendant, too, of course—a beautiful blue diamond, her family's heirloom jewel. Lily Millington had been wearing it. Lucy had a clear picture in her mind of Lily Millington in a white dress, the pendant fixed in place within the hollow of her neck. And now Lily and the diamond and the tickets were gone. It made sense that they were together somewhere. There was just one problem. "My brother met Lily Millington at the theater. She didn't seek him out to become his model. He rescued her when she was being robbed."

The inspector's top lip quivered with pleasure at the opportunity to bend a pair of innocent ears with tales of the seamier side of life. "Another ploy, Miss Radcliffe," he said, lifting a slow, solitary finger, "as devious as it was effective. Another deceitful double act, the two of them in it together. We've seen how the likes of them operate, and if there's one thing certain to gain the attention of a respectable gentleman like your brother, it's the sight of a beautiful woman in need of assistance. He was *helpless* but to respond—any gentleman would have been. And while he was busy restoring the woman to rights, distracted by the rendering of care and concern, the fellow—her partner in crime—returned, accused your brother of being the thief who'd just made off with his 'sister's' bracelet, and in all the ensuing confusion"—he flung his arms out to great dramatic and triumphant effect—"slipped his fingers into your brother's waistcoat and pocketed *his* valuables."

Lucy remembered Edward's account of the night that he met Lily Millington. She and Clare and Mother—even their maid, Jenny, who was listening from where she was pouring the pot of breakfast tea—had exchanged fond, knowing glances when he told them that he'd had to walk the whole way home because he had been so transfixed by the young woman's face, so excited at the prospects that it presented, that he'd managed somehow to lose his wallet. Forgetfulness in the face of inspiration was so in keeping with Edward's nature that none of them had thought to question it—not to mention, his wallet had been as empty as it ever was, so recovering it was of no great consideration. But according to Inspector Wesley the wallet had not been lost at all; it had been taken—stolen from Edward by that man, Martin, at the very moment that Edward had believed himself to have been coming to Lily Millington's rescue.

"You mark my words," the inspector said, "because I'll eat my hat if I'm wrong. A man doesn't spend thirty years wading through the rot and the filth of London's streets without learning a thing or two about the despicable elements of human nature."

And yet, Lucy had witnessed the way Lily Millington looked at Edward, the way they were together. She couldn't believe that it was all a ploy.

"Thieves, actresses, and illusionists," the inspector said with a tap to the side of his nose when Lucy said as much. "Cut from the same cloth, they are. Great pretenders, tricksters all."

Viewed through the prism of Inspector Wesley's theory, Lucy could see how Lily Millington's actions might not have been exactly as they had seemed. And Lucy had observed Lily with the man. Martin. That's what she had called him. "What are you doing here?" she'd said, and "You must go, Martin. I said a month." And the man, Martin, had replied, "You did, but you're a fast worker, one of the best," and he'd held up a pair of tickets and said, "America . . . the land of new beginnings."

But Lily hadn't left the house with Martin. Lucy knew that she hadn't, for Lucy had locked Lily Millington in the hideaway. She was sure she could remember feeling proud when she revealed the hidden chamber.

Lucy tried to say as much, but Inspector Wesley only said, "I know all about the priest hole. That's where *you* were hidden, Miss

Radcliffe, not Miss Millington," and he reminded her of the bump on her head and told her that she should rest, calling for the doctor: "The child is confused again, Doctor. I fear I've worn her out with my questions."

And Lucy *was* confused. Because it was impossible that Lily Millington could have remained in the stairwell hiding place all of this time. It had been four days now since Martin had come to Birchwood. Lucy could remember how it felt within the tiny cavity, how difficult it was to breathe, how quickly the air had staled, how desperate she'd been to escape. Lily Millington would have called out for release long ago. No one could have stayed in there this long.

Maybe Lucy had got it wrong, after all? Maybe she hadn't locked Lily Millington away? Or, if she had, maybe Martin had released her and they'd run off together, just as the inspector said. Hadn't Lily told Lucy that she'd spent her childhood in Covent Garden; that she'd learned the coin trick from a French illusionist? Hadn't she called herself a pickpocket? Lucy had presumed at the time that she'd been joking, but what if Lily Millington *had* been working with that man, Martin, all along? What else could she have meant when she said that she'd told him she needed one month? Maybe that's why she had been so eager for Lucy to run back to the woods, to leave them to it . . .

Lucy's head hurt. She screwed her eyes tight. The bump must have jumbled her memories, as the inspector said. She had always placed the utmost value on being accurate, disdaining those who abbreviated or approximated and did not seem to realize that it made a difference; and so she made a solemn decision not to say anything further until she was 100 percent certain that what she remembered was true and correct.

Edward, naturally enough, refused to accept the inspector's theory. "She would never have stolen from me and she would never have left me. We were going to be married," he told the inspector. "I'd asked her and she'd accepted. I'd broken off the engagement with Miss Brown a week before we came to Birchwood."

It was Fanny's father's turn to wade in then. "The lad's in shock,"

Mr. Brown said. "He's not thinking straight. My daughter was looking forward to her wedding and was discussing plans for the occasion with my wife on the very morning that she left for Birchwood. She would most certainly have told me if her engagement had been canceled. She said nothing to that effect. Had she done so, I'd have had my lawyers involved, I can assure you. My daughter had a spotless reputation. There were gentlemen with far more to offer than Mr. Radcliffe lining up to ask for her hand in marriage, but she wanted to marry him. There's no way I'd have allowed a broken engagement to spoil my daughter's good name." And then the big man broke down, sobbing, "My Frances was a respectable woman, Inspector Wesley. She told me that she wished to spend the weekend in the country where her fiancé was hosting a group at his new house. I was pleased to lend her my coachman. I would never have allowed her to attend the weekend if not for her engagement, and she would not have asked."

This reasoning was good enough for Inspector Wesley and his Berkshire counterpart, particularly when it was further cemented by Thurston, who took the inspector aside to inform him that he was Edward's closest confidant and that his friend had never breathed a word about breaking off his engagement to Fanny Brown, let alone entering a second engagement with his model, Miss Millington. "I'd have talked him out of it if he had," said Thurston. "Fanny was a wonderful young lady and a sobering influence. It's no secret that Edward has always had his head in the clouds; she managed to bring his feet back firmly onto the ground."

"It was your weapon that was used in the murder, was it not, Mr. Holmes?" the inspector had asked.

"Regrettably, yes. A decorative piece only. A gift from Mr. Radcliffe, as it happens. I'm as shocked as anyone that it was loaded and used in such a way."

Lucy's grandfather, having learned about the missing Radcliffe Blue, had decamped by then from the Beechworth estate, and was only too happy to round out the description of Edward. "Even as a child," the old man told the inspector, "he was filled with wild ideas

and wilder inclinations. There were many times when he was growing from a boy to a man that I despaired. I couldn't have been happier
or more relieved when he announced his engagement to Miss Brown.
He seemed at last to have set himself on the right track. He and Miss
Brown were to have been married, and any suggestion from Edward
otherwise signals nothing more than a sad loss of his senses. Natural
enough in the face of such terrible events, especially for one with his
artistic temperament."

Mr. Brown and Lord Radcliffe were right, Thurston said soberly;
Edward was in shock. Not only had he loved and lost his fiancée, Miss
Brown, he was forced to accept that he was responsible for the horrific events, having brought Lily Millington and her associates into his
group of friends. "It wasn't as if he didn't have fair warning," Thurston
added. "I told him myself some months ago that I'd noticed certain
items of value missing from my studio after he and his model had
come to visit. He left me with quite the black eye for even daring to
suggest such a thing."

"What sort of items were taken, Mr. Holmes?"

"Oh, mere trifles in the scheme of things, Inspector Wesley.
Nothing to bother yourself with. I know how busy you are. I'm just
pleased to have been able to offer you some small assistance in clearing up this disturbing matter. To think of my friend being taken in by
a pair of charlatans—well, it makes my blood boil. I reproach myself
for not having put it all together sooner. We're lucky Mr. Brown sent
you to us."

The final nail in the coffin came when the inspector arrived one
morning and announced that Lily Millington had not even been the
model's real name. "My men in London have been asking questions
and looking into the records of births, deaths, and marriages and the
only Lily Millington they could find was a poor child who was beaten
to death at a public house in Covent Garden in 1851. Sold to a pair of
baby farmers and lock pickers by her father as a child. Little wonder
why she didn't make it."

And so, it was settled. Even Lucy had to accept that the inspector was right. They had all been taken in and swindled. Lily Millington was a liar and a thief; her name wasn't even Lily Millington. And now the faithless model was in America with the Radcliffe Blue and the man who'd shot Fanny.

The investigation was closed and the inspector and the constable left Birchwood, shaking hands with Mr. Brown and Grandfather and making promises to contact their counterparts in New York City in the hope that they might thereby at least recover the diamond.

Uncertain what else to do, stuck out in the country where the lazy stretch of summer had come to an abrupt end and the rain had set in, the Magenta Brotherhood returned briefly to Birchwood Manor. But Edward was a wreck and his desolation and anger permeated the very air. He and the house were one, and the rooms seemed to take on the faint but foul odor of his grief. Powerless to help him, Lucy stayed out of his way. His distress was catching, though, and she found herself unable to settle to anything. She was beset, too, with an uncharacteristic apprehension about the stairs where it had all happened and took to using the smaller set at the other end of the house instead.

Finally, Edward could stand it no longer: he packed his things and sent for a carriage. Two weeks after Fanny was killed, the curtains were closed, the doors were locked, and two horse-drawn carriages thundered up the lane from Birchwood Manor, carrying them all away.

Lucy, sitting on the back seat of the second one, had turned as they left, watching as the house receded further and further into the distance. For a second, she thought that she saw one of the curtains in the attic shift. But it was just Edward's story, she knew: the Night of the Following playing on her mind.

CHAPTER TWENTY-EIGHT

BACK in London, nothing was the same. Edward departed almost at once, traveling to the Continent and leaving no forwarding address. Lucy never saw what became of his final painting of Lily Millington. After he had left she dug up the hidden key to his studio and went inside, but there was no sign of it there. In fact, all trace of Lily was gone: the hundreds of sketches and studies had all been pulled from the walls. It was as if Edward had known even then that he was never again going to paint inside the Hampstead garden studio.

Clare, for her part, did not stay long, either. Having given up her pursuit of Thurston Holmes, she married the first wealthy gentleman who asked her and was soon happily enough ensconced within a large, soulless country house of which Grandmother was predictably enamored. She had two babies in quick succession, fat little wrigglers with wide cheeks and milky jowls, and on occasion over the years, when Lucy went to visit, spoke vaguely about having a third if only her husband would deign to spend more than a week each month at home.

By 1863, the year that Lucy turned fourteen, it was only Mother and her left at home. It seemed to have happened so quickly that each was left as stunned as the other. Finding themselves in a room together, they would both look up, surprised, before one of them— usually Lucy—made an excuse to leave, saving each the difficulty of having to invent a reason to explain the lack of conversation.

Lucy, as she grew into adulthood, eschewed love. She had seen what it could do. Lily Millington had left Edward and it had broken him. And so she avoided love. That is, she avoided the complication of locking hearts with another human being. For Lucy had fallen deeply in love with knowledge. She was greedy for its acquisition, impatient with her own inability to absorb new information quickly enough. The world was just so utterly abundant, and for each book that she read, each theory that she came to understand, ten more branched out before her. Some nights she lay awake wondering how she could best divide her lifetime: there simply wasn't enough of it for a person to ensure that they learned everything they wished to know.

One day, when she was sixteen years old and sorting through the items in her bedroom in order that a new bookcase might be moved up from the study, she came across the small suitcase that she had taken with her to Birchwood Manor in the summer of 1862. She had pushed it to the back of the cupboard beneath the window seat when she returned, wanting to forget the entire episode, and hadn't given it another thought in the intervening three years. But Lucy was a sensible girl, and so, despite not having expected to turn up the suitcase, now that she had, she decided that it made no sense at all to avoid dealing with the items inside.

She unlatched the case and was pleased to see her edition of *The Chemical History of a Candle* lying on top. Beneath it were two more books, one of which she remembered finding on the top shelf at Birchwood Manor. Lucy opened it now, gently, because the spine was still hanging by only a few fine threads, and saw that the letters were still there, the designs for the priest holes, precisely where she'd put them.

She set the books to one side and took up the item of clothing that had been packed beneath it all. Lucy remembered it at once. It was the dress that she'd been wearing that day, her costume for the photograph that Felix was going to take down by the river. Someone must have removed it after she fell, for when she woke in the yellow-striped room at the public house, she had been wearing her nightdress. Lucy remembered packing the costume away afterwards, balling it up and pushing it to the bottom of her case. It had given her an unpleasant feeling then, and now she held it in front of her, testing to see whether she was still spooked by it. She wasn't. She was sure she wasn't. Her skin did not heat; her heart did not race. Nonetheless, she had no wish to keep the item; she would put it out for Jenny to cut up for cleaning rags. First, though, because it was something that she'd been taught to do when she was young, she checked the pockets, expecting to find nothing but lint and the inside lining of the fabric.

But what was this? A hard, round item at the bottom of a pocket.

Even as she told herself that it was one of the river stones she'd collected at Birchwood Manor, Lucy knew better. Her stomach knotted and an instant wave of fear flooded her system. She didn't need to look. It was as if by touching it a rope had been pulled and a curtain lifted, and now light shone onto the dusty stage of her memory.

The Radcliffe Blue.

She remembered now.

It was Lucy who had been wearing it. She had gone back to the house in a tantrum, no longer needed for the photograph, and whilst exploring in Edward's room she had come across the diamond pendant. Ever since they had walked together to the village, Lucy had found herself thinking of Lily Millington, seeing her through Edward's eyes, wishing to be more like her. And, holding the necklace, she had perceived a way to feel—just for a moment—what it must be like to *be* Lily Millington. To be stared at by Edward and adored.

Lucy had still been looking at herself in the mirror when Lily Millington appeared behind her. She'd slipped the necklace from her throat and been about to put it back inside the box when the man, Martin, arrived and tried to take Lily with him. Lucy had dropped the Blue into her pocket instead. And there it was still, exactly where she'd put it.

Lucy had come to believe the inspector's story about Lily Millington, but once she found the Radcliffe Blue, the stitch at the center of the tapestry was cut and the rest of the picture, so carefully embroidered, began to unravel. Quite simply: without the theft of the heirloom, there was no motive. And while officials in New York had verified that a couple traveling under the names of Mr. and Mrs. Radcliffe had arrived and been registered at the port, anyone could have used those tickets. The last person Lucy had seen holding them was that awful man, Martin.

Edward had seen him fleeing from the house. He might have used one of the tickets and sold the other; he might have sold them both.

There was also the matter of the secret chamber in the staircase. For Lily Millington to have gone with Martin, she would have had to let him know where she was hiding and he to figure out the trapdoor. Lucy had needed instructions and even then it had been tricky. It would have taken time for the man to find Lily and further time for him to solve the lock's puzzle. But Fanny had arrived so quickly, and Edward soon after that. There simply hadn't been long enough for Martin to liberate Lily Millington.

Besides, Lucy had seen the way that Lily Millington had looked at Martin in genuine fear; she had seen, too, the way Lily looked at Edward. And Edward had loved Lily Millington absolutely; there was no doubting that. He had been a ghost of himself after she disappeared.

That Lily Millington *had* disappeared was not in question. No one had glimpsed her since that day at Birchwood Manor. Lucy had been the last person to see her, when she was locking Lily Millington inside the hideaway.

Now, back at Birchwood Manor, twenty years later, Lucy stood up and plaited her fingers together, flexing her hands in an old gesture of anxiety. She let them fall gently to her sides.

There was nothing for it; no use stalling now. If she were going to start a school in this place, and she felt very strongly that she must, then she had to know the truth. It would not change her plans. There was no way to go back and no point wishing things had turned out differently.

Lucy lifted the chair to one side and knelt down, regarding the stair's rise.

It really was an ingenious design. There was no way anyone would find it if they did not know that it was there. During the Reformation, when Catholic priests were hunted by the Queen's men, such places must have provided great comfort and safety. She had researched since and found that six men's lives were saved by this very priest hole.

Bracing herself, Lucy pressed the edges of the rise and opened the trapdoor.

CHAPTER TWENTY-NINE

As soon as she had looked inside the secret chamber, Lucy closed the panel again. Emotions, suppressed for so long, overwhelmed her and she let out a single great, hiccupping gulp of grief: for all the years since finding the diamond, in which she'd carried alone the secret knowledge of what she'd done; for Lily Millington, who had been kind to her and who had loved her brother; and most of all, for Edward, with whom she had broken faith, leaving him all alone in the world by believing the inspector's story.

When she could finally breathe again, Lucy went downstairs. She had known in her heart what she would find within the staircase hideaway. More importantly, she had known in her head. Lucy prided herself on being a rational woman: she had thus come armed with a plan. She had gone through each of the eventualities from the safe distance of London, and devised a clear set of tasks. She had thought herself prepared. But it was different, being here; Lucy's hand was shaking too much to write the planned letter to Mr. Rich Middleton of Duke Street, Chelsea. She hadn't counted on that, the way her hands would shake.

And so she went for a walk to the river to steady her nerves. She reached the jetty sooner than she had expected and headed towards the woods. Without meaning to, Lucy realized that she was tracing, in reverse, the very path that she had run that day, from the photo shoot back to the house.

Within the copse was the clear spot in the woods where Felix had planned to take the photograph. She could picture them all now in their costumes. She could almost see herself, thirteen years old and filled with the burn of injustice, darting off across the wildflower meadow towards the house. Soon to find the diamond pendant, to take it from its velvet box and put it at her own neck, to show Lily Millington the hiding place and start the terrible ball rolling. But no: she refused to see her phantom thirteen-year-old self take flight. Lucy walked back towards the river instead.

When she had discovered the Radcliffe Blue within her suitcase in London, she had known immediately that she had to hide it; the trouble was deciding where. She had considered burying it on Hampstead Heath, putting it down a drain, throwing it into the duck pond in the Vale of Health—but her conscience picked holes in every idea that she had. She knew it was irrational to imagine that a wily dog might somehow discern the very place that she had buried the jewel, dig it up, and then carry it home; or that a duck might eat it, digest it, and then deposit it on the bank for an eagle-eyed child to find. It was equally irrational to believe that if such an unlikely scenario were to occur, the diamond would then be traced back to her. But guilt, Lucy had learned, was the least rational of the emotions.

And, in truth, the rediscovered heirloom leading attention back to Lucy was only part of her worry. What mattered more to her, and did so increasingly with each passing year, was how much suffering would have been for naught if the official scenario were now to be disproved. Lucy could not bear to think that Edward's wandering might have been prevented; that if she had told the truth sooner he might have grieved for the loss of Lily Millington, but that he might then have been able to put her to rest and got on with his life.

No, the diamond had to stay hidden so that the story would continue to be believed. It had all gone too far now for anything else to be acceptable. But Lucy would know. And she alone would live with her knowledge. Given that there was no way of going back in time to do things differently, eternal guilt and isolation seemed like a fitting punishment.

She had intended to put the pendant in the box with everything else, but now, suddenly, as she stood by the edge of the Thames, such a different river here from the one she knew in London, she felt a need to be rid of it even sooner. The river was the perfect place. The earth gave up her secrets easily, but the river would carry its treasure out to the fathomless sea.

Lucy put her hand into her pocket and withdrew the Radcliffe Blue pendant. Such a brilliant stone. So very rare.

She held it up to the light one last time. And then she threw it into the river and started back towards the house.

The box arrived four days later. Lucy had placed the order in London before she left, telling the man that she would write again to let him know when and where she needed the item delivered. She had considered the possibility that the order would be unnecessary, the money wasted, but the odds, she decided, were not in her favor.

She chose a coffin maker and undertaker by the name of Mr. Rich Middleton of Duke Street, Chelsea, giving him specific instructions as to the unusually small dimensions required, along with a short list of other specifications.

"Triple lead-lined?" he'd said, scratching the thatch of hair beneath his tattered black top hat. "You'll not be wanting all that, surely? Not for an infant's coffin."

"I said nothing about an infant, Mr. Middleton, and I did not ask for your opinion. I have told you my requirements; if you are unable to meet them, I shall take my business elsewhere."

He held up his pinkish, soft-looking hands, and said, "It's your coin. If you want triple lead-lined, then that's what you'll have, Miss . . . ?"

"Millington. Miss L. Millington."

It was a brazen choice, and an unusual nod to sentiment. But she could hardly give her real name. Besides, Edward was dead and it had been twenty years since Fanny was shot. No one else was looking for Lily Millington, not anymore.

When he'd finished writing down the details, Lucy had him read them back to her. Satisfied, she asked him to draw up an account so that she could make a payment.

"Will you be requiring a cortege? Some mutes?"

Lucy told him that she would not.

The small coffin, when it arrived at Birchwood Manor, was brought grudgingly by a railway porter who struggled to lift it from the cart. It had been packed in a wooden travel crate and there was no out-ward indication of what it was that he was delivering; the man was maladroit enough to ask. "A bird bath," Lucy told him. "Marble, I'm afraid." Generous gratuity was paid, after which the man's spirit im-proved considerably. He even agreed to move it closer to its intended position, the garden bed to the side of the front gate. It was where Lily Millington had been standing on the day that Lucy, looking for Edward to tell him about the secret hideaways, had found Lily instead on her way to post a letter. "I want to be able to see it from as many windows as possible," Lucy told the railway porter, even though this time she had been asked no question.

When he had gone, she opened the travel crate to inspect its con-tents. Her first impressions were that Mr. Rich Middleton of Duke Street, Chelsea, had done a very good job. Lead was essential. Lucy had no way of knowing how long the box would remain hidden, but having spent her life reading obsessively about the treasures of the past, she knew that lead did not corrode. She wanted to hide things, certainly; she hoped that they would remain concealed for a very long time; but she could not bring herself to destroy them. To that end, Lucy had specified that the lid must seal securely. Too often, archae-ologists uncovered pots that had survived the ages, only to open them and find that the contents within had perished. She did not want air or water finding their way inside. The coffin must not leak or rust, and it must not crack over time. For it would be found one day, of that she was certain.

Lucy spent the next few hours digging. She'd found a shovel in the field barn and carried it up to the front garden. Her muscles ached, unaccustomed to the repetitive motion, and she had to stop every so often to rest. She realized, though, that stopping only made it harder to start again, and forced herself to push on until the cavity was deep enough.

At last it was time to fill the coffin. First, Lucy enclosed the copy of *Daemonologie* inside, which contained the letter by Nicholas Owen and the plans for Birchwood Manor explaining the priest holes. She had climbed into the attic and been glad to find the box of costumes where they'd left it. The white dress that Lily Millington had been wearing when she modeled for Edward was still amongst them, and Lucy had wrapped the bones from the priest hole carefully within it; now, she set the bundle gently inside the box. Twenty years had not left much behind.

Last, but not least, she put in a letter that she had written (cotton paper, non-acidic), outlining what she knew of the woman whose mortal remains now lay inside the coffin. It had not been easy to learn the truth, but finding information about the past was what Lucy did best, and she was not the kind of person to give up an inquiry. She had needed to rely on almost everything that Lily Millington had told her, and everything that Edward had reported, and the details that came back over time from what the man, Martin, had said that afternoon at Birchwood Manor.

Bit by bit, she had put the story together: the house above the bird shop on Little White Lion Street, the pair of rooms in the shadow of St. Anne's, the early years spent by the river; slipping back across time to the birth of a baby girl in June 1844, to a woman named Antonia, the eldest daughter of Lord Albert Stanley, and a man called Peter Bell. A clockmaker, who had lived at number forty-three Wheatsheaf Lane, Fulham.

Lucy sealed the lid just as the sun was starting to slip behind the gables. She realized that she was weeping. For Edward and for Lily; for herself, too, and the guilt from which she would never be free.

The porter had been right—the coffin was very heavy—but years spent in nature had made Lucy strong. She was also determined, and so she managed to heave the box into the ground. She filled in the dirt and patted it down hard on top.

Any latent religious inclinations that Mr. Darwin had not killed, Lucy's life experience had vanquished, and so she did not say a prayer over the fresh grave. Nonetheless, the moment called for ceremony and she had given much thought as to how she might best mark the spot.

She was going to plant a Japanese maple tree on top. She had already procured it, a lovely sapling with pale bark and the most elegant limbs, long and even, fine but strong. It had been one of Edward's favorite trees; the leaves were red in spring, turning by autumn to a most beautiful bright copper color, just like Lily Millington's hair. No, not Lily Millington, she corrected herself, for that had never been her real name.

"Albertine," Lucy whispered, thinking back to that mild Hampstead afternoon when she had seen the shock of red in the glass house at the bottom of the garden and Mother had instructed her to take two cups of tea "in the finest china." "Your name was Albertine Bell."

Birdie, to those who loved her.

Lucy's attention was on the patch of flattened dirt in the garden bed by the front gate, so she did not notice; but by some strange trick of the dusk, just as she spoke the words, the attic window seemed ever so briefly to glow. Almost as if a lamp had been switched on inside.

XI

I told you. I do not understand the physics of it and there is no one here to ask.

Somehow, without understanding how or why, I was out of the hideaway and in the house again. Moving amongst them as before, and yet nothing like before.

How many days passed? I do not know. Two or three. They were no longer sleeping here when I returned.

The bedrooms were deserted at night, and during the day one or another would arrive to fetch an item of clothing or some other personal effect.

Fanny was dead. I heard the policemen talking about "poor Miss Brown," which explained the gunshot but not the thump.

I heard them speaking, too, of the Radcliffe Blue and the tickets to America. The policemen also spoke of me. They collected everything they could pertaining to me. To Lily Millington.

When I realized what they believed, I was aghast.

What did Edward think? Had he been told the same theory? Did he accept it?

When he finally came back to the house, he was pale and distracted. He stood at the desk in the Mulberry Room, staring out towards the river, turning to gaze sometimes at my clock, the minutes sliding by. He ate nothing. He slept not at all.

He did not open his sketchbook and seemed to have lost all interest in his work.

I stayed with him. I trailed him wherever he went. I cried, I shouted, I begged and pleaded, I lay down beside him and tried to tell him where I was; but my abilities in that area have grown with time. Back then, in the beginning, it just exhausted me.

And then it happened. They all left and I could not make them stop.

The carriages retreated along the coach way and I was alone. For such a long time, I was alone. I evaporated, returning to the warmth and stillness of the house, slipping between the floorboards, settling with the dust, disappearing into the long, dark quiet.

Until one day, twenty years later, I was pulled back together by the arrival of my first visitor.

And as my name, my life, my history, was buried, I, who had once dreamed of capturing light, found that I had become captured light itself.

Part Four

CAPTURED LIGHT

Chapter Thirty

SUMMER 2017

Day broke with the sort of electric clarity reserved for the morning after a night of storms.

The first thing Jack noticed was that he wasn't in the god-awful uncomfortable bed in the malthouse. He was somewhere even less comfortable and yet he felt far more buoyant than usual.

The lush tangle of green-and-purple wallpaper told him where he was: ripe mulberries, and an engraving above the door that read: TRUTH, BEAUTY, LIGHT. He had slept on the floor of the house.

A stirring on the sofa beside him and he realized that he wasn't alone.

Like a kaleidoscope shifting into place, the night before came back into focus. The storm, the failure of the taxi to come and pick her up, the bottle of wine he'd bought on a whim at Tesco.

She was still asleep, delicate, with her short dark hair cut around her ears. She was like one of those teacups in fancy places that Jack had a knack for breaking.

He tiptoed down the hallway and back into the kitchen in the malthouse to make them tea.

When he carried the two steaming mugs back, she was awake and sitting up, the blanket wrapped around her shoulders.

"Morning," she said.

"Morning."

"I didn't go back to London."

"I noticed."

They had talked all night. Truth, beauty, and light—the room, the house had some sort of magic in it. Jack had told her about the girls, and Sarah. About what had happened in the bank, just before he left the police force, when Jack had gone in against orders and come out with seven rescued hostages and a gunshot wound to the shoulder. He had been a hero, all the papers said so, but it had been the last straw with Sarah. "How could you, Jack?" she'd said. "Didn't you think about the babies? The girls? You could have been killed."

"There were babies in the bank, too, Sar."

"But not yours. What kind of a father are you going to be if you can't even see that there's a difference?"

Jack hadn't had an answer. Not long afterwards, she'd packed up the girls and told him that she was going back to England to live closer to her parents.

He'd told Elodie about Ben, too, who had died twenty-five years ago on Friday, and how it had broken his dad. Elodie, in turn, told him about her mother's death—also twenty-five years ago—and her own father, who was similarly weighed down by grief, but with whom she'd decided she was finally going to speak when she returned to London.

She told him about her friend Pippa, and the way she felt about her work, and how she'd always thought it might make her a little odd, but that now she didn't mind.

And finally, because they seemed to have talked about everything else and the omission was notable, he'd asked her about the ring on her finger and she'd told him that she was engaged to be married.

Jack had felt a disappointment far out of proportion with what he considered reasonable, given that he'd known her for the sum total of forty hours. He'd tried to keep it casual. He'd expressed congratulations and then asked her what the lucky man was like.

Alastair—Jack had never met an Alastair he liked—was in banking. He was nice. He was successful. He could be funny at times.

"The only thing," she'd said with a frown, "is that I don't think he loves me."

"Why? What's the matter with him?"

"I think he might be in love with someone else. I think he might be in love with my mother."

"Well, that's . . . unusual, in the circumstances."

She had smiled, despite herself, and Jack had said, "But you love him?" She didn't answer at first, but then: "No," she said, and it sounded as if she might have surprised herself. "No, I really don't think I do."

"So. You're not in love with him and you think he's in love with your mother. Why are you getting married?"

"The whole thing is arranged. The flowers, the stationery . . ."

"Ah, well, then, that's different. Stationery in particular. Not easy to return."

Now he handed her a mug of tea and said, "Come for a walk in the garden before breakfast?"

"You're going to make me breakfast?"

"It's one of my specialities. Or so I've been told."

They went out through the back door near the malthouse, under the chestnut tree and across the lawn. Jack wished he'd brought his sunglasses. The world had been washed clean, everything as bright as an overexposed photo. As they rounded the corner into the front garden, Elodie gasped.

He followed her gaze and saw that the ancient Japanese maple had come down in the storm and was lying now across the flagged path, its gnarled roots pointing towards the sky. "My museum colleagues are not going to be happy," he said.

They went over to perform a closer inspection and Elodie said, "Look. I think there's something down there."

Jack got down on his knees and reached into the hollow, dusting the distant smooth speck with his fingertips.

"Maybe it's your treasure," she said with a smile. "Right in front of you all along."

"I thought you said that was a children's story."

"I've been wrong before."

"I guess we should dig it up."

"I guess so."

"But not until we've had some breakfast."

"Certainly not until we've had breakfast," she agreed. "Because I heard a rumor that it's your speciality, and I'm expecting big things from you, Jack Rolands."

CHAPTER THIRTY-ONE

SUMMER 1992

Tip was in his studio when the news came. A phone call from the woman who lived next door to them: Lauren was dead, killed in a car accident somewhere near Reading; Winston was distraught; the daughter was coping.

He had reflected on that later. *Coping.* It seemed an odd thing to say about a six-year-old girl who had lost her mother. And yet he knew what the woman, Mrs. Smith, had meant. Tip had only met the child a handful of times and knew her as the diminutive person who sat across from him at the odd Sunday lunch, trying to be surreptitious as she watched, wide-eyed and curious, over the tabletop; but he had seen enough to know that she was different from Lauren at the same age. Far more internal. Lauren had exuded a wound-up energy since the day she was born. As if her voltage were set a little higher than everybody else's. It made for a fascinating kid—she was certainly a success—but there was nothing easy about her company. The light was always on.

After he was given the news, Tip put the telephone receiver back in its cradle and sat down at his workbench. His vision glazed as he took in the stool on the other side. Lauren had sat there just last week. She'd wanted to talk about Birchwood Manor, asking him where it was exactly.

"The address, you mean?"

He'd given it to her, and then he'd asked her why—whether she was thinking of visiting—and she'd nodded and said that she had something very important to do and that she wanted to do it in the right place. "I know it was only a children's story," she'd said, "but in some way that I can't explain, I'm the person I am today because of it." She'd refused to be drawn further, and they'd changed the subject, but when she was leaving she said, "You were right, you know. Time makes the impossible possible."

He'd read about the concert she was playing in Bath in the newspaper a few days later, and when he saw who the other soloists were, he'd realized what she'd meant. She'd been planning to say good-bye to someone who had once meant a great deal to her.

She had sat on that very same stool six years earlier, when she returned from New York. He could picture her the day she'd come to visit him; he'd been able to see at once that something had happened.

Sure enough: she had fallen in love, she said, and she was getting married.

"Congratulations," he'd said, but her expression made it clear this wasn't an ordinary announcement.

It turned out that the two parts of the sentence fit together in a rather more complicated way than he'd assumed.

She had fallen in love with one of the other young musicians invited to be part of the quintet, a violinist. "It was instant," she said. "It was fierce and complete and worth every risk and sacrifice, and I knew at once that I would never feel the same way about another man."

"And did he—"

"It was mutual."

"But?"

"He's married."

"Ah."

"To a woman called Susan, a lovely, sweet woman who he's known since he was a boy and whom he couldn't bear to hurt. She knows everything about him, she's a primary school teacher, and she bakes the most delicious chocolate and peanut butter slice, which she brought to the rehearsal room and shared with all of us before sitting on a plastic chair and listening to us play. And when we finished, she cried, Tip—cried because the music had moved her, so I can't even hate her, because I could never hate a woman who is moved to tears by music."

Which might have been the end of it, but there was a third part to the story.

"I'm pregnant."

"I see."

"Not planned."

"What are you going to do?"

"I'm going to get married."

And that's when she'd told him what Winston had proposed. Tip had met the lad a couple of times: a musician, too, though not like Lauren. A good sort, hopelessly in love with her. "He doesn't mind—"

"About the baby? No."

"I was going to say, that you're in love with someone else."

"I've been very honest with him. He said it didn't matter, that there were different types of love and that the human heart did not admit limitations. He said I might even change my mind in time."

"He could be right."

"No. It's impossible."

"Time is a strange and powerful beast. It has a habit of making the impossible possible."

But, no, she'd been adamant. She could never love another man in the same way that she'd loved the violinist.

"But I love Winston, too, Tip. He's a *good* man, a kind man; he's one of my best friends. I know it's not usual."

"No such thing in my experience."

She'd reached across to squeeze his hand.

"What will you tell the child?" Tip had asked.

"The truth, if and when she asks. Winston and I agreed on that."

" 'She'?"

Lauren had smiled then. "Just a feeling."

She. The girl, Elodie. Tip had found himself watching her occasionally, in turn, across the table at Sunday lunch, mildly puzzled because he recognized something in her that he couldn't articulate at once; she had reminded him of someone. He realized now, in the sudden focus of her mother's death, that she'd reminded him of himself. She was a child whose still waters masked her depths.

Tip went over to the shelf where he kept his jar of whatnots and took out the stone, weighing it in the palm of his hand. He could still remember the night the woman, Ada, told him about it. They'd been sitting out the front of the pub in Birchwood; it was summer and dusk, so there hadn't been a lot of light, but enough for him to show her some of the rocks and sticks he'd been collecting. His pockets were always full at that time.

She'd picked each one up in turn and looked at it closely. She had liked collecting things, too, when she was his age, she said; now she was an archaeologist, which was a grown-up version of the same thing.

"Do you have a favorite?" she'd asked.

Tip told her that he did, and handed over a particularly smooth piece of oval-shaped quartz. "Did you ever find something as good as this?"

Ada nodded. "Once, when I was not much older than you are now."

"I'm five."

"Well, I was eight. I had an accident. I fell from a boat into the river and I couldn't swim."

Tip could remember becoming alert then with recognition; he had a feeling he'd heard this story before.

"Down I went, through the water, all the way to the bottom."

"Did you think that you were going to drown?"

"Yes."

"A girl *did* drown in the river over there."

"Yes," she agreed gravely. "But not me."

"*She* saved you."

"Yes. Just when I felt that I could hold my breath no longer, I saw her. Not clearly, and only for a moment, and then she was gone and I saw the stone, shining, surrounded by light, and I just knew some-how, as if a voice had whispered in my ear, that if I reached out and grasped it, I would survive."

"And you did."

"As you see. A wise woman once told me that there were certain items that brought a person good fortune."

He'd liked the sound of that and had asked her where he could get one for himself. He explained to her that his father had just been killed in the war and he was worried about his mother, because it was his job now to look after her and he wasn't sure how to do it.

And Ada had nodded wisely and said, "I'm going to come and see you at the house tomorrow. Would that be all right? I have something I'd like to give you. In fact, I have a feeling that it belongs with you. That it knew you'd be here and found a way to get to you."

But it must be a secret between them, she'd said, and then she'd asked whether he'd found the hidden chamber yet, and when Tip said that he hadn't, she'd whispered to him about a panel in the hallway, and Tip's eyes had widened with excitement.

Next day she'd given him the blue stone.

"What will I do with it?" he'd asked as they sat together in the garden at Birchwood Manor.

"Keep it safe, and it will do the same for you."

Birdie, who'd been sitting beside him, had smiled her agreement.

Tip no longer believed in amulets or good luck, but he didn't dis-believe, either. What he did know was that the idea of the stone had been enough. Many times, as a boy—at Birchwood, but more so after they'd left—he'd held it in his hand and closed his eyes and Birdie's words had come flooding back into his mind: he would remember the lights in the dark, and the way he'd felt when he was in the house, as if he were enveloped, and everything was going to be all right.

Thinking of Lauren and the little girl who was now without her mother, Tip began to have an idea. He had a trove of trolleys in his studio, each loaded with items he had found when he was out walk-ing: things that spoke to him, for one reason or another, because they were honest or beautiful or interesting. He began to pick out some of the finest, arranging them on the bench before him, returning some to the trays, exchanging them for others, until he was happy with the selection. And then he began to mix up the clay.

Little girls liked charm boxes. He had seen them at the markets on Saturdays, lining up at the craft stalls, looking for little cases in which to keep their treasures. He would make one for her, Lauren's daughter, and he would decorate it with all of the items that meant the most to him; the stone, too, for it had found a new child to protect. It wasn't much, but it was all that he could think to do.

And maybe, just maybe, if he did it right, when he gave the gift to her, he would be able to imbue it with the same powerful idea, the same light and love, that the stone had held when it was given to him.

CHAPTER THIRTY-TWO

SHE parked the car on the verge and turned off the ignition, but she didn't get out; she was early. The wave of memories had been behind her all day, threatening to break, and now that she'd stopped, it had rolled over the top of her and spread out in a glittering wash. Juliet was beset, suddenly, with a visceral remembrance of the night they'd arrived off the train, the four of them, weary and hungry, no doubt traumatized after being uprooted from London.

It had been one of the most horrific periods in her life—the destruction of her home, the loss of Alan—and yet, in some ways, Juliet would have given anything to go back. To step through that gate over there, into the Birchwood Manor garden, and know that she would see five-year-old Tip, with his hair like a curtain; Bea, a surly preteen too proud to accept a hug; and Red, just Red, irrepressible, with those stubborn freckles and the gap-toothed smile. Their noise, their squabbles, their incessant questions. The stretch of time between now and then, the impossibility of going back, even for a minute, was a physical pain.

She had not expected it to feel like this. For her connection to the house to pull so hard at her chest. It wasn't a weight upon her; it was a great sudden pressure inside her, pressing against her ribs in its urge to escape.

It had been twenty-two years now since Alan had died. Twenty-two years that he hadn't lived, in which she had gone on ahead without him.

477

She didn't hear his voice anymore.

And now, here she was, her car parked on the verge outside Birchwood Manor. The house was uninhabited; she could see that at once. It wore the patina of neglect. But Juliet couldn't have loved it more.

Sitting in the driver's seat, she took the letter from her bag and read through it quickly. It was short and to the point; not his usual style. Little more than today's date and a time.

Juliet still had every letter that he'd sent her. She liked knowing that they were all there in hat boxes in the back of her wardrobe. Beatrice liked to tease her about her "pen pal," though since Lauren had been born, she didn't have as much energy for stirring.

The clock in the dashboard clicked forward by a minute. Time was passing at a snail's pace.

Juliet didn't much fancy sitting in the confines of the Triumph for another forty minutes. She glanced at herself in the rearview mirror, checked her lipstick, and then, with a decisive breath, hopped out of the car.

She followed the winding lane towards the cemetery, blinking away the ghostly image of Tip stopped along the way to search for odd pieces of quartz and gravel. She turned left towards the village, and as she reached the crossroads, she was pleased to see that the Swan was still there.

After a minute of consideration, she summoned up the courage to go inside. Thirty-four years since she and Alan had arrived from London on the train, Juliet doing her best to conceal her pregnancy. She had half expected Mrs. Hammett to arrive at the door to greet her, to start talking as if they'd only just had dinner the night before, but there was a new young woman behind the bar.

"Changed hands a few years ago now," she said. "I'm Mrs. Lamb. Rachel Lamb."

"Mrs. Hammett—is she . . . ?"

"Not likely. She's moved in with her son and daughter-in-law, down the road."

"Close by?"

"Too close. Forever popping in here to give me advice." She smiled to show that she was speaking fondly. "You might catch her before her midday nap if you hurry. Takes it like clockwork."

Juliet hadn't thought to visit Mrs. Hammett, but she followed Rachel Lamb's instructions anyway and arrived soon enough at the cottage with the red front door and black letterbox. She knocked and held her breath.

"I'm so sorry, you've missed her," said the woman who answered. "Down for the count, and I daren't wake her. She can be testy when she hasn't had her winks."

"Perhaps you could mention me to her," said Juliet. "She might not remember. I'm sure she saw so many guests come and go, but she was kind to my family and me. I wrote an article about her. She and her WVS ladies."

"Oh, well, you should have said so! Juliet of the Laneway! She still has a framed copy on the wall beside her bed. Her claim to fame, she says."

They exchanged pleasant chat for a few more moments, and then Juliet said that she ought to be going, she was meeting someone soon, and Mrs. Hammett's daughter-in-law said that it was just as well, as she had some pantry sorting to be getting on with.

Juliet was turning to leave when she noticed the painting on the wall above the sofa. A portrait of a striking young woman.

"Beautiful, isn't she?" said Mrs. Hammett's daughter-in-law.

"Intoxicating."

"Came to me from my grandfather. Discovered it in his attic after he passed away."

"What a find."

"Quite the hoard, I assure you. Took us weeks to clear it—mostly rat-eaten rubbish. His own father had the house before him."

"Was he an artist?"

"A policeman, back in the day. When he retired, his boxes of old notes were put up top and forgotten. Don't know where she came from. She's unfinished—you can tell by the edges, where the color isn't right and the brushstrokes are rough—but there's something in her expression, don't you think? You can't help but look at her."

The woman in the painting stayed with Juliet as she started the walk back towards Birchwood Manor. She wasn't familiar, not exactly, but the essence of the painting was reminiscent of something. Everything in her face, her expression, radiated light and love. It made her think of Tip for some reason, and Birchwood Manor, and that sunlit afternoon in 1928 when she'd fought with Alan and become lost and then found again, when she'd woken up in the garden beneath the Japanese maple tree.

No surprise, of course, that she should think of that day now. Juliet and Leonard had been exchanging letters for almost twenty years, ever since she wrote to ask him to contribute to a "Laneway" article she'd planned to write but never got around to, about the many different lives led in one house. He'd received the letter too late, as it happened, and by the time he wrote back she was in London again and the war was wearily winding down. But they'd stayed in touch. He also liked writing, he said; he got along better with people on the page.

They had shared everything. All of the things she couldn't write in her columns, the anger and grief and loss. And, by turns, the things that happened to them along the way: the beautiful, the funny, the true.

But they had never met in person, not since that afternoon in 1928. Today would be the first time.

Juliet hadn't told anyone what she was doing. Her children were always encouraging her to go out for dinner with one eligible fellow or another, but this, today, him, was impossible to explain. How could she ever make them understand what she and Leonard had experienced, the two of them, that afternoon, in the garden of Birchwood Manor?

And so he remained her secret; this journey back to the house their own.

The twin gables came into view, and Juliet felt herself begin to walk faster, almost as if she were being pulled along towards the house. She put her hand in her pocket to check that the tuppence was still there.

She had kept it all this time; now, at last, she could return it.

XII

Jack and Elodie have gone for a walk together, the two of them.

She said something about wanting to see the clearing in the woods for herself, and he was only too happy to offer his services as a guide.

And so, here I am, sitting again in the warm spot at the turn of the stairs, waiting.

One thing I know for certain: I will be here when they get back.

I will be here, too, when they are gone and my next visitors arrive.

I might even tell my story again someday, as I did to little Tip, and before him, Ada, weaving together threads from Edward's Night of the Following with the things my father told me about my mother's flight from home, the tale of the Eldritch Children and their Fairy Queen.

It is a good story, about truth and honor and brave children doing righteous deeds; it is a powerful story.

People value shiny stones and lucky charms, but they forget that the most powerful talismans of all are the stories that we tell to ourselves and to others.

And so, I will be waiting.

When I was alive, and the great craze came first upon society—spiritualism and the desire to communicate with the dead—there was an assumption that ghosts and apparitions longed for release. That we "haunt" because we are trapped.

But it is not so. I do not wish to be set free. I am of this house, this house that Edward loved; I *am* this house.

I am each whorl in each piece of timber.

I am every nail.

I am the wick in the lamp, the hook for a coat.

I am the tricky lock on the front door.
I am the tap that drips, the red rust circle on the porcelain sink.
I am the crack in the bathroom tile.
I am the chimney pot and the black snaking drainpipe.
I am the air within each room.
I am the hands of the clock and the space in between.
I am the noise you hear when you think you're hearing nothing at all.
I am the light in the window that you know cannot be there.
I am the stars in the dark when you feel yourself alone.

AUTHOR'S NOTE

I SHARE Lucy Radcliffe's anxiety about the number of subjects to be studied and grasped within the limits of a single lifetime, so one of the best things about being a writer is having the opportunity to explore topics that fascinate me. *The Clockmaker's Daughter* is a book about time and timelessness, truth and beauty, maps and mapmaking, photography, natural history, the restorative properties of walking, brotherhood (having three sons shot that one to the top of the list), houses and the notion of home, rivers and the power of place, among other things. It was inspired by art and artists, including the English romantic poets, the Pre-Raphaelite painters, early photographers such as Julia Margaret Cameron, Charles Dodgson, and Mathew Brady, who first described the camera as "the eye of history," and designers like William Morris, with whom I share a passion for houses, and who drew my attention to some of the unique ways in which the buildings of the Cotswolds mimic the natural world.

Places that lent thread to the weave of this novel include Avebury Manor, Kelmscott Manor, Great Chalfield Manor, Abbey House Gardens in Malmesbury, Lacock Abbey, the Uffington White Horse, the Barbury Hill Fort, the Ridgeway, the countryside of Wiltshire, Berkshire, and Oxfordshire, the villages of Southrop, Eastleach, Kelmscott,

Buscot, and Lechlade, the river Thames, and of course London. Should you wish to visit a house with genuine priest holes, Harvington Hall in Worcestershire retains seven designed by Saint Nicholas Owen. It also sits upon a moated island.

If you are eager to read more about nineteenth-century London and the streets occupied by Birdie Bell and James Stratton, some useful sources include: *London Labour and the London Poor*, by Henry Mayhew (providing insight into such forgotten occupations as "The Blind Street-Sellers of Tailors' Needles" and "'Screevers' or Writers of Begging Letters and Petitions"); *Victorian London: The Life of a City 1840–1870*, by Liza Picard; *The Victorian City: Everyday Life in Dickens' London*, by Judith Flanders; *The Victorians*, by A. N. Wilson; *Inventing the Victorians*, by Matthew Sweet; and *Charles Dickens*, by Simon Callow, being a deeply affectionate biography of one of the greatest Victorians and Londoners. The Seven Dials is still a bustling pocket of Covent Garden; however, should you visit now you will find more restaurants and fewer shops selling birds and cages than when Mrs. Mack was running her enterprise. Little White Lion Street was re-named Mercer Street in 1938.

I was inspired by a number of museums whilst writing *The Clockmaker's Daughter*, which seems fitting given the novel's focus on curation and the use of narrative structures to tell cohesive stories about the disjointed past. Some of my favorites include: the Charles Dickens Museum, the Watts Gallery and Limnerslease, Sir John Soane's Museum, the Fox Talbot Museum, the Victoria & Albert Museum, the British Museum, and the Royal Observatory at Greenwich. I was thrilled to attend the following exhibitions and am grateful to galleries and curators who make such works available: *Julia Margaret Cameron*, the Victoria & Albert Museum, 2015–2016; *Painting with Light: Art and Photography from the Pre-Raphaelites to the Modern Age*, Tate Britain, 2016; *Victorian Giants: The Birth of Art Photography*, the National Portrait Gallery, 2018.

With special thanks to: my agent Lizzy Kremer and all at DHA, my editors Maria Rejt and Annette Barlow, Lisa Keim and Carolyn

Reidy at Simon & Schuster, and Anna Bond at Pan Macmillan. Thanks also to the many people at A&U, Pan Macmillan, Atria Books, and Simon & Schuster Canada, who played a vital role in turning my story into this book and sending it out into the world so beautifully. Isobel Long generously provided information about the world of the archivist; and I am grateful to Nitin Chaudhary—and his parents— for assistance with the Punjabi terms in Ada's story. All errors are of course my own, whether intentional or not. I have, for instance, taken the liberty of situating a Royal Academy exhibition in November 1861 even though during the nineteenth century the annual exhibition of the RA opened in May.

Those who helped in less specific but no less important ways while I was writing *The Clockmaker's Daughter,* include: Herbert and Rita, precious departed friends, still in my thoughts; my mum, dad, sisters, and friends, especially the Kretchies, Pattos, Steinies, and Browns; every single person who read and enjoyed one of my books; my three lights in the dark, Oliver, Louis, and Henry; and, most of all, for too many things to count, my life copilot, Davin.